Rhys slowly rocked the glider with his right leg. "Maddy, I don't know what the Wellmont mold is. What I do know is that you're clever and you're funny and you're beautiful. . . . Look what you've accomplished in the short time you've been here. Most people would've written off the Lumber Baron as a scrape. When you're done with it it'll be the pride of Nugget. From where I'm standing this Gabriella woman wasn't your problem. If your husband couldn't see what I see . . . Well, he doesn't deserve you."

She pressed her face against his shoulder and mumbled, "You might not say that if you'd ever seen Gabriella."

He gently lifted her onto his lap, his soft lips just inches away from her ear. "I don't need to. I've seen you."

Maddy looked at him with such wonder in her eyes that it mesmerized him. He bent his head, gently brushing her lips with his. The kiss started innocently enough. But when she wrapped her arms around his neck, he was lost. He sank his mouth over hers, pulling her firmly against him . . .

GOING HOME

A
NUGGET
ROMANCE

STACY FINZ

KENSINGTON BOOKS
KENSINGTON PUBLISHING CORP.
www.kensingtonbooks.com

KENSINGTON BOOKS are published by
Kensington Publishing Corp.
119 West 40th Street
New York, NY 10018

All Kensington titles, imprints, and distributed lines are available at special quantity discounts for bulk purchases for sales promotion, premi-
ums, fund-raising, educational, or institutional use.

Special book excerpts or customized printings can also be created to fit
specific needs. For details, write or phone the office of the Kensington
Special Sales Manager: Kensington Publishing Corp., 119 West 40th
Street, New York, NY 10018. Attn. Special Sales Department. Phone:
1-800-221-2647.

Kensington and the K logo Reg. U.S. Pat. & TM Off.

First Electronic Edition: October 2014
eISBN-13: 978-1-60183-338-9
eISBN-10: 1-60183-338-5

First Print Edition: October 2014
ISBN-13: 978-1-60183-339-6
ISBN-10: 1-60183-339-3

Printed in the United States of America

To my late father, Steven R. Finz.
Heaven got one hell of a copyeditor. I miss you, Dad.

Acknowledgements

Thanks to Susan Kennedy for your invaluable information about city zoning, licensing and waste treatment plants. I bet you never thought sewage would be so spellbinding. Thanks to Jeff Rinek and Joe Toomey for your expertise on guns, ballistics, and all things law enforcement.

Thanks to my critique partners A.J. Larrieu, Vanessa Kier, Sonya Weiss, and Suzanne Herel. How many versions of this book did you read, A.J.? I'm so indebted and grateful for all of your help, inspiration, and encouragement.

A special thanks to Amanda Gold, Tara Duggan, and Sarah Fritsche for being beta readers, telling me what worked and what didn't and for lending me your names. Amanda, your help working out plot problems was vital!

Thanks to Wendy Miller and Leah Garchik, my besties, for all the dinners, drinks (especially the drinks), and the advice. Wendy, thank you for reminding me that my characters needed to shower and for all your editing expertise. Leah, thank you for your spectacular gift for coming up with names and slogans.

Thanks to my agent, Melissa Jeglinski of the Knight Agency, for believing in my work, helping me make it better and steering me through this new journey. And to my editor at Kensington, John Scognamiglio, thanks for taking a chance on me and guiding my work with the bedside manner of a country doctor.

Last, but never least, thanks to Jaxon, Iris, Janet, Laura, Noah, Kendra, Kaley, Zach, Paulina and Garyn—my family. Thanks for the endless reading and for believing that there isn't anything I can't do. I love you guys. A special shout-out to Jaxon, my husband, who read, proofread, cooked all my meals, and did all the dishes so I could finish this book. You're the best!

Chapter 1

"Pop, why'd you take this stuff?" Rhys stared down at the assortment of crap—because with the exception of the ladies' ring and the handgun, it really was just crap—and shook his head.

When his dad looked up at him with those basset hound eyes Rhys actually felt sorry for the old man.

"You listening? You're looking at grand theft here. That's a three-year sentence."

They'd been at it for nearly forty minutes and Rhys was about to throw up his arms in defeat. Out of professional courtesy the Plumas County sheriff's investigator had given him a heads-up about his dad's arrest. Rhys in turn had called a highly recommended local attorney, jumped on a plane to Reno, and driven the eighty-one miles in a lousy rental car across the Nevada-California line to Quincy, the county seat.

If they didn't resolve this mess soon, he'd miss his flight back to Houston. With the two-hour time difference, he wouldn't get home until midnight, and he had to be in court in the morning to testify on a case he'd solved.

But Rhys was starting to panic. Stan Shepard might be a mean SOB, but he was no thief. And his lack of memory and fits of confusion didn't seem to be an act.

"Pop, you okay? What's going on with you?"

Stan, known simply as Shep by what few friends he had, responded, "You gonna make me some of that Dinty Moore stew, boy?"

"Oh, for Christ's sake." Rhys banged his head against the institutional green wall of the nine-by-nine-foot sheriff's interrogation room.

"You're gonna hurt yourself, son."

He hadn't heard his dad's lawyer come in. For a big guy, he was light on his feet. "Where the hell have you been?"

Del Webber didn't seem to take offense. "Been getting your old man's test results."

"What test results?" No one had told Rhys about any tests.

"Psych eval." Del grabbed a chair and dragged it over to the conference table that anchored the windowless room, motioning Rhys to do the same. "You want the good news first?"

Rhys remained standing. "Yeah, sure."

"Sit down, Detective. This might take a little time."

Rhys sagged into one of the folding chairs and rested his elbows on the table. Shep continued to sit in the corner, staring into space.

"For now, they're holding off on officially charging him."

"How's that?" Rhys had worked for Houston PD going on eleven years now. He knew the drill. "Mental incompetence?"

Del took off his cowboy hat and set it down on its crown, then ran his fingers through what little was left of his hair. "Although there is no definitive diagnosis, it looks like your dad's in the middle stages of Alzheimer's. I'm sorry, son."

Rhys probably should've felt a whole range of emotions, including grief. All he felt was inconvenienced. "They putting him in a state hospital?"

Del shook his head. "I can make this whole thing go away. He probably misplaced a few of his own things and thought these were his." He looked over at the collection of stolen goods: a set of keys, one of those gaudy figurines they sold in shopping mall jewelry stores, a Kodak camera, and some corroded jumper cables. The gun and the ring.

"I don't know about Nugget anymore, but in Texas people don't take kindly to someone walking into their home and making off with their stuff."

Del frowned, running his hands through that thin hair again. "The truth, Rhys, is he probably was disoriented. Didn't even know he was committing burglaries. People around here are pretty forgiving."

Rhys got up and paced the room. "What am I supposed to do with him? He obviously can't be left to his own devices."

"Maybe find one of those assisted-living facilities. Our doctors said there will be times when he's totally lucid. But he'll need medical care and someone to watch over him."

Rhys looked over at his father. They shouldn't be talking about him as if he wasn't sitting in the same room. But Shep seemed more preoccupied with a loose thread on his shirt than he did with their conversation.

"You ready to go, Pop?"

He lifted his head as if seeing Rhys for the first time that day. "You gonna make me some of that Dinty Moore stew?"

Rhys turned to Del. "You want me to write you a check?"

"I know where you live. You'll get my bill in the mail." He grabbed his hat off the table and gave Rhys's shoulder a fatherly squeeze. "I'm truly sorry, son."

Rhys acknowledged Del's condolences with a slight nod of his head and gently tugged his father up out of the chair. "Let's go home."

Home? When had he ever thought of Nugget as home? Even though Rhys had lived there a good part of his life, he'd always felt like an outsider, like someone peering through a picket fence, watching a party he hadn't been invited to. Something about that kind of alienation, the hollowness of it, made Nugget the loneliest place in the world.

He maneuvered his father past the front desk and out the door into the parking lot. It was colder here than it had been in Houston. He wished he'd thought to bring something warmer than a sweatshirt. His dad's denim railroad jacket wasn't any heavier, but he seemed oblivious to the temperature. Rhys hustled him into the front passenger seat and got behind the wheel.

"What do you say we blow this popsicle stand?"

Shep didn't respond, just stared out the window as Rhys headed east on Highway 70. The last time he'd been back was twelve months ago for the funeral of his best friend Clay's father. Shep hadn't bothered coming to the chapel to pay his respects, but Rhys had called on him anyway. Like always, they'd had nothing to say.

It'd been Rhys's only visit since peeling out of town eighteen years earlier. With nowhere in particular to go, he'd just wanted to get far away from Nugget—to a new place, where no one knew him and he could reinvent himself.

About the only good thing in coming back was he'd get to see Clay again. The McCreedys had been ranching in Plumas County for four generations. Clay knew everything about these mountains. And everybody. Rhys grabbed his cell phone and punched in Clay's number. When voice mail came on, he left a message, then tried his lieutenant. His partner would have to pull court duty while Rhys took a few days to get his dad settled.

Thirty-five minutes later he rolled into downtown Nugget. The place was looking a little long in the tooth. But the surrounding snowcapped mountains and hulking pines still awed him. Funny how when he told Texans he was from California they automatically conjured up images of palm trees, sandy beaches, and balmy Santa Ana breezes. It was late September. In a month, Nugget, located in the northern Sierra Nevada, could be socked by sleet and snow.

He drove up Donner Road to the two-family home where he'd grown up. It hadn't been much then and looked even worse for wear now—little more than a double-barrel shotgun shack, housing the Shepards on one side and Old Lady Brown on the other. But it was spitting distance from the Union Pacific Railroad depot, where Shep, up until the time he retired, reported to work every day. The house practically sat on the tracks. As a kid, Rhys had hardly noticed the constant roar of diesel engines and the piercing blows of train horns.

"We're here, Pop." Rhys got out of the car and helped his dad out of the passenger seat, noticing for the first time how frail he'd gotten. He could feel the sharpness of Shep's bones through the flimsiness of his dungaree jacket.

"I'm hungry, Rhys."

That caught Rhys off guard. He couldn't remember a time when his father had actually called him by his name, the only remaining vestige of his mother's Welsh heritage. Other dads sometimes used nicknames:

Shortstop, Sport, Buddy. He was just "Boy." Or if his old man was in a particularly foul mood, "You good-for-nothing little punk."

"Let's get inside and I'll fix you something to eat." Rhys turned the knob and smiled when the door gave way with a little shove of his shoulder. People still didn't lock up in Nugget.

The old plaid fold-out sofa that Rhys used to sleep on still sat against the main wall in the living room. The linoleum floor, nicked and worn with age, had been swept clean and smelled of disinfectant. As he walked through his father's bedroom to the kitchen in the back of the house he noted that the place remained as sparse and neat as the day he'd left it.

Rhys hunted through the pantry for a can of stew, checked the expiration date, and chucked it in the garbage can. "You'll have to settle for soup, Pop."

He grabbed a cast-iron pot off a shelf above the stove, found a can opener in one of the drawers, heated the soup, and reached by rote into one of the upper cupboards for two bowls, which he set on a small Formica table in the corner of the room.

His dad took one of the chairs while Rhys served them lunch. He tested the soup to make sure it wasn't too hot and waited to see if his father could feed himself. "This okay?"

Shep slurped down a few spoonfuls of chicken and noodles and nodded. They ate in silence while the old man cleaned his bowl.

"You want more?" Rhys asked.

"Nah. I'm good."

Rhys finished the last of his broth and pushed his bowl away. "Mrs. Brown still live next door?" He thought his father seemed a little more clearheaded now that he'd had something to fill his belly.

"She died."

"That's too bad." Although Rhys meant it, he'd never liked her much.

Through the thin wall that separated their two houses, he knew she'd heard him crying as a boy on those miserable nights his father left him alone to work on the railroad. Instead of assuring him that she was just next door—there if he needed her—she'd cranked up the volume on her TV set. At least he'd had Johnny Carson to keep him company. "Anyone living there now?"

"Nope." Shep took his bowl to the sink. He gazed out the window as if trying to get his bearings, and fiddled with the faucet uncertainly until a spray of water came out.

"Want me to do that?" Rhys called to him.

Shep didn't answer, just placed his bowl on the drying rack and turned in the direction of his bedroom. "Get some sleep, boy."

Rhys didn't have the heart to tell him that it was only two o'clock. He washed his own bowl and stepped out onto the back porch, resting his elbows on the wobbly railing so he could admire the fall leaves on the trees that dappled the edge of town and inhale the familiar scent of wood smoke from the neighboring chimneys. The trains didn't run as frequently as they used to—he hadn't heard one since being back at the house. But the sound of the Feather River rushing at full throttle made Rhys think of record rain and snowfalls.

As he peered down on the town, he felt nostalgic for the kind of childhood he should've had. What boy wouldn't love growing up in a place like this? A safe and endless playground of rivers and lakes, trees and fields, cow and horse pastures. Snowboarding and sledding in the winter. Swimming and inner tubing in the summer. Fishing, nearly year-round.

Now looking at it, Rhys found it hard to believe that Nugget had ever been prosperous—first, during the gold rush, later, when loggers from around the country discovered the area's abundant fir and pine forests. The railroad eventually followed, so that lumbermen could ship their timber downstate. More recently, the place had become a mecca for weekenders, skiers, hunters, and outdoorsy types. But like every other rural town in America, when the recession hit, Nugget took it in the shorts. Badly.

His father had moved them here from Utah to work as a brakeman for Union Pacific when Rhys was just two. He'd never known his mother, who, according to Shep, had run off with a Mormon dentist to live the high life in Salt Lake City shortly after Rhys was born. Something about Nugget must have resonated with Shep, because no matter how solitary his meager existence got here, he'd never left this little town.

Never.

But tomorrow Rhys would have to start looking for a care facility for his father, and the likelihood of finding one near Nugget was next to nil. Shep would never make it through one of Texas's hot, humid summers. Not that Rhys wanted him living there. He'd made sure over the years to put a lot of miles between him and his father. Sacramento or Reno seemed like the most logical choices. And the sooner Rhys got him tucked in the sooner he could get back to Houston. Back to his life.

"Hey, if you've got cigarettes, I've got beer."

Rhys pivoted fast on his feet and broke into a huge grin at the sight of his best friend. "You scared the shit out of me."

"Well, you know Nugget—full of toughs and ne'er-do-wells," Clay said. "Gotta keep on your toes."

"You learn that in the Navy?"

"What?"

"Sneaking up on me from the side like that."

"Nah. You were just deep in thought."

Rhys gave Clay a big bear hug. "How the hell are you?"

"From the sound of things, better than you."

Rhys eyed the grocery bag Clay carried. "I gave up smoking when I went through the police academy."

"Well, hopefully you didn't give up drinking." Clay pulled a six-pack of Sierra Nevada and a bottle of Patrón from the sack.

"Looks like your taste has vastly improved since high school." The two of them used to shoot Cuervo Gold with Pabst Blue Ribbon chasers while smoking packs of Marlboros they'd filched off his old man.

"Just my booze. I still like my women cheap." Clay laughed and took a seat on the porch steps. "It's good to see you, man. I just wish it was under better circumstances."

Rhys joined him on the stairs. "How're the boys?"

Clay rubbed his temples. "A goddamn handful. Probably payback for everything we pulled. My dad's gotta be laughing in his grave."

Both he and Clay had been raised by single dads. Although Tip had enough love in him for two parents, it couldn't have been easy.

"What's Justin? About fourteen now?"

"Yup. Cody just turned eleven. The biggest little shit you ever saw."

Rhys smiled, but quickly turned serious. "I'm sorry I didn't make it to Jen's funeral. I was in the middle of a big case and—"

Clay absolved him with a wave of his hand. "You came for Tip's. I didn't expect you to come back six months later."

"I should've come for you . . . for the boys."

"Things were pretty much over between us when she had the accident." Clay stretched his legs down the length of the staircase. "But it's been hard on the kids. Apparently even a bad mother is better than no mother."

Rhys had met Jennifer only a couple of times in San Diego. She'd seemed nice enough—though a little overdone for his taste. Unlike Clay, he didn't go for women who put their wares on parade. And Jen with her low-cut tops, her too-short skirts, and that mane of bottle-blond hair was a veritable window display. Unfortunately, she hadn't been satisfied with men just looking.

"The kids like living on the ranch?" Rhys used his car key to pop the cap off one of the Sierra Nevadas and took a long drag.

Clay also grabbed a beer from the pack, but seemed more intent on peeling the label off the bottle than drinking from it. "It took them a while to adjust. They liked San Diego and missed their friends. But they've made new ones and I think they're sort of tickled by having dogs, horses, and cattle. So stop changing the subject. What's the plan for Shep?"

Rhys pulled his hood over his head. Damn, it was getting chilly. "Del suggested an assisted-living-type deal. . . . Thanks for the referral, by the way. Good guy . . . So I guess I'll check out a few in Sac and a few in Reno, see which ones I like best."

Clay nodded. "Sounds like a viable plan. He have insurance for that sort of thing? I hear they can get pretty expensive."

"Shep's never been too open about his finances." He eyed the dilapidated duplex warily. "I'd say it's not great—probably a pension from the railroad and social security. But he had pretty good benefits. Hopefully that carried over into retirement. I'll have to check."

Clay opened his beer and took a swig. "Any way you'd consider sticking around? Maybe hiring one of the ladies from town to help out with him?"

"No can do." From the time he'd landed in Reno and had crammed his six-three frame into a compact rental car, he'd counted the hours until he could get back on that plane and hightail it out of here. "I've got a job in Houston, a good apartment, and a nice schoolteacher I'm seeing. Besides you, there's nothing for me in Nugget."

Clay continued tearing strips of the label off his bottle. He stuffed the shredded paper in his pocket and leaned toward Rhys. "Hear me out on this. There's talk of hiring a new police chief. Ever since Duff retired, the town's been contracting with the sheriff's department out of Quincy. Folks here aren't happy at all with their response time. Sometimes it takes a deputy forty-five minutes to get here. In an emergency . . . hell."

Rhys had to laugh at that one. "Emergency? What around here amounts to an emergency? Floyd Simmons getting stuck in the mud? Someone stealing eggs from Tessa Barnes's chicken coop?"

"That's bullshit now, Rhys. With the weekender population this town's grown to nearly six thousand people. We have our fair share of crime. Maybe not the same caliber of crime you have in Houston. But look at it this way: the less law enforcing to do, the more time to fish."

Rhys smiled. "You got me there." He lifted his chin. "What about Frank or Deets? They still with Nugget's finest?"

Clay tilted his head back and laughed. "Rhys, they were old even when we were kids. Frank died six years ago and Deets is in some retirement home near Las Vegas." Clay pulled another beer from the six-pack, but didn't open it. "Now we're completely reliant on the sheriff's department. So if you took the job, you'd get to hire your own staff."

"I appreciate the vote of confidence," Rhys said. "But it ain't happening."

Chapter 2

Two weeks later

The place was modest to say the least. Maddy had to walk through the bedroom to get to the kitchen, and the bathroom was in the back of the house.

But with a little imagination, she could probably make it habitable. Maybe even cute. Since deciding on her move to Nugget she'd put off house hunting until the last minute. At least this little duplex apartment would only be temporary. As soon as the contractors spiffed up quarters in the soon-to-be-renovated Lumber Baron Inn, she'd move in there so she could supervise the entire overhaul. In the meantime, she could walk to the inn from here.

"So you taking the place?" The guy who'd introduced himself as Rhys Shepard, the duplex owner's son, leaned against the doorjamb.

"Maybe," she said, noticing the way his shoulders filled the doorway. Maddy suddenly wished she'd put on makeup, maybe even worn her hair down instead of piling it up on top of her head like a mop.

She gave the apartment one last walk-through, staring out the windows at the breathtaking views. She could see the river, snow-covered mountains, and the town, which from here looked almost quaint.

"Did the Donner Party come through here?" she asked. Ever since her brother, Nate, had found her holed up in her Pacific Heights Edwardian, inconsolable over her husband's deception, and had dragged her to Nugget, she'd become obsessed with the tragedy. She stared out at a distant mountain peak and thought maybe it happened there. Maybe that's where the snowbound pioneers started feasting on the dead.

She'd have spatchcocked Dave, that's for sure.

She turned to face Rhys. "Is that why this street's named Donner Road?"

"Yeah . . . I think so. If you're not interested—"

"I'll take it." She reached in her purse for a checkbook. "Deposit and first month's rent, right?"

"That'll do you." He continued to stand there while she wrote the check. "So, you're fixing up the old Lumber Baron place?"

"Yes. How'd you hear about it?" she asked.

He grinned, showing a nice set of white teeth against his tan skin. "The whole town's talking about it. No secrets in Nugget."

She caught him checking out her wedding ring as she handed him the payment.

"Let me get you the key." He disappeared into his dad's side of the building and returned a few minutes later. "Here you go."

"Thanks. I probably won't need it until Monday," she said, stashing the key in one of the zippered compartments of her handbag. "That's when the movers are bringing my stuff."

"You know what time? Mine's also coming Monday. I don't think there's enough room in the driveway for two trucks."

Her curiosity must've shown, because he gave her a tight smile and said, "I'm your new neighbor."

"I thought your dad lives here?" The apartment barely had enough space for one person, let alone a second, tall, really built one.

"Me, too, now." He didn't elaborate, just jutted that strong square jaw of his at her in a way that said, *Wouldya answer my original question?*

"Hopefully in the morning. What time's yours scheduled?"

He shrugged. "They're coming from Houston, so whenever they get here. Maybe it won't be a problem. We'll have to play it by ear."

"Texas, huh?" Curiosity was killing her. "Job transfer?"

"Something like that," he said, and Maddy thought she detected a tint of bitterness in his voice. "When's your husband arriving?"

When he's done screwing our best friend's widow. For all Maddy knew Gabby had already joined Dave in Paris. "I'm not sure yet," she answered, gazing out at the railroad tracks. "Do the trains run frequently?"

"Only every four or five hours."

Super!

As if reading her mind, he said, "Don't worry, you'll get used to it," and flashed those pearly whites again.

Maybe it was just Maddy, but the smile seemed slightly sadistic. She got the feeling that moving here didn't rank high in his top picks of places to live and you know what they say . . . misery loves company.

"Well . . . I guess I better get going. I have a meeting with the contractor and the carpenter." Folding the rental agreement, she stuffed it in her purse.

He pushed himself away from the door. "I'm on my way to the bowling alley, too. Want a lift?"

She jerked her head up in surprise. "How'd you know the meeting was at the bowling alley?"

He grinned again. "I told you: no secrets in Nugget. You want that ride?"

She looked over at her new Subaru. The locals told her she'd need all-wheel drive for the rough winters. So she'd traded Dave's right-out-of-the-showroom Porsche Carrera for an Outback and kept the change for her divorce fund.

What the hell. She'd take a ride with a stranger. It was just a short walk back and Maddy could certainly use the exercise. Ever since finding Dave and Gabriella's emails she'd been eating nonstop, lying on the couch, watching the Shopping Channel, stuffing her face with Cheez-Its. At one point she'd thought about taking a pair of scissors to her husband's designer suits, scattering his pant legs and jacket arms across the front lawn. Instead, she'd just wolfed down another morning bun. The Porsche had been Nate's idea. All that business acumen had turned her brother vicious.

"Thanks," she said and got in the passenger side of the Ford Focus while he held the door open.

"It's a rental," Rhys said. "My truck's coming with the movers."

Maddy tried not to roll her eyes. "You grow up around here?"

"Yep."

She fastened her seat belt and waited for him to say more, but he didn't. "So what was that like? Growing up here?"

A deep chuckle rumbled through his throat. It was a good manly sound that gave her a little tingle. "I left as soon as I turned eighteen. So that should tell you how much I liked it."

"Is that when you moved to Texas?"

"Went to Alaska first to work on a fishing boat. Heard through the grapevine that Houston PD was hiring, so I moved there a few years later."

"Oh. So you're a police officer?" Maddy thought his ruffled hair and five-o'clock shadow looked a little scruffy for law enforcement.

"Narcotics detective, actually. After Katrina, I got promoted to sergeant."

"So what brings you back to Nugget?"

He let out a breath. "I found out a couple of weeks ago that my dad has Alzheimer's. I took a six-month leave of absence from the department so I can work things out here."

She reached out and touched his arm as it rested on the console. "That's awful about your dad. I'm so sorry. What about your mom, siblings, can't they help?"

"Don't have any, it's just the two of us." He turned onto the square, parked the car, but left the engine running. "So what's your story?"

"Well, not so much to tell. My brother and I are planning to rehab the Lumber Baron and turn it into a luxury inn."

He looked skeptical. "Luxury and Nugget. Now there's an oxymoron."

Her thoughts exactly. But she stuck to Nate's spiel. "This place is a dream for outdoor enthusiasts. But other than the campsites in the state park and a few motels and rustic cabins, there are no higher-end lodging options. Not unless you schlep all the way to Reno, Truckee, or Tahoe." She removed her safety belt and turned sideways in her seat. "It's not like we're building a Ritz or anything, just a more comfortable alternative to what's already available. Not all adventurers want to rough it."

He made a face. "Y'all know what you're doing?"

Disarmed by his brusqueness, she laughed. "Yeah, I'm pretty sure we do. My husband's family happens to own one of the largest luxury hotel chains in the world."

"Didn't hear you mention him being involved in this little venture of yours. Just your brother."

He was blunt. And perceptive. "My brother owns one of the best known hotel management companies in San Francisco. And my parents operate high-end boutique inns in the Midwest. Does that work for you?"

Rhys cut the motor and turned to face her. "I didn't mean to offend you, sugar. It's just—"

"Whoa, whoa, whoa," she stopped him. "Do I look like a sugar to you?"

He gave her a cheeky grin. "Excuse my Texas . . . What I was trying to say, Miz Breyer"—he drew out both the "Miz" and the "Breyer"—"is have you looked around this place?"

Unfortunately, he had a point. Half the storefronts on the square were boarded up. But if she and her brother wanted the inn to be successful, they had to sell this place as if it was the next Lake Tahoe.

"Maybe we're exactly what this town needs," she said. "Something to kick it in its pants. If everyone came together and spruced up the place and created a clever marketing campaign to attract visitors, Nugget could be a major destination vacation spot. And that would be a win-win for the whole town."

Rhys held his hands up in surrender, looking so contrite that it made Maddy laugh again. They just sat there for a few minutes, not saying anything, until Rhys opened the car door. She followed him into the Ponderosa, where they went their separate ways—Rhys to join a handsome man in a cowboy hat and she to join her brother and their builders, Colin Burke and Pat Donnelly.

Pat was a popular contractor in the area, but Colin was a bit of an enigma. Strapping, scruffy, intensely shy, and very private. His carpentry, however, was exemplary. He'd done much of the restoration for Sophie and Mariah, bringing the Ponderosa's vintage woodwork back to life. In his spare time, he worked on his own home and ran a small Internet furniture business—with rocking chairs as his specialty.

He'd agreed to help restore the Lumber Baron for a very fair price. Because Nate paid cash for the Victorian and its owner couldn't wait to unload the decrepit building, they'd closed escrow in record time. The mansion was theirs—rats, bats and all. Nate, a world-class finagler, had also managed to sprint through the licensing and permitting process to turn the one-time family residence into a hotel. It helped that the vacant Victorian—built by a wealthy timberman in the late eighteen hundreds for his bride—sat on nearly one quarter of Nugget's commercial square. Now all she had to do was make the Lumber Baron beautiful again, fill it with guests, and turn a tidy profit.

The prospect of leaving San Francisco and taking up residence in this dusty, depressed town held about as much appeal as chugging battery acid. But Nate had wheedled, pleaded, and finally convinced her to at least oversee the hotel's restoration and opening.

"After that we'll take it one day at a time," he'd promised.

But she'd known full well that he'd conceived this whole inn idea just for her. Two months ago they'd stood in this very square, in front of the broken-down Victorian, and Nate had told her the painful truth.

"I think you wasted the last five years of your life trying to be the perfect wife, standing on the sidelines so Prince Dave Wellmont could be the hotshot. When you, little sister, used to be amazing."

Tears rolling down her cheeks, she'd turned to him. "I'm not amazing anymore?"

He'd shaken his head. "But we're going to get you back. We're going to buy this place, polish it up to its former glory, and turn it into a five-diamond inn."

"But I don't like it here," she'd sniffed.

Nate had shrugged off her aversion to the town. "It's as good a place as any to find yourself."

At the time, his words had hurt, made her question the kind of person she'd become. But the challenge of starting this project from scratch, and the chance to finally use her innate skills—the ones that had made her family, the Breyers, among the most respected names in hospitality management—gave her hope that breathing new life into the old mansion would somehow make Maddy new again, too.

It also scared her to death.

"Who's that?" Clay drew circles with his finger in the condensation left on the table by his coffee mug.

"Maddy Breyer, new owner of the Lumber Baron mansion and Shep's new tenant."

"Pretty."

"Married." Although Rhys got the impression that there may be problems on that front. Why would she move to the middle of nowhere to renovate a piece-of-shit building without her husband?

He grabbed the menu and scanned the list of lunch items. On his few occasions eating at the Ponderosa, he'd found the food decent. Unfortunately, the restaurant's Western-style saloon décor—dark paneled walls, Victorian light sconces, red velvet curtains, and pleather banquettes—reminded him of a Nevada whorehouse. At least the other half was a modern bowling alley. Ten lanes, shoe rental booth, video-game arcade, and food concession stand.

"You taking the job?" Clay closed his menu.

"Yep. Seems to be the best temporary solution."

"You don't look too happy about it."

Rhys just shrugged. "It'll give me the time I need to work things out here. Either find an assisted-living-type situation for my dad, or . . . something." He didn't know why he cared. It wasn't like Shep had ever given a rat's ass about Rhys. But when Rhys's mom had run out on them, Shep had at least kept him fed and put a roof over his head. That had to be worth something. Or so Rhys told himself.

"Houston's giving you a leave?"

"Six months under our union contract for family care. The department's okay with me taking the interim chief position. I told them it's more of a consulting gig to get Nugget PD up and running again until they can hire someone permanent."

"The lady?" When Rhys drew a blank, Clay said, "The school-teacher you've been seeing?"

"Christy? She wouldn't last one day here." He chuckled, thinking about how crazy she'd go without her weekly Galleria fix. "That was more of a casual thing."

Rhys let his gaze wander over to Maddy's table. Clay had been right about her being pretty. In Houston, a lot of the women wore tons of makeup, stiff hairdos, flashy clothes. He much preferred Maddy's fresh face. He liked the shades of gold and red swirling through her brown hair, which she'd shoved up into a kind of twist. And she did nice things to a pair of jeans and sweater.

Too bad she was already married. Rhys was no saint, but when it came to married women he had a strict hands-off policy. Otherwise, she might be nice for whiling away the tedious Nugget hours.

He turned his attention back to Clay. "I'm not getting back in a damn uniform."

Clay nearly choked on his coffee. "Come again?"

"You ever wear one of those things? They itch."

"Okay. So don't wear it. I doubt anyone will care. As long as you're loaded for bear, that's good enough for this town."

Rhys lowered his voice. "The salary's a nice consolation. I wasn't expecting that kind of money for a small-town cop."

"Surprised me, too." Clay motioned a server over. "But the city charter says the pay has to be competitive with other police chiefs and that's the going rate in California."

"You don't see me arguing." Rhys ordered a club sandwich, a side of fries, and an iced tea. When the server left, he asked, "But can the city afford it?"

"Looks like."

Rhys moved in a little closer to the table. "I know you went to bat for me on this job, Clay, and I really appreciate it. I won't mess you up on this."

"I know you won't. My prediction is they'll give it to you permanently after you prove yourself."

"I'll prove myself," Rhys said. "But Houston's my place."

"What's so great about Houston?"

"I'm due for promotion there. Lieutenant. It's a huge department . . . lieutenant's a really big deal and a decent pay hike." He paused, weighing his words carefully. The McCreedys had always been his salvation here and he didn't want to come off ungrateful. "To tell you the truth, Clay, this place isn't good for me—stirs up a lot of bad stuff. Somewhere else . . . well, I can be a different person."

"Rhys," Clay said. "A place doesn't define you. Let it go, man."

Rhys wished he could. But from the moment he'd crossed Nugget's city limits that old feeling of isolation crept through him like a metastasizing cancer. He looked over at Maddy's table again. The Ponderosa's two proprietors had joined her group and the three women looked pretty chummy. "So what's the deal with the new owners?"

"Mariah and Sophie?"

"Yeah."

Before Clay could answer, their food came and he dug into his heaping plate of steak and eggs like a starving man. "What do you want to know? Are they a couple? Yeah, they are."

"Shep says they're trying to take over the town."

"Yeah, I'm not surprised. They moved up from the Bay Area about a year ago. Made some waves when they fixed up the place."

"Why?" Rhys held up his glass to signal the server for a refill.

Clay shook his head. "It's stupid. Some of the old-timers accused them of yuppifying Nugget."

"Yuppifying?" Rhys had to cover his face so the kid pouring the iced tea wouldn't see him laughing. "So how will these same people feel about the new inn? Because it sounds like Maddy and her brother have all kinds of grand plans to buff up downtown."

"You grew up in this town. How do you think people will react? I'm sure a number of the businesses will fully support it. But it's bound to cause a shitstorm with some of the rest of the town."

"Even if it helps the local economy?" Rhys might have his doubts about a fancy hotel succeeding in a country town snowed-in three months out of the year. But he couldn't believe residents would actually stand in its way. People were hurting. Anything that would bring money to Nugget, or create jobs, would be a boon to the community.

"Look at the good side, when they start throwing Molotov cocktails, you'll get to shoot someone."

Just then, a middle-aged lady in turquoise jeans, a white blouse tied at her waist, and an arm full of clunky bracelets sidled up to their table.

"Clayton McCreedy, I found you a woman," she announced, scooting her butt next to Rhys's in the booth.

"I wasn't aware I was looking for one," Clay said. "Donna, you remember Rhys Shepard, now our new police chief?"

"Of course." Pinching a silverware setting from the next table, she helped herself to some of Clay's eggs. She grabbed a shaker from the caddy and sprinkled the rest of his scramble with salt, then tried another bite. "Not bad. Not as good as mine. But not bad at all." With the napkin, she dabbed the corner of her mouth.

Clay looked around the crowded dining room. "Tater seems to be packing them in. This place used to be deader than four o'clock before they hired a local. The Ponderosa cutting into your business at the Bun Boy?"

"Nah." She waved her hand through the air. "It's good to have a sit-down restaurant. And I like the gals, Sophie and Mariah. They add a little diversity to this white-bread town."

Donna turned to Rhys. "You don't remember me, do you?"

"No, ma'am," he said a little sheepishly.

"What's with the ma'am? Do I look ancient to you? I'm not even old enough to be your mother."

"Sorry." Women around here sure were touchy. "It's a Texas thing. You know . . . being courteous."

"This is California. We're all about being rude." That made Rhys's mouth quirk.

"Well," she continued. "I have a perfect memory of you. People here used to think you were a wild boy, more than likely headed for prison. But I remember pulling into the Nugget Gas and Go . . . you were filling an old can . . . and I couldn't figure out the newly installed pump system. You came over and politely showed me how to work it, then filled my tank. And here you are, chief of police. Go figure!"

She leaned back against the plush seat. "So, you've come back to take care of all the people who didn't take care of you?"

The woman was obviously missing a filter. Rhys kind of liked her, though. "It's just temporary, until I can square away my dad."

"How is Shep?"

"He's getting by."

"You let me know if there is anything I can do." Donna pulled a pen and a small notebook from her enormous purse, scribbled a name and number on the page, ripped it out and shoved it at Clay. "Call her. She's gorgeous, newly divorced and has kids." With a quick pat to Rhys's thigh, she slid across the bench and wiggled out from behind the table. "You single, Chief?"

Before he could answer that he wasn't in the market, Clay interjected. "He's single and looking."

"Well, then, I'll keep my eye out," Donna said, and Rhys watched her size up his vital statistics like a world-class tailor.

After she sauntered off, Rhys pulled the paper from Clay's grip to read it. "What're you, *The Bachelor* now?"

"The women of Nugget have decided it's time I started dating again. But thanks to you, they now have fresh meat." Clay reached over and clapped him on the shoulder.

He looked at Clay pensively and nudged his chin at him. "You ready to start dating again?"

Clay shrugged. "When I can sneak away, I've got a flight attendant I'm seeing in Reno. But I wouldn't call what we're doing dating." He stared into the distance for a moment. "The boys are having enough trouble adjusting. Hell, Rhys, I spent most of their lives on an aircraft carrier in the middle of the Persian Gulf. They hardly know me. The last thing they need right now is me dragging strange women through their lives."

Maybe at some point a woman who wasn't strange would be good for them, Rhys thought, but didn't say. After his own mother had left, he used to fantasize about having a stepmother who would take care of him, make him lunches the way the other boys' moms did. But Shep had never dated.

"Next time you want to sneak off to Reno, I'll hang out with Justin and Cody. It'd be good for them to have a man around."

"You always were delusional. But I'll keep it in mind." Clay pulled a couple of bills from his wallet and put them on the table. "That should cover both of us. I need to get home—feed some cattle before the boys get out of school."

Rhys finished his tea and checked Maddy's table again. Her meeting seemed to be in full swing. Hopefully she didn't expect a ride back to Donner Road, because he needed to beat it home.

And getting too cozy with his new neighbor wasn't such a hot idea.

Chapter 3

Nugget's commercial district wore a suit of dinginess. Although Maddy had walked these streets numerous times before the mansion had closed escrow, she'd never inspected the square the way a discerning tourist might. Not until now.

The park looked well kept. But as she and Nate strolled from the Ponderosa to the Lumber Baron she made a list of transgressions in her head.

Broken signs with missing letters. A jungle of weeds sprouting in the planting strips between the curbs and sidewalks. Building façades drab from age and weather. Yet, despite the overall disheveled appearance, a couple of the downtown shops seemed to be doing a brisk business. There was a combination dance-yoga studio, a resale clothing shop, a sporting goods store, a bike and kayak rental service, and a dumpy kiosk that advertised horseback, boat, river, hiking, and railroad tours. An old-fashioned red, white, and blue pole signified that a barber shop shared the same block with a burger joint called the Bun Boy, where a smattering of people waited in line.

"You taking that place on Donner Road?" Nate asked, interrupting her silent audit.

"Yep. Signed the papers, met the landlord's son, got the key. I'm good to go."

Nate slowed his pace almost to a stop, signaling that he was about to impart some big, bad brotherly wisdom. "Mad, you'll see, this'll be good . . . Dave's an asshole."

Lately, every conversation, no matter how innocuous, seemed to take a detour to Dave. *How 'bout those Giants? And what's the deal with your cheating dirtbag husband?* The comments served as a constant reminder of her poor judgment. How, for the entirety of a five-year marriage, do you not know that your husband's in love with his cousin's wife?

Even before Maddy had come into the picture, Dave had loved Gabriella. Since he couldn't have her, he'd settled for second best. But when Max died, it had changed everything.

"What does Dad think of us turning this place into an inn?" she asked Nate as they reached the wrought iron fence that surrounded the mansion and found themselves gazing through the posts.

Once stately, the fence had gone to rust and ruin. Broken glass bottles, old car parts, and a dirty diaper littered the swath of brown grass that passed for a front yard. Most of the mansion's windows had been busted, the paint was peeling, and the Victorian's ornate gingerbread trim was probably beyond repair.

And if that wasn't bad enough, someone had scrawled "John Sucks Ass" in red paint across the carved oak entry doors.

"He likes the idea—thinks it's a good opportunity. When we get closer to opening, he and Mom want to come and help us."

"That would be nice." Their parents lived in Madison, Wisconsin, and loved coming to California for visits. "Maybe Claire and Jackson can come, too, bring the baby."

He nodded.

"Did you tell Mom and Dad about Dave and me, Nate?"

His eyes dropped to his shoes. "They suspected something when you didn't go to France. So I just told them a little—the barest of details." At least he had the decency to look embarrassed while he lied.

The Breyers were incapable of keeping secrets from each other. Something as minor as a runny nose lit up the phone lines. A breakup, and they'd be on her doorstep. As much as she loved her parents, the whole thing with Dave was hugely humiliating and she'd prefer to get some of her dignity back before they started hovering. Although they'd never said it, Maddy had known that they didn't approve of Dave. They thought he was self-entitled and spoiled and that the Wellmonts were showy.

It wasn't until Maddy was an adult that she realized how well-off her parents were. Their home, though lovely, was modest, allowances were always tied to chores, and summers were spent working in the family business, housekeeping.

"Stop screening their calls," Nate said. "They're worried about you. The only reason they've laid back this long is because they know you have me to lean on—and Sophie and Mariah—who, by the way, say Dave's dead to them."

She appreciated the loyalty of friends. Six years ago the Ponderosa's owners had come into their lives through Sophie's younger sister, a corporate lawyer whom Nate had dated for about fifteen minutes. Back then, Sophie had worked in marketing, and Nate had just started his company. He'd hired her to promote a few of his hotels and something about the two of them had clicked. Dave used to tease that Sophie had the qualities Nate dreamed of in a wife except for one really important one. She didn't do men.

Maddy would add, "Nate, she's your feminine ideal: smart, beautiful, and totally out of your reach."

A year ago, Mariah and Sophie had left San Francisco to find a slower way of life here in the Sierra mountains, ultimately taking over the Ponderosa. Then the Lumber Baron had come on the market and Sophie had immediately called Nate. The opportunity had presented itself at a perfect time—Maddy needed a distraction from her disastrous marriage and Nate wanted to buy his own hotel. And here they were, one big happy family again.

But right now, even Sophie and Mariah's allegiance seemed like cold comfort.

Maddy pushed open the iron gate, which squeaked like something out of a cheesy horror movie. The front porch sagged and bowed, making her question how much longer it would safely hold a person. Despite her misgivings, she climbed up on the veranda and felt it slump under her weight.

"I've got a few ideas for the inn I want to talk to you about," she said as Nate joined her on the porch.

"Great. Let's go inside, it's getting cold."

She motioned for him to go first. "Age before beauty." Even though they had walked through the place repeatedly it still gave her the creeps.

"God, you're such a wimp."

She watched him enter and then hesitantly followed. A long time ago the foyer had been grand, but water damage stained the high ceilings and the wallpapered lath and plaster walls showed signs of mold. The oak floors were badly scarred, but the inlaid wooden medallion in the center of the room remained intact. The moldings and trim work hadn't been so lucky—huge chunks were missing. The elaborately carved staircase—probably oak or mahogany—had been painted hot pink.

Nate led her into the kitchen, where appliances had been ripped out of the walls and the cabinetry's antique leaded glass was smashed. She and Nate sat up on the Formica countertops—a remnant of a seventies makeover.

"Tell me what you've got."

"I was thinking that we team up with Soph and Mariah in persuading the rest of the merchants on the square to form a business association. The place looks like hell, but if we can rev up the town, get people excited about the inn and the money it'll bring, maybe everyone will pitch in to make the square more presentable."

"Yeah, I like it. Sophie's marketing background will come in handy. But I'll be spread pretty thin over the next few weeks in San Francisco. So you two will have to lead that effort."

Nate was only thirty-four and already operated nine hotels in the Bay Area. He planned to drive the four hours to Nugget every few weeks to check on the progress of the Lumber Baron, but for the most part it would be Maddy's baby. That included everything from supervising the restoration to devising a marketing plan.

"Of course," she said. "You want to hear my other idea?"

"Yep."

"How do you feel about adding some Donner Party elements to the theme of the inn?"

Nate looked at her like she'd lost her mind. "You're kidding, right?"

"No."

"Uh . . . 'cause nothing says hospitality like cannibalism?"

"Give me a break, Nathaniel. It happened in 1846. It's a huge part of the town's history—California's history—and Nugget's done nothing to capitalize on it. Look at towns like Northfield, Minnesota, where they play up all that Jesse James bank raid stuff, or Southern cities that stage reenactments of the Civil War. You can't go to a Bodega Bay hotel or restaurant that doesn't make some reference to *The Birds*."

"That was a movie, Maddy."

"You know what I mean. Here, we have a threefer"—she counted on her fingers— "gold rush, railroad, and the most shocking tragedy in California history. People love that stuff."

Nate was paying attention now, studying her intently, as if he thought she'd finally emerged from her pity party and was taking this project seriously. Nate took everything seriously. Even as a kid, her brother's ambition had bordered on pornographic. At fourteen—four years older than her and two years older than Claire—he'd celebrated his birthday by making a list of goals and tacking it to the corkboard that hung over his bedroom desk.

Goal #1: Graduate from Harvard summa cum laude (like what fourteen-year-old even knows what summa cum laude is?). Goal #2: Own the most successful hotel management company in the world by age twenty-five. Goal #3: Only drive a Jaguar. Goal #4: Buy the Green Bay Packers.

He'd accomplished at least some variation of three out of the four.

"So, how do you suggest we implement this Donner Party thing?" he asked.

Maddy wasn't quite sure yet, but had a few ideas. "We don't have to go overboard. Maybe copy some old pictures from the Historical Society and dedicate one wall in the inn to a photo essay about the event. Stock the library with historical accounts, put a little blurb about it in our sales literature—that kind of thing."

Nate wore an ear-to-ear grin.

"What?"

"No wonder Prince Silver Spoon didn't want you working for Wellmont Hotel Enterprises. You'd make him look bad and you're a pain in the ass." He got down from the counter. "Okay, run with it. But don't go nuts."

On Monday, Maddy and Rhys's moving trucks arrived at exactly the same time.

A Mayflower truck and a United Van Lines rig sat next to each other at the top of Shep's driveway like antsy racehorses at the starting gate. Maddy motioned to her driver to come down first, simulating an air traffic controller with her arms.

"Hold on a second, guys," Rhys called up, and turned to her. "Come on, Maddy. Don't make me late for my first day of work."

Her eyes moved down to the gun holstered on his hip and the blinding silver badge on his belt. "What? Gunfight at the O.K. Corral?"

"Ha, ha. Very funny." He smiled, showing these adorable creases, not quite dimples, in his cheeks that she hadn't noticed at their first meeting. "In case you didn't know, I'm Nugget's new police chief."

"Well, I'm paying by the hour." She put her hands on her hips, in a move she hoped would say, *I'm no pushover.* No, the new and improved Maddy didn't let good-looking men manipulate her. Not like Dave had. *Fool me once, shame on me . . .* No way in hell would there be a twice.

He took off his aviators and began cleaning them on his shirt, and sweet mother of Jesus he had some seriously sculpted abs. Unlike Maddy, it was a good bet he hadn't taken three turns in the buffet line at the Atlantis Casino Resort in Reno, where she'd stayed overnight for a last bit of luxury. It was the closest big city, about fifty minutes away.

And now that she could see his eyes, they were hazel, more green than brown. She must've been in a coma that first time she'd met him to have missed so many fine details.

"Thought your husband's a Hilton?" He propped himself against the porch, his dire need to get to work on time suddenly out the window.

"He makes money because he doesn't throw it away," she said. Actually Dave was born into it, but Rhys Shepard didn't need to know that. Maddy had always been the thrifty one.

"Breyer?" He scratched his chin. "Don't remember seeing any Breyer Hotels."

He was fishing for information and she knew it. Nosey parker. "That's because it's my maiden name."

"Aw, come on, sugar," Rhys said in that lazy Texas drawl Maddy suspected he only trotted out on special occasions. "Let me go first and I'll pay for your added expense."

"So, we're back to sugar again, huh?" She shook her head. The man sure thought he was some kind of sweet-talker. "Oh, all right. Go ahead."

Maddy started to walk off, but just so he'd know she wasn't a complete soft touch, called over her shoulder, "I'm subtracting the extra from the rent."

"Thank you," Rhys called back.

"Whatever." She was only doing it because his father had Alzheimer's.

She decided to get a start on the cleaning while she waited for Rhys and his movers to unload their truck. Balancing a box of supplies in one hand and her purse in the other, she pushed the door of her apartment open with her foot and set out to make the place sparkle. An hour later, she wandered outside for some fresh air to find two burly guys loading one ugly-ass plaid couch into Rhys's moving truck.

She looked over at Rhys, who was standing on the porch having an animated conversation with his father. Hmm, it looked like they were going at it, she thought as she tried not to be too obvious about watching them. But he caught her out of the corner of his eye.

"Okay. Your turn." He motioned at the moving van that was leaving.

"Well, it's about time."

He jogged down the steps and chucked her on the chin. "Thanks again for being a sport."

Ten minutes later he had reached the top of the driveway, zooming away behind the wheel of a pickup. She looked back at the porch and

Mr. Shepard was gone. He must've gone inside the house, because Maddy didn't see him leave.

For much of the morning she moved around furniture, unpacked boxes, hung up pictures, and set up her small kitchen. Not much of a cook, Maddy brought only the essentials. She walked through the three-room house to admire her handiwork and thought the place didn't look half bad.

She'd taken most of the pool house and sunroom furniture from her and Dave's place. They were bright and cheery. Most of the pieces in the main house were dark, ornate Wellmont heirlooms Dave's mother Brooke had insisted on. They'd made Maddy feel like she was living in a museum.

The restoration of the three-story house had been her full-time job for the last four years. Brooke had loved the idea, more than likely relieved that it kept Maddy home and out of Wellmont Hotel Enterprises.

Her mother-in-law never let Maddy forget that the Wellmonts owned hotels, while the Breyers just managed them.

The day after she and Dave had announced their engagement, Brooke had taken her to the Rotunda at Neiman Marcus for lunch to celebrate. At least that's what Maddy had thought. But before her salad Niçoise ever made it to the table, Brooke whipped a thirty-eight-page prenup out of her Birkin bag and shoved it in Maddy's face.

"If it's my son you love and not his money, you'll sign this."

Stunned, she'd sat there with the pen dangling from her hand. Summoning all her courage, she'd simply said, "No." Then she got up and walked out of the restaurant, past the St. John Resort collection, down the escalator, around the La Mer counter, and out the glass revolving doors. While falling in love with Dave, she'd never stopped to consider the implications of his wealth. The Breyers might've been rich, but compared to the Wellmonts . . .

With tears blurring her eyes, she'd called Dave from the street on her cell phone.

"I'll fix this, Maddy," he'd told her. "When you're my wife, everything I own is yours."

That night he'd come to her studio apartment above Lupe's Taque-

ria on Valencia and they'd sat on the floor, eating dumplings out of
Chinese takeout cartons. Like he'd promised, he'd fixed it, in effect
telling Brooke to shove the prenup up her liposuctioned ass.

"I threatened we'd leave San Francisco, work for your parents, or
open our own chain of hotels," he'd told Maddy, and her heart had
soared.

The next morning, after Dave had left for work, Maddy put on her
best suit, hailed a cab to the Financial District, took the elevator to
the fifth floor of Wellmont Hotel Enterprises, and signed it. She'd
signed the prenup as a testament to her love for Dave.

What a colossal idiot she'd been.

The only money she had on her own was a $200,000 inheritance
from her grandmother, which she'd plunked down on the Lumber
Baron. Although the amount paled in comparison to Nate's stake, it
would've been enough to live off of for several years until she could
rebuild her career. Her brother insisted that she draw a small salary
until they got the inn up and running.

She wandered onto the porch, thinking that a few pots of flowers
and a nice Adirondack chair might warm up the entry when she
smelled smoke and something like melting rubber, or plastic. It reminded her of Wisconsin and their neighbor who used to burn his
garbage in the backyard—it drove her mother nuts.

She followed the noxious smell to the other side of the duplex
where it seemed to be coming from inside the apartment. When no
one answered her knock, she let herself in.

Shep, wearing a pair of bib overalls without a shirt, was flailing
his spindly, bare arms in the middle of the room, holding a Bic lighter
in one hand and a blanket in the other. Next to him, a stack of moving
boxes filled with sports equipment smoldered. He stared at the pile, a
little smile playing on his lips, as if hoping for the molten rubber to
turn into a blazing beach bonfire.

So far, the embers were contained to the pile of cartons, but if the
boxes went up so would the floors, taking the whole house with it. Vi-
sions of the surrounding forest bursting into an inferno catapulted
Maddy into action. She looked over at Shep, who continued to watch
the nascent blaze with unconcealed joy.

Definitely no help in that corner.

She ripped the quilt from his grasp and used it in an effort to smother the burning boxes. "Stay calm," she told herself, grabbing the phone off a little mail table near the door and dialing 9-1-1. The operator remained on the line, coolly giving her instructions until backup arrived. She dashed into the kitchen, found a mop bucket, filled it with water, and dumped it on the smoky pile like the operator told her. When that appeared to have doused any residual hot spots, she gingerly lifted the blanket to make sure. No burning embers, at least none she could see.

Just a big mess.

She hung up the phone and turned her gaze on Shep.

His bushy gray brows shot up as he looked her over. "Who the hell are you?"

"I'm Maddy Breyer." When he glared at her puzzled, she said, "your new tenant," and reached for the lighter. He pulled the Bic away and shoved it in his bib pocket. "Mr. Shepard, you could've burned the whole house down."

"Would've served the boy right," he muttered.

"Mr. Shepard, are you okay?" Dumb question. Of course he wasn't okay, the man had Alzheimer's.

"He took my damn car keys."

"What do you need the keys for?"

"You daft, woman? That lughead's trying to starve me."

"I won't let you go hungry. If you want, I could go to the store right now and get groceries," she volunteered, but wondered how prudent it would be to leave him alone.

"Why does everyone think I'm a damned invalid?"

"Would you like me to take you to the market, Mr. Shepard? Then you could do your own shopping."

"What I want is for you to get the hell out of my house."

Before he could toss her, a couple of brawny firemen barreled through the door.

"Uh . . . I think we have everything under control now," she said, embarrassed that in the heat of the moment she might've overreacted.

One of the firemen pulled what was left of the boxes apart. Looked like Rhys's tennis shoes were toast. His basketball hadn't fared too well, either. Shep, outgunned, stomped off into his bedroom and slammed the door.

"How'd it happen?" one of the firefighters asked as he sifted through the cartons.

Rhys saved her from having to answer. He came tearing through the house, stopped in front of the carnage and frowned. He and the firefighters huddled together, talking, while Maddy sat on a leather sofa that was wrapped in moving plastic. The same plastic covered the mattress and box spring that leaned against the wall. This was the first opportunity she'd had to look around the room. Except for the charred remains of Rhys's worldly possessions and the stacks of moving boxes, it was identical to her place.

A few minutes later, the firemen left and Rhys just stood over the destruction, running his hands through his hair. "You okay?"

"I'm fine. Sorry about your stuff. How'd you hear?"

"The 9-1-1 call."

Duh—police chief. "I probably should've just handled it on my own, but I panicked. Hope I didn't scare you to death," she said. "Your dad was upset about you taking his car keys. I think the fire was an act of protest."

Somehow she got the impression that he'd already surmised that.

"Would you mind waiting here a sec?" Rhys asked.

Before she could say "sure," he marched into Shep's room.

"What the hell's wrong with you?" She heard him say through the wall.

"Who do you think you are, boy, ruling over me like you're king? You're trying to dominate me."

"Oh, for Christ's sake, you could've set the whole town on fire . . . hurt that nice woman next door . . . All because you're pissed at me over those stupid keys? God, you're a selfish bastard."

There was a loud thump and Maddy considered rushing into the room and breaking up whatever was going on in there. Rhys's next words to his father stopped her.

"You listen and you listen good. You pull another stunt like this and I'll put you in a stinking home. It's your choice, old man, because

I really don't give a shit. Now give me the goddamn lighter and go apologize to Mrs. Breyer."

Shep emerged from his room, tufts of his white hair sticking up on his head, and marched up to Maddy like a petulant child. "I'm sorry." He didn't bother to look her in the eye when he said it. Just turned on his heels and disappeared behind the door.

Rhys rubbed his hands down his eyes. "He would've put the fire out before it got out of control. He was just trying to teach me a lesson—that's the kind of shit he pulls. Look, I've gotta get back. You sure you're okay?"

Maddy nodded.

"If there are any more problems . . . Hell, just hit him over the head with a frying pan."

Maddy followed him out the door. "He's sick, Rhys."

Rhys kept walking, but gave a short laugh. "Nope. That right there's Stan Shepard in all his coherent glory. He's a real son of a bitch."

By the time Rhys got home that evening, the debris from the fire had been cleared away. His bed had been set up at the far end of the room, away from the front door, and made with fresh linens. His clothes had been folded and stored in his dresser drawers. The leather sofa now sat at an angle that separated the room into two spaces— living and sleeping. And a few of his books had been arranged on the coffee table he'd moved here from Houston.

It looked nice.

He checked on his father, who lay in a lump in the middle of the bed. Rhys suspected him of playing possum and gave him a nudge. "Who set up my things?"

"That buttinsky from next door," Shep grunted, and rolled onto his stomach.

Rhys left the room. The last thing he needed was another confrontation. After today's histrionics, he'd made a few phone calls about getting someone part-time to sit with Shep. His doctor had assured Rhys that even a responsible teenager could do it.

"What you need right now is someone who is warm, patient, caring, and responsible," she'd said. "Not someone with a wall full of certificates. When it gets to that point, Shep'll have to go into a long-term care facility."

The problem was finding someone reliable in this small town. He had a couple of leads. Hopefully something would pan out by the end of the week. In the meantime, he'd have to make sure to hide all the matches and lighters.

He walked to the kitchen and found a takeout box from the Ponderosa in the refrigerator. Someone had set the table with a place mat, napkin, and silverware—more compliments of Maddy, he presumed—and heated the meat loaf and mashed potatoes in the microwave. When the bell dinged, he grabbed a beer and ate.

He'd spent most of his day—at least until the 9-1-1 call came over the radio—organizing the office, a nondescript building on the square that had been left vacant after Duff retired. He'd posted positions for five officers and a dispatcher on an online law-enforcement job board. A few people he vaguely remembered from the past had popped in to say hello. He suspected they were curious to see how Stan Shepard's son had turned out.

After cleaning up the kitchen, Rhys started to take the few steps over to Maddy's place to thank her. He walked out onto the back porch and stopped to take in the scent of pine mingled with crisp, clean, cold air. Stars filled the inky sky. He couldn't remember ever having seen so many—at least not in Houston. Even the lights from town, twinkling like Christmas, made him take in a breath.

It had to be forty or fifty degrees out. In Boy Scouts he'd learned to measure the temperature by counting how many times a cricket chirped in fourteen seconds and adding that to forty. Although the method stopped being accurate at temperatures lower than fifty-five degrees, he tried to calculate anyway. But instead of hearing cricket song, he heard something like crying. And it was coming from Maddy's apartment.

His first impulse was to turn tail, go back inside the house and pretend like he hadn't heard anything. But he remembered the apathetic Mrs. Brown and let guilt get the better of him. With his fist poised to knock on her door, her trembling voice came through the apartment.

"You tell me that you've been in love with her our entire marriage, yet you don't want me to leave you? What am I supposed to do, Dave? Wait patiently while you choose which woman you want to spend the rest of your life with?"

Ah—so Hotel Boy's a cheating asshole, Rhys thought as he shamelessly eavesdropped. That answered why she was here and Dave, dickless heir to the Wellmont hotel dynasty, wasn't. Yeah, he'd Googled them both at work today.

Someone ought to kick the guy's ass.

"Did you want me to find those emails?" Maddy asked Dave, somehow pulling the words from her throat without falling apart.

Two months ago, when she'd accidentally stumbled upon the emails, Maddy had sat there transfixed, reading them over and over again, trying to convince herself that she had somehow misconstrued their meaning. And then it all started to come together like a gut-churning montage—the inappropriate attention Dave lavished on Gabby during family gatherings, their bizarrely intimate telephone conversations, and the inexplicable gloominess that always came over Dave at the end of a weekend spent with Gabriella and Max.

"I'm thinking you did it because you're a coward and couldn't tell me the truth," she said, with a challenge. "You know—accidentally on-purpose."

The other end of the line went silent.

Maddy wished they weren't doing this on the phone. But Dave was in Paris for the foreseeable future, brokering the acquisition of a French chain of luxury inns. So they'd been rehashing the same argument long distance.

"Of course not, Maddy," he finally said.

She could visualize him running his fingers through his sun-streaked hair in that harried way he did when something was bothering him. How could she hate him with every fiber in her body and love him at the same time?

"There's no way in hell I meant for you to find out that way. I planned to tell you everything when you came to France. Oh, baby . . . It's so complicated. And you're my best friend—"

"Don't!" Maddy shouted. "*Max* was your best friend. And the whole time, you were in love with his wife. My God, Dave. If the aneurysm hadn't killed him, your betrayal would've. He couldn't have loved you more if you were his own brother.

"And what about Gabby? Is she there with you now?" The thought of the beautiful, graceful, perfect Gabriella wrapped naked in Dave's arms ripped Maddy's heart out.

He exhaled and she could hear the sadness in his voice. "I'm by myself, thinking about you and what we have together. Look, I don't want to do this while I'm overseas. I want us to sit down and talk, so I can explain. Baby, you're everything to me."

She whimpered, trying to wipe away tears while holding the phone. "But I'm not her."

There was a long pause and then a deep sigh. "Can we do this when I get back?"

"Why? So you can avoid having to admit that the only reason you married me was in the desperate hope that I could deliver you from temptation? Did it work, Dave? Did I keep you from sleeping with your best friend's wife?"

Other than the sound of his breathing, Dave's muteness told her all she needed to know. "You've been sleeping with her all along— even before Max died—haven't you?" Maddy's stomach clenched as she squeezed her eyes shut to dam the hot flow of new tears. From the tone of the emails she should have known that Dave and Gabriella had been sharing a physical relationship from the start, but denial was a beautiful thing. "Oh, God."

"It's over now, Maddy. I swear. It's . . . she's out of my system. I love you so much. All I want to do is make this work."

He actually expected her to believe that after all these years of pining for Gabriella to the point of obsession, he was over her. Just like that. Even if he were telling the truth, which given his history seemed doubtful, how could she ever get beyond that kind of betrayal? How could she ever trust again?

"Maddy, you're not going to leave me, are you?" His voice went soft and for the first time she heard true fear.

Her throat tightened and she felt on the verge of hysterics. "I think that's pretty obvious."

"I'm on the next plane out, baby. We'll talk. We'll work it out."

"No. Don't come. I need to be alone. . . . I need to understand why this happened." *And I'm done with you.*

She clicked off and curled up in a ball on her bed, her head swimming with recriminations. But the one that kept floating to the top was the harshest. Nate was right. Somewhere along the way Maddy had sacrificed her entire identity to become Dave's *perfect* wife. And the whole seamless tableau had been nothing but an illusion.

Chapter 4

The Ponderosa was hopping, nearly every table full, including the twelve stools at the bar. The best thing Sophie had ever done was hire Tater. Not that his cooking would win them a Michelin star, but the fact that he was a local and dished up comfort food drew in customers. The town was sort of provincial that way, but she and Mariah were getting used to it.

A year ago, Sophie never could've imagined running a bowling alley–saloon. Or playing Patsy Cline on an old Seeburg jukebox. All she and Mariah had known at the time was that they wanted to flee the rat race before they turned forty, move to a beautiful place and start a family. Then the Ponderosa came up for sale and they couldn't resist buying it and going Western-era redux.

Sophie placed her last order and caught sight of Dink Caruthers motioning to her at the entrance to the bowling center. The mayor and his posse, a group of geezers otherwise known as the Nugget Mafia—nothing got done in the town without their stamp of approval—were her Saturday morning regulars. Every week, they ate the same breakfast—chicken-fried steak and eggs with extra gravy—at the same table. Then they bowled—in the same lane.

Sophie headed his way. "Hello, Mr. Mayor. What can I do for you?"

Disgruntled, he shoved his hands into the pockets of his polyester Dickies and let out an exasperated breath. "Lane three isn't working again. Same trouble as before. The rake isn't sweeping up the pins. The kid you've got in there doesn't have a clue."

"Let me see what I can do." She took off her apron and stowed it in the drink station before entering the alley. Once Sophie got behind the lanes, she fiddled with the hydraulic pinsetter, flipped a few switches to reboot the mechanism, and waited to see if it would reset.

Nothing happened.

"Sorry, guys." Sophie walked down the wooden lane in her stockinged feet. "Someone from the manufacturer is due out to repair it, but unfortunately Nugget isn't on their regular route."

"Isn't Mariah one of those Silicon Valley engineers?" Owen the barber huffed, offering Sophie his arm so she wouldn't slip on the oiled floor. Dink might be the mayor, but Owen was the grand poobah of Nugget's power structure. "Can't she make it work?"

"She's a software designer, Owen, not a technician." She scanned the room to find an empty lane. "I'll move you guys to ten. That one is working fine and you'll have that end of the center all to yourselves."

Earl, proprietor of the Nugget Feed Store, grumbled. The old goat. And Dink whined, "Three's my lucky lane."

"Well, maybe you'll get lucky on ten." Begrudgingly, they followed her to the other side of the room, lugging their balls with them. Their bowling shoes made squeaking noises on the old gymnasium floor that she'd had Colin Burke, the local carpenter, painstakingly refinish.

"You gearing up for the Halloween festival?" Owen asked her.

"Yep. We're on drink duty." At last year's festival, the townsfolk hadn't yet warmed to her and Mariah. Ah, who was she kidding? They had just plain ignored them.

"Don't forget to put one of those posters I brought by in your window," he said. She promised she would, even though the festival didn't need any advertising. It was all the town could talk about.

On a nearby bench, she took a seat and slipped her feet back into her clogs.

"So, Soph," Dink asked. "What do you think of our new interim police chief?"

"I haven't formally met him yet, although he's been in the restaurant a few times. But I hear he's got great credentials." And, according to her staff, he was a generous tipper.

"He's a homegrown boy, you know?"

"I thought he's from Houston," she said, tamping down the urge to call them on their insularity.

"Nope," Owen interrupted. "Grew up here. Truth is, we thought the boy was more likely to wind up on the other side of the law, the way that odd father of his let him run around unsupervised."

"Looks like he turned out okay," she said. And now, according to town gossip, the "odd" father had Alzheimer's. Sad.

"We're gonna give him a chance, see how he does, before making anything permanent," Dink said, and the rest of the Nugget Mafia nodded their heads in agreement.

From what Sophie had heard, the new chief had no desire to stay, just needed a job until he could find a living situation for his father. "You gentlemen okay now? I've got to get back to the restaurant."

"Yeah," Dink said. "But get lane three fixed."

"Yes, sir," she said, and returned to the dining room, where the morning rush had begun to subside.

Maddy sat in a booth in the back. Sophie waved to her, pressed up to the bar and told Mariah she was taking a break.

"You gonna talk to her?" Mariah whispered.

"I think now's a good time, don't you?"

Mariah nodded, reached under the bar, and handed Sophie the thick catalog that had become their required reading. "Want me to come with you?"

"You mind the store," Sophie said. "It'll be touchy for her and I don't want her to feel overwhelmed."

Sophie found Maddy eating a late breakfast and slid into the seat across from her. "You all moved in?"

"Yep," she said. "Now I can focus full-time on the Lumber Baron, getting a business association started and turning this place into tourism central. In fact, I have a lead on a local historian who might be able to help me with the Donner Party angle."

"You're not letting that one go, are you?" Sophie knew that Nate thought the topic might be a little dark for vacationers.

"Heck no. I'm telling you, we play it up and we'll put this place on the map."

Sophie thought Maddy might actually be on to something. The calamity had certainly earned its place in California history. Why not use it to attract tourists? From her days as a marketer, Sophie knew everyone liked a good story.

"Anything new with Dave?"

Maddy wiggled her ring finger. Her marquise-cut diamond was gone and only a pale indentation was left. Sophie imagined that it would take a while for the dent to come back—at least as long as the dent in Maddy's heart.

"Is this it?" she asked quietly. "You filing?"

Maddy nodded. "Maybe it seems rash. I suppose some would argue that the first tenet of marriage is for better, for worse. But what Dave did . . . it's a deal breaker, Soph."

Sophie didn't think there was anything rash about divorcing Dave. Admittedly, she'd once counted him as a close friend. Now, however, her advice to Maddy would be: Take Dave for every dime he had.

"You getting a lawyer?" she asked.

"I'm sure Nate knows someone good." Maddy played with the cottage cheese on her plate.

Nate would hook Maddy up with a shark. She'd need one. Dave's legal team would be top-of-the-line, and given the chance, would skin Maddy alive. "Hang tough, girl."

"Listen," Sophie continued. "I know the timing is awful on this, but I wanted to talk to you about something."

"Soph," Maddy reprimanded. "You can talk to me about anything, anytime."

"Okay," Sophie said, and let out a breath. "We're finally taking the baby plunge. Business has gotten good. And . . . my God, Maddy . . . waking up every day in this breathtaking place is like paradise. It's perfect for raising a family."

Before Maddy could say anything, Sophie held up her hand. "I know how difficult the miscarriages were for you and Dave. I don't want to do anything that would be insensitive to that. But we desperately need your help."

Maddy reached across the table and gave Sophie a hug. "How? Tell me how, and I'll do it."

Sophie laughed and slid the catalog across the table. "Pick one."

Maddy examined the cover for a good long time, then slowly leafed through the directory. "Wow, this is like the Hammacher Schlemmer of men. You're actually planning to find the baby's daddy in here?"

Sophie saw skepticism written across Maddy's face. Or maybe it was *ick*. Honestly, she'd had a similar reaction. How do you choose your baby's DNA from a catalog? Like garden seeds or a fruit basket. It seemed so sterile, so impersonal, so loveless. Not a way to bring a living being into the world. But going with an anonymous sperm donor had been Mariah's decree.

"We just think it's safer legally to go with someone unknown. Fewer complications," Sophie said, trying to put the best spin on it.

"I can see that," Maddy flipped back to the cover of the donor catalog. "Is this place reputable?"

"It's a fully licensed and accredited sperm bank," Sophie said. "We did a lot of checking around and this one comes highly recommended."

She leaned across the table and turned the pages marked with multicolored Post-its. "Mariah likes this one, number four six four five. But I'm partial to number six two three nine—he graduated from Columbia with a master's in journalism. Go through it; see if anyone catches your eye."

Sophie watched as Maddy carefully read through the men's profiles. "This guy looks good." She pointed. "But it says he's sold out."

"Yeah, the ones over six feet go really fast. What about Lithuanian Man?" Sophie showed her #6280. "He's five-eleven."

Maddy perused his CV and screwed up her face. "I don't know. His favorite band's *Maroon Five*."

She pushed aside her plate and let out a sigh. "Soph, I'm jinxed when it comes to picking men. Dave's evidence of that. And this,"

Maddy said, slapping her hand on the book, "seems rather impersonal."

"That's the whole point."

"Don't you want a man you care about in your baby's life?"

"Too many complications," Sophie said sadly.

But the truth was she had one man in particular whom she very much wanted to be a part of their baby's life. Sophie suspected Maddy knew exactly who he was. But even if he offered, which he hadn't, Mariah had made her position very clear.

No. Nate.

After Sophie went back to work, Rhys came in the door, scanned the room until he found Maddy, and headed to her table. In a pair of Levi's and a chambray shirt, the man knew how to rock him some denim. His stride, all loose-limbed and confident, reminded Maddy of one of those gunslingers in an old Western. She wasn't the only one enjoying his entrance. Several ladies had stopped mid-bite to ogle him.

Nugget's new police chief was definitely a looker. Given her lack of faith in men these days, Maddy found it odd that she could feel even so much as a glimmer of attraction for him. But she convinced herself that admiring a gorgeous man was natural—even healthy. Trusting one? . . . Well, that was another story altogether.

Taking the seat previously occupied by Sophie, Rhys handed her a folded piece of paper. "Virgil Ross's number. He'll talk to you."

Maddy gazed at the note. "How do you know this guy, again?"

"Back when I was a kid, he used to talk to our California civics class. Knows everything about the history of the region. He's your Donner Party guy for sure."

"Thank you, Rhys. This is great. You working on a Saturday?" She'd seen his truck parked in front of the police station.

"Yep. Until I get some help, it's just me."

"What about your dad? You need me to sit with him?"

"Nah, I handcuffed him to a tree." Chief Smartass flashed a wicked grin that would've made a weaker woman swoon.

"Great!" she joked. "He's probably setting the forest on fire as we speak."

"Nope." Rhys's lips twitched. "His pyro days are over. I just found a retired nurse to look after him. Betty won't put up with his crap. Unfortunately, she's temporary. Her daughter's about to have a baby in Southern California and she's planning to go down there for a few months." He eyed her half-eaten cottage cheese curiously.

"Want the rest?" She pushed her plate toward him.

Rhys wrinkled his nose. "No thanks."

"Yeah, I'm not a cottage cheese lover, myself."

"Then why'd you order it?"

"I started my diet today," she said on a sigh.

"What for?" He looked her up and down, then pointedly fixed on her naked ring finger—ever the observant detective.

"Just want to get into shape." This morning she could barely button her jeans.

He gave her another once-over. "Nothing wrong with your shape." Then Rhys muttered, "Just your husband."

Flabbergasted, she peered at him, and he said, "Thin walls, Maddy."

"Oh." She turned away, embarrassed.

"Sorry." He held up his hands. "I'm overstepping. But this diet thing is bullshit."

He must've overheard everything between her and Dave and thought Maddy had low self-esteem. Terrific! She was now officially pathetic.

Presumably sensing her discomfort, he deftly changed the subject. "What are you and the ladies of the Ponderosa up to? I saw you and Sophie huddled together when I came in."

Maddy didn't know if Sophie and Mariah's baby news was public record yet. "We were discussing plans for starting a business association."

"Don't get your hopes up, okay Maddy?"

"Why not?" she asked defensively.

"Because folks here are resistant to change. They're bound to look at the three of you as upstarts from the city, trying to turn

Nugget into the next Truckee and price them out of the market. These are ranchers and railroad workers—blue-collar people. They hear about fancy hotels and business associations and instead of seeing the benefits it could bring the whole town, they see developers. Down go the trees, in come the tracts with their mini mansions and golf courses."

"Ha." The idea made her want to howl with hilarity. "Don't be ridiculous."

He threw some cash on the table and pulled her out of the booth, steering her toward the door. "Come with me."

"Rhys, I have stuff to do." She dragged her feet in the middle of the restaurant.

"This will only take fifteen minutes." He put his hand at the small of her back to give her a nudge. When it made her start, he quickly dropped his arm.

He led her to his truck and held the passenger door open.

Once they got on the highway, Rhys picked up a little speed, passed the Nugget Feed Store and turned down a road she'd never seen before. They were only a few minutes driving distance from town, but the new spiffy split-rail fence flanking both sides of the street signaled to Maddy that they were worlds away.

When Rhys pulled through a gate emblazoned with the name Sierra Heights in fancy scroll work her suspicions were confirmed. As he whizzed past a security booth, Maddy asked, "Hey, weren't we supposed to stop and check in or something?" She turned her head to look through the back windshield.

"No one there," Rhys said.

He drove a little farther and there it was—acres of obscenely large log homes with three-story windows, stacked stone chimneys, decorative gazebos, and four-car garages.

"Oh, my God. It's like Jackson Hole on steroids," Maddy said, trying to keep her mouth from hanging open.

As they slowly cruised a few of the subdivision's streets, she got a closer look at the homes' details. Big porches. Glass front doors. And hand-forged iron light fixtures.

"Check this out." Rhys turned his truck down one of the side streets, up a driveway, and into a parking lot. He helped her out of the cab, leading the way down a lighted path to an enormous timber-frame clubhouse. They walked around the building to a series of terraced decks overlooking a golf course.

"Eighteen holes," Rhys said.

"They didn't skimp on anything, did they?"

Rhys gave her a wry smile and led her back to the clubhouse. "Rec room, gym, and pro shop," he said. "There's even an Olympic-size pool." He gestured through a wrought iron arbor to a stone patio with two spas and a complete outdoor kitchen with pizza oven. None of it would have been out of place at a Wellmont Resort, except here the pool brimmed with slimy water the consistency of green Jell-O, and the gardens were overgrown with weeds.

"Who lives here?" Maddy cupped her hands against one of the clubhouse's tinted windows and peeked in.

"No one. The developers fought Nugget tooth and nail to build this subdivision—promised to pay millions in improvements to the city for roads, police, schools, even to fund a clinic. But they promptly filed for bankruptcy as soon as the project came to a close. There are so many liens against the place that all the houses have been taken off the market."

"Wow. What a waste." Maddy walked the length of the patio to take in the view. Despite being what her brother would've called OTT—over the top—the place was sort of gorgeous.

"Yep. Until a few days ago they had their own security detail to at least watch over the place, keep kids and vagrants from breaking in. Now, Nugget's stuck footing the bill for me and my officers to patrol it, when the city's residents didn't want it in the first place."

"Why didn't they?" she asked.

"Look around you, Maddy. These are million-dollar houses. Before this came in, Nugget didn't have a wrong side of the tracks."

"Don't think badly of me," she said guiltily. "But I kinda want one."

Rhys let out a loud belly laugh.

"Stop." She nudged him. "Okay, I can see how Nugget might be upset about this place, but I don't see how it pertains to my inn or a downtown business association."

They headed back to the truck, where he hooked her around the waist and swung her up into the passenger seat as if she weighed nothing. Although it was an innocent gesture, it made Maddy's belly flop like she was free-falling off a tall mountain.

"You never heard the saying, 'once bitten, twice shy'?" he asked her.

Oh, she'd heard it all right.

Chapter 5

Maddy had gotten into the habit of going to the Lumber Baron early in the morning, before the workers arrived and before most of the town awoke. She'd grab a cup of coffee from the Ponderosa or the Bun Boy, sit on the ramshackle veranda of the old mansion, and watch the square come to life.

Every day at seven sharp, Rhys pulled into his parking space, alighted from his truck with a thermos tucked under his arm, and let himself into the police station. At about that time, someone from the yoga studio unlocked the door. A group of men congregated at the barber shop, where Owen, the owner, held court. Merchants turned on their lights and a maintenance truck from Plumas County Parks and Recreation circled the green belt, picking up trash.

No one, except for Rhys, ever came over to say hello. Not even so much as a simple head nod or a friendly smile. She may as well have been invisible. Maddy tried not to take it personally. Rhys and Sophie had warned her that in a town like this, newcomers were viewed with the same wariness as a blind date. Still, it would have been nice to be acknowledged.

She rose from her spot on the porch and stretched her legs. Although the construction crew swore the rickety veranda was safe, they'd be reinforcing it soon. Then she'd have to set the lawn chairs she'd brought on the dirt. No sense trying to plant grass while the workers used the yard to stack their lumber and tramped across it in their heavy work boots.

For now she had a reprieve. The crew, busy completing another project's punch list, wouldn't be here for hours. But she was meeting Virgil Ross, the local historian. She checked her watch, and to kill time, began strolling the property.

Even in downtown Nugget, the air smelled forest fresh, like pine with a hint of vanilla and butterscotch. Someone had told her that Ponderosa sap, when warmed by the sun, smelled exactly like freshly baked cookies. And she was definitely getting hits of bakery.

As she wended her way back to the front of the mansion, a man wearing a tweed newsboy hat, carrying a walking cane with a handle braided in buckskin and decorated with fringe and feathers, stood at the foot of the porch steps calling, "Anyone home?"

"Mr. Ross?" She walked toward him and waved.

He turned to greet her and flashed a warm smile. "Yes, ma'am."

She stuck out her hand. But instead of shaking it, he leaned the cane against the Victorian and sandwiched her palm between his gnarled, milk-chocolate-colored hands. On nearly every finger he wore a turquoise ring; some were delicate with intricate inlay designs that looked like mosaic and others more chunky, with big silver bands.

"I'm Maddy," she said, inviting him to take a chair on the porch. "It's so nice to meet you."

He looked up at the mansion and Maddy could see him assessing how run-down it had gotten. "This house used to be a beauty. I'm glad you're bringing her back." Using the cane to help hoist himself up, Virgil slowly climbed one step at a time.

"I'm glad we are, too," Maddy said, dragging one of the lawn chairs next to his. "I want to stay as true to the period as possible." Then she quickly amended, "Of course we're turning it into an inn so we'll have to incorporate twenty-first-century amenities."

"Of course," he said and grinned. "People do like their indoor plumbing."

"And their Wi-Fi," she added. "But I very much want the inn to be a symbol of the area's history."

One of the only reasons Maddy had been attracted to Nugget was its rich past—the Maidu Indians, who'd hunted and gathered in these mountains; the gold and copper miners, who'd struck it rich; the nineteenth-century cowboys, who'd driven their cattle through forests and over high desert just so they could settle here. And of course there had been the loggers and the railroad men. Nugget's welcome sign proclaimed the town to be the "Pride of the West," and Maddy could see why. She just didn't understand why the town didn't work it more, especially the Donner Party angle.

"Chief Shepard says your grandfather was one of the first settlers here and that you know everything there is to know about this area's history," she said.

He chuckled. " 'Everything' might be overstating it, but I appreciate Rhys's endorsement. He's right that my granddad was the first white man"—Virgil made quotes with his fingers—"to put down roots in Nugget," he said, adding that in addition to being African-American, his grandfather had been part Native American.

"He built a trading post on the edge of town, which became popular with the miners. But he settled here about four years after the Donner Party got stranded in the Sierra." Virgil stared out at the perilous mountain range that surrounded Nugget like a fortress. Even though a freeway ran through the pass now, these mountains could still be treacherous in winter. "And it's the Donner Party, as I understand it, that you want to talk about, correct?"

"Honestly," she said, "I can't fathom why Nugget hasn't done more to showcase the fact that it happened right here. The tragedy is so gripping. There's the railroad museum, chronicling the importance of the Western Pacific in the Sierra, endless amounts of gold rush attractions, but other than Donner Memorial State Park, nothing to, you know—"

"Exploit it?" he said, amused.

"Well, yeah," Maddy reluctantly admitted. "At the risk of sounding ghoulish, it's a pretty captivating story. So why shouldn't Nugget use it to promote the town a little more? We don't have to be disrespectful, or tacky." She thought about all the Donner Party cannibalism jokes she'd heard over the years and inwardly cringed.

"What exactly did you have in mind?" he asked.

"I was thinking of turning one wall of the inn into a sort of Donner Party exhibit: photos, various written accounts of what happened, maybe even some artifacts if we could get them."

Virgil sat there pensively, as if considering how involved he wanted to be in this little project, and eventually started nodding. "It's doable," he said, pushing the newsboy cap back on his head and scratching. "Even though the best relics already went to the park service, we might be able to get a piece of pottery, or a remnant of clothing from some descendant's attic."

"Are there any relatives around here?" Maddy asked excitedly.

"A few scattered throughout Northern California. The Virginia Reed-Murphy house is just up the road."

"Virginia Reed-Murphy?" Maddy had read quite a bit about the Donner Party, but the name didn't ring a bell.

"It was Virginia Reed back then," he said. "When she was twelve her family left Springfield, Illinois, to come to California. Her dad was a big businessman hoping to strike it rich out West. They met up with the Donner family, so they could all travel together and eventually picked up more people along the way.

"But you know how that turned out . . ."

Maddy knew that the trip was a catastrophe. They followed a shortcut that was supposed to shave hundreds of miles off a nearly three-thousand-mile trek. An ambitious lawyer named Lansford Hastings had written about the shortcut in a book. The problem was, Hastings had never actually tried the route himself. It turned out to be deadly.

"The trip was a suicide mission," Maddy said.

"Yep." Virgil nodded. "When the group of travelers finally made it to the Rocky Mountains, they caught up with an old friend of the Reeds. The friend warned them not to take Hastings's shortcut, that the trail wasn't wide enough for wagons. When the caravan got to Oregon, most of the travelers took the advice of the Reeds' friend and went the safe route. But Virginia's dad convinced the Donners and a number of other families to take Hastings's cutoff."

"Seems to me it should've been called the Reed Party," Maddy said. "Why Donner?"

"Ah," Vigil said, warming to the tale. "Now that is a very good observation. I suspect that it was called the Donner Party because George Donner was elected captain by the group. They didn't like Virginia's dad—thought he was pompous. And his decision was hasty, because somewhere between Utah and the Nevada border the Reeds lost their oxen and couldn't take their wagon any farther.

"They had to sleep on the ground with their dogs on top of them for warmth," he continued. "It turned out that not only was Hastings's shortcut perilous, but it was more than one hundred miles longer than the safe route. All the travelers who'd taken the well-traveled road made it to California in five months."

Virgil sat back in his lawn chair. "Not the Donner Party. By October, things were getting pretty bad. Lots of fighting and blaming. One day, Virginia's dad caught one of the teamsters beating his oxen with the handle of a bullwhip. He tried to stop it, but the driver turned the whip on Reed and hit him in the head. So Virginia's dad stabbed the driver to death with his hunting knife."

"Oh, my goodness," Maddy said, surprised that she didn't know anything about this part of the story.

"The group wanted to lynch Virginia's father. One of the pioneers grabbed a rope and was ready to hang him. Virginia's mom got down on her knees and begged them to spare his life. So they showed him mercy by banishing him from the group. The next day he left his family with the Donners and rode west out of camp."

"Did Virginia ever see him again?"

"Every day, as they traveled, she searched for a sign of him. Sometimes he'd leave missives stuck to trees. But then the letters stopped." Virgil looked at his watch. "We'll have to pick up the rest of the story another time."

Maddy wanted to protest. She knew how it ended for the Donners, but what about Virginia and her family? Obviously Virginia had survived if she'd built a house around here. But how? "You think the Reed-Murphys would talk to me?"

"Virginia died in 1921. A descendant hasn't lived there since," Virgil said. "A slew of different owners, mostly weekenders, have occupied it. My guess is whoever lives there now doesn't even know who Virginia Reed is, or that she and her husband built it as a summer home."

"See what I mean," Maddy said. "The residents here don't even know what they have. Maybe we could get the whole town involved. Set up a little museum in the square, or a visitor center, maybe hold a day to commemorate the historical event."

Virgil patted her knee, his eyes crinkling at the corners in amusement. "All that might be a little ambitious. But let me look into some things and get back to you. I've got a few ideas. You've got a little time, right?"

"Absolutely," she said.

After Virgil left, Maddy came down the steps and headed to her car.

"Hiya." A woman with red hair jogged up, waving. "I'm Pam, owner of the yoga-dance studio." She pointed to a building adjacent to the Lumber Baron. "For days I've wanted to come over and welcome you to the square, but the hours kept getting away from me. Busy time. Anyway, hello and welcome."

She looked up at the mansion and grimaced. "You've got your work cut out for you."

"Yeah," Maddy said, thrilled to finally have one of the merchants introduce herself. "The place is pretty disgusting. But we'll make her shine again."

"Well, watch yourself. I've seen some sketchy people hanging around—probably just squatters, but I didn't like the looks of 'em. I called the sheriff a few times, but with the whole county to patrol— not a top priority. It'll be better now that we have our own police department again. But I felt you ought to know, especially if you're here alone."

"I appreciate it," Maddy said. Hopefully Pam was overreacting. There were lots of shady-looking characters in San Francisco, mostly all harmless.

"Uh . . . I know this is short notice, but, if you're not busy this afternoon we're having a meeting for the Halloween festival. We could sure use some fresh blood."

"Halloween festival?" Maddy remembered Mariah mentioning something about a holiday carnival, but hadn't paid attention to the details.

"Yep, we hold one every year on the square. With everything spread out the way it is, the kids have a tough time trick-or-treating.

So all the merchants hand out candy, there's a couple of booths, apple bobbing, pumpkin decorating, that sort of thing. If you're interested, the meeting's at my studio around fourish."

"I'm absolutely interested."

When Pam left, Maddy texted Nate, telling him to put the festival on his calendar.

"Shit." Rhys knocked over a glass of water as he searched his nightstand in the dark for the phone. He squinted at the glowing numbers on his alarm clock. One a.m. "Hello."

"Sorry to wake you, Chief."

"Connie, that you?" He finally found the light switch and flicked it on.

"Yes, Chief. We've got a four fifteen on Trout Lane in Sierra Heights."

"Uh . . . What? Connie, just talk in English."

His new dispatcher, with her cherubic face and geeky glasses, reminded Rhys of Velma from the *Scooby-Doo* cartoon. Owning a police scanner, being willing to take emergency calls at home after hours and having memorized the entire California Penal Code had won her the coveted position. Rhys would definitely have to rethink the penal code situation, since he was still on Texas's.

"A disturbance, Chief. Someone called it in about four minutes ago and Wyatt's off tonight." Wyatt, his sole officer, had been foisted on him because his parents were friends with the mayor. The kid was green as grass.

"All right." Rhys already had one leg in his Levi's and was hopping around on the other. "Text me the house number. I'm on my way."

Shit, shit, shit! Shep. He couldn't leave him alone. Lately, Shep had been having his worst moments at night, waking up in a cold sweat, forgetting where he was. Rhys had even found him outside, taking a leak in the pitch black, because he couldn't find the bathroom. His doctor said it was typical of dementia, but it had scared the hell out of Rhys.

Given that Nugget shut up quieter than a tufted titmouse after nine o'clock, he'd figured this would never be a problem. Wrong.

He quickly finished getting dressed, holstered his Glock, walked across the porch, knocked on the door, and whispered, "Maddy, open up." What the hell was he whispering for? He tried again, this time louder. "Mad—"

"What's wrong?" She opened the door with her hair all tousled, in an oversized Giants sweatshirt, wearing fuzzy pink bunny slippers. He took one look at her, flushed and sleepy eyed, and a wave of lust hit him like a fist to the gut.

He backed away from the doorway to give himself a little space and almost forgot the reason he'd come. *Get your head back in the game.* "Sorry to do this, but it's an emergency. Could you sit with Shep just until I get back? I have to go out on a call."

"Yeah. Sure. Of course. Let me just throw on a robe."

While she disappeared back into her apartment, he checked his phone for Connie's text. He knew the address and could be there in minutes, but if this turned out to be a real emergency, he had taken way too long. He'd have to work out a better system or the good folks of Nugget may as well save their money and go back to contracting solely with the sheriff.

"Okay." Maddy came flying out the door.

"Thanks. I owe you big-time."

He ran to his new city-issued all-wheel-drive. The police SUV had been purchased with federal block-grant money earmarked for community improvements. His personal truck was fine for light duty, but Nugget needed vehicles equipped for the rigors of daily police work—especially in three feet of snow. So he'd snatched the money before someone got the bright idea of buying all new office furniture for City Hall. He had enough cash left over from the grant to buy two more if he shopped right. He jumped into the rig, turned on the flashing blue and red roof light, and sped away.

The disturbance on Trout Lane turned out to be the heavy bass thump, thump of about two dozen kids throwing a house party. The problem: It wasn't their house.

This was exactly what Rhys had feared. Now that Sierra Heights' developers had let their security team go, the subdivision acted as an attractant to every vexation this side of the county.

Rhys stood outside the house, and for shits and giggles shouted through a bullhorn, "Come out with your hands up." The kids scattered like roaches, running pell-mell for their cars, or to hide in the forest.

"Hey, where you going?" He grabbed one who looked familiar by the collar and shined his flashlight in the boy's face. "That you, Justin?"

"Uh-oh," Justin muttered as he came face-to-face with the police chief. "My dad's gonna kill me."

When Clay got to the police station he found Justin making himself at home, sprawled out in one of the chairs, playing on his iPhone.

"Go wait in my truck," he told his son. Even to his own ears he sounded like an autocratic naval flight officer. Not a dad. No wonder he couldn't close the distance between him and his boys—especially Justin, who treated him like an interloper. Like a stranger.

When his dad died and Clay had hung up his wings to come home to run the ranch, he had hoped to bond with his sons—to become a real family. But then Jen had died too, and the chasm between him and Justin grew even deeper.

He watched through the window as Justin got into the passenger seat, then turned to Rhys. "I should've beat the crap out of him and left him in jail overnight." It's something Tip would've blustered, but instead ordered up a week's worth of mucking horse stalls. Man, he missed his father. Tip would've known how to handle two preteens.

"He was one of the few kids who wasn't drinking," Rhys said. "Give him credit for that." He walked into the bathroom and dumped his coffee down the drain.

Clay scrubbed his hand under his cowboy hat. "Thanks for bringing him in."

"Hey, that's what I'm here for. To serve and protect." Rhys grabbed the key off a hook behind the dispatcher's desk and the two of them walked out together. "Go easy on him, Clay. He's trying to fit in here. I know it's not an excuse, but it wouldn't kill you to cut him a little slack."

Clay stood on the sidewalk, watching Rhys drive off, then climbed into the cab of his truck. "Buckle up," he told Justin, who was still on that damned phone. "What were you thinking breaking into that house like that?"

Without looking up from the screen, Justin mumbled, "Kids do it all the time."

"Justin, put the phone away. How do you mean they do it all the time?" Clay started the engine, pulled out of the square and headed toward the ranch, managing a sideways glance at his son.

Justin got a guilty look on his face, like he knew he'd just stepped in it.

"Justin?"

"It's no big deal." He fidgeted with one of the Velcro tabs on the sleeve of his ski jacket. "They just find homes, places where people have gone away for the weekend, or homes that are empty."

"To throw parties?" Clay asked, disgusted. He'd certainly pulled his fair share of shenanigans growing up in this town, but breaking into private property? Pretty audacious. And pretty damned self-entitled.

"Yeah, I guess."

"You guess? Or you know?" It was like pulling teeth with the boy.

"I know," Justin spat.

Clay turned down McCreedy Road, and even though it was a mile away he could see his big farmhouse lit up as bright as Union Square. Cody must've turned on every lamp in the place.

"It's not like anyone got hurt," Justin said so cavalierly that Clay had to clamp down on his temper. Getting liquored up before taking the wheel was a particular sore spot with him. But Justin didn't know all the details of his mother's death. And Clay wanted to keep it that way.

"Not yet." Clay tried for calm. "But all those kids drinking and driving, someone's bound to get hurt. Or worse. Not to mention that you kids trashed that house. Who's gonna pay for the damage?"

"I've got money from working around the ranch. I'll pay for it."

"You bet your ass you will." Clay pulled into the driveway and before Justin could open the door, he put his hand on the boy's shoulder. "This isn't like you, son. You're always so responsible. What's really going on here?"

Clay might not be the most communicative. Hell, he'd been raised single-handedly by a cattleman and had spent much of his adult life in the cockpit of a fighter jet—not a lot of talking going on. But he and Justin would never connect if they didn't open up.

The kid just sneered. "You're the one who wanted me to make friends in this hick town. So I'm making friends."

Yeah, great friends—burglars and vandals. But before Clay could make the point, Justin made a beeline for the house.

A person could break his neck out here in the dark. Especially Shep on one of his sporadic midnight bathroom runs, Rhys thought as he walked from his SUV to the house, making a note to himself to install some outdoor lighting.

When he got inside, he found Maddy curled up on the sofa, wrapped in his blanket with her nose in a book. He tilted his head sideways to read the title.

Maddy lifted her eyes above the cover. "Everything okay?"

He sighed and threw his keys on the mail table. "A bunch of kids broke into one of those houses in Sierra Heights and held themselves a little party."

"Really?" She let out a laugh. "I guess there's not a whole lot to do in Nugget."

He scooted her legs over and sat next to her on the couch. "When we were kids we got our kicks shooting potatoes at mailboxes with homemade spud guns."

She marked her place in her book and set it aside. "The Ponderosa should host a youth bowling league. That might keep them out of trouble."

"Maybe." He grinned. "But I doubt bowling can compete with sex and drinking."

"Probably not." She pushed the blanket off and began gathering up her stuff.

Man, he didn't want her to go. She looked so good cuddled up on his couch, soft and drowsy. Pointing at her book, he said, "You're pretty hung up on that whole Donner Party thing, aren't you?"

She settled back in. "It's fascinating. Don't you think?"

He shrugged. "I guess it's a big part of the history around here, but I never really gave it a lot of thought. You get in touch with Virgil?"

"Yes," she said. "And he was great. I'm more obsessed than ever. Not so much with the gory parts about them eating each other to stay alive. But how they persevered. They came to California to find a better life, a better home. And they wound up pushing themselves to unthinkable limits to survive. What blows me away is when they were finally rescued, they settled around here. Did you know that one of the survivors built a house right here?"

"Nope." Damn, she was cute.

"Yeah. Crazy, right? I want to find it, but Virgil says the people who live in it now probably don't even know."

Rhys thought she had great lips. Like that movie star's. Pink and pouty. And her big brown eyes reminded him of that Billie Holiday song Shep used to play. *They sparkle. They bubble. They're gonna get you in a whole lot of trouble.*

"Do you know that after newspapers published stories of the Donner Party's disastrous trip people stopped coming to California?" Maddy said. "It wasn't until the gold rush, two years later, that prospectors started flocking here again."

"Money'll do it every time." Rhys couldn't believe he was actually sitting here talking history with her. He watched Maddy unsuccessfully try to hold back a yawn and looked over at his bed. "You should've slept."

"I was afraid if your dad went out the back door I wouldn't hear him. I dead-bolted it. Sorry. I should've told you."

"That's okay. Now I know for next time." She grabbed her book and readied to leave.

"So what's the deal with your husband?" he blurted, before she could get up and go. *Smooth, Rhys, real smooth.* He had no business prying into her personal life. They hardly knew each other.

"What?" she asked with an eye roll. "You haven't been listening through the walls again?"

It's not like he'd bugged the place, but it was kind of hard not to hear Maddy fight with her husband over the phone. "Enough to know that the two of you are still having problems. Why isn't he here fixing them?"

She turned away. "He's in France, cutting a big hotel deal. And I told him not to come."

"Why?" He moved a little closer to her on the couch.

"Because I'm leaving him. He's in love with someone else," she said, adding incredulously, "And with me, too. Or so he says. But you apparently already know that."

Rhys waited a few seconds, then very softly asked, "Is he sleeping with this other person?"

She went stock-still and Rhys feared that this time he'd gone too far. Way too private.

She sniffed a few times and pulled her legs up underneath her on the couch. "He was, but says he's not anymore. Dave fell in love with Gabby before he knew me—when she was with his cousin. He married me so he wouldn't make a play for her."

"Nah. He must've loved you."

"No," she said. "Not at first."

"He tell you that?"

"In so many words." Something elusive shone in her eyes. Shame? Sadness? Whatever it was it made Rhys want to pound the crap out of her asshat husband. "I don't even know why I'm telling you all this. It's so humiliating."

"Nothing to be humiliated about." He took her hand.

"He's promised me that it's over between them—that he wants us to work it out."

"You don't want to try?" He certainly hoped not. The dude was a double douche bag.

She pulled her hand out of his. "I don't think he's really over Gabby. And she's certainly not over him. According to Dave, even before Max died she wanted to leave him for my husband."

"But Dave didn't want to leave you?"

She didn't answer right away, staring off into the distance. "I'd just had my second miscarriage."

"Ah Christ, Maddy, I'm so sorry."

She flushed. "That was way too much information, wasn't it?" Clumsily, she started gathering up her things, trying to avoid eye contact. "It's late, I better get going."

Code for conversation over.

"Hey," he said, lightly pressing the pad of his thumb along her lower lip. "Don't be embarrassed."

Although he hankered to touch her more, offer a little comfort—

or even a lot of comfort—it was a bad idea. She was a train wreck. And he didn't need the drama or the distraction from his end goal— getting the hell out of Nugget. "I'll walk you home."

"Rhys, I live two feet away."

"Humor me," he said. "I'm the police chief."

He escorted her to her door. "Thanks, Maddy. You really saved my ass tonight."

She waved him off. "Give me a break. It was nothing."

"I'll buy you breakfast," he offered.

"I can't. I have a meeting at the inn." She backed into her doorway and despite the voice in his head telling him to stand down, those big bedroom eyes of hers made him want to follow her in. "Rain check?"

"You bet." Before he could do something stupid, like kiss her, he walked away.

When Rhys got to the station the next morning, a tall man with short-cropped salt-and-pepper hair stood there waiting. His Oakley sunglasses and tactical cargo pants immediately pegged him for an off-duty cop. Or a fed.

"You the new chief?" he asked, not so discreetly taking Rhys's measure.

"Interim chief. Yeah, that would be me." Rhys unlocked the door and ushered him inside. "What can I do you for?"

The man grinned, showing a row of perfect teeth that made Rhys think of denture commercials. "Heard you might be hiring."

"I might be." Rhys hung his key ring on a hook behind his desk and looked around the empty room. It could certainly use a few bodies. Even with Wyatt, Rhys handled most of the calls. He couldn't keep up the pace and still take care of his dad.

The man handed Rhys a manila envelope. "My résumé."

He plopped down in one of the office chairs Rhys had salvaged from a city hall storage closet and waited. So to appease him, Rhys pulled out the neatly typed page and scanned its contents.

"Twenty-one years at LAPD, huh? A bit overqualified for Nugget, don't you think?" Rhys looked at the name printed at the top of the résumé. "Hell, Jake Stryker, you've got more experience than I do."

Jake lifted his chin, clearly expecting Rhys's reaction. "I've got a cabin up here that I've been coming to for years," he said. "I'd like to make it full time, but I've got a few ex-wives I'm keeping in style and a few kids I'm putting through college. My pension from LAPD won't be enough."

"There's no way we can compete with your LA salary," Rhys said.

"Yeah, I figured that. But I can probably make it work." He looked determined.

Rhys got up from his chair and sat on the corner of Connie's desk. "Looking to draw a second pension, huh?" Back in Houston he knew plenty of cops taking early retirements after maxing out on their pensions, then accepting kickback jobs to collect a second one. Wasn't anything wrong with it, but in a small department like this, he didn't want any deadweight.

"Besides me, one officer and a dispatcher, you'd make four until I can find a few more to hire," Rhys said. "That means plenty of nights, weekends, and holidays. Not a whole lot of time for fishing and hunting. You still interested?"

Jake sat up and leaned forward. "Where you from, Chief? I detect a trace of a drawl."

"I'm from here," Rhys said emphatically, and then wondered why he'd been so insistent. For years he'd tried to burn the memory of this place out of his head.

"I'll be honest with you," Jake said, meeting Rhys's eyes. "I'd like a second pension. But I have every intention of earning it. I know you see me as an older guy—probably think I'm a burnout. But I love my job and I'm good at it. I'd just like to do it here, in God's country. But if you have doubts about me, call anyone at LAPD. They'll tell you I'm good people."

Rhys perused Jake's résumé again. "We don't get many homicides in Nugget."

"I worked patrol a lot of years," Jake said. "Dealt with drunks, domestic violence, break-ins—probably much of the stuff you get here."

There was no question that Jake's experience would be an advantage, but Rhys wasn't entirely convinced that the senior cop wouldn't look to skate. He rubbed his chin.

"How do you feel about getting back into a uniform?"

Jake took in Rhys's jeans, long-sleeve shirt, cowboy boots, and grinned, shaking his head. "I can do that."

Rhys sat there for a while just looking at him. "Okay."

"Okay, I'm hired?"

"I didn't say that." Rhys pulled up straighter. "Let me make a few calls. This number good?" Rhys held up the résumé.

"Yep."

When Jake left, Rhys pulled his department budget out of his desk drawer and went through it line by line. Even if he set Wyatt up with a mentor and got him up to speed, six officers weren't enough for a town of nearly six thousand residents. They'd have to continue to rely on the sheriff's department for backup.

Maybe in a few months Rhys could persuade the mayor to drop the city's contract with the county sheriff and beef up Nugget PD. The town deserved its own force. When cops lived in the place where they worked, they tended to care more. It also made residents feel secure.

He could make this happen. And before leaving, he'd help pick his successor—someone with Stryker's experience who could keep the department going.

Rhys kicked his feet up on the desk and smiled. Maybe this wouldn't be so bad after all.

But by the time he got home everything went to shit.

Chapter 6

Two dark-haired urchins sat in Rhys's kitchen, ratty backpacks at their feet, eating grilled cheese sandwiches. A waifish woman in a drab business suit leaned against the counter.

The children—the girl might have been in her mid-teens—stared at him with more interest than he got from the police groupies at the bar across the street from the Houston police station.

Betty, his dad's caretaker, rushed to him and reached up to pat his back consolingly. "I'll talk to you in the morning, hon." She sprinted out the door so fast Rhys didn't bother to stop her.

"Pop?"

"Where have you been, boy?" Shep was unusually agitated.

Rhys gave the kids a strained smile, trying to seem friendly and not too self-conscious. But there was something about them that made him uneasy. The woman tried to fade into the background as if she wanted to give them a chance to greet each other without intruding. But he didn't know these children.

"Uh, Pop, can we talk in the other room?"

Shep made no move to leave the kitchen. "Make 'em something to eat, wouldya."

The girl looked at the boy, the woman looked at Rhys, and Rhys looked at the food on the kids' plates.

"Who are they?" Rhys asked, lowering himself into one of the chairs. He regarded the girl, then the boy, and back to the girl again, trying to get a fix on them. All the while he could feel acid backing up in his throat.

The woman appeared to be equally befuddled. She pushed away from the counter, offering her hand. "Allow me to introduce myself. I'm Annie Stover from San Joaquin County Child Protective Services."

Before she could say more—like what the hell she was doing here—Shep stammered, "I'm not sure who they are. But . . ."

Either the old man was confused, or pretending to be. Duck and cover.

Because whatever bad news the social worker was here to deliver involved Shep. Rhys at least knew that much.

"But what!" he asked, his voice louder than he wanted or intended it to be.

The girl burst into tears, uncontrollable sobs, actually. The boy narrowed his eyes at Rhys and got up to stand by his sister (or presumably his sister).

"Stop crying, Rosa," Shep demanded. "Tell him who you are, girl."

The social worker Annie tried to step in, but the girl forcefully asserted, "I'm Lina and this is Samuel." She stabbed Shep with a *what-on-earth-is-wrong-with-you?* glare. "Momma died."

The room went silent and Samuel went back to his chair and looked down at his grilled cheese.

"She's gone," she repeated, laying her hand gently on Shep's shoulder. "A car ran her over. Annie explained this to you already."

Shep suddenly got very still and like a baby waking from a nap and picking out a face from the general mayhem of shapes and colors, he focused clearly on the children at the table, then put his face in his hands and wept.

In his whole life, Rhys had never seen his father shed one tear. Not in physical pain, nor in sadness. As far as Rhys had known, Stan Shepard only had one emotion. Anger.

Rhys got up and went into the bathroom, returning with a roll of toilet paper.

"Someone needs to tell me what's going on here." He looked meaningfully at Annie.

Lina tore off a wad of the tissue, dried her eyes, and blew her nose. "We had nowhere to go, so Annie brought us here."

"Your mother is dead?" Rhys tried to keep a soft tone and to appear calm. They were just kids, after all. But he was starting to lose it.

"Yes," she said.

"Why? Why would you come here?" The acid moved into his mouth, leaving a bitter taste—metallic and sour.

Her expression turned shocked, almost angry, like why would he ask such a stupid question. "Because you're our only family."

Shep seemed to shrink right in front of him and that's when Rhys knew for sure.

"Pop, you want to chime in here?" A part of him still held out hope that he was wrong. Could be that they were just distant cousins and if he gave them money, they'd go away.

Shep turned to Lina and looked so damned apologetic that for an instant Rhys didn't recognize him. "I never told him," he said.

"Why not?" she asked, so utterly bewildered that it was painful to watch.

Shep lifted his shoulders in response, wiping his eyes with the back of his hand. "He wouldn't have understood. He wouldn't have liked it."

Lina shook her head as if to clear it of confusion. "But he's our half brother."

If it hadn't been like looking in a mirror, Rhys wouldn't have believed it. The only physical differences between him and the kids— besides age, and in Lina's case, gender—were his fairer skin and hazel eyes. Theirs were brown.

Still, the idea that Shep had actually been able to maintain a relationship with someone, had fathered children and kept it a secret, was so far-fetched that Rhys couldn't help rejecting the evidence staring him in the face. Rookie mistake.

The burning sensation in his throat returned. Maybe it had never left, Rhys didn't know. "Why don't you start at the top," he told Lina, without so much as glancing at his father.

Annie started to interrupt, then seemed to think better of it, letting Lina take the lead. He got the feeling she was assessing their family dynamic—and finding it a whole lot fucked up.

Forty-five minutes later, Lina told him how a hit-and-run driver had left Rosa to die on the road as she was walking home from work. Child Protective Services had come to their house near Stockton, tracked down Shep, and had gotten them to Nugget. To their father.

Rhys was still trying to wrap his head around that last one. Had Shep been married to this woman? Had he had a relationship with these kids all these years? Stockton was more than four hours away by car. Farmland. What would Shep have been doing there?

He didn't know what rocked him more, the fact that his father had carried on a whole other life, or that he'd completely cut Rhys out of it. What a joke, he reminded himself. Rhys had never been part of Shep's life—just an appendage.

"How did you know this woman, Pop?"

Shep just stared at him vacantly and started keening again.

Annie came forward and smiled at the children. "Your brother and I need to talk outside for a few minutes."

Ya think?

He led her to the front porch and plopped down on the steps. "Grab a seat," he said, pointing at Shep's lone chair.

"I wasn't aware you didn't know about them," Annie said, primly perching on the edge of the rocker. "Someone else has been handling the case. I was thrown in at the last minute and no one told me. I'm so sorry. Obviously this came as quite a bombshell."

Understatement of the year.

"According to the case file, your father met Rosa Silva when he was with Union Pacific. She worked for an almond packing company that used the train to ship product. We couldn't find a marriage license, but your father's name is on both children's birth certificates. Lina says that although his visits were sporadic, he'd been going back and forth to Stockton since she was born—seventeen years. Then about a year ago he abruptly stopped. Rosa had told Lina that they'd broken up."

Rhys wondered if perhaps his father had already begun experienc-

ing symptoms of the Alzheimer's and it had taken a toll on their relationship. Or, more than likely, knowing Shep, visiting his kids had
become too much effort, so he cut them off. Bastard.

"It's apparent to me, Mr. Shepard, that your father is suffering
from some mental health issues." She paused, clearly waiting for him
to fill in the blank.

"Alzheimer's."

"I'm terribly sorry."

"Yeah," he said. "So the thing is he's in no condition to take on
two kids. If you had called, I could have saved you the four-hour
trip."

"My predecessor did call, Mr. Shepard. Repeatedly. No one answered and no one returned her messages." Rhys would have, if he
had known.

"Rosa died ten days ago," Annie said. "Some of the neighbors
were good enough to take the children until we finally reached your
father."

Rhys shrugged. "I don't know what you want me to do. You
saw him."

"What about you, Mr. Shepard? You're their half brother and according to your father, you're the police chief here."

"Interim police chief. I'm only here to find my dad a permanent
situation. In six months I go back to Houston—to the police department there. My hours are crazy. Not a good situation for kids. Don't
they have an aunt, an uncle, relatives somewhere?"

"No, they don't," she said tersely. "They only have you."

"Look . . . Annie, right? I don't even know these kids. I'm a single
thirty-six-year-old narcotics detective . . . work a lot of nights . . . live
in a one-bedroom. Them . . ." He motioned inside the house, feeling
panicked. "Not happening, Annie."

She stood up and walked to the other side of the porch, gazing out
into the forest. "It's pretty here," she said, almost like she was talking
to herself, then let out a breath. "I guess I'll have to make other
arrangements."

"Don't get me wrong, I'd like to help out, do what's right. But I
couldn't give those kids what they need. You said the girl's seventeen.

Maybe the courts can emancipate her. She seems very mature. Very responsible." God, he felt like a prick.

"And how," she asked with unconcealed hostility, "should she go about supporting herself and her brother? As far as social services can tell, your father hasn't been paying child support."

No revelation there.

"I will absolutely take care of that," he said. "Whatever they need." Great, now he was one of those assholes who threw money at the problem.

"What they need, Mr. Shepard, is their family. Otherwise they go into the system—foster care." She let that hang in the air like a gun to his head.

Intuitively, he knew there were good, caring foster families. But as a cop, he'd seen the horror stories. They'd probably get split up. He thought about the girl. Alone. Living with God knows who. At least she could go her own way in a year. Not the boy, though. He was just a kid—twelve at the most.

Rhys wanted to hit Shep. Wrap his hands around his throat and choke the sorry life out of him for putting him in this untenable situation. He took in large gulps of air, trying to regulate his breathing, and with resignation asked, "Could it just be temporary . . . until I can make appropriate arrangements?"

"That would be a good start, Mr. Shepard."

He let out a breath. "What do I have to sign?"

"So you'll take them, then?" she asked.

"Yeah." Because coming back to Nugget wasn't bad enough.

And if taking responsibility for these kids—total strangers—didn't send him around the bend, he now had the unenviable task of telling them that their father was losing his memory and that it would only get worse; the only person they had left in the world would forget them altogether in a few years.

Clay towed the monster trailer down the driveway as Rhys directed him to a pad by the side of the house near the electrical hookups. After a few deft maneuvers, Clay managed to lay the RV right in the spot. It was no easy feat, but he was used to landing jets on the world's smallest runways—flight decks no larger than five hundred feet.

He jumped out of the truck and had a look. Rhys had predicted that the trailer would take up the whole yard and he was right. The thing was fricking huge.

When Rhys had called with the bizarre story of Shep's second family, Clay had come up with the idea of bringing over Tip's fifth wheel. He'd also offered a barn on the ranch that his late wife had converted into her design studio, but it wasn't much larger than Shep's place.

Unhitching the trailer, he tossed Rhys the keys. "Have a look."

Rhys checked out the exterior of the motor home from various angles before ducking inside the door. "Whoa!"

Clay watched, amused, as Rhys walked the length of the living area, dazzled by all the gewgaws. At least that's what Clay's dad used to call the built-in flat-screen TV, the leather-upholstered recliners with cupholders, the full kitchen. Even skylights.

"I was expecting something a little more bare bones," Rhys said.

"You know Tip—always liked living large. Used to haul this thing to cattle auctions." Clay pointed down the hallway. "Head's in there."

The bathroom was small, but it had an enclosed shower and enough storage for towels and toiletries.

"Check this out." Clay led him into the bedroom.

Rhys bounced on the queen bed. "Damn, Clay. This beats the hell out of Shep's actual house."

"You planning on having the kids live in here?"

"That was the plan," Rhys said. "But when I told them about it, they didn't like the idea—afraid to be out here alone. It would work for me, though." He played around with the remote control, surfing the channels on the Dish. "But someone needs to keep an eye on Shep at night."

"The girl's old enough to do that, right?"

"She'll have to, if they want to stay in the house," Rhys said.

"You told them about the Alzheimer's?"

"Yeah. The girl, Lina, had already figured out something was wrong. Shep keeps calling her by her mother's name."

Clay sat down next to him and looked up at the low ceiling. "It'll get old fast, Rhys. What you're doing for those kids . . . It's a good thing. But you need better digs, man."

"Eventually Maddy'll move into the inn," Rhys said. "Then, if they want, they can convert the duplex into a single-family home."

"Maybe you should rent it out and find something more suitable. Now's a good time to buy, and if you need help with a down payment—"

"I've got some money put away." Rhys got off the bed and tested the drawers in the built-in dresser. "But I'm not staying, Clay. Six months, that's all my union contract gives, and I'm going back to Texas, back to Houston PD. This trailer will be fine until then . . . Unless you need it back?"

"It's yours for as long as you want it," Clay said. He certainly had no use for a fifth wheel and his friend had gotten dealt a cruddy hand. "If you go back to Texas, what will you do with those kids? With Shep?"

"All the medical professionals I've talked to say that it's inevitable—Shep'll need round-the-clock care. As for the kids . . . beats the hell out of me." Rhys shoved his hand into his hair. "Everything's happened so fast, I haven't had time to think that far."

"Well, you better get to figuring it out. People aren't like dogs— you can't send them back to the pound when they become inconvenient."

If Clay knew his friend, Rhys wanted to send Shep straight to hell for putting him in this predicament. Clay understood the feeling. Lately, he'd been cursing Jennifer for wrapping her Lexus around a tree, leaving him alone with two boys to raise. It wasn't enough that he had a cattle ranch to run.

"I think the girl, Lina, will be eighteen by then," Rhys said. "She can be the boy's legal guardian at that point. But . . . me . . . and those kids . . . that was never part of the bargain."

"Tough situation. I don't envy you. What about school?"

"Yeah. I guess that's left to me to figure out, too."

"Bring 'em over to the ranch, introduce them to Justin and Cody."

"Yeah, okay." Rhys paused. "Thanks."

"Forget about it," Clay said, knowing that Rhys was awkward about accepting help, or even acts of kindness, since there had been so little of it in his life. But to the McCreedys, Rhys was family, so he'd better get used to it. "So, what's going on with the brunette?"

"Maddy?"

"You got any other hot brunettes living next door to you that I don't know about?"

"The guy she's married to is cheating on her," Rhys said.

"The hotel guy?" Clay asked and Rhys nodded. "She leaving him?"

"She says she is. The giant rock's off her finger. Funny thing, when I first found out who she was, I figured her for one of those spoiled high-maintenance chicks. She's actually pretty awesome— sat with Shep when I had to go out on the Sierra Heights call, helped unpack my stuff. And, as you so astutely pointed out, she's easy on the eyes."

Clay raised his brows. "You interested?"

"Nah. I've got enough complications."

"Probably wise," Clay said. "Dollars to donuts, she gets back with the hubby."

Chapter 7

Buzz saws screeched and hammers banged so loudly that Maddy signaled for Nate to follow her outside. "I couldn't hear you in there," she said.

"That's the sound of money, Mad."

Nate had driven the four hours from San Francisco the night before to deliver the latest architectural plans. The drawings had been revised repeatedly to meet Nugget's rigid aesthetic requirements. The city hadn't minded when the building sat rotting, but now that she and Nate had gotten permission to turn it into a twenty-room inn, there were all kinds of rules about maintaining "the rustic charm" of the town's commercial district. Apparently no one else in the square had to adhere to the requirements.

"You like my place?" she asked Nate, who'd spent the night on her fold-out couch after they'd had a long dinner with Sophie and Mariah.

"Uh...not that much. The layout's a little funky, don't you think?" He'd whined about having to walk through Maddy's bedroom to get to the kitchen and bathroom. "And I could hear the guy next door snoring. Are there like ten people living over there?" Generally, Nate liked to complain.

"Well, it's only temporary—until I can move in here." Given the

Shepards' new overcrowding situation, they could definitely use her side of the duplex. But the truth was she felt comfortable living there. Safe. And having Rhys as a neighbor . . . well, you couldn't ask for a better view. Or a better listener, considering how he'd let her dump all that crud about Dave on him. He'd even acted indignant on her behalf. At the end there, when he'd walked her home, she'd surely thought he was going to kiss her. Crazy, but despite being cheated on, lied to and screwed over, she would've let him.

Clearly, she needed to get her head examined.

"So the cop lives in the motor home?" Nate asked.

"That just happened, but, yes." One day she'd come home to find two kids on the other side of the duplex and a behemoth trailer parked in the yard. Rhys hadn't said too much about them other than they were Shep's children and that their mother had died in a hit-and-run accident. She'd talked to the kids a few times in passing. Polite and beautiful and so sad that it broke her heart.

She looked up at the cross-gabled roofline of the Queen Anne and held her breath, pointing up at one of the workers testing the pitch. "That safe?"

Nate rolled his shoulders. "I guess. They're roofers; they ought to know what they're doing."

Maddy frowned at the massive piles of debris ripped from the mansion that now covered every inch of the yard. "I didn't think it possible, but the place looks even more hideous than when we first bought it."

"I told you, the demolition phase is ugly. In a few days they'll haul all this refuse away and we'll have a clean slate to work with. You take a look at the blueprints yet? They're off the hook."

"Not yet," she said. "So, what do you think about Sophie and Mariah having a baby and *The Big Book of Sperm*?"

He chuckled. "Sort of a non sequitur there, but yeah, I'm aware of *The Big Book of Sperm*. What's wrong with it? Sophie's thirty-eight—she has to get cracking on this. A lot of people, even straight couples, use donors."

Maddy was surprised that her brother was taking it so seriously. While Nate was methodical in his business dealings, he was careless, even immature, in his personal life, dating and dumping women faster than his housekeeping staff could change a bed. She didn't think he gave a lot of thought to family and babies.

"What's going on with that divorce lawyer I recommended?" Nate asked. "She serve him yet?"

"Yep." The court documents had all been signed, sealed, and as far as she knew delivered. It had been a little tricky with Dave being in a foreign country. But her lawyer was . . . very diligent. Before she could say more on the topic, their carpenter, Colin, came out on the porch.

"We have a problem," he said.

Both Maddy and Nate turned to see their entire construction team filing out of the building and spilling onto the yard.

"I evacuated them," Colin said.

"What's going on?" Maddy asked with alarm.

Colin came down the steps and pulled Maddy and Nate aside. "I'm pretty sure I just found a drug lab in your basement."

"Well, let's pull it out of there, so we can get back to work," Nate said.

"Uh-uh." Colin directed himself at Maddy. "We need to call the police. There are drums of stuff down there—quite possibly flammable, explosive, even toxic. They were stowed behind a false wall I just ripped out. That's why we never noticed it before."

Nate blew out an exasperated breath, while Maddy dialed Rhys. He got there ten minutes later and waved her over while surveying the crew.

"Who's the biker-looking dude with the bandanna around his head?" he asked in a hushed tone.

"His name is Colin Burke," Maddy said. "He's the one who found it."

"Ah, Colin the chair guy. Shep has one of his rockers." Maddy nodded and Rhys asked, "Who's that?"

"That's my brother Nate. Let me introduce you." She called Nate over from talking with the workers and made the introductions.

Nate gave Rhys one of his obnoxious, overly firm handshakes, which was embarrassing for everyone involved, including Maddy. Rhys either didn't notice, or pretended not to.

"So you're my sister's neighbor," Nate said, spreading his legs wide and folding his arms over his chest, taking the overly protective dork thing to new levels.

"Yep. That would be me." They just stood there for a while until Rhys nodded in the direction of the building. "I should probably get inside, check things out. Nice meeting you."

"Likewise," Nate said. "Watch your back in there."

Watch your back in there? Maddy rolled her eyes.

Rhys headed over to Colin, talked to him for a few minutes, and told everyone to wait on the sidewalk behind the falling-down wrought iron fence.

"He seems like he knows what he's doing," Nate said.

Maddy watched Rhys disappear inside the mansion; hand on his hip holster, all badass and hotness. She reminded herself that it was perfectly normal for a woman in the throes of an ugly divorce to find another man—not her husband—attractive. Her heart might be dead, but the rest of her body parts worked just fine. "He used to be a narcotics detective, you know?"

"Yeah, you told me when you first moved in." Nate regarded her intently.

"What?"

"Nothing. You call Mom and Dad?"

Maddy shuffled from one foot to the other. "Uh-huh. Left a message."

Nate scowled at her, but before he could lecture her on the ills of avoiding her parents, Colin came over. The carpenter caught Maddy off guard by reaching out and giving her an awkward pat. Some might see him as aloof, even intimidating with his bushy beard and powerful build. She knew he was just socially awkward. Sometimes Maddy got the sense that he'd spent so much time alone making his furniture that he hadn't had a lot of human contact.

"Sorry," he said. "I know you're both anxious to get going on this project."

"Don't be ridiculous," she said. "Thank God you found it when you did. Someone could've been hurt."

Rhys came out of the house and Maddy and Nate automatically started walking toward him. He held up his hand and motioned for them to meet him at his SUV.

"This is a crime scene now, so I need you to stay off the grounds,"

Rhys told them, glancing over at the workers milling around on the sidewalk. A few of the merchants also looked on curiously.

Owen had come out of his barber shop and crossed the square. "Everything okay?"

Before Maddy could respond, Rhys told Owen, "I'll be over in a few minutes to let you know what's going on, but for now we have to keep the area clear." He turned back to her and Nate. "You may as well send your crew home."

"Is it really a drug lab?" Maddy asked.

"Meth, from the looks of it," he said.

"How can you tell?" Nate wanted to know.

"Bunsen burners, lots of cooking equipment, drain cleaner. I'm leaving the drums to a hazmat team, but if I had to guess, I'd say ether." Rhys lowered his voice. "Stuff's worth money. What worries me is whoever left it might come back looking for it."

"What do we do now?" Maddy asked.

"Wait for us to process the scene—pull all that equipment out of there, make sure the chemicals haven't made it uninhabitable. Then you can go back to work."

"How long will that take?" Nate asked.

"Three days. Maybe a week, depending on whether you have to send in a cleanup crew."

"A week—"

"Nate." Maddy fixed him with an admonishing glare. "Why don't you get the workers off the clock, while I continue our conversation with the chief."

"Yeah, okay."

Maddy waited for Nate to walk away. "Don't mind him. He's just frustrated."

"No doubt. It sucks. Hopefully we can get this done quickly and find the culprit," Rhys said, absently pushing a stray hair that had come loose from Maddy's twist away from her face.

"I just never expected something like this right here in the middle of town," she said. "I know meth has become a problem in rural areas, but this seems fairly brazen. Doesn't it?"

He rubbed his chin. "Nah. It's so commonplace in the Sierra that these guys set up wherever they find a vacant building. A place like this is actually ideal because they can come in at night and steal electricity and water from the neighboring businesses. For an abandoned cabin in the woods, they'd need a generator if they wanted light."

From the distance of the street, Rhys tilted his head, regarding the basement's now-open cellar door. "The stuff down there looked cobwebby, like it's been behind that wall awhile, so maybe this was just a convenient storage unit for them until they could find somewhere else to do their cooking." He shrugged. "Who knows? I'll check with the sheriff. They'll have a hot list of known parolees and probationers in the area. But what I'm hoping is that this jogs some memories . . . maybe a merchant saw someone, something . . . that looked funny."

"Pam from the yoga studio saw something," she said, suddenly remembering their first conversation. "She told me a few days ago that some sketchy people were loitering around the building, thought they might be squatters, that I should be careful."

"I'll talk to her," he said, and Maddy got the impression that her piece of news didn't sit well with him.

"Can Colin go, too?"

"Not yet. I have to take a formal statement from him since he's the guy who found it." He glanced over at Colin. "What do you know about him?—seems real nervous."

"Oh, he's just bashful," she said. "But he's a sweetheart. In fact, he's the one who insisted we call the police. If it had been up to Nate, the guys would still be hammering away." Maddy shook her head.

Rhys darted another sideways look over at Colin. "Shep seems to think he's had some troubles."

"Hmm, I don't know anything about that. He's an amazing carpenter, though. Before we hired him he showed Nate and me the house he's building up on Grizzly Peak and it's gorgeous. He also did a lot of the woodwork in the Ponderosa. Honestly, Rhys, he strikes me as a very nice man. And responsible."

Rhys shoved his hands in his pockets and let his gaze quickly flicker over her. He did that a lot, she noticed. "Okay," he said, and then, for some odd reason, he reached over and gave her a little kiss on the forehead. Just as abruptly, he walked over to where Colin stood.

"I think our police chief is sweet on you," Nate said as he came up behind Maddy, giving her a jolt.

"You're crazy."

"He just smooched you in front of everyone. And I'm crazy?"

"It was a brotherly little peck." She slugged him in the arm. "So don't go exaggerating things."

"Brotherly?" Nate shook his head. "I don't think so."

She let it drop, wrapping her arms around herself to ward off the cold. Mid-October in San Francisco usually felt like summer, but here, it was more of a brisk fall. "Maybe we should've inspected this place better before we bought it. I'm worried this is going to turn out to be a big problem."

"I certainly don't like having to stop work," Nate said. "But we bought a blighted building and the basement had a false wall. The only reason we found it in the first place is because of the demolition."

"I know. It just gives me the jitters." Maddy watched Rhys stretch yellow crime scene tape across the fence. "I have to go to a meeting for the Halloween festival. We're making goodie bags. There's nothing you can do here. Want to come meet Pam from the yoga studio and the other ladies?"

Nate glanced at his watch. "Nope. I think I'll get an early start back to the city. Traffic through Sacramento at rush hour is a bitch."

"Okay." She gave her brother a hug. "Drive carefully. Oh . . . and Nate, you're coming back for the festival, right?"

"I wouldn't miss it for the world," he said sarcastically. Nate thought he was a little too good for all mankind, but Maddy loved him anyway.

She waved goodbye to Nate, but before leaving in her own car, Rhys called her over.

"Hey." He clasped her by the shoulders. "Promise me you won't go in the Lumber Baron by yourself for a while."

"Okay," she said.

"Drug-sniffing dogs is what I heard," Grace Miller, queen bee of the Baker's Dozen cooking club, told the other four women assembled around a folding table covered with craft supplies and bags of

Halloween candy. "They had the entire sheriff's narcotics task force combing through that mansion."

Besides Grace, Maddy recognized Donna Thurston, who along with her husband owned the Bun Boy and Ethel of the Nugget Market. She'd met all three ladies at the first meeting. And of course Pam. Maddy didn't know the fifth woman, an attractive blonde who looked closer to her own age.

They were so captivated with Grace's exaggerated version of the Lumber Baron incident that no one had noticed when Maddy snuck in. Pam's yoga studio was about the size of a gymnasium, one side covered in floor-to-ceiling mirrors and a long ballet barre that ran across the wall.

"I saw the whole thing," Pam said dismissively. "There were no dogs and it was just Chief Shepard."

Someone else started to make an observation when the group finally glimpsed Maddy standing next to the upright piano.

Grace was the first to hop up from her chair and extend her arms for a hug. "You okay, dear?"

Maddy barely knew her, but she walked into the plump woman's embrace and into a cloud of Jean Naté. Who knew they still sold the stuff? "I'm fine," she said. "The whole thing is just a little disconcerting."

"Well, of course it is," Grace said, absently fluffing her head of gray curls. "But a slice of Amanda's upside-down pear cake will fix you right up." She pulled a chair out from the table for Maddy and patted the seat.

"We're just lucky you found it before the place went up like a bomb," Pam said. "Does Chief Shepard have any leads?"

"Not yet, but he wants to talk to you about those guys you saw hanging around the place."

"Damn," Pam said. "I wish I'd snapped a photo of them with my phone."

"Can you go back in?" Grace wanted to know.

"Not for a few days. They have to make sure the place isn't contaminated."

Someone pushed a plate of cake in front of her. Maddy, who

rarely found a sweet she could resist, didn't have much of an appetite. But she took a bite to be polite.

"Oh, my God." The rich flavors of something—Maddy had no idea what, maybe cinnamon and ginger—exploded in her mouth. "You actually made this?" she asked Amanda.

"I sure did," Amanda said, smiling proudly.

"When Amanda and her husband aren't training prize-winning quarter horses, she's generous enough to bake for every school, Kiwanis and Cattlewomen Association fund-raiser there is in this town—and there are a lot," Grace said.

"You could seriously sell this and make a fortune." Maddy tried not to inhale the whole piece.

"Do you cook, Maddy?" Grace asked.

"I microwave." If Maddy wanted to be completely truthful she did mostly takeout.

Grace held her heart like she was having a coronary. "Join the Baker's Dozen, dear, and we'll teach you how to cook."

"I don't think there's any hope." Ever since the incident with the double-boiler—how was Maddy supposed to know that you didn't melt the chocolate directly in the water?—she'd given herself a pass as far as the culinary arts. Not everyone was cut out to be Nigella Lawson. "But after this cake, definitely yoga."

"Excellent." Pam clapped her hands. The yoga instructor had to be in her early forties, but her body rivaled that of a thirty-year-old. "You have to come to the morning group."

"I'm in it," Amanda announced. And Maddy thought, *Why?* No muffin top hanging over that girl's jeans, not like Maddy's.

Pam rebuked the other three women with a piercing glare.

Grace held her palms up. "What? You think the Nugget Feed Store runs itself?"

Pam just shook her head. "You make time for what's important. After the meeting I'll give you a schedule," she told Maddy, grabbing a clipboard and pulling her chair closer to the table. "Okay, ladies, what do you say we get started?" She pointed to the candy bags on the table and everyone dutifully started stuffing. "Sophie and Mariah are doing the soft drinks, water, and have kindly offered to supply free beer and wine."

Pam looked down at the clipboard. "Baker's Dozen, how we doing on desserts?"

"Good," Amanda said. "I'm in charge of cupcakes, Grace is doing caramel apples, Donna and Ethel are handling cookies, brownies, and pecan squares."

"Perfect." Pam checked it off her list. "Can you guys show up a little early and set up tables?"

"You bet," Donna said. Of all the women in the group, Donna was the fashion plate, her blond hair stylishly layered with highlights so good they almost looked natural. Maddy put her at fiftyish.

Pam put down the clipboard. "Maddy and I are in charge of the stage, fortune-teller's tent, and decorating the park."

Maddy tied off a bag with a piece of orange yarn and turned to the group. "Okay, at the risk of sounding a little off-the-wall, what would you think about adding a Donner Party element to the festival. Too crass?"

Donna's eyes widened. "Oooh, Oooh . . . we can make ginger-bread men with missing arms and legs." Amanda laughed, but in that nervous kind of way, and Ethel looked faintly appalled.

"Okay, bad idea. But I think Nugget should do something to commemorate the event. Maybe once a year we could host a Donner Party History Day. And while I'm on the topic, what do you guys think about organizing some kind of downtown merchants' association?"

"Uh, thank you, Jesus," Donna raised her face reverently to the ceiling. "Then we could force Portia Cane to do something about that ghetto kiosk of hers."

"So what's the deal with her anyway?" Amanda wanted to know. "Are she and Steve an item? Because I kind of got the impression that she played for the other team."

"Hold on, ladies. Slow down for the new girl." These Baker's Dozen women were definitely in the running for Maddy's new best friends. So far, they traded more gossip than they did recipes. "Who's Portia Cane?"

"She and Steve own the tour guide business across from you," Ethel said. "You'll meet her at the festival. She's in charge of the skeet-shooting booth."

"Well, are they together, Gracie?" Amanda asked, and told Maddy, "Steve is Earl's brother."

"Who's Earl?" Maddy asked.

"Grace's husband," the other women answered in unison.

"As far as I know they're just business partners. But don't ask, don't tell, right?"

"You know, Donna," Pam said, crossing her arms over her chest. "Portia's not the only one with a ratty business. What about all those boarded-up storefronts on the square?"

"You talk to Trevor about that. That's his, not mine. His family had those buildings long before our marriage. I'll take full responsibility for the Bun Boy, the best-looking frosty in the Sierra, if I do say so myself."

"Yes it is," Ethel said.

"Right back at you, beautiful."

"So," Maddy said, "what do we have to do to get an association going?"

"Ha," Pam said. "To do anything in this town takes an act of Congress. The trick is getting the Nugget Mafia—Steve, Earl, Trevor, Ethel's husband, Stu, Mayor Dink Caruthers—on board."

"Don't forget Owen," Grace said. "He's Don Corleone." And they all laughed.

She'd seen all those men on the mornings she went to the Lumber Baron, gathering at the barber shop, drinking coffee, reading the paper. It was sweet.

"Clay still giving hayrides in his flatbed at the festival?" Grace asked.

"He sure is," Pam said, and the ladies started to giggle. Middle-aged women giggling like schoolgirls.

Maddy looked around the table. "Am I missing something here?"

"Have you seen Clay McCreedy?" Donna started fanning herself.

"Chief Shepard's friend, the one with the cowboy hat?" Maddy asked.

"There are a lot of men in this town with cowboy hats, including my husband," Grace said. "But there is only one Clayton McCreedy." And they started giggling again.

Maddy glanced over at Amanda, who shook her head. "Don't

look at me. I grew up with the guy—we used to share the same kiddy pool. But they . . . they're obsessed."

"If the man I think you're talking about is Clay McCreedy . . . and I'm pretty sure he is . . . I'll grant you he's hot. But he's not nearly as hot as Chief Shepard." As soon as the words left Maddy's mouth she wished she could take them back. Because now everyone in the room was staring at her.

"Mmm hmm," Donna said. And they continued to peal with laughter.

"Now that one turned out just as fine as fine can be," Grace said. "To come back and take care of that jackass father of his . . ."

"Gracie Miller!" Ethel tsked. "The man's got Alzheimer's." Grace and Ethel were the matrons of this bunch—both somewhere in their sixties—but Maddy noticed that Ethel kept the other women in check when they went too far.

Grace lifted her hands. "I know, I know. But the way he neglected that boy . . . We should all be ashamed for not having called Child Protective Services. It's just a miracle Rhys grew up as good as he did."

"That's because Tip McCreedy took him under his wing," Donna said. "Now there was a man." The women collectively sighed and Donna told Maddy, "After his wife Patrice passed, he raised Clay from a baby and never even looked at another woman."

"Can you imagine if he'd still been alive when Jennifer came sashaying through this town, flashing those Pamela Anderson boobs to any man who'd give her the time of day?" Grace shook her head.

Amanda whispered in Maddy's ear, "Jennifer's Clay's late wife."

Maddy was dying to know more, but as the newcomer she didn't want to seem nosey.

"You see Shep with those kids?" Ethel asked. "They came in the store the other day. Shep told Stu they were his and that their mother recently died. Apparently, Rhys didn't know squat about them until they showed up on his doorstep with a social worker." The other women hummed their disapproval. Maddy didn't say a word.

"Those poor children," Grace said. "The man wasn't fit for fatherhood even when he was healthy."

"Rhys'll wind up caring for them," Donna said.

Why Shep would've kept Rhys's own flesh and blood a secret

from him, Maddy didn't understand. But if it was true, which she suspected it was, it made her heart ache for Rhys.

The women resumed filling candy sacks and the topic turned back to the festival. They discussed the fortune-teller booth and Maddy suggested renting a canvas party tent and gussying it up by draping it with fabric remnants and scarves. Pam liked the idea and said she had an old crystal ball lying around somewhere.

The longer Maddy spent with Pam and the Baker's Dozen the more relaxed she felt. In San Francisco she'd inherited Dave's friends— women who served on this or that board with him, the wife of a college buddy, his mother's goddaughter. They all wore designer clothes and had a distinctive way of talking through their noses.

Maybe it was the fact that when she had arrived here, dismayed at finding a chemical cache in her basement, these women—practically strangers—had hugged and fed her. Maddy wasn't precisely sure, but as conversation came to a lull and the ladies took to their task of filling bags in earnest, she blurted, "I'm getting a divorce."

The room went so quiet all Maddy could hear was the low purr of the radiator.

"Oh, dear," Grace said.

"I know." Maddy's voice quavered. "It's terrible. But when my husband—his name's Dave—married me, he was in love with someone else. This other woman, though, happened to be married to Dave's cousin, Max. Max died a few months ago, leaving Gabby, the other woman, available." Even to her ears it sounded like *Days of Our Lives*.

"So he left you for this Gabby woman?" Donna asked.

"Not exactly." It was more complicated than that, she wanted to say, feeling proud of the fact that she could finally talk about it without breaking down. Even the pornographic slide show of Dave and Gabby writhing in ecstasy, playing like a constant loop inside her head, had mercifully gone dark.

"He says he loves me and has gotten Gabby out of his system," she said.

"Oh, honey, you're right to leave the asshole," Donna said.

The rest of the women gasped. "Donna!" Ethel chided.

"Oh, give me a break," Donna bit back. "You're all thinking the same thing. I just had the cojones to say it."

"She's right," Pam sighed.

Grace reached over and covered Maddy's hand with hers. "No one can tell you what to do in a situation like this. It's your heart and you have to follow what it tells you. But you absolutely have our shoulders. You just tell us what we can do to help, dear."

"Well," Maddy sniffed. "Someone could cut me another piece of that cake."

Chapter 8

"You want a refill on that iced tea?" Sophie wiped the counter until it gleamed.

The lunch crowd at the Ponderosa had thinned to just a few tables and only Owen sat at the bar. The barber's patronage made Sophie want to pump her fist in the air. It used to be that other than his standing Saturday bowling date with the rest of the Nugget Mafia, Owen got his lunches at the Bun Boy.

And since he pretty much ran this town behind the scenes, Owen eating alone at the Ponderosa signaled real progress to Sophie.

"Yeah, hit me again." He pushed his glass at her.

"Slow day at the barber shop?"

"Nope. Just taking a well-deserved break."

"Good for you."

"Getting ready for the Halloween festival?" he asked her.

"Yep," she said. Mariah had even decorated the Ponderosa with flashing skull lights and orange and black crepe paper.

"You two find a baby daddy yet?"

Sophie missed the shaker she was refilling and poured salt all over the counter as she nearly choked. "Owen, how do you know about that?" Jesus, you couldn't keep anything private in this town.

"Oh, don't go getting your panties all in a bunch, your secret is safe with me. But you might not want to talk so loud when you're on the phone."

She shot him a dirty look. "Or you might not want to eavesdrop on people's personal conversations."

"Why wouldn't I want to do that? A man can learn a lot of interesting stuff that way. If you haven't found anyone yet, I'm here to offer up my services."

Sophie felt that Cobb salad she'd just eaten coming up on her. "What are you talking about, Owen?"

"Me," he said. "Stud for hire. But in your and Mariah's case, free. Okay, maybe a few lunches . . . and bowling."

"You have got to be kidding me." The man couldn't be a day under seventy.

"Okay, forget the bowling. You gals have to make a living. Diapers and college ain't cheap." He downed the rest of his tea and reached for his wallet to pay his bill. "Well, whaddya think?"

"Wow, Owen. I don't know what to say." And she really didn't. "Uh, it's a super generous offer. But we already have someone in mind."

"Someone from that book?" Owen said, getting down off the stool.

"So you know about that, too?" Sophie asked, annoyed.

"You girls aren't exactly subtle, pawing through that directory like it was porn. The other day Mariah left it on the bar while she was making coffee. Had a look at it myself and I've gotta say, if you're going the turkey baster route, Lithuanian Man looks like your best bet—good pedigree on that one. But if it doesn't work out—"

"We've got it covered, Owen," Sophie snapped.

"Suit yourself." And with that, he sailed out the door.

"What was that about?" Mariah came in from the kitchen carrying a glass rack and started arranging clean stemware on the shelf.

Sophie grabbed a stool on the other side of the bar. "Owen volunteered to father our child."

Mariah let out a laugh. "Seriously? Oh, that's hysterical."

"No, it's not." Hostility edged her voice and she knew it wasn't really about Owen and his absurd offer. "He saw the book, which you carelessly left on the bar."

"Oh, Soph, lighten up. It's a small town—everyone knows everyone else's business."

"I'm glad you feel that way," Sophie said. "Because Owen gave Lithuanian Man a thumbs-up."

"See." Mariah let out a bark of laughter. "I told you he was a good choice."

"Well, I think he's a terrible choice."

"I know, Soph. We've been over this what—fifteen, twenty times? My feelings haven't changed about Nate."

According to Mariah, friends were risky donors. They were more likely to get attached to the child and sue for custody. Unfortunately, statistics backed her up on this. And so did the courts. Judges tended to rule in favor of biological parents—regardless of promises, contracts, and lawyers. Mariah had done her research. Even though anonymous donors occasionally came out of the woodwork, fighting for involvement in their child's life, it happened far less often.

But Sophie could swear that besides legal reasons, Mariah had other issues with Nate. The fact that she wasn't even willing to talk about it, not even with a family law attorney, seemed so out of character for her usually reasonable partner.

So Sophie pressed. "You'd prefer to go with a complete stranger over someone we know and love?"

"Yes," Mariah said emphatically. "You don't even know that Nate would be willing to be a donor."

"As long as you're against it, I won't get the chance to find out. Tell me the truth. Are you jealous of Nate?" They'd never broached this subject before, but Sophie thought it was high time to get everything out in the open.

"Not jealous," Mariah said. "But definitely threatened."

Sophie's jaw nearly hit the ground. Her relationship with Mariah had always been rock solid. So how could Mariah feel threatened?

"Not the way you think," Mariah said. "I'm not worried that you're secretly in love with Nate. But think about it, Sophie. If he's the father and you're the mother, what do I bring to this family?"

Sophie walked around the bar and turned Mariah to face her. "You would be as much the baby's mother as I would be. Nate being the child's biological father wouldn't change that. It would be the same as if we had adopted a baby."

"No it wouldn't," she said. "Typically, when you adopt a baby both biological parents aren't still in the picture. Don't you see how it would be for me, Sophie? I would be nothing."

Mariah could never be nothing. For Sophie she was everything. But she couldn't force her own ideal of a perfect father down Mariah's throat. The problem was the alternative for her was just as unpalatable.

The day of Nugget's big Halloween festival arrived and despite forecasts of near-freezing temperatures, the weather remained clear and by Sierra mountain standards, moderate. The low fifties. Maddy had been told that on numerous occasions the cold had forced the festivities to be moved inside the community center. Because of Nugget's elevation it was the sixth snowiest city in the nation, getting an average of two hundred inches a year.

An anomaly for California. And most unfortunate for the Donner Party.

However, thanks to global warming, Maddy could forgo the parka, and put on a fitted puffer jacket. She tucked the legs of her skinny jeans into her boots, put on a ribbed turtleneck, and flat-ironed her hair. She even took extra care with her makeup.

The entire town had gotten into the spirit of the party and the square's shopkeepers expected a full turnout.

She parked in front of the Lumber Baron Inn, which was still cordoned off with police tape, and wandered over to the square.

Maddy gazed up at the black and orange paper lanterns and twinkle lights she and Pam had strung from the trees. The closest she'd gotten to this kind of community spirit during the holidays in San Francisco was Drag Queens on Ice. She never missed it.

They'd erected a stage in the center of the park for the bluegrass band and the square's proprietors had set up card tables loaded with candy in front of their shops. The Baker's Dozen had their own table, laden with goodies. Tubs overflowed with soft drinks, and Mariah and Sophie worked behind a makeshift bar outside the Ponderosa, serving beer and wine. Not even seven o'clock and the open house already crawled with people.

Owen organized a pumpkin carving contest in front of his barber shop. He wasn't exactly friendly when he saw Maddy, but he did ask if she'd been able to go back inside the Lumber Baron.

"Not yet," she said. "Just waiting for Chief Shepard to give us the thumbs-up."

Pam, decked out in full gypsy regalia, read tarot cards in the tent Maddy had created. And sure enough, Portia Cane—the Baker's Dozen's androgynous nemesis—had constructed a toy skeet-shooting gallery at the edge of the square. She wore an Indiana Jones hat and fatigues.

At the Lumber Baron table, Maddy and Nate handed out cookies stamped with the hotel's new logo. Not exactly homemade, but Maddy thought the shortbread, imprinted with a miniature version of a Victorian, was truly inspired. Her idea of course.

"How we doing?" Maddy asked.

Nate didn't answer, just showed her the untouched cartons of cookies.

"That sucks." Maddy noticed that people were lining up for the Ponderosa's free drinks. "Maybe we should've done Jell-O shots."

"Maybe," Nate said. "But to be honest, I'm not feeling the love. Sophie warned me that we might not be welcomed with open arms." He gave an apathetic shrug. "Hey, we got our permits."

She gazed out over the square and saw Rhys with Shep and the kids. His hands were shoved in his pockets and he was looking down at his feet. Maddy sensed that he'd rather be anywhere than here. Sam followed him around like a puppy, emulating his walk and stance. It would've been adorable if it weren't so sad. Those children had missed out on having a big brother during their formative years, and Rhys had missed out on having a family.

So far, the kids seemed to be a great help with Shep. Lina and he would walk together nearly every day to the library and market. In the evenings before Rhys got home from work Maddy would some-times join Shep and the children on the porch. She'd offered to take them to Reno the next time she went. They were ill-prepared for the cold weather coming from central California, and the clothes they had seemed rather worn. She'd gotten the sense that they hadn't had much money.

As she rearranged their table a couple wandered over. The woman had at least three inches on the man and wore an orange hoodie with a rather large fleece appliqué of a bear. He, too, wore a bear sweatshirt, but his wasn't 3-D, just a screen print of Yogi and Boo-Boo.

"Hi, we're the Addisons—Sandy and Cal," Sandy announced, giving Maddy the impression that she was supposed to know those names.

"Nice to meet you," Maddy said, hoping that if they kept talking something would eventually spark her memory. "This is my brother Nate. We're the new owners of the Lumber Baron."

"We know who you are," Sandy said—apparently Cal didn't talk. Then they just stood there. Awkward, really.

Maddy grabbed one of the boxes. "Cookie?" she offered.

"No thanks," Sandy said. Cal reached for one, but Sandy slapped his hand away.

Nate watched the whole interaction from his folding chair, tipping it backward until he balanced on two legs.

"Beautiful night, isn't it?" Maddy said.

Sandy shrugged. Cal might've nodded, Maddy couldn't tell. It was their turn to talk, but they continued to dawdle, hands stuffed into the pouches of their sweatshirts. If Maddy wasn't mistaken, Cal was checking out her chest. Or maybe he was just eye level with her boobs. She didn't want to judge.

"I'm sorry," she finally said. "I get the feeling I should know who you are, but I don't." *Sue me.*

"We own the Beary Quaint."

"Oh, for goodness sake. We meet at long last." Maddy reached across the table to shake their hands, but Sandy backed away. People in the hospitality industry usually veered toward warm and friendly. But, okay. "I've been meaning to come over, introduce myself and brainstorm with you guys."

"Brainstorm? Brainstorm about what?"

"Well," Maddy said, not wanting to sound too pushy. "I thought we could work together to bring a little more tourism to Nugget."

"We're not having any problems attracting guests, are we, Cal?" Sandy looked at her husband for affirmation and he shook his head like a good soldier. "The same families have been coming back to the Beary Quaint for generations. We're booked solid for years out."

"That's wonderful." Maddy looked at Nate for a little help. As the only other Nugget lodging option outside of the state park and nearby Graeagle, she was hoping they could partner up to entice the town to clean up the commercial district. Maybe together they could even convince the Chamber of Commerce to promote the city's historical past. The Donner Party.

But no. Nate just sat there, the back of his chair resting against a tree, his hands laced behind his head. Sure would be a shame if he fell and cracked his skull open.

"Are you sure you'll even be able to open?" Sandy asked, her eyes growing wide with feigned concern.

"You mean the paraphernalia we found in the Lumber Baron's basement?" Maddy tried to slough it off. "Just a minor setback."

"I wasn't talking about the meth lab." Sandy flashed Maddy a malicious smile, tugged on Cal's arm, and they left.

"What do you think she meant by that?"

"Who knows." Nate landed his chair on all four legs again. "The woman's on crack.

"And there is no way they're booked solid. Have you seen that place? Chain-saw bears all over the place. Bear cozies on the toilet seats. Serious Bates Motel shit going on there. I don't want us aligning ourselves with those people."

"They do not have bear cozies on the toilet seats."

"Swear to God," Nate said. "Hey, don't look now, but your police chief boyfriend's checking you out."

"Is he really looking over here?"

"He's looking . . . and he's headed our way," Nate said.

Rhys lifted his chin in greeting, while his eyes examined Maddy with open male appreciation. "You look nice."

"Thanks." He looked better than nice in a waffle Henley that hung loose over his jeans. The shirt concealed the top of his gun holster, but did nothing to conceal the man's sinewy chest. Maddy could make out every muscle. Like a twit, she reached into one of the boxes. "Want a cookie?"

"Sure."

"It's nice that you brought Shep and the kids. They seem to be having a nice time. Is everyone settling in?"

Rhys drew in a breath. "I suppose. Look, I'm sorry about all the extra noise; about you having to park your car at the top of the driveway until I can get a bulldozer in there to clear more yard; about the fact that you now have a monster camper outside your window. I know this isn't what—"

"Rhys, are you serious? Those kids lost everything. I can walk a few extra feet to my car. But I know how horribly cramped you all must be and I just want you to know that as soon as the innkeeper's quarters are ready at the Lumber Baron, you'll have my side of the duplex back."

"Actually, that's what I came over to talk to you guys about." He waved Nate over. "I wanted to let you know that we're done processing the Lumber Baron. It's all yours starting tomorrow."

"You have any leads?" Nate asked.

"Not yet. These folks tend to be nomadic. Eventually I'll get something. But in the meantime, you and your workers need to keep your eyes open, no one should be there alone after dark. I was serious when I said these guys might come back for their stash. As for you moving in there, Maddy . . . Bad idea. Hold off on that. At least for a few weeks."

"Okay," Maddy said. "Do we need to fumigate?"

"Nope. Those drums were sealed tight. Hazmat didn't find any leakage."

That seemed to make Nate happy. They hadn't budgeted for chemical decontamination.

"Should we remove the yellow crime tape, or do the police have to do that?" She wanted it gone as soon as possible. "The tape's not so good from a marketing standpoint."

"I've got you covered." He winked at her, making her insides slam. She really needed to get a grip where he was concerned. Like maybe getting over the last man who screwed her over, before moving on to the next one.

When he walked away, she found Nate grinning at her obnoxiously.

"You're an imbecile," she said, and took off across the square to get her cards read.

Pam waited for Maddy to grab a seat at the table they'd draped with a fringed velvet shawl and took her palm in her hand.

"This is so cool, Pam." Maddy peeked out through the tent's opening and everywhere she looked people, young and old, were enjoying themselves. At night, with only the glow of the string lights, a few jack-o'-lanterns, and the moon, the place actually looked magical.

"We did pull it together rather nicely, didn't we?" Pam leaned across the crystal ball. "I know things have been rough-going with the inn. But it'll work out, you'll see."

"Chief Shepard said we can go back in, that there was no contamination."

"That's gotta be a relief."

"It is," Maddy said. "But the Addisons sort of put a crimp in my night. I had high hopes that we could work together making this a tourist town. But they came over to our table and made it very clear they weren't interested."

"I'm not too surprised. They were the big game in town until you came along. It's pretty silly of them, but they've been known to be petty. Give them some time, maybe they'll come around."

"Yeah, maybe." But Maddy didn't think so.

Fred, Pam's husband, popped his head inside the tent. "Hello in there. Half the town's lined up outside."

"If you want a break I could take over for you," Maddy said. "I don't know how to read palms or tarot cards, but I could fake it."

"I'm fine."

"Okay, then I'll see you at yoga on Monday."

On Maddy's way out, Pam called, "Your heart line ends at your second finger. That means you're a generous soul—a giver. But most of the time it's at your own expense."

She considered Pam's fortune as she returned to the Lumber Baron table. It was true; she'd made a lot of concessions in her marriage, like quitting her career, spending time with people she didn't particularly like because Dave thought of them as "good connections." Performing the part of a perfect Wellmont for so long, she'd forgotten what it was like to be good old Maddy Breyer. At least here, she could be whoever she wanted.

Back at the table, Nate was going stir-crazy. "I think I'll hit Soph and Mariah's. You okay here for a while?"

"Sure," Maddy said.

As he started across the square, she called, "You staying with me tonight?"

He shook his head. "Sophie and Mariah offered me unlimited use of their guest room. And they have running water. But let's do breakfast. Unless you and the cop have plans?"

Before she could fire off a snide remark she backed up into something expansive and granite-hard.

Strong arms reached out to steady her and a pair of warm lips landed next to her ear. "I presume he's talking about me. Wasn't aware we had plans?"

She turned to face him, fairly sure that her face had turned various shades of red. For some reason she couldn't stop staring at his chest. And, as if her eyes had a will of their own—lower. "Uh . . . Nate was being an idiot . . . I'm sorry, Rhys, but I'm really in no shape to date."

"Okay." His mouth quirked teasingly. "Good to know, since I don't recall having asked you out."

Then he walked away, leaving her more than a little mortified.

As he made his way across the square, Rhys shook his head. He'd never had a woman rebuff him while looking at him like he was a giant lollipop. No doubt about it, Maddy wanted to lick him from head to toe. And for more than a minute there, he'd been tempted to press her up against the nearest building.

The woman was making him crazy. Sometimes he swore he could smell her perfume through their connecting walls. Rhys had idled on the porch in the cold more times than he could count, just so he could "accidentally" bump into her. Like a freaking eighth grader.

When he wasn't loitering on the deck, he was lying in the trailer, visualizing her naked. Or visualizing them both naked. Together. In bed. On the hood of his truck. Over his desk. Behind the Bun Boy. There should be laws against the places his mind went.

Although she'd smacked him down pretty hard a few minutes ago, she wasn't immune to him, either. Not by the looks she'd been giving him. The question was what did he do about it?

Maddy was mending a broken heart. And Rhys only had 152 more days—not that he was counting—to go until freedom. Texas. Away from here. Ordinarily, it would've been the perfect setup for a light, no-strings-attached friends-with-benefits type of situation. But Maddy didn't strike him as doing light or no-strings-attached.

No, she was hearth and home and apple pie. And his gut told him she was the kind of woman who gave bad husbands a second chance because she believed in the institution of marriage.

It was probably for the best. Keep things simple.

Rhys was just about to head across the square when Owen called to him, "Hey Chief, what's going on with the Lumber Baron?"

He stopped so Owen could catch up. As a kid, Rhys had always wanted the barber to cut his hair. All the other boys in town went to him. But Shep had complained that it cost too much and used to trim both his and Rhys's hair on the porch, like they were fucking hillbillies.

He'd already briefed Owen and the other merchants about the status of the investigation. Now he apparently wanted hourly updates. "I still don't have any suspects, Owen," Rhys said testily. "But Maddy and her brother are free to go back in." He started to walk away.

"I guess that's good," Owen said, scratching his head. "Heard you went off to Houston and made captain in the police force over there."

Rhys hid a smile. "Not quite captain, just detective-sergeant." Although he'd passed the lieutenant's exam and was waiting for a bump in rank. Unfortunately, those jobs came up as often as the Astros won a Series.

"Well, we're all real proud of you, son. The way you've come back to handle Shep's situation . . . We're all just real proud."

Taken by surprise, Rhys just nodded. The fact that anyone here was keeping track of his accomplishments since he'd left town came as a revelation.

He was about to call it a night, when Clay pulled up to the square in a flatbed strewn with hay and a dozen or so costumed kids. Rhys walked over to give his friend a hand lifting the little ones off the truck. Some of the adults he recognized from his elementary school days, back when he wore the same pair of dirty Toughskins to class and suffered pitying looks from their parents. Even then, he'd vowed to bust out of this nothing town the first chance he got. But here he was. Stuck in Nugget again.

"Hey Chief, any luck catching those meth cookers?" asked Gavin Becker, his eleven-year-old arch-nemesis all grown up. When he thought no one could hear him, Gavin used to taunt Rhys by singing "I've Been Working on the Railroad." He used to lord it over the other Union Pacific kids that his dad managed the Silver Legacy casino—like that was some big deal.

"Not yet," Rhys said.

Gavin hoisted a little girl dressed as a butterfly into the air and gave her a kiss. "Glad to have you back, Rhys. Sorry about your dad, man. But I gotta tell you, it's a comfort knowing you're running the police department here. Now Duff . . ." Gavin shook his head. "Let's just say that was a different era. But I'm raising kids now and knowing that you have all that experience . . . it helps me sleep at night."

He slapped Rhys on the back and invited him to stop by the house for a beer anytime.

First Owen, now Gavin.

"What crawled up his ass?" Rhys asked Clay when everyone left.

"He's still a dick. But he finally found a woman who'd actually have sex with him."

Clay waited for Rhys to stop laughing. "Speaking of, I'm seeing that woman I told you about in Reno this weekend. She's got a friend. You interested?"

Rhys wasn't. He was much more interested in Maddy. But since that wasn't happening, he found himself saying yes.

Chapter 9

Monday dawned cold and gloomy. Rhys thought the weather mirrored Sam's mood.

"Eat your oatmeal," Lina cajoled as she sipped coffee at Shep's old Formica kitchen table. "You have a big day ahead of you, *mijo.*"

"I don't want to go to school," Sam whined.

Rhys was sorely ready to tell him he didn't have to go. The only thing worse than attending Nugget Elementary School had been Rhys's days at Nugget Middle School. Both, he was positive, had scarred him for life. The kids mocked his junky clothes, they teased him incessantly about his weird father, and generally made his life a living hell. If he hadn't buddied up with Clay in the second grade, he might've been an elementary school dropout. It's not like anyone, including his dad, would've noticed if he'd just quit going.

At least in high school he had been able to play up the story he'd invented about being emancipated from his father and living in Shep's apartment as a fifteen-year-old bachelor—free to carouse as much as he wanted. The latter part had been mostly true. The lie had sufficiently impressed the dumber desperate girls enough to have them sneaking over to his place on the nights Rhys knew his dad would be away, traveling with the railroad.

"What are you worried about?" Although he didn't want to get involved any more than he had to, Rhys asked anyway.

"I don't know." Sam played with his food and Lina scolded him to eat. "What if the other kids don't like me?"

"Why wouldn't they like you? From what I can tell you're a pretty likable guy," Rhys said.

But from what Rhys knew about fifth graders there was a distinct possibility that the kids would be mean just for the hell of it. Unfortunately, there was no putting it off. The boy living with the police chief couldn't be a truant.

Both kids had gone to a year-round Catholic school in Stockton, which shockingly Shep had paid for. Rosa had worked in an almond processing plant on an assembly line. Rhys doubted she made more than minimum wage. Still, the only demand she'd made of the old man was that he pay the tuition. She'd been smart to insist on it. Stockton had a gang problem and the public schools could be rough.

Not for the first time, he wondered what Lina and Sam's lives had been like there. Had they left a lot of friends? Did they miss their home? According to their transcripts, they'd both been good students.

Lina was so good that she'd completed all her requirements early and should have been college bound. But that plan got blown to hell when her mother was killed. Until they could come up with a new plan, she would help take care of Shep while his nurse, Betty, was gone. Lina spent most nights on Rhys's laptop, researching Alzheimer's, coming up with specialists they should contact, finding trials in which Shep could participate. Rhys mostly just humored her.

"Let's go, Sam," he said, looking at his watch.

"Thank you, Rhys," Lina said, her face wreathed in gratitude.

He and Sam grabbed their jackets and headed up the driveway. The boy scrambled into the truck and Rhys made sure he was buckled in. Ten minutes later, Rhys queued up in the school's crescent-shaped drop-off behind a trail of parents.

"Let's do this," Rhys said eagerly, sensing that Sam's feet were getting colder with each passing second.

Sam hesitated, pressing his face against the window and staring out at the cliques of boys and girls assembling in front of the gray building.

Rhys scanned the crowd, feeling satisfied that Sam was dressed like all the other boys—jeans, sweatshirt, and Converse high- tops.

Rhys got out of the truck and opened the passenger door. "What do you say we find your classroom?"

"Hi, Uncle Rhys."

Rhys turned around to find Cody McCreedy standing there. He'd had so much to occupy him these last couple of days, he'd forgotten that Cody and Sam were about the same age.

"Hey, Code."

"This your brother?"

Rhys stiffened. "This is Sam." He watched the boys size each other up. "How would you feel about showing him around on his first day—maybe introduce him to a few of the other kids?"

"Who's your teacher?" Cody asked Sam.

"Mrs. DeLeo."

"That's my teacher, too." Cody smiled and looked up at Rhys. "Okay, I'll take him to class."

When Rhys tried to follow, Cody stuck out his hand. "Don't take this the wrong way, Uncle Rhys, but it would be better if you didn't come."

"Why's that?"

"It'll make Sam look like a loser."

"Got it," Rhys said. "I'll just head over to the main office to sign some enrollment papers. You guys can pretend you don't know me."

He watched the boys' backs disappear behind the school's double doors and ambled into the administration office. A stick-thin woman with curly gray hair greeted him from behind the counter.

"May I help you?"

"I'm here to enroll Samuel . . . Samuel . . . Shepard."

"Ah, Chief Shepard. Principal Rice said you'd be stopping by." She leaned over the counter and pursed her lips in a straight line. "Where's the young man?"

"We ran into Cody McCreedy on the way. They both have Mrs. DeLeo, so Cody took him to class."

"Oh," she said stiffly, her face puckering like she'd sucked on a mouthful of Lemonheads. "Sign in, please." She pointed to a sheet on the counter and with an efficiency of movement that belied the stick up her ass, grabbed a stack of forms, a clipboard, and a pen from various desks. "You'll need to fill these out."

The smell of the building hadn't changed—a combination of ammonia, must, and old gym shoes. There was an earthquake preparedness poster on the wall and student drawings of the food pyramid.

With some effort, Rhys managed to fold himself into a combination chair-desk and cursing the trolls who'd invented the unholy furniture combo, he sifted through the forms. A lot of the questions he couldn't answer. He'd brought the transcript so he knew the basics—Sam's birth date, the name of his old school, his academic record. But as far as whether the boy had any allergies, or whether he had a seizure disorder, Rhys didn't have the first clue.

"Some of these his sister will have to fill out," he told the woman. "I'll bring them back tomorrow."

"That's fine," she said. "As long as we have them by the end of the week."

He placed the completed forms on the counter and made to leave.

"Chief Shepard?"

He turned back to the counter.

"You have to give us an emergency contact."

Without even thinking, he wrote down his name and his telephone numbers.

The second week of November, Jake Stryker started his new job with Nugget PD. Finding that stockpile in the Lumber Baron's basement finally lit a match under Rhys to make the hire. Frankly, he'd wanted someone younger. Someone more likely to have the fire in his belly.

But between the meth lab and the fact that he now had a desolate development with million-dollar homes to patrol, Rhys also wanted a person with experience. And true to Stryker's word, the boys down in LAPD's Rampart Division had given him glowing reviews.

They'd also given him a nickname.

Jake had been known as the Silver Fox because of his graying hair, his way with the ladies, and the fact that he'd landed a few bit police roles in Hollywood movies. Rhys could see why. Jake was straight out of cop central casting—a good natured Dirty Harry. He'd already turned heads in Nugget.

When Rhys got to the station, Jake was already there, chatting up Connie. He liked that Jake was early.

"I'll just check my messages and we can go," Rhys called from his office.

"Where you guys off to?" Connie asked.

"I'm taking Jake on a tour of Sierra Heights."

"Ah . . . Where the other half don't live." Connie poured coffee into a to-go cup and placed it on Rhys's desk. She'd donated a fancy European coffeemaker that ground and brewed to the office after up-grading her personal one. Her sister lived in Seattle and had turned her into a coffee snob. She ordered their beans from some specialty roaster in Oakland. It seemed like a lot of trouble to Rhys, but it was damn good coffee.

"Okay," Rhys said. "We're out of here. Radio if anything comes up."

Before hitting the road, Rhys took Jake over to the Lumber Baron to show him the basement. Sometimes Maddy hung on the porch while the crew went in and out. He glanced over, but no sight of her.

Colin was working in the yard. When he spotted Rhys, he turned off the table saw and flipped up his goggles. "Anything yet?"

"Nope. You mind if I show Officer Stryker where you found the stuff?"

"No problem." Colin slid the goggles down and went back to cutting trim.

Rhys led the way down a flight of steps to the cellar door and reminded himself to tell Maddy or Colin to get a lock. It wouldn't keep out anyone who really wanted in, but at least it would slow them down. The basement was fairly spacious with enough height for them to walk around without having to duck their heads.

"That's where we found the barrels of ether." Rhys pointed.

Jake toed the residue on the ground from where they'd dusted for prints. "So they're fixing this place up, huh?"

"Yeah. They're turning it into an inn."

"Nice." Jake felt the basement wall with the back of his hand. "This would make a great wine cellar. You thinking these guys will be back for their stash?"

As a narc, Rhys had seen it happen dozens of times in Houston. Tweakers too stupid to realize they'd been raided, returning to the scene of the crime. "If they're from around here, they may already know we took it. If not . . . yeah, they'll be back."

They climbed out of the basement and walked toward the front of the Victorian. Rhys scanned the porch again and felt a twinge of disappointment.

"You all moved in?" he asked as they crossed the square to where his truck was parked.

"Yep. Had an efficiency apartment in LA, so I kept most of my stuff here anyway."

"How long you have the cabin?" Rhys clicked his key fob and they both piled inside the cab.

"Oh, fifteen years at least," Jake said. "I've been bringing my girls up since they were little."

"How many you have?"

"Five—three in college." He beamed and whipped out his phone. "That's my oldest, Sarah. I got her that kayak when she graduated from high school. That one's Janny—straight A student. Tara's the baby, loves horses."

"Nice-looking family," Rhys said, as Jake continued to show him picture after picture of his daughters.

"Not a boy in the bunch." Jake chuckled, but Rhys heard a little longing, too. "You have any?"

"Kids? Hell no."

"So you came from Houston PD, huh?"

"Yep," Rhys pulled out of the square, hopped on Highway 70 and turned onto Sierra Heights Road. He drove through the scrolled gates, past the empty security booth. "I worked narcotics, but my goal is homicide. I'm guessing it's even tougher in LA than it is in Houston. You don't think you'll miss it?"

"Nope. It sucks the life out of you." Jake stared out at the huge homes. "Wow. I see what you mean."

"Yep, sort of our version of Bel Air."

Jake continued to gape. "In all my years living here, I never checked this place out. So, what's the deal?"

Rhys headed for the clubhouse, explaining that the developers had run out of money, stiffed their subs, who subsequently filed liens against the property. He parked and Jake followed him out of the truck.

"They can't sell any of these houses until the liens are lifted?"

"Right," Rhys said. "In this economy I don't know who'd buy them anyway."

He showed Jake the common grounds like he'd done with Maddy. The pool, the golf course, the pro shop. "Honestly, with our lack of resources we can't worry too much about vandalism. As far as I'm concerned that's the developers' problem. My fear, however, is that this place will become an encampment for squatters and I don't want them making trouble for our residents."

Jake nodded. "The power and water must be shut off. It'll be freezing soon. We'll have to watch for chimney smoke."

Rhys jiggled the rec room door handle to make sure it was still locked. "I'd like this to be part of Wyatt's beat, but the kid's pretty inexperienced. So maybe you could patrol the subdivision with him a few times, tell him about things like chimney smoke, show him the ropes."

"Sounds good," Jake said. "I also think you and I should hit some of the back roads in these mountains, see if anything leads to our meth friends."

Just as they were heading back to the truck, Rhys's radio crackled and Connie's voice came over the air. "Chief, we've got a two seventy three-point-five up on Shadow Lane."

"You got a house number, Connie?"

"It's the McCall place."

Ah crap! He knew the house. Last he'd heard, the family had moved away; only Mini lived there now.

"On our way," he told Connie.

"Spouse reported being badly beaten," she warned.

Mini getting married was news to him. "Send paramedics, okay?"

"Will do," she responded and signed off.

He pulled his portable police beacon from the floor of the backseat, attached the flashing light to his roof and took off, siren blaring. The Southside quarter, right outside town, hadn't changed much. Rows of run-down Craftsman bungalows. Not too long ago, he would've prescribed a wrecking ball. But Maddy's optimism for Nugget was rubbing off on him. Because, now, looking at Shadow Lane, he could actually see potential. The modest-sized homes with their front porches, tapered square columns, and gabled roofs had character. With a little TLC this could be a good neighborhood for young families.

When they got to the McCall house, a naked man crouched behind a corduroy couch on the porch, holding his bleeding head.

"What the hell took you so long?" The man kept darting his eyes around, as if expecting someone to haul out of the house at any second.

Jake immediately headed for the rear in case someone tried to bolt out the back door.

"Come down, sir," Rhys ordered from the street.

Seemingly satisfied that the coast was clear, the man got up and staggered down the steps, grabbing for the railing.

"EMTs are on their way." Rhys quickly checked the man's head, determining the wound to be superficial. Just the same, he could have a concussion, so Rhys told him to wait in the truck. The thought of the guy's bare ass rubbing on the leather seats made Rhys cringe and kick himself for taking his Ram instead of the department rig.

That's when Mini came barreling out the tattered screen door. Barefoot, she might've tricked the scale to one eighty. Other than the pink streaks in her bleached-blond hair and the jowls, she hadn't changed much in twenty years.

"Mini, you stay right there." Rhys kept his hand on the butt of his gun, but didn't draw.

"I'll kill that son of a bitch." Waving an empty wine bottle in the air, she pounded off the porch like a charging rhinoceros.

Jake rounded the corner, weapon ready.

"Dammit, Mini. I told you to stay put." Rhys grabbed her arm and knocked the bottle out of her hand.

Neighbors began pouring out onto the sidewalk, jockeying for a good view. McCalls had been creating spectacles in this part of town for as long as Rhys had known them. He'd hoped Mini would've turned out different.

Rhys kept his voice down, but cross as hell, said, "Now I have to cuff and read you your rights in front of everyone, when we could've just had a conversation." He did both.

"What about him?" Mini bobbed her head at Rhys's truck. "You cuff him, too?"

"No. Unlike you, he follows directions." He watched as two Cal Fire medics arrived and moved the victim from Rhys's truck to the back of their van, where they applied first aid. "What the hell's going on here, Mini?"

"He won't get a job, just lies around the house getting drunk. Won't even put on his clothes."

"So you crack him over the head?"

"No. I hit him for wrecking my car. I just got it paid off and he goes and rear-ends someone on his way to get a pack of smokes."

"When did that happen?" Rhys was thinking he couldn't have gone out to get cigarettes in his freaking birthday suit.

"Last night," she answered.

"You waited until this morning?" he asked incredulously and heard Jake snort.

"I just saw the damage," Mini said. "Went outside to water the plants and the whole front bumper's trashed." She stopped talking and gave him the once-over. "I heard you were back. You're looking good, Rhys Shepard."

He rolled his eyes heavenward. "Mini, do you realize how much trouble you're in?"

"What? You're actually arresting me?" she asked, as if bashing a guy over the head wasn't a felony offense. Mini was probably under the mistaken impression that Rhys should cut her a break because of their past.

In high school, besides Clay, she'd been the closest thing he'd had to a friend. They'd met their freshman year on the student quad. Mini had tried to bum a cigarette off him, he'd told her to get her own, and for whatever reason she'd taken that as an invitation to stick to him like glue. Despite his efforts to lose her, they'd eventually started skipping second-period Spanish together and smoking weed in the woods. They'd even hitched a ride once to Reno to see a Wilco concert.

"I don't have a choice," he said.

She tossed her head. "He'll just drop the charges."

"How do you know?"

"Because I dropped them last time. The bastard fractured my arm, so he owes me one."

"Jeez, Mini, you're married to this guy?"

"Hell, no! We're just living together."

"Well, it doesn't exactly sound like a love connection," Rhys said.

"It has its moments." Her whole face softened, reminding Rhys of Mini's knack for making the best out of a bad situation, like her alcoholic, abusive train wreck of a family. Maybe that's why she'd been able to stay here; living like her parents did, when he'd had to get the hell out.

"You want to get a beer sometime?" she asked. "Talk about old times?"

"Ah, Mini, there's nothing I'd like better," he said, thinking that in that revisionist mind of hers she was already humming Bruce Springsteen's "Glory Days." "But right now I have to take you in."

"Whatever." She gazed over at the paramedics' van.

He knew Mini was right. In a few hours, after his mad wore off, the boyfriend would call the attack a misunderstanding. Even though the district attorney could still file charges; without a victim, or a witness, the case would be too difficult to prosecute. And the whole damn cycle would start over again.

Rhys walked Mini to the truck and helped her into the cab. Jake got in next to her. "I'll tell you what," Rhys said. "Enroll yourself in an anger management program and we'll get that beer."

Rhys slanted a glance at Jake, wondering whether the older cop thought a police chief shouldn't be associating with the likes of Mini McCall. But Jake was grinning his ass off.

Chapter 10

Maddy swayed back and forth in her new glider—a Colin Burke original—taking in the mountains and the trees.

So far autumn had only brought scattered flurries of snow and an occasional overcast morning. But today, nothing but blue skies. The mild weather was especially fortuitous given that construction on the inn had already suffered the meth-lab setback, and in two weeks many of the workers would be away for the long Thanksgiving weekend. Maddy planned to spend her turkey day with Nate, Sophie, and Mariah at the Ponderosa. Without Dave, it would be surreal—lonely, but at the same time liberating. She'd hated celebrating with his parents. They'd turned what had been in her own home a convivial family holiday into a ceremony, expecting everyone to dress to the nines and eat with the right forks.

Luckily, she'd never have to do it again.

"Mornin'." Rhys walked out onto the porch with his hair wet, sipping a cup of coffee. Ever since the Halloween festival she'd felt a little awkward around him. But since they lived next door to each other she needed to get over it.

Maddy must've stared longingly at the steam rising off his mug, because Rhys said, "Lina made a fresh pot in the kitchen. You want a cup?"

"I'd die for one."

"Aw, don't do that," he said, and popped back into the house only to return a few minutes later with a second mug.

"Mmm." She didn't usually take sugar, just cream, but he'd sweetened the coffee and Maddy had to admit that it tasted delicious.

"Nice swing." He tipped his head to check out the gliding mechanism. "Colin's?"

"Yep."

"How much it set you back? Maybe I'll get one before I leave—rent a place in Houston with a porch."

"He made me promise not to tell. For me: special deal." She patted the space next to her on the bench built for two, and together they rocked while drinking their coffee. "The kids seem like they're settling in."

He gave a half shrug, signaling he didn't want to talk about it. She thought he was missing out on an opportunity to get to know them, but kept her mouth shut. In so many ways Lina and Sam reminded her of Rhys. Lina had his take-charge thing going on, overseeing Shep's care as well as Betty had. And Sam was a natural-born flirt. The eleven-year-old could talk her into playing endless hours of Hangman while they sat on the porch. Maddy hated Hangman.

"If it's okay with you," she said, "I told Lina I would take her and Shep to Reno the next time I go. She and Sam could use a few things."

"Yeah, sure. That's really nice of you." He grinned at her and damn if her knees didn't knock. *What was it about this guy?*

"You going into the station?"

"Yep," he said. "The new hire, Jake Stryker's, been opening for me."

"That's great. He'll keep you from having to put in so many extra hours, won't he?"

"That's the idea. How 'bout you? Going to the inn?"

"Mm hmm."

He propped his booted feet up on the railing. "Maybe I should book now, before you're flooded with reservations."

"Rhys, you get first dibs." As she said it she had an unsettling thought. What if he was serious about booking a room in her inn? She doubted he'd stay there by himself. "You thinking of bringing a date?"

He gave the question some consideration. "It's a romantic place, right?"

"Of course." She couldn't tell whether Rhys was teasing, but suddenly her stomach turned a little queasy. The idea of him staying in her hotel with a woman bothered her. A lot.

"Well, then I guess I ought to. Maybe I'll ask Portia," he said, letting out a shout of laughter. She socked him in the leg. "What?"

"Come on; don't tell me you're not seeing someone." She waited, and when he didn't respond, muttered, "Probably multiple women."

He did a double take. "How do you figure that?"

She twisted herself sideways on the glider so she could face him. "You're a player."

"I'm a player?" He sounded peeved.

"I don't mean it in a bad way. You're single, good-looking. Why wouldn't you date?"

"Yeah, well, I don't kiss and tell, sugar." He started to get up, but Maddy pulled him back down.

"Oh, no you don't. Spill!"

He looked at her challengingly. "Then you have to tell me the latest with Dave?" He said "Dave" like the name was a pair of dirty socks.

"You first," Maddy insisted.

"Fine. But a deal's a deal. Don't renege when you find out I don't have much to tell." He put his coffee mug on the floor. "I've gone on one date since I moved back to Nugget—a coworker of a flight attendant Clay sees. That's it. The end."

"Well, do you like her?"

"Not much, no."

For some reason, that pleased her enormously. "How come?"

He scrubbed his hand through his hair. "I don't know. No chemistry I guess. Now your turn."

Maddy put her mug down next to Rhys's and exhaled. "I filed," she said quietly. "His lawyer must have gotten word to him in France, because he's been calling me like crazy."

"What's he saying?" He tugged her close so she could lean into him. Oddly, the intimacy of that gesture felt incredibly natural and she burrowed in deep.

"I haven't been taking his calls, but he's refusing to sign the papers." Maddy closed her eyes and without realizing it she'd nestled her head against Rhys's shoulder.

"I feel so stupid," she continued. "I thought we had this amazing life together—that my husband wouldn't even look at another woman, let alone cheat on me. My own parents have been married for nearly forty years. That's what I thought it would be like for Dave and me. Now I wonder if I deluded myself into only seeing what I wanted to see. You ever feel that way?"

"I have," he said, surprising her. "Not with someone I loved, but on the job all the time. I think it's natural to want to believe the best in people. And when they let you down, you wind up blaming yourself for being gullible. But this is on him, Maddy, not you."

"Poor Max. I wonder if he knew, or if he was as much in the dark as I was."

Rhys shrugged. "So he died, huh?"

She nodded sadly. "From a blood clot in his brain. He was a wonderful man. I think part of the reason Dave's been trying to work it out with me is to make up for his betrayal of Max. He really did love him."

"Yeah, that's some kind of love," Rhys said, and Maddy was struck by how contemptuous he sounded.

"The fact is," she said, "Gabby fits the Wellmont mold a million times more than I ever will."

Rhys went back to holding her, and his arms felt warm and solid. His thighs hard and strong. The scent of his shampoo and aftershave—something woodsy like pine needles—made her want to bury her face in the crook of his neck.

He slowly rocked the glider with his right leg. "Maddy, I don't know what the Wellmont mold is. What I do know is that you're clever and you're funny and you're beautiful . . . Look what you've accomplished in the short time you've been here. Most people would've written off the Lumber Baron as a scrape. When you're done with it it'll be the pride of Nugget.

"From where I'm standing this Gabriella woman wasn't your problem. If your husband couldn't see what I see . . . Well, he doesn't deserve you."

She pressed her face against his shoulder and mumbled, "You might not say that if you'd ever seen Gabriella."

He gently lifted her onto his lap, his soft lips just inches away from her ear. "I don't need to. I've seen you."

Maddy looked at him with such wonder in her eyes that it mesmerized him. He bent his head, gently brushing her lips with his. The kiss started innocently enough. But when she wrapped her arms around his neck, her full breasts pressing against his chest and her rear end pushing against his groin, he was lost. He sank his mouth over hers, pulling her firmly against him. His hands roamed over her back and shoulders and his tongue slid inside her mouth.

She opened for him, tentatively at first, but then he felt her breath catch. "Ohhh," she whimpered, and he could feel himself growing so hard that he was straining against his fly.

He cradled her head and took the kiss deeper, maybe even a little rough. But the sweet taste of her made him crazy. Hungry. She pushed against his erection, clinging to him, filling him with heat and yearning. Rhys cupped her ass, pulling her tighter so she could feel the full length of him.

"We should stop," she said, but kept kissing him.

"Let's go inside the trailer," he whispered, a little breathless.

"Bad idea," she groaned against his mouth.

"Ah sugar, let me make you forget about Dave." It was a bullshit line, but she felt so damn good. God, he wanted her.

"Oh, Rhys, we need to stop." But he could feel her resolve weakening and was pretty sure that if he carried her into the fifth wheel he'd get her clothes off in no time flat.

It took everything he had, but Rhys slowly released her. He lifted her off his lap. "You okay?"

She nodded.

He waited for her to find her equilibrium. Feeling slightly unbalanced himself, he said, "I better get going."

"Yeah. Me, too." Maddy grabbed her purse off the porch and took off for the stairs like someone had set her on fire.

"Hey, hang on a second." Rhys caught up to her. God, he'd acted like a horny high school kid. "I didn't mean to take advantage of your situation. That was a jerk move. I'm sorry, Maddy."

He turned to walk away when she called, "Rhys?"

"Yeah?"

"Thank you."

Maddy was still light-headed when she arrived at the inn. No one had ever kissed her like Rhys had.

No one. Ever.

Colin waved to her from the new veranda, shaking her out of her stupor. The crew, following the adage of making hay while the sun shined, worked on the exterior of the house. On the days it snowed, they would move the whole team inside to focus on her innkeeper's quarters. Still, there were a few guys in the bathrooms, working on toilets, sinks, and tubs.

Maddy poked her head into the powder room on the main floor. Since the demolition, the place had undergone a dramatic change. Other than the equipment, lumber, and tools that now cluttered the property, the garbage had been toted away, the graffiti sanded off the doors, and the horrific fencing removed.

The decking on the porch and its railings had been repaired and looked sturdy enough to hold a platoon. Maddy envisioned overhead fans, wicker furniture, and giant potted ferns—a place where guests could enjoy a cold glass of lemonade on a warm day and watch the town go by.

She looked at her watch. In a few minutes she had an appointment with a representative from a linen distributor. Somehow, Nate had sweet-talked the guy into driving all the way from the Bay Area to Nugget so he could meet her on-site with samples.

While she waited, the constant drum of hammering lulled her back into thinking about that kiss. And Rhys. And what it would've been like if she had met him first. Before Dave. The two men were so different—suave Dave and rough Rhys. But there was also a gentleness and a kindness in Rhys.

She wondered whether he'd ever been married and found it odd that she'd never thought to ask. A guy that good-looking wouldn't stay single for long.

Dave took good care of himself, worked out five days a week with a personal trainer. But he had nothing on Rhys, who could crush him like a tin can.

Ah, Dave. She'd thought he'd hung the moon, bowling her over with his lavish attention. She'd been barely twenty-five and managing the reservation desk at the Wellmont. He'd pop by on his way up to the corporate offices to flirt, bringing her silly souvenirs—Fisherman's Wharf snow globes, cable car Christmas ornaments, Alcatraz visors—from the gift shop. She'd been incredibly flattered and a little starstruck. Ultimately she bonded with him over the one thing they had in common—the hotel business. But after the first miscarriage, he'd convinced her to put off coming back to the Wellmont indefinitely.

"The hours are long, Mad. I don't want to be one of those couples racing around, always trying to get ahead. I want us to spend time together. Quality time," he'd told her. "Plus, I want us to try as soon as we can to get pregnant again."

Looking back on it now, he seemed almost desperate, making her wonder if after she'd failed to keep him away from Gabriella, Dave thought a baby might help him find his conscience.

Ironically, it had been the times they spent with Max and Gabby that had been the best. Max, a gregarious winemaker, would pop a cork on one of his famous Napa Cabernet Sauvignons, pour her a glass, and they'd spend the next hour pretending to be wine critics.

Max would swirl his goblet, stick his nose into the bowl, and take a big whiff. "I'm getting hints of horseshit. How 'bout you?"

Maddy, who knew nothing about wine, would swirl, sniff, and sip and in her most pompous voice say, "No, I believe that's bat guano with a horseshit finish."

They'd go on like that until they were sloshed, rolling on the floor laughing.

Max had been the only Wellmont who'd ever made her feel part of the family. It still plagued her whether he knew about Dave and Gabby—about their weekend trysts when the four of them were together at Max's vineyard. Or had Max been as clueless as she had?

Maddy checked her watch again. Not surprising the linen guy was late. People often miscalculated how long it took to get to Nugget from the city.

"It's looking good." Pam strolled over, shielding her eyes from the sun with her hand as she stared up at the gable Colin painstakingly tacked to the roof peak.

"As long as this weather holds we'll make the deadline," Maddy said.

"When's that?"

"Summer." When she saw Pam's eyes grow wide, she said, "Ambitious, I know. But that's Nate. He wants this Victorian lady earning her keep. We're keeping crews on seven days a week."

Pam cringed. "I didn't want to tell you this until I knew how serious it was. But word on the street is there's a petition circulating to shut you down."

"What?" Maddy knew people here weren't happy with the noise and mess from the construction, but this news knocked her for a loop. "On what grounds?"

"Apparently, Sandy and Cal Addison have a bug up their butt that the Lumber Baron is going to tax Nugget's antiquated sewage system. They're trying to get your lodging permits pulled and want to bring it before the city council at the next meeting."

Dumbfounded, Maddy asked, "Can they do that . . . pull permits that they've already issued? I mean, if the city thought it had a sewage problem it shouldn't have agreed to let us put in a twenty-room hotel. We never would've bought the place without the lodging permit. This is crazy. What kind of city does something like this?

"Jeez," Maddy continued. "I should've paid better attention when those Addisons hinted at something like this at the Halloween festival. But Nate wrote them off as nut jobs. You know how much money we've already poured into this place?"

"I'm so sorry, Maddy," Pam said. "I didn't want to tell you, but unfortunately they do have political juice around here. They sponsor a lot of city-run programs and the council members kowtow to them. Two years ago they granted Buzz Henderson a commercial ordinance to sell Christmas trees on his property right off the highway. The Addisons bitched and moaned that it was causing traffic backups, and, sure enough, the city rescinded the ordinance. And quite frankly, this town has always been resistant to change. I thought there would be a war over the Sierra Heights development.

"Look." Pam squeezed Maddy's hand. "This whole ploy may backfire on them. But in the meantime, I'd talk to Bud Coleman over at the Nugget Wastewater Treatment Plant and find out what the city's sewage capacity is and where it's at right now."

"I'll do better than that," Maddy said and headed for her car, shouting to Colin to stall the linen rep until she got back.

"What?" Pam called.

"I'm going over to the Beary Quaint and talk some sense into those people."

"I wouldn't do that, if—"

The sound of Maddy's engine drowned out the rest of whatever Pam had to say. The motor lodge was only about ten minutes on Highway 70 from downtown Nugget. On her way, she texted her brother, then pulled into the Beary Quaint parking lot.

Eww, Nate wasn't kidding. There were chain-saw bears everywhere—the entrance, the yard, the walkways. Creepy. Like the bear version of a Chucky doll.

It was a shame, really. If they hadn't tchotchked up the place, it wouldn't be half bad. The eighteen motel rooms were designed to resemble mini log cabins. The office—a chalet. Kitschy, but cute.

Just a few yards off the highway flashed a neon sign of a bear sleeping in a sleigh bed. "Vacancies," it read.

"We're booked solid," Maddy mimicked.

The sign was vintage 1920s and was worth a good amount of money. It was the first thing she planned to smash, if the Addisons didn't see reason.

Maddy didn't bother to wait for Nate to text back, since she knew what he'd say anyway. "Call our lawyer."

But why get billed hours when they could work this out like sensible business people, she thought as she marched up to the Beary Quaint's entrance.

Maddy spied Sandy behind the glass doors and caught her eye. *See*, Maddy thought to herself, patting down her hair, *the woman is coming outside to have a rational conversation. Two hoteliers hashing it out like adults.*

Wait a minute, was Sandy dead-bolting the door?

"Sandy," Maddy called through the glass. "Could we please talk."

No answer.

Maddy pulled the knob and banged on the window. "Oh, for God's sake, I just want to talk to you."

"Get off my property, or I'll call the cops," Sandy's muffled voice came through the door.

"Seriously, Sandy? Is this how you want to play this? At least send Cal out if you're so afraid of me."

"I'm not going to tell you again," Sandy yelled. "Get off my property!"

"Fine," Maddy shouted, pretending to head for her car. When she got to the corner of the building she raced around the office, searching for the back door before Sandy could dead-bolt it.

Too late.

"Sandy, come on." Maddy pounded on the slider.

Sandy made a big show of picking up the phone and dialing.

Very well. Maddy would just wait her out. She walked back to the front of the motel and sat on a bear-carved bench.

"You can't stay inside forever," she muttered, swinging her legs, studying the intricacy of the burl wood's design.

Ten minutes later, Rhys pulled up in his police truck. Crazy Town had actually called the fuzz, Maddy couldn't freakin' believe it.

"Hey." He did his chin bob thing as he sauntered down the walkway in his mirrored aviators. It was a good look for him.

"Hey," she said back.

"Let's go."

"What, you're arresting me? On what grounds?"

"I'm not arresting you. But this is private property and the owner wants you vacated."

"Well, what if I want to book a room?"

The corner of his mouth curved up ever so slightly. "Come on, sugar, let's go."

"I don't want to go. I want that yellow-bellied coward of a woman to come out here and talk to me. And I want you to stop calling me sugar."

"What you really don't want," he said tightly, "is Sandy Addison getting a restraining order against you, telling everyone and his brother that you tried to attack her. It doesn't look professional, you know what I mean? So get in the car and drive away. Come on, I'll follow you out."

"Attack her . . . I barely even talked to the woman. I can't believe you're taking her side." Maddy stood up and wiped the back of her pants.

"What are you, ten?" He lowered his voice. "I'm trying to mitigate the damage you've done here. Now get your goddamn ass in the car."

"Fine."

She'd managed to drive two miles before he lit her up, forcing her to pull into a circular turnout on the side of the road. He got out of his truck and motioned for her to unlock her passenger door, then slid in.

"What did I do now?"

"Stop with the drama, would you? What you did back there was unbelievably stupid."

"All I did was go over there to reason with her. You don't even know what's going on."

"The Addisons are trying to petition the city to revoke your permits on the grounds that Nugget's waste system can't handle the extra sewage."

She glared at him. "How long have you known?"

"I found out twenty minutes ago when you decided to make your house call."

"Rhys," she said. "They're trying to put the Lumber Baron out of business. Every dime I have is invested in that inn."

He all but rolled his eyes.

"Oh, you think because my soon-to-be ex is wealthy that means I'm Mrs. Money Bags? Well, you don't know a damn thing about it. Now get out of my car, I need to meet the linen rep." She was on the verge of losing it and she wanted to do it in private.

"Maddy, you can win this thing. You just have to go about it the right way. Your first move should be calling a very good lawyer—"

"Oh, my God, why didn't I think of that?"

He threw up his arms. "Whatever, Maddy. Try to stay out of trouble." He slammed her car door shut, got into his truck, and drove away.

She just sat there with the weight of her inn's future on her shoulders, wondering what it would've been like if he'd kissed her again.

Chapter 11

The following days turned much colder and the snow began to pile up faster than the plows could clear it. Rhys paced in front of the plate-glass window of the police station.

They said when temperatures dipped like this, people stayed home—made babies. Then why, he wondered, did crime rates soar during extreme weather? He still wasn't any closer to catching the people who'd stowed their chemicals and equipment in Maddy's basement.

Rhys continued to wear a hole in the floor. Back and forth in front of that plate-glass window.

"You're a worrywart, Chief," Connie teased as she made a fresh pot of coffee. "Those warm Houston winters made you soft."

No. It was just too damn quiet. "You ever hear of the calm before the storm?"

Jake came in, jangling the bell over the front door, and brushed the snow off his jacket. "Holy hell, it's cold out there." He rubbed his hands together.

"Coffee's on," Connie told him. "And Tater brought over some sweet rolls this morning."

Jake held up a Bun Boy bag wet from either grease or weather, Rhys couldn't tell. "Got some chili and fries. But coffee never sounded better." He went over to the machine and poured himself a mug.

"Wife number two called," Connie said. "Janny needs a new clutch."

"Janny can take the bus," Jake mumbled. When Rhys and Connie exchanged amused glances, he added, "Who needs a car at college? She lives in a sorority house five minutes off campus, for Christ's sake."

"Where's Wyatt?" Rhys asked. "Staff meeting should've started five minutes ago."

"Oh, sorry, Chief," Connie piped up. "I forgot to tell you, Wyatt responded to a call at the middle school."

"What's going on there?" Rhys didn't like being kept out of the loop.

"The principal called right before you got in. Two students got into a tussle." When Rhys lifted his chin for her to continue, she said, "You know how kids are when cabin fever sets in. I'm sure Mr. Crocket overreacted."

Typically, the school didn't call in the police for a playground scuffle unless it was serious. Before he could give it another thought, Wyatt came in the door. Snowflakes clung to his military-style crew cut, but other than that the kid seemed unaffected by the cold.

He nodded to everyone in the room and filled a cup with coffee. "What's up?"

"You're late," Rhys told him.

Wyatt looked nervously over at Jake. "He's just giving you a hard time, kid."

Wyatt had instantly clicked with Jake, who'd taken him under his wing. The kid already showed progress. He'd grown up in Nugget and served a few years in the army. After his hitch, he came home and the mayor told Rhys to hire him. Rhys had suggested that Wyatt enroll in some classes at Feather River College in Quincy or even the University of Nevada. No one knew better than he the disadvantage of not having a college diploma. After being passed over for detective twice at Houston PD, Rhys had taken day classes while working night patrol to earn a degree in criminal justice at Sam Houston State University.

"What's up at the middle school?" Rhys asked.

"The Becker boy and Clay McCreedy's son got into it." Wyatt paused and Rhys could tell he was uncomfortable. Everyone knew that Rhys and Clay were tight.

"Why'd the school call us in?"

Wyatt swallowed, looking even more ill at ease. "Justin had a knife . . . was threatening to cut Will Becker's dick off."

Rhys tensed. "How did you resolve it?"

"The school confiscated the knife and suspended him for a week. I wrote up a report and released him to his father's custody." He hesitantly added, "Tomorrow, I'll submit the report to the DA. Right?"

Dragging his hand through his hair, Rhys said, "That's the procedure." Even though Justin was his honorary nephew, he didn't want his staff thinking he played favorites. But if the district attorney brought up charges against Justin, it would kill Clay.

Jake interjected, "How old's the kid?"

"Fourteen," Wyatt said.

"We're not talking a Ka-Bar or a bowie knife here, are we?" Jake asked.

"Nah," Wyatt said. "Just a little Swiss Army penknife."

"Hardly seems worth submitting to the DA," Jake said. "Why don't we make a deal with both sets of parents for the kid to do some kind of community service? Shovel the sidewalks or some crap like that."

"Sounds good to me." Wyatt looked at Rhys for approval.

"I'll leave it up to your judgment, Wyatt." When Rhys caught Jake's eye, the Silver Fox shrugged and nonchalantly popped a fry in his mouth.

Clay was under an old John Deere when Rhys came walking up his path.

"What's wrong with the tractor?" Rhys asked.

"Nothing that can't be fixed. Now, my son I'm not so sure of." Clay knew Rhys's visit was more than a social call.

"Clay, don't be so hard on him. He's just a kid."

He crawled out from under the tractor, handed Rhys a wrench, and stood up, shaking off the snow. "I think I'm screwing this up."

"Your boy got into a playground brawl," Rhys said, leaving out the crucial fact that Justin had pulled a knife on another kid. To Clay's way of thinking that was more than just a playground brawl.

"As I recollect you were in a hundred of 'em," Rhys went on. "So don't turn this into a federal case."

Clay held out his hand for the wrench and stashed it in a toolbox that lay open next to the tractor. It was something like twenty-five degrees outside. So Clay led Rhys into the barn, where he kept a few dairy cows, and lit a kerosene heater. They both sat on a bale of hay and warmed their hands.

"It's not just the fight at school, or the break-in at the cabin. It's a whole passel of problems. Justin's got a chip on his shoulder as big as this barn, and Cody's so clingy that half the time it feels like I have a third leg. The shrinks say it's normal for a kid who's lost a parent. But it doesn't feel normal."

"What's Justin so angry about?" Rhys asked, edging closer to the heater.

"Some of it's teen angst and raging hormones. But a lot of it's over his mother—anger at the way she lived her life, anger at her for dying."

"Why'd he threaten to cut off Will Becker's dick?" Rhys asked.

Clay rubbed the back of his neck. "The kid made some crude remark about Jen."

"Can't blame a kid for standing up for his mama."

Clay got the feeling that Rhys was remembering his own past. When the town bullies made fun of Shep.

"I guess not," Clay said, his expression uneasy. "This gonna go down on his permanent record?" He tried to make a joke of it. But Clay didn't want the possible ramifications of Justin threatening a boy with a weapon to screw up his future. What if his son wanted to follow in his footsteps and attend the naval academy? Something like this could keep him out.

"I think Officer Maynard has come up with a compromise . . . as long as the Beckers go for it."

"Yeah?" Clay raised his head. "What's that?"

"Community service."

Clay nodded with relief. "A part of me wants to say treat him like anyone else. But he's my—"

Rhys cut him off. "Clay, this is what we'd do for any other fourteen-year-old. Justin doesn't have a record—he's a good kid."

Clay scrubbed both his hands over his face. "These kids make Annapolis look like a cakewalk." One of the cows called from its stall, so he got up, grabbed a hay hook and snapped open a bale of alfalfa. He threw a flake into the animal's feeder and the sound of contented munching filled the barn. "So how's your home life?"

"Bursting at the seams. The fifth wheel's a lifesaver, though. You don't want it back, right?"

"It's all yours. You going to the basketball game tomorrow?"

"Nope. Gotta work."

"Come on, Rhys. The kid's excited he made the team."

"As I recall pretty much anyone with working legs makes the team. Wait, I take that back. When we were in fifth grade, Larry Riggs got to play center. Remember him, the kid in the wheelchair?"

Clay laughed. "Yeah, but that boy could shoot. Sam needs you there, man."

"I'm not making any promises," Rhys said.

"Do what you gotta do." Clay passed his hands over the heater again. "I hear a petition against your girlfriend's inn is making the rounds."

"She's not my girlfriend. In fact, I don't think she's talking to me anymore."

"How come?"

"I had to force her off Sandy Addison's property," Rhys said, and for the first time that day Clay felt like laughing.

"Pissed her off, huh?"

"Oh, yeah," Rhys said. "The woman might look sweet, but you don't want to rile her. Take my word for it. Any chance the city will yank her lodging permit?"

Clay cocked his head to the side. "Ooh wee, boy, you're gone for this girl, aren't you? Hell, Rhys, she's on the rebound. Don't get in over your head with this one."

"Yeah, thanks for the advice. What about her permit?"

"There's always a chance they'll revoke it," Clay said. "From what I understand the Addisons are making a good case. And they have pull around here."

126 • *Stacy Finz*

"But not more pull than the McCreedys, right?"

"Nope."

When Rhys left, Clay went into the house and yelled up the staircase for Justin to come down. It took at least three bellows before his sullen son dragged his ass into the kitchen where Clay poured them each a glass of milk.

"What do you want?" Justin sneered.

"I suggest you watch the attitude." Clay dropped into a chair across from his son.

"I've got homework."

"You can finish it when I'm done. You'll have plenty of time during your week of suspension." He watched Justin drain the milk. The boy was starting to shed some of his gangly adolescence. Soon he'd be as tall as Clay. "We all miss your mom—"

"You don't miss her. You don't even care what people in this town say about her."

Clay pinched his eyes closed. "Small towns gossip, Justin. It's just a fact of life. That boy, Will Becker, when his dad was young, he used to taunt your uncle Rhys mercilessly about his father."

"Yeah, and I bet Uncle Rhys kicked the crap out of him." Justin gave Clay an accusatory glare.

"No, Justin. Uncle Rhys didn't give Will's dad the time of day. He wasn't worth the trouble."

"Well, I'm gonna kill the next guy who says one bad thing about Mom."

"Then I guess Cody and I will be spending a lot of time visiting you in prison," Clay said. "I can tell you this; it would break your mom's heart. Is that how you want to celebrate her memory—getting kicked out of school, doing hard time?"

"You couldn't care less about her memory," Justin shouted, his voice cracking as he swiped at his cheeks. "You hated her. You think I don't know about the divorce? . . . About how you made us move here and ruined our lives. It's your fault she's dead." He jumped up, knocked the chair over and pounded up the stairs to his bedroom.

Clay started to go after him, but thought better of it. The boy needed time. And so did Clay.

* * *

"Hi, Chief Shepard."

"Hey, Chief," the voices continued to chorus as Rhys walked through Nugget High School's gymnasium. The elementary school didn't have an indoor basketball court, so the fifth graders played at the home of the Prospectors on Wednesday, and the middle school's team got to borrow the court on Thursdays.

Shep hadn't wanted to come to the game—shocker—so Lina had stayed home with him, forcing Rhys to have to endure these hallowed halls once again.

As he scanned the bleachers, looking for Clay, the greetings kept coming, making Rhys feel a little self-conscious. No one had been this friendly when he'd actually attended this school.

Finally spotting Clay, Rhys climbed to the third row and grabbed the seat next to him. Amanda sat behind them with her husband. Either they had a fifth grader who played, too, or the Gaitlins were extremely hard up for entertainment.

"Hey, you made it," Clay said and handed him a carton of Milk Duds.

He greeted the others and watched as both teams came onto the court to sing the national anthem. Sam and Cody, heads taller than most of the other players, stood out in their purple and gold uniforms. The team had always been called the Hotshots, slang for the fast long-distance freight trains given first priority on the tracks. Today, they were playing the Blairsden Bulls.

Someone announced the starters, but Sam wasn't on the list. Rhys watched him go to the bench with a few of the shorter players. Cody made first-string center and the kid had some moves.

Rhys elbowed Clay. "Cody's got game."

"Not bad, huh?"

"Where's Justin?"

"Home." Clay sighed. "We're taking some space."

Rhys arched a brow. "Some space?"

"The kid's got issues with me—some of them justified." Clay pointed across the gymnasium. "Isn't that Shep over there?"

Rhys followed Clay's finger and there stood his dad, Lina, and Maddy staring up into the bleachers. Rhys waved them over and they made their way toward his side of the grandstand. Shep had never been to a game before. As far as Rhys knew, Shep had never been to the high school, hadn't even come to his graduation. Tip had, and afterward had taken both Clay and him out for steaks in Reno.

"I thought you weren't coming," Rhys said and Shep just shrugged.

"I wanted to see him play," Lina said, sitting next to Rhys. "Maddy brought us."

"Hi," Maddy said a little shyly—maybe she was embarrassed over her Addison meltdown, who knew?—and Clay made room so she could squeeze in between the two of them.

"Thanks for bringing them," Rhys said to Maddy, then leaned over Lina. "Hey, Pop, the team's called the Hotshots."

That tugged a little smile out of Shep. If nothing else, the old man knew his railroad terminology.

"Where's Sam?" Lina surveyed the boys running across the court.

"They haven't put him in yet," he said, noticing that the girl was shivering under her thin jacket.

Neither kid had the proper attire for the Sierra's frigid winters. Lina had bought a couple of things with Maddy, but no coat it would seem. He couldn't stand seeing her cold, so he took off his ski jacket and draped it over her shoulders.

"Why not?" she wanted to know.

"They save the best for last," he lied and swiveled to face Maddy, who was gabbing with Amanda, but stopped when he caught her attention.

Rhys reached for her hand and poured a few Milk Duds into her palm, then passed the box to Lina. "How's the trespassing going?"

She gave him a tight smile. "I've mended my wicked ways."

"Glad to hear it. San Quentin's damp this time of year."

"Yes, you're very funny. Nate says we have nothing to worry about, so I'm channeling my inner Zen and doing a lot of yoga."

"Yoga?" He didn't necessarily agree with Nate, but he didn't want her tangling with Sandy Addison again.

"Mmm hmm. With Pam. Amanda, too."

"Maybe you should turn the Lumber Baron into an ashram."

"Maybe you should watch the game."

At halftime the teams switched goals and Sam got called in to substitute for Cody, who'd already scored five baskets. The Hotshots were up by seven points. Sam jogged to the center of the court with a slightly shorter boy from the Bulls to do the tip-off. The ball went to the Bulls. Sam tried to steal, but tripped over his own feet and took a mean header onto the court.

The spectators muttered a collective "Ah," and Rhys and Lina jumped to their feet. But Sam got up and quickly positioned himself just outside the three-point arc.

"Good boy," Rhys quietly cheered. That fall looked painful.

When Charlie Gaitlin managed to block a pass, the home team crowd roared. Charlie tossed the ball to Sam, who prepared to shoot. *Okay, here's your chance, kid,* thought Rhys as he waited, holding his breath. But in the middle of his shot, a stocky Bull mowed into him.

The referee blew his whistle and motioned foul, awarding Sam three free throws. He missed every single one.

With only two minutes left in the quarter, Sam was called for traveling and double dribbling. The coach finally pulled him, and put Cody back in to win the game.

"*Ay Dios*, he's not very good, is he?" Lina said.

"He just needs practice," Rhys replied, but the truth was Sam sucked. Hard. "He play much in Stockton?"

"No," Lina said. "He liked soccer."

Great, kids' soccer season wouldn't start up again until spring. After the game they waited for Sam to change in the locker room. Rhys expected him to be down in the dumps, but the boy bounded out as chipper as if he'd brought the team to victory.

"Did you see me, Papa?"

"You were terrific," Shep said, and Rhys wondered how the old man would know since he'd slept through most of the game. To be fair, since the Alzheimer's, Shep's sleep cycle had become erratic. The doctors said it was par for the course.

Maddy came up alongside Rhys. "Maybe we should go out for burgers or something, to celebrate Sam's first game." Rhys felt sure it was her subtle way of telling him the kid needs this, don't be a dickhead.

"Yeah. Dinner. You guys want the Ponderosa, or the Bun Boy?"

After deciding it was too cold to sit outside at a picnic table, they headed to the bowling alley. Maddy took Shep and the kids in her

Outback and Rhys went in his truck. Good thing he had his own parking space, because when he got to the square it was packed. Why wasn't everyone home baking pies for Thanksgiving?

They started for the Ponderosa when Maddy suddenly turned toward the sporting goods store. "What the hell is that?" she asked, stomping through the park, Rhys at her heels.

A banner hung over the shop's door. "Save Our Sewers, Flush the Lumber Baron," it read. The same banners hung on Portia and Steve's adventure tour kiosk, the used-clothing store, Owen's barber shop, and the kayak and bike rental shop. The Ponderosa, the Bun Boy, Pam's dance studio, and the police station were about the only places that didn't have a banner.

"I'm going to kill those Addisons," Maddy shrieked.

"Shush." Rhys grabbed her around the waist and pulled her close so that only she could hear him. "Don't ever threaten to kill someone in front of a cop."

"For crying out loud, it's a freakin' figure of speech. Would you look at that." She pointed at the banner, whipped out her phone, took a picture and texted it to Nate. "We are so screwed."

He had to admit it didn't look good. "You call a lawyer?"

"Not yet," she said. "Until now I didn't think it was necessary and was trying to save money. Big mistake! Right after Thanksgiving, I'm calling the fanciest hotel lawyer in the business. Josh will ruin those Addisons."

Just then Donna Thurston came tottering across the square in three-inch heels. "Now, honey, don't you go getting yourself all worked up over these nitwits—a bunch of inbred goat-ropers is what they are. For years I've watched this town try to freeze out every newcomer. Everyone's afraid the place will turn into Lake Tahoe—overrun with tourists and development. As if." She harrumphed. "You hold your ground just like Sophie and Mariah did when these idiots gave them hell for fixing up the Ponderosa."

"Thank you, Donna." Maddy choked back a sob. "And thank you for not putting a banner on the Bun Boy."

"Of course I'm not putting a banner on the Bun Boy. It's absolutely ridiculous to think that a small hotel could overtax a waste system that has served this town for as long as I can remember. And I've lived here my whole life. Besides, that banner is fugly."

Maddy half laughed, half cried.

"Fight back, girl," Donna said.

"Let's go eat." Rhys started leading her back toward the Ponderosa.

"Don't you two look cute together. You dating?" Donna asked.

"No," they said in unison.

Thanksgiving dinner was at Sophie and Mariah's sprawling apartment above the Ponderosa. While redoing the restaurant and bowling alley, they'd completely gutted the upstairs and had turned it into fabulous living quarters with killer views of the surrounding mountains and river. After the baby came, they'd probably look for a place with a yard. In the meantime, the apartment was perfect for entertaining family and friends.

At least Nate would be there and could see those asinine banners for himself. Because a pic-text just didn't do the whole "Flush" campaign justice. Although she could have done without his date. At the last minute, he'd decided to invite his latest squeeze, a designer from Restoration Hardware. According to Nate, she was young, beautiful, and busty.

Goody!

As Maddy pulled her car into a space near the Ponderosa she noticed Rhys's truck in front of the police station and decided to take a detour. The door jingled when she walked in and Rhys came out of his office.

"Hi," Maddy said. He was wearing a long-sleeved thermal under a Houston Astros T-shirt and a pair of faded jeans. Other than the badge peeking out from his hemline, he looked like a man who planned to spend his day hunkered down on the couch, watching the Macy's Parade. "How come you're not home, eating turkey?"

"Someone's got to hold down the fort. Come on back."

She followed him into his office where she noticed a game of Texas Hold 'Em on his computer screen. "You look mighty busy."

"So far, all is quiet on the Western front." He flashed her a boyish grin as if to say, *I know that you know that this work thing is a load of crap. I'm hiding out here in the Bat Cave.* "You on your way to Sophie and Mariah's?"

"Mm hmm." She hung her coat over the back of a chair and flashed a saccharine smile. "It's gonna be awesome. I get to sit next to Nate's new child girlfriend with the amazing rack."

He chuckled, then let his gaze take a pleasure ride over her chest. "Your rack ain't so bad."

Maddy looked down at her cashmere sweater. "Push-up bra."

"Uh-uh," Rhys said, his mouth curving up rakishly, making her stomach do all kinds of crazy acrobatics. "I felt them, sugar. Up close and personal, if you recall."

She did. They'd been smashed against his chest while they'd played dueling tongues on the front porch. Just the memory made her insides melt.

"Don't go to dinner," he said, giving her boobs another once-over. "Hang with me. We can spend all day talking about the Donner Party."

"Or," Rhys lifted his brows, "we can work on some of those kisses you supposedly don't want."

"Or," she said, her voice dripping censure, "you could go home and celebrate Thanksgiving with two children who just lost their mother."

She sat in the chair where she'd hung her jacket and gave him a hard stare. "Don't punish them, Rhys. It's not their fault that they were kept secret from you. And it's not their fault that they don't have anyone."

"Nope. It's not their fault," he said, and he glared right back at her. "And for that reason, I'm giving them my guardianship. But don't expect me to do more, Maddy. I don't know them, and this is not going to end happily ever after, we're-a-freaking-Lifetime-movie family now. I don't do family. And I'm going back to Houston. The end."

"You'll just leave them alone when you go?" Maddy asked, not believing it for a second. He may not be a family man, but Rhys placed his responsibilities above all else. Case in point: Shep. When he left Nugget, he'd make provisions for his siblings. Maddy knew it.

"Lina will be eighteen by then." Instead of saying more, he came around the desk, tugged her out of the chair, and slowly backed her against the wall.

"What are you doing?"

"Shutting you up."

"How?"

"By keeping your mouth busy."

That's when he went in for the kiss. And this time Maddy didn't even try to stop him. One wet, hot kiss wouldn't hurt, she told herself. They'd just get it out of their systems. No biggie.

But then he pressed his hard body against her and let his warm breath and satin-soft lips float against her mouth like a whisper, and she was a goner. He moved over her so slow and sweet and sexy that it made her muscles clench and her heart stand still. And when he deepened the kiss, his tongue boldly tangling with her own, it made her want to do things with this man that she shouldn't be ready to do. Not so soon after Dave.

"Let me see that push-up bra," he murmured, inching up her sweater.

"Don't press your luck, buster." She swatted his hands away, whispering, "I've gotta go, Rhys. They're waiting for me for dinner."

"Blow it off." He was kissing her neck now, pulling her closer so she could feel the ridge in his pants grow thicker against her belly. God, she was so, so tempted.

"I can't." She dragged herself just far enough away from his hold to keep from changing her mind. "It would be incredibly rude. Come with me and I'll call the kids. We'll all have dinner at Sophie and Mariah's. There's plenty for everyone."

"I have to cover the office," he said, but something like yearning flickered across his face. "Thanks for the offer, though."

She straightened her clothes, tried to catch her breath and walked behind Rhys's desk. Well, at least she wouldn't let those poor children spend Thanksgiving alone. She picked up the phone and dialed. "Hi, Lina. This is Maddy. I know this is short notice but would you, Sam, and Shep like to have Thanksgiving with my brother and some friends of mine?"

When she got off the phone Rhys looked at her curiously. "What'd she say?"

"She's already made a big turkey and all the fixings. They're just waiting for you to come home to eat."

As if Maddy needed to be reminded, Rhys said, "My home's in Houston."

Chapter 12

Maddy came home after dinner to find Dave's angry voice on her answering machine.

"I guess you're still avoiding me," he railed. "Will you stop acting like a child and pick up the goddamn phone?"

She did a quick calculation in her head. It was nine thirty in the morning in Paris, and she'd put Dave off long enough. She picked up the phone and dialed his number.

"Hi."

"Hey." He sounded aggravated. "I'm getting tired of this screening crap. I've been trying to get ahold of you since you filed those ridiculous divorce papers. At least have the decency to drop me an email—let me know you're okay. Jeez, Maddy, I worry."

"I wasn't screening—I was out." What did he think, she would just sit around on Thanksgiving, waiting for his calls and out of spite not answer the phone?

"With whom? Sophie and Mariah?" he asked.

"Mm hmm. And Nate." And Rhys. Kissing.

"It was just me, eating bad hotel food," he said. "I miss you, baby." When had Dave become so smarmy?

"What's up, Dave?" she said through clenched teeth.

"I wanted to talk to you about this divorce bullshit."

"There's nothing to talk about."

"The hell there isn't," Dave said, raising his voice. There was a long pause and then he said, "I want you to come to Paris for Christmas."

Maddy took the phone into her room and sat on the edge of the bed. "Why?"

"What do you mean, why? Because you're my wife and I miss you. This damn sale is taking twice as long as it was supposed to and I would like us to spend time together . . . away from distractions."

"What part of divorce don't you understand, Dave? It's been a month and you still haven't signed the papers."

Dave got quiet, then said, "You don't want to do this, Maddy. You're hurt and you have every right to be. I swear I'll spend the rest of my life making it up to you. If you're still too furious with me to come to France, I understand, baby. But don't give up on us. We'll go to marriage counseling when I get back. We can split our time between the Lumber Baron and San Francisco. Whatever you want."

She wanted to ask him, "What about Gabriella? How is it that you don't love her anymore?" It made her wonder if Dave always wanted the woman he couldn't have—the one who posed the most challenges. Maybe all men were like that. Even Rhys.

"Maddy, I don't want to fight with you." Fatigue and longing laced Dave's voice. "I just think it's important that we focus on our marriage right now."

"That's the thing, Dave. I've been focusing on our marriage for a long time. Now, I need to focus on me."

She'd be damned if she'd tell him about the Addison mess. Everything always came so easy to Dave. That's why she had so much wrapped up in making a success of the Lumber Baron. Money, for one. But most of all—tangible proof to herself that she was something other than Dave Wellmont's second choice.

"So what're you saying, Maddy? That we're through? Because I'm sensing a real reluctance on your part to work this out."

"Don't put this on me. Maybe you need a reminder of why we're in this position in the first place."

"What are you saying, Maddy?"

"I think the divorce papers make what I'm saying very clear. Sign them and let's be done with this."

"Baby." His voice was barely a whisper. "Don't do this. It's impulsive. Just come to Paris . . . away from distractions . . . so we can discuss this."

"You mean away from Gabriella?" She could hear Dave heave an annoyed sigh on the other end of the line.

"From everything," he finally said. "Just you and me, in the most romantic city in the world. It'll be good, Mad . . . help us turn up the heat."

"Mine never went out." But she wasn't altogether sure that was true. Lately, she'd hardly missed him. She'd been distracted by the inn, and if she wanted to be honest with herself, a certain police chief.

"I have to go now," she said, feeling suddenly drained. Her failed marriage. The banners. The inn. It was all too much.

"Okay," he said. "But Mad, you'll think about Paris, won't you?"

He never took no for an answer. "I'm hanging up now."

But before she could click off, Dave said, "I love you, Maddy."

After yoga class Maddy hurried to the Lumber Baron to call her lawyer. On her way, she passed the barber shop—the "Flush the Lumber Baron" banner still hanging from the building. As usual the Nugget Mafia gathered inside, drinking coffee. Mayor Dink Caruthers sat in Owen's chair getting a shave, and Grace's husband, Earl, waited, reading the paper.

"Hey, fellows," she called inside the door, showing that she could be the bigger person.

Owen actually waved. She ought to put a horse head in his bed—make him an offer he couldn't refuse. The jerk.

"Sophie and Mariah find a live one yet?" Owen called across the shop.

The Nugget Mafia had become obsessed with the couple's quest to have a baby. The old coots had somehow gotten their hands on the Big Book and were laying odds on candidates. So far, Lithuanian Man was the favorite.

"Boundaries, Owen. Boundaries." Maddy walked away, shaking her head.

When she got to the inn, she took off her coat and hat, hung them on the rack in her temporary office, and grabbed the phone. Because of the snow, the men were working inside. She scouted out a quiet corner near her desk and sat cross-legged on the floor.

"Hey, Maddy." Josh Mendelssohn answered directly, which surprised her. Usually his secretary picked up. "Nathaniel filled me in on your sewage situation." Josh handled all the legal business for Nate's hotels.

"Can they actually revoke our permits?"

"Probably not," he said, but Maddy knew a caveat would follow.

"But," he continued, and there it was, "the residents could potentially file a lawsuit accusing the city of ignoring the inn's so-called adverse environmental impact on the town, which would hold you up until it got resolved in court."

"Great!" They couldn't afford for the place to sit vacant even for a few months. "Is there any way to stop this?"

"You could offer to pay for an upgraded waste system, but I suspect that would cost more money than you have."

"You got that right," she said. A citywide sewage structure, even just improvements, could cost tens of millions of dollars.

"You and Nate need to hire a waste management expert to look at the capacity of the system. If these Addison people are talking out of their asses, end of story. If not . . . Well, we'll cross that bridge when we get there."

"Should we stop with the renovations in the meantime?" Maddy didn't want to pour money into the building if they couldn't open.

"That's for you and Nate to decide," he said. "I'm not going to lie to you. Depending on how far these people take it, the courts could tie you up for years."

Maddy blew out a breath. "Okay, Nate and I will have a discussion. Thanks, Josh."

When she got off the phone, Colin stuck his head in. "Some guy named Virgil stopped by earlier. Wanted me to tell you that he has a surprise for you. He was on his way to Reno, but he said you should give him a call this evening."

Maddy concluded that it must have something to do with their Donner Party plans. She got up off the floor. "Thanks, Colin."

"No problem," he said.

The phone rang and Nate's number came up on the caller ID. "What the hell do we do now?" she answered.

"You talk to Josh?"

"Just got off the phone with him. He's the voice of doom."

"We pay him to give us the worst-case scenario, Maddy."

Maddy paced the room, stopped at the bay window and peered outside. They'd accomplished so much in such a short amount of time. "Should we stop the work?"

She could almost hear Nate thinking on the other end of the phone.

"Nope," he finally said. "Let's go for broke."

"Really?"

"Yep. Screw these people!"

"Okay," Maddy said, half of her thrilled because they weren't giving up, the other half screaming, *Are you insane?* "I'll see what I can do on my end about swinging public sentiment our way." How? She didn't know. People in this town were not only loyal to the natives, but anything new—even a small inn—had them fearing overdevelopment.

"Okay," he said. "I'll be up this weekend to help you with crisis management."

After they said their goodbyes, Maddy went outside to clear snow for the workers. Between Pat's efficiency and Colin's eye for detail, they were quickly turning the old-mansion-from-hell into a thing of beauty. Because of the weather they still hadn't been able to paint the exterior, but that didn't keep the townsfolk from occasionally standing outside the new wrought iron gates, gawking.

"Looking good," Rhys called from the street.

Maddy stopped shoveling and waved. "Come see the inside."

Rhys walked through the open gates and let his gaze sweep over her. "You look good, too." He reached out and touched the hand-knit red hat her mother had sent her last Christmas. "I like this."

Red had always been her color. She also knew her fitted coat showed off her new yoga curves, which Rhys was not-so-covertly admiring.

She smiled up at him. "So do you."

He wore Levi's that rode low on his hips and a pair of pointy-toed cowboy boots she liked. But it was the green sweater peeking out from under his jacket that brought out those sexy eyes of his.

Rhys scanned the property. "Where is everybody?"

"Lunch."

He took the shovel from her and finished clearing the steps. "I don't like you here alone."

"After nearly two months, you really think they'll come back?" she asked.

"In an abundance of caution, I'd like you to humor me." He leaned the shovel against the wall and looked out over the square at the banners. "You call your lawyer yet?"

"Yep. He says we should hire a sewage expert. In the meantime, Nate says we should keep working."

Rhys tipped his head in the direction of the barber shop. "There's your ticket. Get their backing and you're golden."

"The Nugget Mafia?"

Rhys chortled. "Is that what you call them?"

"That's what the ladies in the local cooking club call them. You have any suggestions for how I could win their favor? I'm open to anything—short of sleeping with them. Although . . ."

Rhys glowered at her. "Not funny." After two scorching kisses, the man had become possessive. Now that, Maddy thought, was interesting. "Why don't you take me on that tour now?"

Maddy led him into the stately foyer, where he let out a low whistle. The walls had been repaired and the trim work had been replaced. A new stained-glass skylight flooded the room with colored rays of sunlight.

"I'm still deciding whether to do wallpaper in here. Any thoughts?"

He laughed. "I don't think I'm your guy for that sort of advice. But I'd go with your gut. You've got an amazing eye."

She looked at him skeptically. "How do you know?"

He held his arms out. "Look at this place. I never could've imagined something this awesome. Every time I drove by it I thought someone should douse it with gasoline and light a match. But you . . . you saw this!"

"Well, to be honest, Nate saw this—and dollar signs. I pretty much felt the way you did."

"Show me the rest."

She guided him through the front parlor. "I know it's still rough. But can you visualize it?"

"Damn." He kept turning in place, scoping it out, like she'd performed a miracle.

They made their way to the dining room, where the fireplace and gumwood mantel had been stripped of layers of garish paint.

"This is where we'll serve the inn's complimentary breakfast and wine and cheese in the evenings." She grabbed his arm. "Come see the kitchen."

She watched Rhys take in the stainless steel countertops and appliances. Colin had managed to save the original cabinets, but not the beveled glass door insets. So Maddy had tracked down antique wavy-glass on the Internet and Colin used it to make his own.

"Wow," Rhys said. "A cook's dream."

"Someday we might do chef's dinners. But for now, we're keeping it simple—home-baked muffins, granola, oatmeal, omelets. Heavy hors d'oeuvres in the afternoons."

Rhys came up behind her so close that Maddy could feel his breath on her hair. "You cook?" he asked.

"No." She turned around to face him and he boxed her in, putting his hands down on the island countertop on each side of her.

"I guess you had servants to do that for you." There was no sarcasm in his voice, just curiosity.

"Only a cleaning lady once a week and a gardener every other. Dave rarely made it home in time for dinner, and when he did, we'd go down the street for falafel or Vietnamese food."

"Why no cook?"

Maddy thought about it. They certainly could afford one. "It's just not me."

"And Dave?"

"He could probably go either way. He grew up with a cook, maids—a butler."

"What about you?"

"Yeah." Maddy laughed. "Her name was Mom."

Rhys smiled and tucked a stray strand of hair under her hat.

"Rhys?"

"Hmm?"

"Have you ever been married?"

"Nope," he said.

"How come?"

He backed away from the counter and lifted his shoulders. "Never met anyone I felt that strongly about."

"You think you might have commitment issues?"

He let out a half laugh. "Maybe. I haven't given it a whole lot of thought."

With the way he grew up—having a father he couldn't depend on, a nonexistent mother—she wouldn't be surprised. "What're you doing for Christmas?"

"Christmas? We just got through Thanksgiving." He played with the buttons on her coat. "Show me upstairs." His voice grew husky. "We can christen one of the guest rooms."

"Is that all you think about?"

"Pretty much."

She leaned into him. The man was kind of irresistible. Aw, who was she kidding, the man was sex dipped in Valrhona chocolate. "First, tell me about your plans for Christmas."

"You're stalling," he said, and brushed a kiss across her nose. "Nothing. Shep and I don't do holidays."

"Oh, Rhys, you have to this year . . . Lina and Sam . . . losing their mom . . . They'll need their family."

"Not again, Maddy. You already know where I stand on this." He looked away for a minute. "What're you doing for Christmas?"

"My mother wants me to go home to Wisconsin." They'd finally had a heart-to-heart. Renée Breyer, who'd gotten her daughter through chicken pox, measles, and too many bad haircuts to count, vowed to help Maddy get through her divorce, too. "Dave wants me to meet him in France."

Rhys went rigid. "So that other woman . . . what's her name?"

"Gabriella."

"She's really out of the picture?"

Maddy shrugged. "He's ignoring the fact that I filed for divorce and wants to spend more time together." Like that was going to happen. When Dave had said they needed to turn up the heat, she'd wanted to reach through the phone and rip out his throat. "Of course I'm not going."

"No?" Rhys moved to the sink on the other side of the kitchen and stared out the window. "The crew's here. I've gotta get back to work." And he left her standing there.

Sophie thought she recognized the boy sitting at her bar, nursing a Coke, watching the window. But she couldn't quite place him.

After school, the kids usually went to the Bun Boy for a soda. Or on days like this, hot chocolate. The frosty was famous in Nugget for its cocoa. Donna Thurston liked to brag that she made it just like the Parisians, from fine bittersweet chocolate—"None of that powdered caca."

For all of Sophie's background in marketing, Donna knew how to keep a message simple. It was a gift, really.

With the dining room nearly empty—except for the boy and a few after-lunch stragglers—Sophie and Nate huddled in the corner, strategizing on the inn situation. Mariah was out, running errands.

Sophie moved toward the drink dispenser. "Would you like a refill on that?"

The boy looked around, like she might be talking to someone else. But he was the only one sitting there. "Is it free?"

"Yep," she said, and filled his glass with the soda gun. "Can I get you anything else?"

"No thanks." He alternated his gaze between the window and the door.

"You waiting for someone?"

"My ride," he said, and Sophie bent over the counter to find a suitcase sitting next to his stool. Nate followed her gaze to the luggage, and shrugged his shoulders.

A teenager walked in and grabbed the stool next to the boy. "You got the money?"

The boy stood up, dipped into his back pocket, and pulled out a twenty. "Here's half now. I'll give you the rest when you get me to Reno International."

"How do I know you won't stiff me?"

"How do I know you won't dump me off somewhere in the middle of the desert after you get all your money? You ever hear of insurance, dude?"

As the two became embroiled in heated negotiations, Sophie grabbed the phone and stepped halfway into the kitchen. If she had to wager a guess the boy was running away and the pimply-faced teen was his driving accomplice. She quickly dialed the phone.

Not long after, the police chief strode in and headed straight to the bar.

"Crap," the younger boy uttered. He clearly knew who the chief was, even though Rhys Shepard wore plain clothes. Something told Sophie that the chief had instantly recognized the boy, too.

"I'm out of here," Pimply said, and scrambled for the door.

"Give me back my money, then," the boy called.

Chief Shepard grabbed the teen by the collar. "You owe him some money?"

The boy practically threw the twenty at the chief and took off like a rocket.

"Hey, Justin." Rhys homed in on the boy's luggage and handed him the bill. "Going on a trip?"

Justin lowered his eyes and said, "Back to San Diego. Home!"

"Your dad know?" Rhys took the stool vacated by the teen and called across the bar, "Sophie, could we get another Coke and a cup of coffee, please. Oh, and how 'bout two slices of apple pie." He nodded a greeting at Nate, who nodded back.

"Coming right up." She'd finally figured out who the boy was. Clay McCreedy's oldest.

Rhys turned back to the kid. "Justin?"

"I left him a note."

"Maybe we should call him and tell him you've had a change of heart. What do you say?"

Justin sipped his soda. "Do I have a choice?"

"Nope," the chief said as Sophie set down their two plates. "Now eat your pie."

"I hate it here, Uncle Rhys." Justin's voice broke, and he hung his head, but not before Sophie saw his eyes grow moist.

"Yeah, I know the feeling," Rhys said, staring at the rows of liquor bottles behind the bar. "But you're only fourteen, so you've got to stick it out. In the meantime, try to make the best out of it. Forget about Will Becker and get to know your dad."

He swiveled his stool so he could face Justin, and Sophie heard him say, "He loves you and your brother like crazy, you know? When I was your age I would've done just about anything to have a father like yours. Give him a chance, Justin."

Sophie didn't know about Justin, but she'd watered up like a Roman fountain. She wanted a child so badly that sometimes her womb ached with it. Yet, she and Mariah were no closer to picking a donor than they had been when they'd first gone to the sperm bank. It was Sophie's fault, of course. None of the choices, not even the over-achievers with their Ivy League degrees and perfect health, felt right. But how could she tell Mariah that?

Nate reached across the bar and slapped her arm. "What's up with you?"

She nudged her head at Rhys and in a soft voice that wouldn't carry, said, "He was good with the boy. That's all." And she wiped away the tears staining her cheeks.

"Soph?" Nate asked. "What's the damn holdup?"

She shrugged. "It's complicated."

"Biology 101, babe." Nate could always tease a smile out of her. "You don't like anyone in *The Big Book of Sperm*?"

She looked at him, wondering how much she could share without betraying Mariah's confidence. "Mariah has a few donors in mind, but I'm more on the fence."

"Why's that?"

Because I want you. I want Mariah and my baby to have all the characteristics that have made you my best friend for nearly a decade. The kindness you're forever trying to hide under that rough exterior. The unflagging loyalty you have for family and friends. The

moral fiber that sets you apart from the hordes of unscrupulous busi-
nesspeople I have met over the years as a marketer.

"I'm uncomfortable with the idea of going with someone I know very little about, someone who may pass along his terrible genes."

"You want me to do it?"

Agog, Sophie stared at him. "Just like that, you'd do this for us? You don't even have to think about it?"

"I've thought about it," Nate said in his typical nonchalant manner. "Frankly, I was surprised you and Mariah never asked."

"It's a big thing, Nate. Lots of details to be considered, like how much of a role you'd play in the baby's life, how this would fit into your own plans for a family, and ultimately, can you, without a doubt, say you'd be able to relinquish your child, your own flesh and blood, to another couple to raise?" And even if he could answer all those questions satisfactorily, it was too much to ask of Mariah.

"The three of us just need to sit down and talk about it," Nate said. "See if we're on the same page."

"We're not." Sophie closed her eyes. Despite Nate's offer being the answer to her prayers, she wouldn't even broach the subject again with Mariah. As much as it broke her heart, it wouldn't be fair. "We love you too much, Nate, to let the complexity of this tear us apart."

And ultimately it would.

Chapter 13

"Whaddya doin', boy?" Shep walked out onto the porch as Rhys unloaded a couple of boxes of motion-sensor lights and low-voltage LED path lanterns from his pickup.

Now that Rhys had Jake he could afford to take a little R&R every now and again. So he was spending his first day off in weeks doing household chores.

The bulldozer guy he'd hired had removed about a half-dozen trees, which Rhys planned to chop up and give to Clay for firewood, and had cleared and leveled a good-size pad near the duplex for the cars. Since there was enough room left for shooting hoops, he'd also purchased a portable backboard system that he needed to assemble. It wouldn't hurt Sam to practice.

"I'm installing some lighting out here before Lina and Maddy kill themselves in the dark." He looked up at his father, who wore a T-shirt, a pair of lightweight cargo pants and house slippers. "Pop, go in and change into something warmer. It's twenty degrees out here."

Rhys kicked himself for telling Lina to go to town. She liked to walk to the library and he'd figured she could use a break from the old man. But Shep had become a real handful and Lina seemed to be the only one who knew how to manage him. He'd gotten both kids cell phones so they could better coordinate Shep's care and rides. Between school, Shep's doctor appointments and errands, he felt like a part-time bus driver. As soon as he got the time, he'd teach Lina how to drive and give her Shep's truck.

The girl was a quick study, her obsidian eyes always cataloging her surroundings the way Rhys's did when he was on the job. Sometimes, when she thought he wasn't paying attention, she'd watch him. He got the sense that she didn't approve of the way he treated Shep—thought he was disrespectful. Well, tough. She didn't know anything about their history. The kid should be going to college anyway, not taking care of an ungrateful poor excuse for a father.

Shep sat on a rocker watching him work. Rhys noticed that he still hadn't changed his clothes. Fine, he thought. If the old man wants to catch pneumonia, that's his problem.

"Instead of messing with those lights, you ought to be out with that girl next door," Shep called down.

"Who? Maddy?"

"You see any other girl next door?"

"What, you two best friends now?" Rhys rolled his eyes. "She's married."

Shep shrugged his stooped shoulders. "She looks pretty single to me."

"Well, she's not," he said, hoping to put an end to the conversation.

Rhys slanted a ladder up against the side of the duplex that faced the driveway, climbed up, and unscrewed the old rusted light fixture so he could replace it with the new motion sensor. Maddy might be on her way to getting divorced and willing to share a few mind-blowing kisses with him, but she wasn't over her husband. Not by a long shot. And why should she be? A guy like Dave Wellmont could give Maddy Paris. All Rhys could offer her was a fifth-wheel trailer down by the railroad tracks. He didn't even own the damn thing.

What did it matter? He wasn't sticking around, anyway. By this time next year he'd be back in Houston, back at the department where they were holding his job. And hopefully a promotion.

Shep stood up, walked to the edge of the porch and craned his neck so he could get a glimpse of Rhys working. "I tell you that girl's ripe for the picking."

Rhys came down, walked to the back of the house to the circuit-breaker box, flipped on the power, and shouted, "Hey, Pop, go inside and turn that light on for me."

He heard Shep shuffle across the porch, and a few seconds later, the screen door slammed. Rhys waved his hand in front of the new sensor and the light came on. He was moving the ladder to the other side of the duplex to replace the second fixture when Shep came down the stairs.

"You gonna go after her?"

Rhys's gaze traveled over the old man and he shook his head. "For thirty-six fucking years you've done nothing but ignore me, and now, all of sudden, you're concerned about my love life. Didn't I tell you to put on something warmer?" He turned his back on Shep and headed for the circuit box again.

By the time Rhys had the second motion-sensor light installed and a bulb screwed in, it had begun to snow. Small wet flakes dusted his hair and stuck to the shoulders of his down jacket. If the snow got any heavier he'd have to report to duty before the accident calls piled up. Rhys came down the ladder and turned the breaker on.

He didn't see his dad on the porch, so he yelled into the house, "Turn on the other light switch, wouldya?" Rhys waved his hand in front of the newly installed sensor. Nothing happened. "Pop, you turn it on?"

There was no reply, and the fixture still didn't work. Rhys stomped into the house, flipped the switch himself and peeked into his dad's room expecting to find Shep napping. But the bed remained neatly made. "Pop?" he called into the kitchen, but no one answered.

He banged on the bathroom door, waited a few seconds and opened it. Empty. "Pop, where the hell are you?"

Rhys dashed out of the duplex, and called some more. He quickly searched the yard, his truck, and the back porch. Maybe Shep had mistaken Maddy's side of the duplex for theirs. She'd left for work hours ago, but like everyone else in Nugget, she kept her doors unlocked.

"Pop?" He searched from one end of the apartment to the other, calling his father's name.

He was out of places around the house to look and dark clouds had started to move in. How does someone disappear in less than fifteen minutes?

He heard a car coming down the driveway and looked up to see Maddy's Subaru.

She pulled up in front of the duplex and rolled down her window. "What you doing out in the snow?"

"Looking for my father," he said. "He was out here while I was installing motion lights. I thought he went inside the house, but now I can't find him."

"I didn't see him on Donner Road. Want some help looking for him?" Maddy got out of her car.

She wore a white coat, furry boots, and her cheeks were pink from the cold. Rhys couldn't tear his eyes off of her. The woman was hotter than a twenty-dollar pistol. And if Rhys didn't watch it he'd get burned.

"He couldn't have gone far," he said, glancing up at the sky. "Why don't we divide and conquer? I'll search the areas up Donner. You mind taking Grizzly Peak Road? He used to walk that route a lot."

"Sure. Where are the kids?"

"Lina's at the library. Sam's at practice."

She glanced at the basketball-net set lying near his truck in an unopened box and grinned at him. He followed Maddy up the driveway, waited for her to take the quick jog over to Grizzly Peak before accelerating up Donner Road's steep grade.

Rhys drove slowly, occasionally shouting his father's name out the window. The road dead-ended at the top of the hill, where a fire trail led into the forest. In Shep's younger days he'd hiked the trail a hundred times.

The snow came down harder now, and the wind whipped flurries against his windshield, making it difficult to see. Rhys pulled over to the shoulder, got out and examined the ground for fresh prints. He walked to the other side of the road, where he peered down an embankment and called his father's name.

Soon it would be dark and even colder. If Shep had fallen down the ravine or had become so fuzzy that he'd gotten lost in the woods it could take hours, even days, to find him.

Rhys rubbed his hand over his face, cursing himself. He should've prepared for something like this—made Shep wear a damn tracking device. Back when he was in uniform, he'd spent a whole day once searching Houston's downtown tunnel system for an old lady suffering from dementia. It had been summer, dripping wet with humidity, and he'd finally found her, dehydrated and passed out on a bench. When the woman came to, she couldn't even remember her name.

As soon as he got Shep back, he'd put a freakin' cowbell around the old man's neck. It would serve him right for disappearing on him.

For being a shit father.

While climbing to the end of the road Rhys flashed on the summer before he went to high school. A group of the popular boys had shown up at his house at bedtime to kidnap him. It was a harmless game they played—snatching someone, taking him into the woods, so they could camp out, telling ghost stories all night. He'd always suspected that Clay had arranged it to help Rhys's social standing. But when the kids knocked on his door, Shep came out in his underwear and fired a shotgun into the air. The boys ran off while Rhys cowered in a corner from humiliation.

Several days later, out of the blue, Shep said, "Those kids were up to no good. They would've hurt you."

Rhys looked up at the sky and down at his watch. At most he had two hours of daylight left.

Where the hell are you, Shep?

He stared out over the mountains for as far as he could see. Nothing but trees. He hiked the fire trail for about a mile before the path became too overgrown to continue. "Pop," he shouted, hearing his voice echo through the forest.

It was possible that Shep had headed to the main road and taken his old route to the railroad station. But Maddy hadn't seen him when she drove in. Just the same, Rhys started back down the hill. He was halfway to his truck when his cell phone rang.

He grabbed it from his pocket. "Hello."

"I found him," Maddy said.

Rhys dropped his head to his chest.

"You there?"

"Yeah." He took a moment to send up a silent prayer of gratitude and to pull himself together. "He okay?"

"He's fine. He's at Colin Burke's place. I was almost at his house when Colin called. He doesn't have your number. I'm here now, so I'll bring him home."

"Hey, Maddy . . . Let me do it, okay?"

A few minutes later he pulled up to the house number Maddy had given him. Although the chalet-style log cabin was still under construction, its grandeur floored him. The striking stonework and mammoth picture windows reminded him a little of the houses in Sierra Heights, but more tasteful.

Before he could knock on the door, Colin pulled it open and grunted a greeting. "He's in the kitchen eating," he said.

Rhys wiped his boots on the scraper and entered the massive foyer, running his palm over hand-hewn logs, dovetailed at the corners. "Nice place you've got here."

"Thanks."

Maddy had been right, Colin's work was incredible. But how could a guy who made his living selling rocking chairs and who took on the occasional carpentry job afford a place like this? The front room with its enormous stone fireplace and sweeping views of the Sierra made him catch his breath.

"Wow." Rhys stopped to stare up at the skyscraper-high ceilings.

Colin stood stiffly in the corner waiting for Rhys to get his fill. Not much of a talker, Rhys observed.

"Sorry about the inconvenience with my dad," he said as he followed Colin into an equally breathtaking dining room, which had been set up as a temporary work space with sawhorses and tools.

"No problem. Um . . . he seems a little confused, though. Keeps calling me Rhys."

"He's got Alzheimer's," Rhys said.

Colin just nodded his head, like he didn't quite know how to react.

When they got into the kitchen—a shell without cabinets and an old stove that appeared temporary—Rhys found Shep hunched over a farm table, bundled in a couple of heavy blankets, eating.

"He was really cold," Colin said.

"Hey, Pop."

Shep gave him a cursory glance and went back to eating his chili.

"Mind if I borrow those blankets?"

"Not at all."

"Thanks for taking him in and feeding him." Rhys turned from Colin and dropped to his haunches beside Shep's chair. "You ready to go, Pop?"

"Okay, Rhys." Shep stood up.

"Looks like you're missing a slipper." Rhys pointed at Shep's bare foot.

Shep looked down, puzzled. "Must've lost it," he mumbled.

Rhys put an arm around his father's shoulder and led him to the front door. "That's okay. I'll get you another one."

Always keep your feet and head warm, boy. It'll prevent you from getting sick. His father's words suddenly popped into Rhys's head. Wisdom to live by.

Rhys had been eight years old, running around the house in the dead of winter in his bare feet.

Shep had gone into his bedroom and pulled a pair of woolen socks from his bureau drawer. "Put these on, boy."

Rhys had slipped into the worn socks, liking the way the fleece lining had instantly warmed his too-small feet.

"You keep 'em," Shep had said.

Twenty-eight years later and Rhys still had them.

Maddy waited on the porch for them to get home and held the front door open as Rhys carried Shep into the house. He continued directly to the bedroom.

She sat on the couch in case he needed her for anything, thought about making coffee, but didn't know how she'd get to the kitchen without intruding on them. In the bedroom she could hear Rhys rustling around, dresser drawers being opened and closed, bedsprings squeaking and him murmuring for Shep to get some sleep. Finally, Rhys wandered back into the living room, a grim expression on his face.

"He okay?" she asked.

Rhys rubbed his temples. "Yeah."

"How about you? You okay?" She gave him a sympathetic smile.

"Yeah. Thanks for helping me find him." He sneezed and walked over to the thermostat, turning the dial up to sixty-nine degrees.

"Come sit down, Rhys. You look tired. You want me to make you some tea?"

He shook his head. "Need to call the station . . . weather's bad."

"You can take a little break first." She got up, steered him to the sofa, and pushed him down. "It was a little scare, Rhys. That's all."

Rhys just nodded as he stared off into space.

Maddy pulled the zipper down on his jacket. "Get this off. It's wet and you're catching a cold." He sat very still as she tugged the parka off him.

Maddy hung it on the coatrack by the door to dry and grabbed a blanket off his bed to drape over Rhys's shoulders. "Better?"

Rhys rested his face in the palm of his hands. "God, I screwed up."

She sat on the floor facing him. "Don't you think you're being a little hard on yourself? Really, Rhys, how'd you screw up?"

He rubbed his hands over his eyes. "I yelled at him. I let him get under my skin."

"You think that's why he took off?" she asked skeptically.

"I don't know. But I wasn't paying enough attention. It was my day off. I wanted to get the lights done and I didn't want to put up with his shit." Rhys took the blanket off, laying it down on the couch next to him. "I should've been watching him better. When I think about how badly this could've ended—" He broke off with a muttered curse.

"Rhys, it's impossible to keep an eye on him at all times. You're doing the best you can." She squeezed his knee. "You're a good son."

Rhys looked away and Maddy got the impression that he was embarrassed. He got up, walked over to Shep's bedroom, and opened the door a crack. His father was sound asleep. He walked over to the hall table, picked up the phone, and dialed.

"What's going on?" he asked, pacing the room, holding the phone to his ear with his shoulder. "Send Wyatt out to the car accident and Jake to the drunk in public—he's better equipped to deal with that sort of thing. You sure you don't need me to come in, Connie?"

Maddy started for the door, but Rhys waved his hand to stop her. When he hung up the phone he gazed at her and simply said, "Stay."

They tiptoed through Shep's bedroom to the kitchen to rustle up a couple of sandwiches and went back into the living room to eat. Maddy noticed that he kept his cell, the cordless, and a police radio with him at all times.

She pointed at the assemblage of electronics. "That much crime in Nugget?"

"If you would've asked me before I took the job, I would've laughed," he said. "But unfortunately this town has grown up . . . I've got a methamphetamine manufacturer on the loose and the lure of an empty subdivision."

He told her about his high school friend, Mini, and her domestic violence case.

"You think she'll really take those anger management courses?" she asked.

"Maybe." But he looked doubtful. "Unfortunately, hitting and fighting is all she's ever known."

"Is that why you left?" Maddy suspected that besides Shep neglecting Rhys, there might've been abuse. Maybe she was getting too personal, but she couldn't help herself.

"It wasn't like that so much," he said, his voice distant. "Shep was tough. But mostly I never felt like I belonged here. I used to think that if I traveled, saw the country, there'd be a place that spoke to me. A place that instantly felt right . . . like home."

"Not Houston?" Maddy asked.

"No," he said regretfully. "But it's better than here. How 'bout you, Maddy Breyer? Where's home?" His eyes traveled over her, and a spark of awareness slithered down her spine.

Their legs touched and even through the denim, Maddy could feel his heat. She remembered how nice it had been that first time she'd snuggled against him on the glider and was tempted to move closer. Curl up in those strong arms. The shadow of dark stubble that covered his jawline made her ache to feel it against her face.

But Rhys instantly moved away from her, putting up an invisible wall. Maybe he was still traumatized by Shep taking off. Maddy didn't know. Still, she missed having his hands all over her.

So instead, she stammered an answer to his question. "Nugget for now." Maddy wrung her hands. "But if the Addisons have their way I'll be out on my ass."

"What's going on with your expert?"

"He just started. But, if he says the Addisons are right, I don't know what we'll do. It's not like we have enough money to upgrade the whole system."

Rhys reached for her hand and covered it with his much larger one. And that powerful attraction she'd been feeling for him pulled at her. "It'll be okay, Maddy." He dipped his head slightly.

She thought he'd kiss her, even half closed her eyes in anticipation. But he got up from the couch and looked in on his dad.

Feeling a whole lot awkward, she said, "I better get home."

As Maddy gathered up her coat, Lina walked in the door, covered in snow.

"It's cold." She shivered, looking from Maddy to Rhys. "What's wrong? Is Papa okay?" She rushed to Shep's bedroom door, but Rhys stopped her before she could go in.

"He's sleeping," he said, and Maddy frowned at how short Rhys sounded.

"Is that a new coat?" Maddy asked her. It was purple and fitted, with a snazzy little belt and a fur-trimmed hood.

Lina nodded, looking down at it proudly. "It's from Rhys."

"You picked that out?" she asked, not even trying to disguise her surprise.

"No. I just paid for it," he said gruffly.

"Well, it's very pretty." She got to her feet and Rhys went to walk her out.

"We need to have a conversation when I get back," he told Lina. Maddy wished he was a little softer with his sister.

When they got to her door, he stood there, hands jammed in his pockets, rocking on his heels. They both talked at the same time, sputtering until he said, "You first."

She lightly touched the sleeve of his jacket. "Today with Shep wasn't your fault, Rhys. What you're doing for your dad is incredibly selfless. But even with Lina, it's an overwhelming job. I'm your friend, let me help, okay?"

"Yeah." He nodded. "Thanks."

She smiled up at him. "What were you about to say before?"

"I forgot." He looked away and backed up. "See you in the morning, Maddy."

She started to reach for his arm, stopped herself, and went inside the house.

Rhys had nearly asked Maddy about Paris. Whether she intended to go. It'd be a stupid move, if you asked him. But she hadn't. And right now he had more important things to think about anyway. Like what the hell to do with Shep?

He found Lina in the kitchen, standing over the stove, stirring something. "You making dinner?"

"Mmm hmm." She barely looked at him.

"Shep took off," Rhys started. "I turned my back on him for five minutes, maybe ten at the most, and he was gone. Maddy found him at a house up on Grizzly Peak. He thought the owner was me."

Lina turned down the flame and sat at the table. "Why didn't you call me?" Her phone sat on the kitchen counter and she reached for it, checking for messages.

Rhys tilted his head to look at her. The resemblance between them really was uncanny. Same deep-set eyes, same indentations at the bridge of their noses, same pronounced cheekbones. The most distinct differences that Rhys could tell were the shapes of their faces—his square, hers heart-shaped—and she was a tiny little thing.

Rhys glanced at his watch, glad that he had at least an hour before Sam got home. Clay said he'd take the boys out for supper after practice.

"Lina," he said as gently as possible, "he's getting worse."

The other day Rhys stood in the kitchen while Shep struggled to make a sandwich, confused by how to layer the meat and bread. Even before that, he had found him sitting with the television remote control in his hand, stymied by how to change the channels. It had been tough for Rhys to watch. The old man was a prick, but he'd always been a self-sufficient one. "Today, if he'd fallen down an embankment, or gotten lost in the woods . . . Jesus, he wasn't even wearing a jacket."

Rhys paused, trying to choose his words. "We can't watch him twenty-four hours a—"

"I can," Lina interjected. "If I had been here, this would not have happened."

He flinched. "Maybe not, but he needs professional care. He needs to be in a place where they can help him use the bathroom, the shower."

"*No voy a tener a mi padre en uno de los lugares—con extraños.*"

"Lina," he said. "Your English is better than my Spanish."

"No. I will not put him in one of those homes, to live with strangers."

Pretty soon Shep wouldn't know the difference. "This could go on for years. You're only seventeen years old . . . there's college . . . a whole life ahead of you."

"What do you care?" she spat. "You hate us and you hate him."

"I don't hate you. I hardly know you." Rhys got up and started pacing the room. "Ah, Lina, don't cry . . . Okay, okay, we'll see what the doctor says. Come on, now."

He went to pat her, give her a quick, reassuring squeeze, but she threw herself into his arms and buried her face in his shirt, sobbing. Something besides empathy and protectiveness sparked inside of him. It was more like an indefinable bond. And in that instant, maybe for a quarter of a beat, he reveled in the resounding connection he felt with this girl, which only made him resent Shep more.

Chapter 14

A hearing was imminent. The Addisons had whipped the town into such a frenzy over the inn, that the city council had been pressured to put the matter on its meeting agenda. At least with Christmas coming up, town officials had tabled the issue until after the New Year, which gave Maddy and Nate time to build a case—and if need be, serve the city with a lawsuit.

In the meantime, the Addisons' "Flush the Lumber Baron" campaign had moved beyond the square. One of their repugnant banners swung over the Nugget Market like Old Glory rippling in the wind.

"Ethel, I thought you were in my court," Maddy huffed in despair. Because if the few friends she had in this town were against her, then she really was in deep doo-doo.

Ethel stood in the parking lot, staring up at the sign, shaking her head. "I told Stu not to put that thing up. I'm sorry, hon. What can I say, he's convinced that your twenty rooms are going to back up the system and we'll all be swimming in sewage."

"Where is he?" Maddy marched into the store and found him behind the butcher counter.

"Stu, I'm really, really disappointed in you," she barked, noticing that shoppers had stopped pushing their carts in the meat aisle so they could listen. Let them get an earful! "I can't believe you're buying those Addisons' line of bull. Do you know how much business the Lumber Baron will bring this town, your store? Our guests will be wanting everything from suntan lotion and sundries to sandwiches and sodas. Not to mention that we'll be buying our ingredients here for our continental breakfasts and snacks for the rooms."

"Don't get me wrong," Stu said, holding up his hands. "I like you Maddy, and I want the business. But this waste issue concerns me. A new system could cost millions and the city can't afford it."

"Stu, do you think the city would've given us our permits in the first place, if there was a real problem?"

"Don't know," he said. "But I don't want them taking any chances."

By the time she got back to the inn, Nate was waiting for her. He'd allegedly come to check on the progress of the renovation, but Maddy knew his real motivation was to force a sedative down her throat.

"You need to calm down," he said, sprawled out on the love seat in her office, both arms spread across the top of the backrest. "Running around like a crazy woman isn't going to win us a lot of friends."

"What do you suggest we do, then? Sit on our hands?"

"Wait for our sewage expert. I talked to him today and he'll have something for us after the holidays. Until then, there's not a whole lot we can do."

He let out a breath. "Now, what's this I hear about you telling Mom that you're going to Sophie and Mariah's for Christmas?"

"Too much to do here."

"Ah, that's bogus, Maddy. Come on, we'll make it a quick trip— fly to Madison on the twenty-third, be back by the twenty-seventh."

"With all this going on?" She waved her hands in the air. "I can't think of a worse time for me to leave. Someone needs to keep an eye on those Addisons."

"Nothing'll happen over Christmas," he said, and then a light-bulb seemed to go off in his head. "You got something going on with the cop?"

She blinked. "First of all, his name is Rhys—not 'the cop.' What-ever gave you the idea he and I have plans?" Rhys didn't do Christ-mas. Or family. Or commitment. It might be good to remind herself of that from time to time. But she'd gotten him a gift anyway. It didn't mean anything, just something for him to remember her by when he went back to Houston.

"Why else would you lie?"

"If I didn't lie, she and Dad would've come here. Besides, it's not technically a lie since I'll probably hang with Sophie and Mariah anyway."

"And what would be so terrible about our parents coming here?" He got up and examined the blueprints tacked up on her office wall. When she didn't answer, he prodded, "Maddy?"

She sat on the floor in front of him, her legs tucked under her. "Remember that first hotel you operated . . . what was it called?"

"The Conquistador."

"Right, the Conquistador. Remember how much you loved those ancient Saltillo tiles and the crumbling fountain in the courtyard? Remember how you told me that you knew, even though Dad wouldn't say it, that he thought you were taking on more than you could handle? Yet, you signed the contract anyway, because deep in your gut it felt right, like you'd found your destiny in that old hotel. You thought the Conquistador would be the foundation on which you built your future. And then, eight months later, the place went belly up." Maddy saw his cheeks grow pink.

"It took me three months before I could face Dad again," Nate spoke to himself as much as to her. "Okay, I get it."

He got to his feet. "Wanna have lunch at the Ponderosa?"

"Oh, I can't. Virgil has a professor friend in Stanford's history department who wants to make a Donner Party documentary about Nugget. I'm meeting with Virgil to talk about it. He says this professor guy has a big name, lots of published books. I want us to be the project's key backer and have the film debut here. Wouldn't that be great?"

"Awesome." He rolled his eyes. "But maybe a little premature, given our current predicament."

"I know," she said. "But I'm trying to think positively."

"How 'bout dinner?"

"I have plans to go Christmas shopping with Pam and Amanda." Maddy also wanted to get new jeans to reward herself for all the yoga she'd been doing. "But I'll make sure to be back in time for dinner."

Virgil lived in a sprawling log cabin in the woods, filled with books, Native American rugs, and local artifacts. Maddy sat on a comfy leather sofa, a fire crackling in the hearth, while Virgil made coffee. In the distance, she could see the sun glimmering off Donner Lake. Now the lake mostly served as a recreational area for fishermen and water-skiers, but in 1846 it had been a death camp for the Donner Party.

"So this guy really wants to make a documentary, huh?"

Virgil laid a tray with cups and saucers on the coffee table. "If he can get the funding. A lot of the Donner Party history has been well documented, but he's hoping to put a new spin on it by telling the story through the eyes of modern-day Nugget."

"Like how Virginia Reed came back to build a house here?"

"Exactly," he said.

"You know you never did finish telling me her story."

Virgil stirred his coffee. "Where were we?"

"Virginia's father had just been banished from the group. He would occasionally leave letters tacked to trees for his family as they traveled with the caravan. But then the notes abruptly stopped."

"Ah," Virgil nodded, getting comfortable. "As winter approached they raced the clock to get over the mountains into California. Indians shot twenty-one of their remaining oxen with poisoned arrows," he said. "Virginia wrote in her diary that she could hear the Indians up on the bluff, laughing and mocking them.

"They were nearly out of food when they finally limped into Truckee. But help came. A scout from Sutter's Fort in Sacramento, who'd gotten word from other travelers that they were still out there, brought them seven mules weighed down with food and two Indian guides. The riders told them they had another month before the high pass of the Sierra would be snowed in."

"But that wasn't the case." Maddy had read this part of the story.

"You're right," Virgil said. "The weather report was wrong. They camped fifty miles from the summit for five days to rest their animals. When they reached the ridge near Donner Lake they called it a day, and made camp. That night it snowed hard. In the morning the group rushed to the pass. But it was too late. Five feet had fallen and they couldn't get through. The higher they climbed, the deeper the snow. Even the Indian guides couldn't find the road."

Maddy shook her head. "Sutter's Fort was only one hundred and fifty miles away and they'd missed it by one day. It seems like fate was out to get them."

"Yes, it does," Virgil said. "And the Reeds were lucky that no one, at least publically, laid the disaster at their feet. Because the snow and sleet kept coming without any sign of letting up. So they all went back to the lake and built a winter camp. The Reeds found a deserted cabin, which they shared with another family. The Donners lived in tents.

"They butchered their remaining cattle for food. Every day they would search the summit for a relief party, but none came. Soon, they found themselves in twenty feet of snow. The meat was running out, so they began boiling hides, charring bones, and mixing it with leaves, twigs, and bark—anything they could find."

"But it wasn't enough," Maddy said. Even though she knew this part of what happened, she wanted to know more about Virginia.

"Nope." Virgil poured himself another cup of coffee from the server. "One of the Reeds' servants was the first to die. By mid-December fifteen of the party's hardiest members and the two Indian guides made a plan to hike out."

"Anyone from Virginia's family?" Maddy asked.

Virgil shook his head. "They weren't the strongest of the bunch, so they stayed behind. With the two Indians leading the way, the volunteer group made a dash for the summit. They made it over, but then got lost—probably delirious from hunger. They ran out of provisions on the sixth day and were slowly starving to death.

"Someone suggested that they draw lots and whoever got the longest slip of paper be sacrificed. Patrick Dolan was the first to pull a death ticket."

"But no one could kill him, right?"

"That's right." Virgil smiled at her, obviously proud she'd done her homework. "The first to die was one of the teamsters," he continued. "After that, Patrick went berserk and some of the others had to restrain him before he fell into a coma and died. Someone built a campfire, while the others cut Patrick's limbs off. They roasted his arms and legs and ate the meat."

Maddy must've looked disgusted, because Virgil said, "Hey, it revived them. But the Indians would have no part of eating human flesh.

"The surviving ten cut up the rest of the dead, wrapped up the meat, and marked it, so they'd know not to feed it to a member of that person's family. But they went through the food in three days. Then someone suggested murdering the Indians. One of the members of the party warned them and the Indians ran for their lives into the woods."

"But they didn't get far," Maddy said. "They lay in the snow, starving to death. William Foster, one of the fifteen who'd gone mad, found them and shot each one in the head. The rest ate them."

It really was one of the grossest stories Maddy had ever heard.

"For eighteen more days they walked aimlessly through the mountains," Virgil went on. "Only seven made it back to the lake alive. There they found more people dead from starvation."

"What about Virginia's family? Were any of them among the dead?" Maddy asked.

"Nope," Virgil continued. "Virginia prayed to God to spare her and her family's life. But no relief came. And by mid-February Virginia lay in her cabin dying. They were all near death.

"Then a miracle happened." Virgil paused for dramatic effect. She could see why he'd made an impression on Rhys back in his school days. "A seven-member rescue party came over the summit. When they reached the camp, the rescuers were sickened to find dead bodies strewn across the snow."

"Didn't the Donner Party eat them all?" Maddy asked.

"The emigrants who remained at the lake hadn't yet resorted to cannibalism. Fifty-five people, including all the Reed children and their mother, had managed to survive. But the rescuers could only take out twenty-four and there was barely any food left.

"Virginia, her mother, and her brother James were in that first group out. Her baby brother Thomas and Virginia's little sister Patty stayed behind. As they made their way across the mountains, they met up with a second relief party."

Virgil smiled. "Guess who led the group?"

Maddy didn't have a clue.

"Virginia's father. James Reed had survived and had come back to rescue them."

Maddy got chills. "I thought for sure he was dead."

"He got back to the lake in time to get Patty and Thomas," Virgil said. "But ten more emigrants had died and the survivors had roasted their flesh—even their hearts and livers—for nourishment. James found cabins filled with half-consumed bodies—skulls, hair, and bones.

"A few more rescue parties came, and by the end of April the last survivor was pulled from the mountains. The death toll was staggering—forty-one people."

"But all the Reeds got out alive, made it over the pass?" Maddy asked hopefully.

"Yes," Virgil responded. "The Donners weren't as fortunate. All the adults died and four of the children. They couldn't even find George Donner's wife's body. One of the survivors eventually admitted to eating her remains."

"It's better than a Hollywood horror movie," Maddy said.

"Yes, it is," Virgil admitted. "And that's why our Stanford friend wants to revisit the whole episode."

"We could do a big summer screening in the square." The Lumber Baron could sell it as a package—that is, if the Lumber Baron still existed when the film was finished.

Virgil chuckled. "Perhaps. In the meantime"—he handed her a stack of history books—"study up. We want to look sharp when we meet with the professor."

On her drive to the Nugget Feed Store, Maddy thought of a dozen ways she could use the documentary to market Nugget as the next big tourist town. All she had to do was save the inn.

Amanda and Pam waited by a big incubator just beyond the entrance, playing with a dozen baby chicks.

The store was about the size of a big-box warehouse. Outside there was a small nursery where they sold seasonal plants, pottery, garden provisions, and a charming array of birdhouses and scarecrows. Right now it was lined with Christmas trees. Inside, the store was separated into various departments—saddles, horse gear, ranch equipment, and livestock supplies. There was even a dizzying selection of housewares.

Grace stood behind the cash register, setting up a counter display of Christmas ornaments. She stopped what she was doing and reached over the counter to give Maddy a hug. "We just got a big shipment in, so you girls go play. There are plenty more sizes in the back."

"Where's Earl?" Amanda asked, leading Pam and Maddy to an area filled with rounders of women's clothing that was nearly the size of Nordstrom's shoe department.

"In the back, helping Clay load grain," Grace said, then reached for a ringing phone.

Maddy eyed the myriad racks filled with embroidered Western shirts, denim skirts, and blinged-out hoodies with doubt. The walls were lined with rodeo pictures and the back shelves held stacks of jeans. "I love Grace," she whispered to the other two women. "But I don't see me in Wranglers."

"Two months ago that would've been a problem," Amanda acknowledged. "Now, you're in for a treat. What size are you?"

"A twenty-eight or a twenty-nine."

Pam pushed her through a set of swinging saloon doors into a dressing room with a rawhide bench and a full-length mirror. "Strip," she ordered, and Maddy obediently complied.

They shoved a pile of jeans at her. "Try these on," Pam said.

"Aren't you guys trying some, too?" Maddy asked.

Amanda popped her head over the pony wall in the next dressing room and held up a fitted sweaterdress that looked straight out of the Sundance Catalog.

"Cute!" Maddy said.

"With boots, right?"

"Oh, yeah." Maybe Maddy would get some boots, too.

She shimmied into a pair of jeans with white side stitching and marveled at how well they fit. "I like these," she said, checking out her butt in the mirror. "Either the yoga's working, or these are miracle pants."

"Come out," Pam urged.

"They're a little long, though." Maddy exited the dressing room on her tiptoes and found Amanda assessing the dress in the three-way mirror. It looked even better on her than it did on the hanger.

"The pants are longer for riding," Amanda said. "Otherwise the legs hike up too short in the stirrups." That wouldn't be a problem for Maddy.

"Turn." Pam shrugged on a leather duster she'd pulled from the sale rack while she made Maddy model the pants. "You definitely have to get those."

"How much are they?" Maddy tried to see the price tag on the back.

"Seventy-nine," Amanda read.

"You're kidding me? I paid three hundred for my Sevens. And these fit about a million times better."

"We tried to tell you," Amanda said. "Should I get this dress?"

"Yes," Maddy and Pam said in unison.

"Ladies."

All three of them turned to see Rhys leaning against one of the clothing tables.

"Nice jeans," he said, surreptitiously trying to get a look at her ass. She felt her cheeks heat. "What are you doing here?"

"Giving Clay a hand—big grain order. You getting those?" He motioned to the pants.

"Maybe. You think I should?"

"Definitely." He pushed away from the table, and strolled away.

"That was interesting." Pam had been watching the exchange like it was the French Open.

"Very," Amanda chimed in. "You two an item?"

"Honestly," Maddy said, "I don't know what we are." There'd been those kisses. But the last time she'd been with him, he'd run a little cold. But then again, who was she to talk? She wasn't even officially divorced yet. And she probably should've kept her mouth shut about

Dave's Paris invitation. That seemed to have driven Rhys's sudden standoffish behavior.

As Amanda watched Rhys and Clay leave the store, she said, "If I was you, I'd get to tapping that. Grace was right, that boy turned out good." Then she disappeared inside the dressing room to try on a few tops and a down vest.

In Maddy's mind Rhys was better than good. He was smart, caring, and dependable. Not to mention so ripped that he made her drool. He just came with more baggage than a transatlantic flight.

By the time they got to the cash register, Maddy had three pairs of jeans and a pair of Old Gringo cowboy boots. She'd gotten a set of sterling silver and turquoise bangles, earrings for Sophie, and a suede fringe jacket for Mariah.

"Ooh, it looks like you girls done good," Grace cooed. "Maddy, you're entitled to a little retail therapy after what those Addisons are doing."

"Did you look at the petition?" she asked Grace, interested to know how many signatures they had so far.

"I did not—told Sandy I wanted no part of that petition, or those ridiculous banners. Now you listen to me, dear. I grew up in this town, and while I'll admit people here are slow to accept anything new at first, they always come around. You'll see."

"You think?" Maddy must've looked as glum as she felt, because Grace came around the counter and gave her a squeeze. The woman was a hugger.

"Let me tell you something," Grace said, handing Maddy her shopping bags. "For thirty years all we sold here were sturdy Western jeans, work shirts, and whites for the 4-H kids. Occasionally, during the holidays, we'd get in a few fancier-style boots, some hand-tooled belts. Then, a few months ago, my daughter, Lucinda, asked if she could take over the apparel department, do the buying. Earl was so happy that she was taking an interest in the business he turned it over to her, then nearly crapped his pants when he saw this." She motioned to the clothing displays. "For weeks all I heard from the customers was how we were ruining the place—turning it into Saks Fifth Avenue instead of focusing on animal husbandry.

"Bitch, bitch, bitch. Well, Maddy, between you and me, our sales have never been better. We've got ladies coming over from Quincy to shop here. And as much as the men complain that we're taking up valuable tack and feed space with all the clothes, I see them picking up a little something for their wives when they make their alfalfa orders."

Maddy smiled at Grace. "The place is great. Lucinda's done an amazing job. And I really do appreciate the encouragement," she said.

Clutching her new purchases, Maddy said goodbye to Pam and Amanda. Yeah, the shopping had been therapeutic, but not a complete antidote. It would take more than a pair of nice-fitting jeans to fix her problems.

When she got to the duplex, Nate was waiting to take her to dinner. He and Rhys stood next to Shep's International Harvester Scout, heads together, like they were trying to unravel the Da Vinci code. Lina sat in the driver's seat, both hands white-knuckling the steering wheel.

"Remember, SMOG—signal, mirror, over the shoulder, and go," Rhys directed.

Nate nodded his head vigorously, then trying to appear casual made a dash for higher ground—the porch steps.

"Okay," Rhys shouted over the Scout's caterwauling engine. "Show us what you've got."

Lina started to pull out, hitting the gas too hard so that the tires sputtered in the driveway, kicking up clumps of dirt.

"SMOG, SMOG." Rhys thrashed his arms.

Lina shut off the engine. "I already did that."

"You have to do it every time. Signal, mirror, over the shoulder. Then gas!" He held on to the side of the truck and seemed to be praying for patience.

Shep and Sam came onto the porch and joined Nate on the steps. Maddy walked over to where they were standing.

"How long has this been going on?" Maddy asked. Only an hour ago, Rhys had been at the feedstore.

"Not long," Nate said, glancing down at his watch. "You missed the part where she almost backed into the trailer."

Maddy visually measured the distance from the driveway to the new car pad. "It's a little tight for a driver's ed course. Shouldn't they be doing this in an empty parking lot with Rhys in the truck?" Maddy's father had taught her in the Dorn True Value lot after hours. They'd driven in circles so many times that both of them had gotten dizzy.

Nate shrugged. Rhys continued to bark commands at Lina, who looked about ready to give up and cry.

"Let's practice your U-turn," Rhys said.

Lina jerked the truck forward, accelerating too hard, and then overcompensated by slamming on the brake. Rhys raised his face to the sky in frustration and told her to take a breather. Just as they were about to start all over again, Maddy wedged her way in between Rhys and the truck.

"Hey, Lina," she said, opening the driver's door. "Why don't you scoot over into the passenger seat."

"What are you doing?" Rhys demanded, sliding his aviators down his nose so he could glare at her over the rims, his face strained.

"Taking her to Sierra Heights, where we can do this right." Before Rhys could protest she jumped up into the seat and restarted the engine.

"Can we come?" Sam yelled down from the porch.

"Get in," she said.

Both he and Shep hopped into the backseat and they drove off, leaving the big, bad ruffled police chief in Maddy's rearview, scratching his head.

The whole way to Sierra Heights, Maddy demonstrated to Lina how to check her mirrors, change lanes, adjust speed. She explained about defensive driving. When they got to the empty development, Maddy headed for the clubhouse parking lot.

"Ready to do this?"

Lina nodded nervously and switched seats with Maddy. They circled the lot about five times, very slowly at first, so Lina could test the weight of her foot on the gas pedal and experiment with the brake. Then she sped up, feeling slightly more at ease controlling the vehicle.

Just when Lina started getting the hang of it, Nate and Rhys pulled up in Nate's Jag. Lina stopped the Scout, activated the emergency brake the way Maddy had taught her, and shouted out the window with glee, "I can drive."

"Yeah?" Rhys's smile spread so wide that Maddy nearly melted into a puddle right there in the truck. He opened Maddy's door, lifted her out of the passenger seat and took her place. "Let me see how you do."

Lina practiced with Rhys some more in the parking lot, Shep and Sam in the backseat, pretending to hang on for dear life. Maddy took her brother on a quick tour of the Heights—that's what Nate had taken to calling it.

"Wasn't that the name of a really bad TV show?"

"Probably," Nate said. "I should buy this place, turn it into a time-share."

They'd probably go bankrupt on the Lumber Baron, but her numbskull brother wanted to turn a deserted subdivision into a time-share. When they got back to the Jaguar, Lina was ready to call her driver's lesson quits and Maddy and Nate were ready to go to dinner.

As they drove away in separate vehicles, Nate asked, "Who do you think will teach Sophie and Mariah's kid how to drive?"

"One of them, I suppose."

Nate hooted with laughter. "You ever ride with either one of those two women? Scary!"

"Maybe you could pitch in with that," she said, and slid her brother a glance.

"I offered."

"You did?" She looked at him to make sure they were both talking about the same thing. They were.

"Soph declined."

"Really," Maddy said. "I'm surprised to hear that. It seemed to me it was what Sophie wanted."

Nate lifted his shoulders. "Something's up with them, Mad. And I don't want to get in the middle of it."

* * *

Rhys sat in the Sacramento waiting room of the geriatrician's office trying to read the latest issue of *Outside*, but couldn't focus. Shep was here for a routine checkup, but he'd dragged Lina along for a reality check.

Despite her stubborn demand to continue Shep's care, she needed to know what she'd be up against. As thin as Shep had gotten, he was still too big for Lina. And given the personal nature of his care, Rhys thought a man would be more appropriate.

"Mr. Shepard, the doctor will see you and your sister now." The nurse stood in the doorway, waiting for Rhys to follow her back to a cheery office cluttered with family photos and framed certificates. He took a seat in one of the two upholstered chairs facing the doctor's desk, and Lina took the other.

"Where's my dad?" Rhys asked the nurse.

"One of the assistants is helping him get dressed," she said. "Dr. Singh thought it would be good for the three of you to have a few minutes alone."

"Hello, Mr. Shepard, Miss Shepard." Dr. Singh brushed into the room, looking well-scrubbed in a navy blue pantsuit.

Rhys stood up, shook her hand, and waited for her to sit before taking his chair again. "He's getting worse, isn't he?"

She nodded. "The disease is progressing, Mr. Shepard. Although his symptoms may continue to come and go intermittently, as his brain degenerates, his faculties will start to decline."

Rhys kept his eyes locked on the back wall where a poster hung of an elderly couple sitting in a cornfield. Something about the starkness of the image resonated with him. He exhaled. "How long?"

"Stages of Alzheimer's often overlap, so it's difficult to say for sure." She modulated her voice in what Rhys assumed was meant to be soothing. "During his visit today your father seemed clearheaded. But given the problems you've described—his trouble distinguishing familiar faces, his behavioral changes, and his inability to complete easy tasks—I'd say he's experiencing severe cognitive decline."

Rhys's eyes flicked from the poster to the doctor. "What does that mean?"

"In my opinion, he's likely entering the later stages of Alzheimer's."

He'd already deduced that. What he wanted, what he drove nearly three hours for was so that Lina could hear it. "Is there anything to slow it down?"

"I can prescribe Razadyne and Namenda to help lessen your father's memory loss and his confusion. But it would only be temporary. I'm afraid there is no cure for Alzheimer's, Mr. Shepard."

Rhys knew there was no cure, but he'd hoped—for Lina and Sam's sake—there was something that could give Shep a little more time. "Can we still keep him at home?" Without even looking, he could feel Lina tense.

"Temporarily, yes. But eventually, he'll require intensive round-the-clock care. At that point you'll want to consider a residential facility." She reached into her bottom desk drawer and handed Rhys a packet of pamphlets. "I know that you've had some time to prepare for this. But it's still a lot to digest."

"Lina," Rhys said. "Do you have any questions for Dr. Singh?" He needed her to understand what they were in for.

"No," she said, her voice breaking.

The doctor scribbled on a prescription pad, ripped off the slip, and handed it to him. "Let me get your father."

On the drive home, somewhere between Lincoln and Auburn, Shep casually announced, "So, I'm losing my marbles?"

"Yep." Rhys kept his eyes on the road.

"You putting me in a home?"

"No, Papa."

"Good girl," Shep said and Rhys wanted to kill the self-centered bastard. "You gonna marry Martha?"

"You mean Maddy?"

"Yeah, Maddy," Shep said.

"You got your seat belt on?" Rhys did a quick check. "Why the hell did you take it off?"

"The damn thing strangles me."

"Well, put it back on. Haven't you seen the signs? 'Click it or ticket.'"

Shep struggled with the belt for a few seconds and finally got it fastened. "I like her, Rhys. She's good for you."

No. The woman was not good for him. Every time he thought about her in those ass-hugging jeans at the Nugget Feed Store he got a painful hard-on. But mostly it was the way she'd inserted herself into his life that was wreaking havoc on his head. Teaching Lina to drive. Helping with Shep. Offering endless advice.

He'd been taking care of himself since he was old enough to walk. Since his mother had left. And he'd learned the hard way that it never paid to become reliant on anyone else. Especially not Maddy. Because she was so filled with life and kindness that he'd lose himself in her.

"We've been over this before," Rhys said. "She's married."

"Bah!" Shep blurted.

Rhys narrowed his eyes. "Mind your own business, old man."

"I think she likes you." Lina surprised him by chiming in. Usually, she gave him a wide berth.

"Well, maybe I'll send her a note at recess and find out," Rhys said, and Lina poked him through the back of his seat.

"I can't imagine why she would like a *pendejo* like you. But there is no accounting for taste."

"A jerk? You think I'm a jerk?" He watched her in his rearview mirror while grabbing his heart. "That really hurts my feelings, Lina."

She giggled, reminding Rhys that the very capable young woman sitting behind him was still a teenager. Wrapped up in his own problems, he'd sort of taken for granted all the tasks—cleaning, laundry, cooking—she did around the house, including caring for Shep. She was too young to have so many responsibilities.

They drove the next hour in silence, Rhys lost in the quandary of what to do with his three wards come April. He could send Lina to college in the fall and she could live on campus. A girl with her smarts should have every opportunity. Sam was the real dilemma. Worse came to worst, he'd take the kid with him to Houston. Not optimal. But what choice did he have?

For Shep, it was just a matter of finding the right assisted-care facility. Despite Lina's argument to the contrary, it was the practical and prudent way to go.

"You okay back there?" Rhys took another glance in the rearview and saw Lina playing *Angry Birds* on her phone.

"Yes. Is Papa asleep?"

Rhys looked over at Shep. "Yeah." Nowadays he was always asleep. And in a few months, he wouldn't know a nursing home from his apartment.

Chapter 15

Maddy crossed the square from her office to the sporting goods store. It wouldn't hurt to do a little lobbying, maybe buy a big-ticket item to butter up Carl Rudd, the owner. With only a few days until Christmas, last-minute shoppers jammed the store. Lots of snowshoes, skies, and sleds moving.

"Hey, Maddy," Carl greeted her with a big smile. The nice thing about the "Flush the Lumber Baron" campaign is that it had elevated her status in the town from nonentity to everyone's favorite antichrist.

"Carl, I'm thinking of getting a bike. What would you recommend for around here?"

"That depends. You want it for mountain biking, for road, or a little of both?"

"I want it so that when I pedal it, it goes," Maddy said, and Carl chuckled.

"Not much of a cyclist, huh?"

"What gave it away? But, seriously, I thought in summer, when the inn's full of guests, they'll be needing lots and lots of sporting equipment. And since I'll be sending them over here, I really should set a good example by being a little more athletic. Don't you think?"

"Ah, Maddy, all that charm won't keep my toilets from overflowing." He draped his arm over her shoulder good-naturedly and directed her to the bicycle aisle. "I think a gently used street bike is your best bet." Carl turned to one of the sales boys. "Chris, you mind helping Maddy here?"

Chris trotted over and Carl pointed out a few bikes for him to show her. "You're in good hands."

"Hey Carl, do you really believe that our tiny inn's enough to overtax Nugget's entire waste system?" Maddy folded her arms over her chest.

"What I think, is that system is old. And if it means blocking new businesses to finally get the city to fix it, then I'm all for it."

"So, you'd put us out on the street just to make a political statement?"

"Oh, Maddy, when you say it that way, it sounds so harsh."

She plastered on a saccharine smile and flipped him the bird. Then she bought a beach cruiser.

When Maddy got home, she found Rhys tugging a couple of shopping bags out of his truck.

"Need help with that?" she asked as she popped her wagon's liftgate.

"Nah, I've got it. What do you have back there?" He stopped to look inside her Subaru and admired her bike.

"I bought it on impulse," she volunteered.

Rhys put his bags down on the tailgate of his truck and pulled out the bicycle. "Nice," he said about the white wicker basket, and smirked.

"I like it." She planted her hands on her hips. "And that's what counts."

He tried to wiggle the basket, but it fit snugly. "Girly. But utilitarian."

"That's me."

He let his eyes drift over her in a way that made Maddy feel warm all over, even though it was about eighteen degrees out.

"Would you mind if I stored it in the shed?" she asked him.

"Not at all." He wheeled it over to the detached garage and gave the door a forceful pull. "We don't usually keep it locked, but I'll get a padlock at the hardware store tomorrow and give you a key."

"I can get it," she said. "I don't want to put you to any trouble."

"No trouble." He went back to wedging the bike in between a couple of ancient power tools.

Maddy looked over at his collection of Target bags. "Been doing a little Christmas shopping, eh?"

"Yep. Went to Reno." He came out of the garage and pulled the door back down.

"What you get?" Apparently, Grinch Boy had changed his stance on not celebrating Christmas.

He shrugged, "Just a few things for Lina and Sam. I took to heart what you said about this being their first holiday without their mother. I got something for Clay's kids, too."

"Ah, that's so nice. What did you get your dad?"

"Nothing." He stuck his hands into his pants pockets. His nose was red and Maddy could see his breath.

"Nothing?"

"We don't get each other presents."

"Not even when you were a kid?"

"Nope."

"Seriously? You didn't get anything?"

"It's no big deal, Maddy." He turned away from her and walked toward his truck where he'd left the bags.

Well, she'd gotten Rhys something—whether he wanted it or not.

"It's cold," he said, lugging his packages to the stairs. "You should get inside before you get sick."

She started toward the door when Rhys stopped her. "You going to France?"

"Huh?"

"With Dave?"

"Of course not. I told you I wasn't going." Why the hell would she go anywhere with Dave?

"How come?"

"Uh, let's see: Because my ex is a man whore, who I'm in the midst of divorcing. Why in the world would you even need to ask?"

Rhys shrugged. "I figured you'd want to try to work things out with him."

"Well, you figured wrong."

"What are you doing for Christmas, then? Because you're welcome to come with us to the McCreedys'."

"I've been invited to Sophie and Mariah's, but thank you."

"Yep," he said, carrying his bags to the fifth wheel. "I guess I'll see you around."

"Rhys," she called. "You want to get together after you get back from Clay's?"

"Uh . . . Sure."

"Great." Maddy opened her door. "We can have a drink." Or whatever.

She told herself that they may as well enjoy each other's company until he went back to Houston. But if she really wanted to be honest with herself she was crushing on him hard, and the prospect of him moving away made her want to vomit.

On the other hand, it was an excellent reminder that men always left when there was something better dangling in front of them.

Chapter 16

Christmas morning, Maddy spent much of the day lounging in her pajamas, talking to her family in Wisconsin, and opening presents. From Dave she'd gotten a bottle of French perfume and a ridiculously expensive pair of diamond studs that screamed guilt gift. She'd gotten him nothing.

They'd talked earlier by phone; him mostly begging for her to take him back, her mostly screaming at him to sign the goddamn divorce papers. He'd made it obvious that he thought she was only going through the motions to scare him and that he still hoped to win her back. Hence, the over-the-top gifts. But no amount of material things would change her mind.

It had dawned on her recently that she missed the familiarity of Dave more than she actually missed his companionship. Even before she'd learned of his affair, they'd seemed to have less and less to talk to each other about. She had to take some responsibility for that. Because, let's face it, spending most of her days getting mani-pedis, shopping, and working on their house didn't exactly add to her repertoire of scintillating conversation topics.

Since the move to Nugget, he seemed to sense the monumental changes in her, and his panic had become palpable. Maybe her new-found independence had suddenly made her seem more attractive to him. She didn't know. And more important, she didn't care.

She slept on and off, curling up with the books Virgil had lent her. When evening fell, Maddy slipped into a sparkly blouse and a pair of black velvet cigarette pants and carefully applied her makeup before heading off to Sophie and Mariah's for Christmas dinner.

Once she got there, the night had seemed somewhat stilted, devoid of the usual festiveness of one of their affairs. Maddy suspected that it was because her friends still hadn't decided on a donor. Lithuanian Man, despite his love for Maroon Five, was still the frontrunner. But Sophie and Mariah couldn't seem to pull the trigger, signaling to Maddy that Nate had been right. There was trouble in paradise.

Maddy stayed through dessert, then begged off early. Even though she knew they'd never see her that way, her new single status made her feel like an interloper.

For the last five years she'd spent Christmas with Dave. And despite everything he'd done, they'd made good memories together. What do you do with those recollections, she wondered; neatly pack them away in a closet? Eventually, yes, Maddy supposed. But for now, those moments seemed too sacrosanct to suddenly start new ones. Next year, she promised herself.

Back at home, she dragged Rhys's surprise onto the porch and tied it with a big red bow. At one point, she'd nearly brought it back inside the house to save for another time, fearing that Rhys would find the gift presumptuous. Especially now that she knew he and his father didn't exchange Christmas presents. But she'd been planning this ever since Rhys had talked about feeling out of place in Nugget. So she left it on the porch and waited.

Finally, at about nine o'clock, she heard his footsteps climbing up the stairs, and the scraping of Shep's shoes. She ran to the front window and pressed her face against the glass. But the angle was wrong and she cursed herself for not planning better. She dashed to the bathroom to check her hair, ran back to the living room, and marked time on the couch, gazing into the lights on her tiny tree.

The knock came about fifteen minutes later. She opened the door and there he stood, gorgeous, in a forest green field coat with snowflakes frosting his hair.

He crushed her in a warm embrace and whispered, "Thank you."

"Do you like it?"

He lifted her chin and softly pressed his lips to hers. "Yeah," he said into her mouth and she realized that he was a little choked up.

With Maddy's input, Colin had designed and crafted the rocking chair especially for Rhys. But the inscription engraved on the headrest—*Here's To Finding Home*—had been all her idea.

When she saw that he was still halfway outside, she pulled him over the threshold and shut the door. "Thanks for being such a wonderful friend to me, even if you were sort of a dick about that whole Addison deal."

"A dick?" he said with affected outrage. "I'm the law, sugar."

She let her eyes roam over him. "I'm gonna let the sugar thing slide, since it's Christmas. You want beer, wine, tea, hot apple cider?"

"Cider sounds nice." He followed her into the kitchen and watched her prepare a pouch of mulling spices. "I got you something, too."

"You did not. What is it?"

He grinned. "It's in the trailer, be right back."

She fixed them each a mug, brought it out on a tray, and placed it down on the coffee table. When he came back in, she didn't see a package on him. He caught her looking and patted his pocket.

"Good things come to those who wait," he said, taking in her outfit. "You look great."

"Thanks. Just wanted to be festive . . . you know . . . for Sophie and Mariah's thing. Did you have a nice time at Clay's?"

"Yeah. How 'bout you?" He sat down next to her on the sofa and took a sip of the cider.

"Mm hmm. I could reheat that," she offered.

"The cider's good, plenty warm. What did y'all have for dinner?"

"Oh, you know, the usual. How about you guys?"

"Clay made prime rib," he said. "I did all the sides."

"Get out. You cook?"

"Restaurant quality, sugar."

She laughed. "I had no idea you cooked."

"I do a lot of things, Maddy." He looked at her in a way that made his meaning clear. "I've got leftovers in the fridge if you want to see for yourself."

"I'm fine. Maybe tomorrow if there's any left." She shifted on the couch to better face him. "Did the kids like their gifts?"

"Oh, yeah. Although I probably should've gotten Clay an Xbox, too. He's gonna hog the thing."

"You got them an Xbox? Pretty big ticket, don't you think?" Oh, she wished she'd been there to see the expression on Rhys's face when the kids opened his presents. "What you get Lina and Sam?"

"Nothing too exciting." He smirked, and Maddy sincerely hoped he was lying. Not cool to give your nonrelatives better gifts than your siblings.

"Did they have a good time?"

"Sam did. Lina . . ." He shrugged. "She's pretty unhappy with me these days."

"Why's that?"

"You really are quite nosey."

"I am not. Why's she unhappy with you?"

"Pushy, too." Rhys stretched out on the couch. "We're in a disagreement over Shep's care. She wants to keep him home indefinitely. When the time comes, I want to put him in an assisted-care facility with professionals."

"So you can go back to Houston?" she asked.

"Because it's the right thing to do. But I'm sure that's what Lina thinks."

"Can I make a suggestion?"

"Can I stop you?" He grinned at her, and despite the gravity of their conversation she really, really wanted to make out with him. Did that make her a bad person?

"You could hire in-home professionals," she said. "That's what we did with my grandmother. Costwise, it works out to be the same as a good rest home."

"And where would I put them, Maddy?"

"They can move into my side of the duplex as soon as the innkeeper's quarters are completed," she offered, knowing that it was the perfect solution. "I could definitely get the guys to speed that up."

"You're not moving into the Lumber Baron until I nab the meth-heads who stowed their stash in your basement." He put his hand on her knee and left it there.

Ordinarily his high-handedness would've put her on the defensive, but she was too distracted by what his hand was doing. Or more accurately what it wasn't doing. She scooted closer to him on the couch and touched his hand. He moved closer and looked at her. Really looked.

"What do you want to do, Mad?" His eyes lowered to her lips. When she didn't say anything, he reached over and kissed her.

She whimpered into his mouth.

"You like that?" He lowered her onto her back, leaned over her, brushing his lips against her throat. "Mmm, you smell nice."

She had a momentary twinge of guilt. Dave's French perfume, which she'd generously dabbed on her pressure points, was what smelled so good. But when she felt Rhys's weight settle on her, all thoughts of Dave evaporated.

He still had the field coat on and Maddy pushed it open with her hands. Rhys leaned up on one elbow and managed to shrug it off with amazing dexterity. Then he began unbuttoning her blouse, trailing kisses across her neck and swirling his tongue around her ear.

"Mmm," she moaned.

Encouraged, he worked his way back down to her lips and explored the inside of her mouth with his tongue. God, this man could kiss. He tasted like apples, cinnamon, and cloves, and she couldn't get enough of him. She grabbed him around the neck and pulled him closer so they could take the kiss deeper, more intense.

He shuddered as she ran her hands over his arms and chest and down his belly. Maddy wanted to feel his skin, but before she could get his shirt off, Rhys pressed his erection against her. She spread her legs for him as he rocked into her.

The friction made her crazy, so she grabbed his perfect backside and held it firmly against her, pushing her pelvis into his hardness until she felt ready to explode. "Oh, God."

He was devouring her again with his mouth. Or maybe he'd never stopped. But now the kiss felt hungrier, more frenzied, almost desperate. Rhys went back to her shirt, opening the last of her buttons and spreading it open. He lifted up on his elbows so he could gaze down at her breasts.

"So beautiful." With a finger he traced the lace of her bra, dipped his mouth down and gently tugged the cups with his teeth. He pushed her breasts together with his big hands so he could take both nipples in his mouth at once, sucking and laving them with his tongue until they ached.

"Oh, Jesus. I want you, baby." He reached for the waistband of her pants, let his fingers dip into her panties, and within seconds was pulling down her zipper. And just like that his hands went completely limp. "You hear that?"

"What? No. Don't stop."

He forced himself to sit up, straddling her with his knees, and pressed his ear to the wall.

"Let's go in the bedroom?" Maddy pleaded, barely able to breathe.

Rhys shut his eyes. "Shep's awake."

Maddy reached up and tried to pull him back down.

"We've gotta quit, sugar."

She wanted to scream. "Why? Lina's in there."

Rhys pulled her up and into his arms and cuddled her close, kissing her hair. "I'm sorry . . . He's having night issues. Bathroom stuff that Lina can't handle. In a minute she'll be banging on the trailer, looking for me." He let out a deep sigh and stood up. Scooping his jacket off the floor, he reached inside the pocket for a small, prettily wrapped box. "I need a second." He looked down at his crotch and shook his head.

Putting on his jacket, Rhys took a few minutes to catch his breath and walked over to Maddy's little Christmas tree. "What's this?" He held up the velvet box containing Dave's diamond earrings.

Before she could respond, he flipped the lid up and Maddy saw his face instantly deflate.

"From Dave?" He tried to act indifferent, but she could tell he was angry.

She nodded, silently cursing herself for leaving the stupid box in plain view.

"Nice." He put the earrings back under the tree. "See you around."

"Rhys—"

He walked out before she could form a coherent sentence, tossing the small parcel he'd been holding into the trash can with her wet umbrella. Once she heard his screen door close, Maddy fished out the package, tore off the wrapping paper and opened the plain white box to find a silver locket. Nestled inside the pendant was a tiny picture of the Lumber Baron.

She touched the photograph with her fingertip, then went into the bedroom, where Maddy used the dresser mirror to clasp the necklace around her neck. Dave's earrings she shoved to the back of her underwear drawer, next to her wedding ring.

Before Rhys left for work he took another look at Maddy's rocker in the light. The chair was beautifully rustic, made from honeyed lodgepole pine. While most of Colin's chairs were chunky, this one had a refined quality. Instead of using rounded logs, Colin had built the chair with flat wooden slats. It could be something that might be handed down from generation to generation.

Women had gotten him gifts before. Shirts. Cologne. CDs. An occasional tie. But nothing like this. He ran his hand over the inscription. Last night he'd gotten caught up in the moment, thinking that maybe he and Maddy could have something. Then Dave's diamonds shocked him back to his senses like a bucket of ice water being dumped over his head.

But he'd always treasure the chair.

His cell phone rang and Rhys answered it, glad for the distraction. "What's up?" He climbed into his truck.

"Chief, Jake just responded to a two-eleven at the Nugget Market. Suspect got away."

Shit! Robberies didn't happen in Nugget. "Anyone hurt?"

"No. The checker's a little flipped out. He's just some kid who helps out on weekends and holidays. Jake's there now."

"Okay, Connie. I'm on my way." Rhys jumped in his truck and turned on his portable siren.

Jake had the department rig. But Rhys had managed to find two seized all-wheel vehicles that were practically new. They were due in any day now. If the weather forecast for the week turned out to be right, they'd need those trucks.

By the time he pulled into the market's parking lot, a small group of residents had assembled. Rhys could tell from their animated body language that they were discussing the robbery.

"Hey, Chief," one of the old-timers in the group called out to him.

Rhys waved, noticed the "Flush the Lumber Baron" banner hanging over the store, shook his head, and went inside. Jake was talking to a teenager, scribbling down notes in a steno pad. The boy must be the cashier, Rhys thought, putting his age somewhere between fifteen and seventeen. The owners of the Nugget Market stood off to the side.

"Ethel. Stu." He tipped his head. "You have an office in the back, somewhere we can talk?"

Stu nodded and led them behind the deli counter to a small room with a desk and a chair, but not much else. Ethel shut the door.

"Were the both of you here at the time of the robbery?" Rhys asked.

"Ethel was home. I was in the back, breaking down boxes. Jesus, in all the time we've been here nothing like this has ever happened. Thank God, no one was hurt. But that dirtbag got the entire till—more than five grand. Being that yesterday was Christmas, we didn't make our usual bank run."

"You got insurance?" Rhys asked.

Stu nodded. "Not sure if it covers holdups, though."

"Show me where you were breaking down those boxes."

Stu directed him to a refrigerated storage room separated from the market by a set of swinging doors. Rhys peered through the doors' two oval-shaped glass windows. The meat counter blocked his view of the rest of the store. "What did you see?"

"Not a damn thing. Didn't even know anything was wrong until I heard one of the customers yelling to call 9-1-1."

"You have any security cameras in or out of the store?"

"Nah." Stu played with the string on his butcher apron. "Occasionally, one of the high school kids will lift a pack of cigarettes or a candy bar. Hardly worth the expense of a security system."

"You notice anyone suspicious in the store during the last couple of days . . . Someone you didn't recognize, who looking back on it might've been casing the place?"

"No." Stu shrugged.

Rhys looked at Ethel, who shook her head.

"We've been awful busy these last couple of days with the holidays and all," she said. "Even if someone came in, we might not have paid attention."

Rhys addressed both of them, "I'd appreciate it if you didn't tell anyone how much money got stolen. I'd like you to ask the other employees to also keep it under their hats."

"Even the insurance company?" Stu asked.

"You can tell them," Rhys said. "It would just be better not to publicize how much money you keep on hand."

"That's not our typical—"

Rhys held up his hand. "I get it, Stu. But we don't want any potential robbers out there thinking the Nugget Market is Fort Knox."

"Oh, God, you don't think he'll come back?" Ethel asked.

"I don't. But for the next couple of weeks one of us will drop by every couple of hours. In the meantime, anyone seem suspicious, you call it in. Okay?"

"Yes, Chief," both Stu and Ethel said together.

He wished he could say something more hopeful, but he didn't want to make any promises he couldn't keep. By now the robber could be in Nevada, playing blackjack with their hard-earned cash. When Rhys walked back to the front of the store Jake stood waiting for him.

"You get a description from the kid?"

"Male. Caucasian. Average height. Slight build. He wore a hood and sunglasses." Jake lowered his voice. "But the checker saw a scorpion tattoo on the back of his left hand. He also thought the suspect might be on something—seemed twitchy."

Rhys brightened at the mention of the tattoo. "A scorpion, huh?"

"Yeah, I thought you'd like that." Jake smiled. "I'll do some checking with the Department of Corrections, the sheriff, and neighboring departments. See if we can find the owner of that scorpion."

"He have a gun?"

Jake looked over at the boy, who was now being consoled by Ethel. "The kid says yes. But when I pressed him, he acknowledged that the guy had his hand in the pocket of his hoodie the whole time. Might've been a pistol. Might've been his fingers."

"No car description or license plate number?" Rhys asked.

"Actually, Chief, he's sitting right outside all wrapped up for you in a big Christmas bow."

Rhys stifled a grin. "Hope you like the graveyard shift, Stryker."

A crowd milled outside while Rhys and Jake finished collecting evidence. News of the robbery spread faster than a brushfire, and residents wanted a first-hand account. So half the town showed up to buy milk.

Rhys got in his truck and headed to the office. As soon as he parked, his cell phone pinged, signaling a text message. He grabbed the phone from the console and wondered what kind of trouble Shep was getting himself into now. But the text wasn't from Lina.

Thank you for the locket. Love it! Wearing it now. How did you get the picture of the inn so teeny?

Rhys hit the delete button and stuck the phone in his back pocket. The locket was a joke compared to Dave's earrings. What the hell had he been thinking, giving her a cheap trinket like that? That was his problem, he hadn't been thinking. At least not with his big head.

Now he felt inferior, which he knew was stupid. Even childish. But he could chalk up his general feelings of inadequacy to the lingering effects of this town. Everything about Nugget made him feel low. Even his next-door neighbor's soon-to-be ex, who didn't even live here.

The last thing he needed to do was stick around and watch Maddy get back with her husband. Because Diamond Dave was doing everything in his power to close the deal. When that happened, they'd probably live part-time in Nugget so Maddy could oversee the inn.

That's why Rhys needed to get the hell out.

Chapter 17

During the next few days, Rhys watched as word of the robbery had folks cleaning their guns.

He knew Trevor Thurston opened the Bun Boy packing heat. That Portia Cane kept a Smith & Wesson behind her counter at the tour kiosk and hung a caution sign decreeing, "We don't dial 9-1-1."

Some of the residents had gone so far as mounting loaded hunting rifles in the cabs of their pickups. Even Tater, Nugget's mild-mannered chef, had taken to wearing a nine-inch bowie knife in a sheath dangling from his belt.

Not happy about the direction this was moving in, Rhys asked Mayor Caruthers to call a town meeting.

By six p.m. the auditorium at Nugget City Hall was standing room only. For the occasion, he'd donned the chief's uniform and couldn't wait to get the damned thing off.

Across the room he saw Maddy sitting with Pam, Amanda, Grace, Mariah, and Sophie. Their eyes met briefly, but Dink sidled up to him and he broke the contact. He hadn't seen Maddy since Christmas night, and other than her text, they hadn't talked.

The robbery investigation had kept him busy. And the forecast of an upcoming storm had been upgraded to a blizzard. It was scheduled to hit Nugget in the next few days. Rhys figured he'd be busy with car accidents and didn't expect to come up for air anytime soon.

When the audience got settled, the mayor introduced him and to Rhys's surprise, the room broke out in thunderous applause. He climbed the steps to the stage and flicked on the microphone. Ordinarily, he would've just sat on the edge of the platform and spoken in a loud voice. But tonight he needed to be authoritative.

Not folksy.

"What the hell are you people thinking bringing shotguns and pistols to work?" That got the attention of the boisterous crowd. "This isn't the Wild West! This is a town filled with families. Kids!

"Make no mistake about it," he continued angrily, "I find any of you carrying a concealed weapon without a permit . . . I'll throw your ass in jail." Instead of the expected heckling, Rhys got a lot of guilt-stricken faces. Good, because this conduct was unacceptable.

"Okay," he told the audience. "Let me tell you where we're at on this. Detective Stryker . . . Raise your hand, Jake, so everyone in the crowd can see you."

Jake, who stood against the wall in the back of the room, held his arm up.

"In a few minutes here, we'll start passing around copies of a composite sketch of our suspect. Detective Stryker is running down a number of leads. We can't talk about specifics, because it'll compromise the investigation. But what I can tell you is that our robber left some telltale signs."

"You think he'll be back, Chief?" someone shouted from the back of the room.

"Maybe. But more than likely this was a one-time deal. We have reason to believe the suspect was a drug user—someone just passing through and desperate. That doesn't mean you shouldn't be alert and on your guard. And when you see something suspicious, call us. Let us do our job."

Owen rose from his seat. "Is there any chance there's a connection between the robbery at the market and the drug lab found in the Lumber Baron?"

"Any kind of abandoned building is a magnet for homeless people, druggies, and criminals." Rhys stopped for a second. "Is the drug operation in the basement of the Lumber Baron somehow linked to the robbery at the Nugget Market? Too soon to tell. But as the police chief responsible for the safety of this town I can sure tell you I'm relieved that the Lumber Baron's no longer vacant."

He took advantage of the question to press an important point. "Ms. Breyer has informally been trying to establish some sort of business association. I say take it a step further: Fix up downtown and organize a neighborhood watch." He stopped himself. "That does not mean strapping on a bandolier."

There were some chuckles from the crowd.

"What would a neighborhood watch entail?" Pam asked.

"You've already conquered half the battle by stepping up the police presence in downtown by hiring your own force and reopening the station on the square." Rhys thought his statement might sound a bit self-serving, but he knew from experience it was the truth. "The next thing I'd suggest is getting the streetlights fixed. I haven't seen them working since I got here. Not only is it dangerous, but it tells criminals that no one's minding the store."

Feeling more at ease, Rhys sat on the edge of the stage. "I'd put a little pride of ownership into this place. It's no secret that boarded-up storefronts are an invitation to crooks."

A number of heads turned sharply to the owner of the Bun Boy.

"Can't you get those rented out, Trevor?" Pam demanded.

"Why don't you lease one, Pam?" Trevor bit back.

Rhys held up his palm to the crowd. "We're not going to get anywhere pointing fingers and shouting at each other. What's the problem, Trevor? Maybe we can come together as a community and solve it."

"We're in a damn recession. That's the problem. No one's looking to rent space in this economy. You think I like having half my income boarded up?"

"I hear you, Trevor. And I think everyone is sympathetic," Rhys said. "I'm just throwing this out as a suggestion. What if the town came together . . . maybe threw a little paint on those properties . . . did a little housecleaning? In return, whoever needed some extra space could borrow it until you get it leased. That way it doesn't sit empty, attracting a criminal element. And in the meantime, a prospective renter sees a well-kept building and a thriving business."

"I might be willing," Trevor said. "Whoever wanted to use it would have to pay for any painting supplies or whatnot. I'm not running a charity."

Carl, of the sporting goods store, said, "I might be interested. I've been toying with the idea of doing some seasonal displays—just don't have the room."

"Me, too," Pam said. "My clients have been asking me about yoga clothes, mats, ballet costumes, and shoes for the little ones." A number of women nodded their heads in agreement. "But my studio's packed. I don't even have space to sell protein bars and powders. I'd love the chance to try it out and see how it goes without having to shell out a second rent. But Trevor, if I find that business is good, I'd take out a lease."

"Sounds good," Trevor said. "Anyone interested can talk to me after the meeting."

Mariah tentatively raised her hand, reminding Rhys of a schoolgirl, which made him grin. He bobbed his head at her to go on.

"I'm actually a decent gardener," she said. "When spring comes, I'd be happy to plant flowers in the strips along the sidewalks. Maybe I can persuade Colin to build a few window boxes and planters."

Several people murmured their approval.

Maddy was next to raise her hand. "What if we organized a spring cleaning for the square—say the first weekend in April—after the snow thaws? We could make a party of it. The Baker's Dozen could bring snacks and the Lumber Baron, if we're still around then," she looked around the room meaningfully, "will spring for the supplies, paint, whatever."

More murmurs of approval, so Maddy continued, "And if Stu and Ethel need help in the store until they're caught up financially, or just so they feel more secure having extra people around, I'd be happy to volunteer. I could stock shelves, work the cash register."

"I think we're off to a good start," Rhys said, hoping he didn't sound as exhausted as he felt.

"Later this week I'll come by your shops with some neighborhood watch signs to hang in the windows. In the meantime, keep your eyes open, keep your ears to the ground, and keep your guns at home."

New Year's Eve Rhys took Shep and the kids to the Ponderosa. Not the way he normally would've rung in the New Year, but Clay had his kids and Rhys was avoiding Maddy. She'd been so preoccupied with the Addisons' petition that she probably hadn't even noticed his herculean efforts to duck her.

He'd been thinking about her more than he should and wanted to put a bullet in any romantic notions either one of them might have. She was married, he was leaving. End of story.

So here he was with his mentally deficient father and the two urchins. Good times!

Of course, the minute they walked into the restaurant, Shep started complaining. "It's like the holidays threw up in here."

Sophie and Mariah had hung black and silver streamers and balloons from the ceiling and a giant Mylar "Happy New Year" banner over the bar. They were handing out hats, party blowers, and noisemakers. At least Lina and Sam seemed taken with all the revelry.

"Hi, Chief," Sophie said, and escorted them to a roomy booth. Despite himself, he wondered if Maddy would come in to celebrate with the Ponderosa owners.

As soon as they were seated, he noticed Jake and two of his daughters sitting at a booth at the far end of the dining room. The girls, Jake's from his third wife, were up from Los Angeles for the weekend. Rhys watched Stryker hang on their every word, which made him grin.

"Why'd you pick this place, boy? We're always coming here."

Rhys glared at his father. "Because I like it." Also, it was the only sit-down restaurant in town. He winked at Sam, pointed at the menu the boy studied with such intensity that it made Rhys want to laugh, and asked, "What looks good?"

"I don't know. What should I get, Lina?"

Lina continued to examine the specials.

"I'm going for the pork chop and mashed potatoes," Rhys announced, hoping to break the ice. "Pop?"

"How the hell should I know? There's too much on this damn menu and none of it's any good. We should've gone to that steak house in Reno."

Rhys held back his temper. "Pop, they've got five different steaks. Pick one, or I'll pick one for you."

When the server came everyone ordered, except Shep, who sat with his arms folded across his chest and a mean scowl across his face.

Rhys rolled his eyes. "He'll have the porterhouse with the baked potato." He looked over at Sam again. "Good choice on the burger."

Across the room, Jake paid his bill, draped an arm around each daughter, and left. Rhys noticed Lina watching them closely and couldn't help but feel a pang of sympathy.

As they tucked into their dinners about a half-dozen diners trickled by to say hello and to thank Rhys for rebuilding the police department. Nice to know he was making a difference. At Houston PD he rarely got to hear from the public, unless the department made the news for screwing up.

"Hey, Chief." One of the diners waved.

"How you doing?" He waved back, then looked at Lina and Sam. "I have no idea who that was."

They laughed. "But everybody knows you," Sam said, clearly impressed.

When the four of them finished their meals, Rhys insisted on dessert. Sam wanted an ice cream sundae, Lina chocolate cake, and for his father and himself, Rhys ordered two slices of apple pie à la mode.

"What do you say we do a little bowling?" he asked the kids.

"We don't know how," Sam said.

Rhys looked over at his father, who'd wolfed down the pie. Miracle of miracles, Shep had actually found something to like. "Shep'll show you. He's a champion bowler, aren't you, Pop?"

Everyone seemed surprised when Shep nodded his head in agreement. "Was on a league . . . long before those two lesbos ruined the place." He pointed at Mariah who was drying and putting away glasses behind the bar.

Rhys smacked his hand down on the table. "That's enough." He didn't bother to point out that before Mariah and Sophie took over, the bowling alley had been on its last legs.

Instead, Rhys turned his attention to Lina, who'd become very quiet. "Something wrong?" he asked her.

Lina shook her head, barely meeting his eyes. "No."

"Come on. Let's bowl." Rhys paid the bill and the four of them found an available lane where they sat on wooden benches, pulling off their boots and sneakers and lacing up their rented bowling shoes. Sam watched intently as a family next to them took turns trying to knock down all ten pins.

Rhys showed him how to hold the ball and the right way to deliver it down the lane. The first time Sam gave it a whirl, the ball went straight, but veered into the gutter about thirty feet down, missing the entire row of pins.

Lina laughed. "Let me try." She had slightly more success, knocking down two pins with her first roll.

Rhys watched them play a few frames, enjoying their enthusiasm for the game. Shep fell asleep, his head lolling on Rhys's shoulder, his snores keeping rhythm to the crashing of pins.

Sandy Addison strode over from one of the lanes farther down the alley. Rhys had seen her and Cal bowling earlier and had hoped to avoid them. Out of courtesy, he gently propped Shep's head against the bench so he could get up and say hello.

"You work for the taxpayers, Chief," she fired before Rhys could even shake her hand.

"Pardon me?"

"No one appreciated your blatant lobbying for that Breyer woman at the town meeting the other day. You could lose your job for that."

Lina put down her bowling ball, came over, and flanked Rhys like a body guard.

"My job is to keep the public safe," he said. "Vacant buildings attract crooks—methamphetamine manufacturers. So, yeah, I have a vested interest in seeing the Lumber Baron open."

"It's not your job to advocate. Remember you're the interim chief. And at the rate you're going, very temporary at that." She lumbered off in a huff.

"That woman bugs the shit out of me," Rhys muttered, noticing that like Lina, Sam now bordered his other side.

Sophie watched Sandy and Rhys from the other side of the center, shaking her head. Good for Rhys for standing up to her. Sandy managed to intimidate everyone else in this town.

Donna came up behind her, wearing a "Happy New Year" tiara. "That Addison woman's a stone-cold bitch. She thinks she owns the town, when everyone knows I do."

"Come on, Diva Donna." Sophie grabbed her by the arm. "Let's get drunk."

"Guess you're not preggers yet," Donna muttered as Sophie dragged her to the bar and snagged two empty stools.

Mariah served all three of them Manhattans before getting called away to make a pitcher of margaritas.

"Business is good, girlfriend." Donna glanced around the packed dining room. The bowling alley was just as crowded.

"Yes, it is." Sophie felt good about what she and Mariah had accomplished here. Her fervent wish was for Maddy and Nate to beat this farcical "Flush" campaign and enjoy the same success as the Ponderosa. "Where's Trevor?"

Donna pointed at a corner booth, where the Nugget Mafia played cards. "I'm thinking of becoming a lesbian, too."

Sophie laughed and Donna reached over and patted her tummy. "Where you at on this whole baby thing?"

Sophie blew out an audible breath. "Still zeroing in on the right donor."

"Out of all the choices in that book, you mean to tell me you can't find one?" It seemed that everyone in Nugget knew about the sperm bank catalog.

"Actually," Sophie said. "There is one in there that meets our criteria—smart, successful, healthy, handsome."

"So what's the problem?"

"I don't know," Sophie said. "It doesn't feel right going with someone so unfamiliar, someone with DNA I can't trust."

"You have someone you know in mind?"

Something about Donna made Sophie want to confide, which was nuts, because they'd only recently become friends. And that was mostly due to the fact that they both owned restaurants on the square.

Plus, Donna was a loudmouth, saying whatever was on her mind in all its unvarnished glory. But to reserved people like Sophie and Mariah, she was refreshing. The woman would have absolutely no qualms telling Sophie whether she was being selfish. And that's what Sophie needed to know so she could put this whole thing with Nate to rest.

"Honestly," Sophie said, "yes. But Mariah is against the idea."

"Why? Is this fellow you have in mind a serial killer?"

"He's Nate Breyer, Maddy's brother."

"Oh, honey, you've picked good. He's adorable." Donna stopped herself. "Mariah's not worried that you and he—"

"No, no. It's nothing like that. Mariah fears that unlike with an anonymous donor, who is completely out of the picture, the baby will be more connected to Nate and me. Especially because none of her DNA is involved."

"Well, of course she does," Donna said emphatically. "Nate'll be around all the time, and that'll make Mariah feel like the odd parent out."

Sophie sucked in a breath. "So I'm being unfair by wanting him?" This is exactly what she needed to hear.

"No," Donna said, taking a long sip of her Manhattan. "You're being unfair by making this baby all by yourself. The solution is simple: Nate's sperm, your uterus, Mariah's eggs. Then everyone's got a horse in the race."

Sophie thought about it. Mariah's eggs. They'd always taken for granted that Sophie would be the birth mother. But they'd never stopped to consider that Mariah could be biologically involved without having to actually carry the baby. With in vitro fertilization it was completely possible for them to use her eggs. Just a little more complicated.

It was such an obvious solution that Sophie wondered why they'd never thought about it. As long as Mariah was amenable and everything checked out medically, this could be the answer to their dilemma. "Donna, you're brilliant."

"Of course I am." And modest, too.

"I smell a conspiracy," Mariah said, rejoining them at the bar. "What did I miss?"

"That I'm a genius," Donna said.

Mariah cocked her head in question.

Sophie beamed, looked up at the antique clock hanging over the back bar, and whispered in Mariah's ear, "I'll tell you in the New Year."

Chapter 18

Maddy stood on the porch, moving her feet to keep them from turning into blocks of ice. She wanted to catch a ride with Rhys to the inn because driving in this weather was not for the faint of heart. And walking was definitely out of the question. Mostly, however, she wanted to clear the air with him.

He'd been avoiding her ever since the earring episode, and she missed not having his very broad and muscular shoulder to lean on. But Maddy didn't know how much longer she could stand the cold. Although she'd bundled up, even put on her snow boots, the temperature had dropped into the low teens and the wind whipped so fiercely that it made her face sting.

She was just about to give up, when Rhys came out wearing a knit cap, a ski parka, and gloves, holding a thermos.

"You're gonna freeze out here, Maddy."

"I wanted to see if I could ride in with you." She shivered, watching the trees bend and sway with the wind until they looked ready to snap like twigs.

"Yep." Rhys opened the passenger door for her and lifted her up. Ice covered his windshield, so he turned on the defroster, pulled a scraper from the glove box, and jumped out of the cab.

Maddy opened her door a crack. "Want me to help?"

"Stay in the truck," he grunted.

When he finished the task, he hopped back in and fastened his seat belt, glancing over at Maddy to make sure she'd done the same. Then he turned away before they could make eye contact—just like he'd done at the meeting.

"Everything okay? You seem grouchy this morning," she said.

"Tired. Hungry." She ignored his terse, one-word answers.

"You didn't have time for breakfast?"

"I overslept and have to get in to see if our new trucks arrived. Big storm's due to hit."

"It looks like it's already here, if you ask me." She hadn't seen weather this bad since she'd gotten to Nugget.

"Nope." He tested the back of his hand against the windshield. "It's gonna get a lot worse."

"Well, drop me off at the Ponderosa. I'll get you something to eat and bring it over to the station."

He looked over at her.

"Watch the road," she said.

"Why? Is it doing tricks?"

"You're funny." Maddy snickered. "What do you want? French toast?"

"Nah. I don't want you walking in this."

"Okay. Then we'll go over and eat together." The construction crew could live without her for an hour or so.

He didn't acknowledge her offer, just parked his truck in the spot marked *Chief Shepard*, turned off the engine, and came around to help Maddy out. When they got into the office Jake and Wyatt were drinking coffee and eating egg sandwiches from the Bun Boy.

"They come yet?" Rhys asked.

"Nope," Jake answered.

"Dammit!" Rhys walked across the room to his glass office, sorted through a stack of messages, and picked up the phone.

Jake grabbed a chair from the back and brought it over to Maddy. "Here you go." He hovered over her, smiling, while she sank down and waited for Rhys, who was barking at someone on the other line.

"You waiting for the boss?" Jake asked.

"I'm taking him to breakfast."

"He could probably use a good meal." Jake glanced over at Rhys's office, then back at Maddy. "The robbery's gotten the town jittery. Rhys puts a lot of pressure on himself. He's a top-notch cop, the town's lucky to have him."

Maddy watched Rhys return a few calls and asked Jake, "You think you'll catch him?"

Jake shrugged. "Hard to say. The guy could be clear across the country by now."

Rhys hung up the phone, crumpled a handful of pink callback slips and tossed them in the garbage. After organizing some paperwork, he walked over to where Maddy, Wyatt, and Jake sat talking. "The rigs are supposedly being dropped off this afternoon. I'll be over at the Ponderosa if anyone needs me."

"You ready?" he asked Maddy and she got to her feet.

He helped her into his truck like he always did. The guy had the best manners, or maybe it was a he-man thing like the "sugar" endearment he was so fond of using. Dave was too progressive for that. The only time he used the word "sugar" was as a sweetener. Then, again, Dave was a cheating asshole.

Rhys, for all his swagger, seemed to genuinely respect everything about Maddy—especially how seriously she took her work at the Lumber Baron. He was certainly complimentary enough about it.

They pulled up in front of the Ponderosa and fought against the wind to make their way inside the restaurant. No usual breakfast crowd today. Maddy suspected that everyone had stayed home with the heat cranked up. Mariah stopped arranging bottles behind the bar, waved a greeting, and gestured for them to take the corner booth.

"It's toasty in here." Maddy stripped off her layers, stuffing her hat, scarf, and gloves into the pockets of her coat and hanging it from a hook on the back wall. When she turned around she found Rhys staring at her.

"What?" she asked him.

He shook his head. "Nothing."

She scooted into the booth. Instead of sitting across from her, Rhys took the same bench, his thigh resting next to hers. She grabbed a menu, passed it to him, and took one for herself.

He rubbed the dark stubble that covered his face. "I need to shave."

"You need to eat." Reaching up, she brushed a lock of hair away from his eye. "You look tired, Rhys."

"Frustrated," he muttered, looking around the room for a server. When no one came, he got up, grabbed the coffeepot off the hot plate, and poured both of them a cup.

When a waiter finally moseyed over, Rhys ordered an omelet, bacon, potatoes, and toast. Maddy got a stack of pancakes.

"Thank you for the other night," she said.

He made a *what for?* expression. "We do something I don't know about? You slip me a roofie?"

She laughed. "For plugging the inn at the meeting."

"Oh," he said, faking disappointment. Rhys gulped his coffee too fast and fanned his mouth. "Hot."

"What you said last night might really help the inn, and I appreciate it more than you know," she said. "But your job is political. I don't want you putting your livelihood on the line for me. It's not worth it."

"I didn't do it for you. I did it for the town."

Their food came. Rhys took a bite of his omelet, washed it down with another slug of coffee. "Before you bought the Lumber Baron, it posed a real problem for Nugget. Not only the threat of dope dealers, but the possibility of kids going in there and getting themselves hurt. It was a liability, Maddy."

"But you also took up my cause of starting a business association, when you yourself told me the shopkeepers of Nugget wouldn't buy in."

"Not because I didn't think it was a good idea, just because I didn't think that folks here would like having an outsider telling them how to run their town."

"And you're not an outsider?"

He appeared to contemplate the question while he poured hot sauce on his potatoes. "I used to think I was. Now, I'm not so sure."

She smiled up at his handsome face. "That's good, right?"

He shrugged. "What's good is this robbery has motivated the town to make changes. Hopefully, it'll also change their attitudes toward the inn."

"I'm keeping my fingers crossed, but I don't have high hopes. I counted five new banners yesterday. People are starting to put them on their houses."

"You hear from your expert yet?"

"Any day now. The holidays slowed him down, but hopefully he'll have a good prognosis."

"Well," he said, "if it doesn't work out, you could always hock the earrings. Or go back to Dave."

She narrowed her eyes. "My future with Dave has nothing to do with whether the inn lives or dies."

"But he's a nice little ace in the hole," he said with cruelty.

"Is that what you think . . . that I always have my rich husband to fall back on?" She'd never loved Dave for his money. Maybe, at one time, she'd been reliant on him for her identity, her happiness. But in Nugget, that was all starting to change.

"I don't know. You tell me."

"I can't even believe you'd say something like that." Did this man to whom she'd confided her worst insecurities know so little about her? She climbed over him to get out of the booth and grabbed her coat off the hook. "I have to get to work."

Before she could pull money out of her wallet for the check, Rhys dropped a wad of cash on the table. "I've got it and I'll drive you—it's too cold to walk."

"Not for me." She fled for the door and was outside, halfway down the street, fighting against the gusts, when she heard snow crunching behind her.

"What do you expect me to think, Maddy?" Rhys called to her back. "The guy sends you earrings that cost more than my fucking truck?"

She whirled on him. "I didn't ask him to send them to me. He's trying to make amends for loving someone else. You think I don't know that? I hate them."

"Have you sent them back?" he asked, challengingly.

She looked down at the snowy ground.

"Yeah, that's what I thought," he said. "What's really going on here, Maddy? One minute you say you're divorcing the guy, the next you're accepting his extravagant gifts. Why are you hanging on to him?"

Hanging on to him? That was rich. She'd done everything in her power to lose Dave. What did it matter to Rhys anyway? He was leaving in a few months.

"I'm not hanging on to him," she barked. "There was no way for me to know the gift was extravagant until I opened it. You seriously think I can be bought for a pair of diamond studs?"

Maddy didn't wait for him to answer, just pulled the locket around her neck out from under her layers of clothes to show him. "This is pure and beautiful and means everything to me, but apparently you're as big an idiot as Dave is."

Rhys reached for her and in a voice just loud enough so that she could hear it over the wind, said, "Send the earrings back." And then he kissed her, pressing his lips so softly against hers that the gentleness of it broke her.

Hours later, Maddy tried to pay bills in her makeshift office at the inn. But all the crap in her life was making it difficult to concentrate.

Colin must have sensed her melancholy mood, because he stopped hammering, came down the ladder, and anxiously hovered over her.

"I'm okay, Col." But she knew her eyes were watery and her nose pink.

"You sure?" He timidly grazed her shoulder with his hand and just as quickly withdrew it.

Maddy got the sense that he didn't have much experience with women, though he was quite good-looking. And unbelievably sweet. She sniffled. "Yep. You think we're wasting our time fixing up this old place, Colin?"

"Nah," he said, taking in the room the way an explorer might examine a map. "We're doing a good thing bringing her back."

"Why can't the rest of Nugget see that?"

"They might come around and surprise you," he said.

"How long have you lived here?"

"Not quite two years."

Maddy realized she knew very little about this carpenter who'd poured what seemed like his entire heart into her project. "Where'd you live before?"

He frowned and looked away. "A place I don't like talking about, if you don't mind."

"I'm sorry, Colin. I didn't mean to pry." But of course her mind ran wild. Prison? War? Prisoner of war? She forced herself to stop—the man deserved his privacy—and changed the subject. "I don't know if I told you, but Rhys loved the chair."

"I'm glad," he mumbled, and headed back to the ladder.

"Hey, Colin?"

He lifted his chin.

"The furnishings for the inside of the inn really should be period. But what do you think of your rockers for the porch?"

He stood there for a few seconds as if trying to imagine how his chairs could blend with a Victorian veranda. "It might look okay. I'll work up a couple of designs on paper . . . See what you think."

"Maybe you could—" But before she could say more, a loud banging sound coming from outside made them both jump.

Colin hurriedly followed the direction of the noise, Maddy trailing behind him.

That's when she realized neither of them had on coats. She ran to fetch them, but by the time she returned Colin had already ventured out into the cold. By now a few of the other workers had also come running to seek out the source of the noise.

She shrugged into her coat, layering Colin's on top, and slowly made her way down the porch steps. The snow was coming down pretty hard, so Maddy ran her hands along the siding of the house to find her way. "Colin?" she yelled, but her voice was lost in the din of the wind.

She tripped over something and caught herself before she hit the ground. The frigid air made her face sting, and her hands were so numb she could barely feel her fingers. Colin must be freezing.

"Where did everyone go?" she shouted. And this time was rewarded with a faint response coming from somewhere in the distance.

Farther up, at the back of the house, she caught a glimpse of red—

maybe someone in a bright jacket. But it was getting tougher to see as the snow came down harder and the winds picked up speed.

The storm was just getting started, but Maddy could tell it would be a doozy.

She slowly made her way toward the speck of color, continuing to use the exterior wall of the Victorian as her guide, careful not to slip on black ice.

It took her nearly ten minutes to make the trek. When she finally reached the destination, Maddy found a few members of her construction crew huddled over something.

She pushed her way through the circle and her heart sank. "Oh, no—Colin?" Maddy squatted on the ground next to his prone body.

"He's breathing," one of the workers said as he felt Colin's wrist for a pulse. "But we shouldn't move him."

Someone had covered him with a wool coat and Maddy quickly pulled off Colin's parka so she could drape it over him as well. She worried about him suffering from exposure.

"The fire department's on its way," said the worker, who cautiously ran his hands up and down Colin's back, looking for injuries.

Blood ran from his scalp, through his hair, down his neck, leaving a pool in the snow. It seemed like a lot of bleeding to Maddy.

Next to Colin lay a sturdy tree branch. She looked up to see where it might have fallen from, but was distracted by the same banging noise they'd heard from the house. She whipped her head around to find the culprit—the trapdoor to the basement had come off its hinges, and the wind violently slapped it against the side of the house. The lock Rhys had told her to put on the hatch remained secured.

It seemed like forever, but finally Rhys and three paramedics carrying a stretcher came bounding toward them.

"Step away," one of the firefighters ordered.

She and the workers fanned out, giving the paramedics room to get to Colin so they could staunch his head wound.

Rhys approached Maddy, his gait frantic. "You all right?"

"I'm fine. But Colin—oh, God, Rhys."

He wrapped his arm around her shoulder and pulled her close. She could feel some of his tension drain as soon as he touched her.

"The caller didn't say who was down—just an accident at the Lumber Baron." Rhys exhaled. "What happened?"

"I don't know. We were in the house, heard a noise, Colin came outside to see what it was . . . He must've gotten hit in the head by the branch." She pointed at the tree limb.

Rhys let go of her and walked over to examine the piece of wood. He looked up, and Maddy could tell he was trying to trace the limb's possible trajectory the same way she had. "Did anyone see it hit him?" he asked.

The worker who had checked Colin's pulse stepped up. "By the time we got here Colin was down."

"Is that where y'all found the branch?" Rhys asked.

The guys in the crew mumbled a collective "Yes." The paramedics had lifted Colin onto the gurney and were trying to move him without losing their footing in the snow.

"Is he going to be okay?" Maddy asked.

"Should be, ma'am. His vitals are good. We're transporting him to Plumas District Hospital in case he has a concussion."

"I don't have a car with me. Can I come with you?"

"You his wife? Or a member of the family?"

"I'm his employer." Maddy didn't know Colin's family, but she should probably call someone.

"We can only take immediate family," the paramedic said apologetically.

She didn't want Colin to be alone at the hospital. If she got a ride home, she could get her car. But the thought of driving in this weather scared her to death. And Rhys seemed to have disappeared. He'd been nosing around the trapdoor on the basement just a second ago.

Before she could go looking for him, her contractor called out, "I'll take you, Maddy. Just let me lock up and get the crews out of here." Pat tossed her his keys and told her to wait in his truck with the heat on.

But by the time they made it to State Route 70, the California Highway Patrol turned them back to Nugget. The storm was too bad to make it through the pass. Maddy only prayed that the ambulance would have better luck.

Chapter 19

Not since living in Alaska had Rhys seen weather like this. Twenty-four inches of snow had been dumped on Nugget and most of the Sierra. It was hardly a record, but it had come down so hard and so fast that it had wreaked havoc on the area's infrastructure. The major highways were shut down. The power was out on the south side of town. And someone had knocked Colin Riley over the head.

Rhys was sure of it.

He'd finally been able to reach Colin at the hospital. All Colin could remember was trying to secure the trapdoor. Then boom—lights out. The doctors at District said he had a mild concussion and they wanted to monitor him overnight.

Rhys didn't believe there was any way in hell Colin could've sustained those injuries from a flying branch. Since he'd been standing under the eaves of the Victorian when he got knocked out, it seemed unlikely that the branch could've fallen from above. No, his wound seemed more consistent with someone swinging that branch like a baseball bat.

Someone looking for his stash.

Now, besides dangerous weather and an armed robber, Rhys had to deal with a deranged druggie. He and Jake had processed the scene, questioned witnesses, but no one had seen anything. Tomorrow, he'd start all over again.

"You're getting good at this," he said to Sam. The two of them had camped out on the couch to play a little *NBA 2K13* on the Wii Rhys had bought for Christmas. If only the kid could play this well on the court.

Lina stared out the window, biting her lip.

"It'll be fine," he told her. "Come over here and play basketball with us."

The new rigs had finally come in, and Jake and Wyatt were supposed to drop one off in case he got called out in the middle of the night. He handed Lina the Wii remote control and alternated between checking the dial tone on the phone and the signal on his cell. The cell was dead. But by some miracle the landline was still working. He used that one to dial the station.

"What's up?"

"Not much since the last time you called," Connie chirped into the phone. "What was it? Fifteen minutes ago?" In the short time she'd been working for Rhys, Connie had developed a smart mouth. "We're fine, Chief. Get some rest in case we need you."

"How're those rigs working out?"

She laughed. "Wyatt and Jake are in love. I swear they'd drive them to the bathroom if they could. Last I heard they were on their way to you with one of them. I'll call you if anything comes up."

"See that you do." Rhys hung up and checked on his dad in the bedroom.

Even over the noise of the Wii, he could hear Maddy vacuuming next door. He'd have to deal with her in the morning—tell her his theory about Colin. Now more than ever, he didn't want her going into the Lumber Baron alone.

"Someone's here," Lina said.

Rhys opened the door and Wyatt stood at the threshold with a set of keys while Jake waited in one of the other Chevy Tahoes. "Tell him to come in."

Wyatt bounded down the steps like a puppy, immune to the freezing conditions. Shep padded into the living room, looking annoyed.

"What's with all the racket? You people could wake the dead."

Lina made a place for him on the couch and tucked a lap blanket around him. Rhys rolled his eyes.

"Hey," Jake said, and he and Wyatt came in. Both of them did a quick perusal of the living room, Wyatt fixing on Lina.

He introduced everyone. "Y'all want coffee?"

"Wouldn't mind a cup," Jake said.

Rhys led them through Shep's bedroom to the kitchen. He could only imagine what they must think of the dump. Both sat at the table, while Rhys searched for the filters. The setup was nothing fancy, not like Connie's, just a Mr. Coffee.

Lina came in and nudged him away. Wyatt kept looking at her. Rhys knew all too well what those looks were about. The moron didn't even have the common sense to be sly about it.

"You scored, man." Jake broke the silence. "What were they, drug seizure vehicles?"

"Yup. For a few extra bucks I had 'em pimped out with Data911s." The high-tech computer systems might be overkill for Nugget, but he wanted to bring the department into the twenty-first century.

"They handle beautifully, especially in the snow," Jake said.

"It took some hunting around," Rhys said. "But I'm happy with them."

When the coffee was done, Lina grabbed a few mugs from the cupboard. Wyatt bounded out of his chair so fast, Rhys thought he might hurt himself.

"I'll get that for you, Lina." Wyatt took the creamer from her hand.

"Thank you, sweetheart," Jake said as she handed him one of the cups.

"I could've done that," Rhys glowered, and Lina, embarrassed, excused herself to check on Shep.

As soon as she was out of earshot, Rhys turned on Wyatt. "She's seventeen. Don't look at her, don't stand near her, don't even so much as breathe on her. You hear?"

"Yes, sir." Wyatt let his gaze fall to his shoes.

"Oh, boy." Jake couldn't stop grinning. "Good thing you don't have five daughters."

They finished their coffee and Jake tapped Wyatt on the arm. "Let's go, son."

On his way out, he slapped Rhys on the back. "Cut the kid some slack. She's a pretty girl."

Well, that pretty girl was his goddamn sister.

"It's open," Rhys called.

Maddy let herself inside the fifth wheel and found Rhys laid out in a recliner, eating a frozen dinner, watching the 49ers on a big-screen TV. One of those fan-style space heaters kept the trailer nice and toasty. This was her first visit to Chez Rhys and her mouth must've fallen open because he chuckled, then went back to watching the game. Since Rhys didn't look inclined to leave the comfort of that chair anytime soon, she took the liberty of showing herself around.

"Wow!" she uttered loud enough for Rhys to hear her in the other room. The master bedroom was compact, but plush. "It's like a real house."

She checked out the bathroom, swung through the kitchen, and tested the other recliner.

"Beer's in the fridge," Rhys said, engrossed in the game.

She got to her feet, pulled out a Trumer Pils, twisted off the cap, and snooped inside the cabinets. Melamine dishes, a few mismatched glasses, and a bag of pretzels. Ha, what more did a person need?

Actually, pretzels and beer were the perfect ending to a harrowing twenty-four hours. She'd barely opened her eyes this morning when Colin called. The hospital had released him and he'd needed a ride back to Nugget. So Maddy had jumped into her car and made the trip to Quincy. Thank goodness the roads had been plowed and reopened. She'd dropped him at home before dashing to work.

"You get a lot done at the inn today?" Rhys asked.

"Yes, I did, and I'm pissed at you."

"Huh?" He switched off the game and pulled the recliner upright.

"I heard about your little brouhaha with Sandy Addison at the bowling alley New Year's Eve."

"Brouhaha? Is that like a Wellmont word?"

"Cut the crap, Rhys. Why are you fighting with that woman when she could have your job?"

"It's hers anytime she wants it," he said. "What are you getting yourself all worked up over? You can't stand the woman."

"This is not your fight. Your job is political and she's got a lot of clout in this town."

Rhys pretended to tremble. "She's beary, beary powerful."

Maddy blew beer out her nostrils. "Stop it," she said, doubling over from laughter. "Why didn't you tell me that you had an argument with her?"

"Because it wasn't a big deal. She got in my face, telling me how to run my department. So I got in hers. She can't do anything to me, and even if she could, I don't care. This job is temporary."

"Even so, it's good to have options. What if you decide to stay?"

"I won't," he said. "Now, let's talk about the inn."

"What about it?" She sat back in the recliner.

"Don't go there alone," he said in a voice Maddy had come to recognize as Rhys's cop tone.

"I didn't. We had the whole crew."

"I know," he said. "I cruised by to make sure."

She stared at him, perplexed. "What's going on?"

"I think someone attacked Colin the other day . . . Someone looking for his supply. I wanted to talk to you about it this morning, but you were already gone."

"I had to get Colin and they'd just cleared the roads. I was afraid I wouldn't get back before they got icy again. Oh, Rhys." Maddy covered her mouth with her hand. It had never occurred to her that what had happened to Colin could be anything other than an accident. "What does Colin say about it?"

"Can't remember a thing before falling flat on his face." He turned to look at her. "That's why you living there right now is out of the question."

She stood up on shaky legs.

"Where you going?" Rhys asked.

"I have to call Pat, let him know to warn the crew. I don't want anyone else getting hurt."

"It's done."

"You caught someone?" She sat down.

"I wish," he said. "I told Pat. You were out picking up lunch."

"When you said he might come back, I thought you were over-reacting," she said. "So, what do I do now?"

"Hope that he returns to the scene of the crime when we have the place under surveillance." As soon as the words left his mouth, she could tell Rhys regretted it. "Maddy, don't tell anyone about the sur-veillance. If word gets out—and if you tell even one person in this town, word will get out—it totally defeats the purpose."

"I won't," she promised, resting her forehead on the heels of her hands. "This so sucks."

He reached over and massaged the back of her neck. "It'll work out."

"You think you'll catch him?" she asked, and he nodded confi-dently, continuing to work loose a series of tight knots in her neck.

"But for now you're staying put. No moving into the innkeeper's quarters."

"Yeah, okay." What a disaster this was turning out to be.

She gazed around the trailer again, taking in little touches she'd missed. "This place isn't what I expected."

He grinned. "Pretty nice, huh?"

"I'll say." She took a sip of the beer and ran her hands over the arms of the recliner. Real leather.

She put her beer down on the side table and turned to face him. "I mailed the earrings back to Dave today."

He shoved his hand through his hair. "Yeah, I've been thinking about that . . . and it wasn't any of my damned business. It's just that a guy like Dave . . ."

"What, Rhys? Just say it."

He took in a deep breath. "I know you care for the guy . . . but Maddy . . . an honorable man doesn't marry a woman he doesn't love, then mess around on her with his brother's wife. Someone that low . . . well, he's never gonna be decent."

"It was actually his cousin's wife." For whatever reason she felt compelled to correct him. Always good to set the record straight.

"I'm sorry, Maddy, but you deserve a hell of a lot better."

"I know," she said, crying a little. By now, she really thought she'd gotten all these tears out of her system. "My lawyer says that even if he doesn't sign the paperwork, I can get a default judgment. It'll just take longer for the divorce to go through. And since I signed a prenup, there's not that much to work out in settlement."

He heaved out a sigh and eyed her barely touched beer. "You gonna drink that?"

She held it out to him and when he reached for it their hands touched.

Taking a sip, Rhys placed the bottle on the lamp table. He lifted her out of her chair so he could take her place and settled her onto his lap. For a few minutes he just sat there, resting his forehead against hers.

He cupped the back of her head in his hands, his eyelids growing heavy. Then he covered her mouth possessively and kissed her. He tasted so good—like beer and man.

His erection pressed deliciously against her backside as his hands snaked up under her sweater and fondled her breasts.

She moaned into his lips, "What are you doing?"

"I'd like to finish what we started Christmas night, if that's okay?"

"Because you feel sorry for me?"

A small laugh escaped his lips. "Yeah. I just go around having sex with all the women I feel sorry for. You're killing me, Maddy." In one swift move, he lifted her into his arms and headed to the bedroom.

He laid her down in the middle of the bed, and began shucking off his clothes. Her mouth went dry at the sheer beauty of him. His broad chest, sprinkled with dark hair that trailed down the center of his honed abdomen and disappeared inside his boxers, was solid as a brick wall. She hadn't known she could want someone this badly.

Grabbing the hem of her sweater, Maddy pulled it over her head. She started to unclasp her bra, but Rhys got into the bed next to her and caught her wrists.

"I'll do it," he said, kissing her neck and throat, feasting on her mouth, while his roughened fingers leisurely eased the straps of her bra down her arms. He caressed her shoulders, running his hands down her sides and spanning her waist. "Mmm," he murmured against her belly, slowly bathing her in kisses.

He worked his way up until his mouth found hers again. This time he lingered at her lips, nipping and licking, then delving like an explorer. One of his legs hooked over her hips and she could feel him grow harder against her.

A tremor seized her as he deftly undid two tiny hooks at her back, freeing her breasts and taking each one in his hands reverently.

"Cold?" he asked, stroking her nipples with his thumbs until she wanted to scream from the throbbing pleasure of it.

"No," she whispered, moaning as he straddled and bent over her, taking the tip of her breast into his mouth and suckling. "Ohhh."

He grazed her stomach with those clever hands of his, unbuttoned her pants, and inched inside her panties, feeling her with his fingers. "Oh, you're so wet."

Maddy reached for the elastic band of Rhys's shorts. The contact made him suck in his breath before pushing her hands away.

"Not yet, sugar."

"Please," she whimpered.

He took her mouth in a scorching kiss, rolling her on top of him, and pushed her pants down over her ass. "Ooh. I like this," he crooned next to her ear, fingering the lace of her thong. In one fluid motion he tugged both her underwear and pants down her legs until they tangled around her ankles, palming her cheeks and molding them with his hands.

She kicked off the jeans, and he turned her onto her back. Their mouths came together again as he reached between her thighs. Every part of her body hummed with pleasure as his fingertips caressed her.

She writhed against his hand, bowing and squeezing her eyes shut to keep from erupting. "Please," she pleaded, desperate to feel him inside of her.

"Come like this first. I want to watch you."

With her eyes still closed, she could sense him gazing down on her, watching the way she moved, absorbed in her passion. When the time got close, Rhys quickened the friction, rubbing her, penetrating her deeper with his fingers, until she shattered into a million pieces.

She rocked her head back on the pillow and his lips moved over her throat. "Oh, God," she whispered.

He reached down on the floor, fumbling for his jeans, and pulled a foil package from his wallet. Yanking off his shorts, he rolled on the condom, spread her legs with his knees and entered her with one hot hard thrust.

Filling her to what felt like capacity, he slid his hands under her bottom, angling her so he could go even deeper. To match the rhythm of his driving beat, she wrapped her legs around his hips and her arms around his back, feeling his muscles bunch every time he drove into her.

"Good?" he asked.

It was more like transcendent. But so caught up, she could only moan her response. He'd slowed the pace until she arched against him, his chest hair tickling her nipples. He kissed her deep and sexy, his tongue keeping time with the measure of his thrusts.

Lifting his head, he gazed into Maddy's eyes as he moved inside her. She heard herself gasp as heat and pressure coiled in the pit of her stomach.

"Close, baby?" He altered the tempo, picking up speed.

"Oh, yes. Ohhh."

"Say my name, Maddy," he moaned. "I need you to say it."

She clung to him, undulating wildly to meet his fervent demand. And something in her broke, something so primal and emotional that she felt her eyes well up with tears. "Rhys," she sobbed, as her body ignited into intense spasms. "Oh—oh, Rhys."

Once she'd shouted his name, his kisses became searing again, and his strokes more powerful. Hard, fast, and forceful. It was almost too much. Then he rocked into her one last time, shuddered, gasped, and collapsed.

He lay there for a second, still slowly moving inside of her. "Am I crushing you?"

She pulled him tighter against her, spreading little kisses across his face, chin, and shoulders. "Uh-uh," she said, drowsily.

"Sleepy?" He lifted up on his elbows, making Maddy cry out in protest.

"Come back."

"Hang on a sec. I've got to get rid of this." He motioned to the condom and rolled out of bed.

Maddy lay there, listening to the faint sounds of water running in the bathroom. She stretched her legs, trying to reach the edge of Rhys's queen-size bed, and wiggled her toes. Oh, she felt good.

The RV was surprisingly comfortable. Even the wind slapping its metal frame sounded melodic. And the sheets smelled like Rhys—that same combination of pine and tree bark that awakened Maddy's senses like aromatherapy.

When Rhys returned, he pulled her on top of him. "Better?"

She nodded and reached for the blanket. He tugged it over them, snuggling her head under his chin. As she drifted off to sleep, she wondered at the carelessness of letting herself grow attached to this man. Maybe she and Rhys had simply found each other out of temporary necessity—two people stuck in Nugget, both going through particularly rough patches in their lives, trying to find security and empowerment in each other.

He was leaving to go back to Houston. And she was in no shape to tumble into another relationship. She was still trying to figure out who she was, who to trust, or if she could even trust herself anymore. This was supposed to be her time for self-reflection, sorting out all the things that had gone wrong with her marriage and learning how to stand on her own two feet.

Still, it didn't stop her from going a second round when they both woke up.

Rhys sat at the station, dripping grease from a Bun Boy burger all over a stack of papers, when Clay came in the door. He reached in the bag for a wad of napkins and sopped up the mess. Rhys hoped he didn't want his fifth wheel back.

"Got time for a break?" Clay asked, lifting the brim of his cowboy hat.

"What does it look like I'm doing?" Rhys pointed to his boots propped on the desk.

"This will require you to leave the office for about thirty minutes."

Rhys sat up. "Everything okay with the boys?"

"Yeah, yeah." Clay dismissed his concern. "Got something to show you."

Rhys figured whatever it was it must be important for Clay to leave the ranch in the middle of the day. He grabbed his keys and jacket off the hook and yelled to Connie that he was stepping out for a while.

"We'll take my truck," Clay said.

Rhys climbed into his Ford and they headed past the square, onto the main road out of town. A Dwight Yoakam and Buck Owens duet blared on the stereo, and Rhys turned it down. "What's up with all the mystery?"

"No mystery. Just thought you needed a little fresh air." Clay was full of shit, but Rhys was a patient man. "Trailer still working out?"

Better than Clay would ever know. Rhys smiled. "Real good."

"Not getting sick of it?"

"Nope." Rhys noticed that they'd left the highway and had turned onto McCreedy Road. Clumps of snow patched the sides of the street, but a lot of it had melted into a slushy mess. "We going to the ranch?"

Clay slid Rhys a look. "Those kids getting tired of sleeping on bunk beds in Shep's living room with no privacy yet?"

"Given that their other option was foster care, I'd say life's good."

They passed Clay's house and continued farther up the paved street. Rhys had a foggy memory of riding horseback in these pastures when they were kids, looking for stray cows for Tip.

They drove two more miles before Clay pulled into a circular driveway paved in red brick that led to a big white house with a wraparound porch that reminded Rhys of a miniature version of the Lumber Baron. The yard was filled with crabgrass and a dead sunflower wreath hung on the door, making him think the place was either abandoned or neglected.

Clay got out of the truck, walked up the steps, and fiddled with a lockbox hanging off the porch railing. It took him a few minutes, but finally the key popped out and he unlocked the door.

Rhys followed him inside. The house was empty of furniture, but looked to be in remarkably good condition. The oak floors gleamed and the staircase banister looked freshly painted in a glossy white that matched the interior moldings and baseboards. Light filled the front room, which smelled like lemon polish.

The dining room had a fireplace and a built-in hutch that looked original to the house. The kitchen, too modern to be original, had one of those restaurant stoves, a giant refrigerator hidden behind cabinet doors, granite countertops, and something Clay called a butler's pantry—a little room with an extra dishwasher, sink, and lots of cupboards. There were several other rooms on the main floor, including a sun porch and a guest room with its own bathroom and fireplace.

"Why you showing me this?" Rhys asked, as if he didn't know the reason. Clay wouldn't be satisfied until he'd anchored Rhys to Nugget like a barnacle to a jetty post.

"Take a look upstairs." Clay led the way to the second story.

Three good-size bedrooms, a couple of bathrooms, and a master suite. The attic had been converted into two smaller rooms with sloping ceilings and dormer windows. He walked through the rooms with his thumbs hooked inside his pockets, taking in the amazing views of the Feather River and the Sierra mountain range from the windows.

Back in Houston, he'd occasionally spent a Sunday going to open houses. Before he came here, he'd been saving to buy something. Most of the homes he could afford had been new, jammed right next to each other with hollow-core white doors, thin walls, and postage-stamp-sized backyards. He much preferred an older-style place like this.

"What do you think?" Clay asked, lifting his brows expectantly.

"That I can't afford it, and even if I could, I'm not looking to set down roots here since I'm going back to Houston."

"You don't even know the price yet."

"The place has five fucking fireplaces, Clay. A water faucet next to the stove. God forbid someone should walk three feet to the sink to fill a pot. That brick driveway alone is probably worth fifty g's."

"So, I guess you won't be wanting to see the guest house?" Clay said flippantly.

Rhys grinned. "All right, show me the fucking guest house."

They went back downstairs, through the mudroom, and out the back door into an expansive yard. Sure enough, a trail of redbrick pavers ran to a small cottage that looked straight out of a storybook with a slate roof and a porch that mimicked the main house. Clay unlocked it and they stepped in.

The inside was gross. Dated linoleum floors. Grimy walls in desperate need of a paint job. Outdated appliances. And it smelled moldy. But the problems were mostly cosmetic. Maddy could have it looking like a dollhouse in no time. Rhys kicked himself for going there. This was not his house. And Maddy was not his woman. Although the sex had been beyond outstanding.

"Wanna see the three-car garage?" Clay asked.

Rhys shook his head. "Give it up, McCreedy. I gotta get back."

As he followed Clay to the front door to return the lockbox key, Rhys said, "You moonlighting as a real estate agent now?"

Clay scratched his chin and nodded his head in the direction of the stairs. "Sit down a second. I wanna talk to you about something."

Rhys planted himself on the fourth rung and watched three deer— a mama and two little ones—across the lane pick through the slush for acorns. The road, he noticed, was nicely maintained, but not a lot of traffic. Besides this house and Clay's, he doubted there were any others up the street, which probably dead-ended at a fire trail.

"I don't think this place would take too much to get into," Clay said, grabbing a spot on the porch where he could hang his legs off the side. "It's in foreclosure—the owner, some tech guy, who only came up on weekends, lost his job and couldn't afford to make the payments."

"How do you know about it?"

"Plumas Sierra Credit Union holds the note. I do business with a guy over there and since this property abuts my land he thought I might be interested. And to tell you the truth, I'm real interested."

"Why didn't the owner come to you in the first place, instead of foreclosing? Might've saved his credit."

"He did. But he bought at the peak of the market. I wasn't about to pay the kind of money he needed to meet his loan. Place isn't worth it. The bank's price is more in line with current property values. At this point they're just looking to unload it."

"What do you need another house for?" Rhys asked.

"The place comes with prime grazing land—about a thousand acres."

Rhys nearly choked. "Never mind the house. You thought I could afford a thousand acres of California real estate?"

"Hell no." Clay laughed. "But I can. And like you said, I don't need a house. But you do."

"Yeah. So what's your point?" Rhys stood up.

"I'm buying the place," Clay said. He jogged down the stairs and with his foot drew a primitive map in the dirt. "This is the house and about three acres of yard." He pointed so Rhys could see. "Here's the land I want. With a little county finagling I could break this off, and sell you that."

"You could sell it to anyone—and for a load of money."

"I don't want just anyone living next door to my spread."

Even if Rhys wanted to settle permanently in Nugget, he wasn't about to take a handout from his best friend. And what Clay offered absolutely smacked of a handout.

"Thanks, buddy. But not happening."

At the end of the second week in January, Maddy and Nate got their sewage report. Nate drove from San Francisco so they could go over it together, before they teleconferenced with their expert and Josh, their lawyer.

"Jeez, you need a PhD in poop to understand this thing," Maddy complained as she and her brother sifted through the documents. "Yay or nay?"

"I can't figure this damn thing out." Nate looked at his watch, grabbed the phone, and speed-dialed. "Josh, you ready to do this? Wait . . . wait . . . I'm putting you on speaker. Okay, go ahead."

"I've got Doug here," Josh said. "Doug, why don't you explain what's going on?"

"The bottom line," Doug said, "is the Nugget Wastewater Treatment Plant is designed to take 18,600 pounds of waste a day from commercial users. It's currently running at close to seventy-five-percent capacity. A twenty-room inn should only produce roughly twelve pounds of waste a day, meaning there's no way you could come close to pushing the system over its limit.

"But," he continued, "I can see why the city would be concerned. The plant's equipment is outdated and desperately needs to be upgraded and optimized. If I were them—"

Josh cut him off. "My argument would be that the system could go at any time due to wear and tear, not quantity. In other words, the Lumber Baron would not be the straw to break the camel's back."

"We win, right?" Maddy said.

"Unfortunately, it's not that cut-and-dried. Like I said before, local businesses and the residents can sue the city. I don't think they would have a leg to stand on, but it could hold you up for years."

"So we're right back where we started," Nate said.

"No. Now you actually have a viable defense to the capacity issue. The Addisons are just plain wrong, which in the court of public opinion should blow their credibility to shit."

"That's what we want to do." Nate put the report back in sequence and tapped the packet on the desk to get the pages even.

"The hearing's at the end of the month, right?"

"Yes," Maddy and Nate said at the same time.

"Doug, you'll be ready to go?" Josh asked.

"You bet."

"Then I'll talk to you guys later in the week."

"Thanks, Josh." When they hung up, Maddy turned to Nate. "You think we're screwed?"

"I don't know. It could go either way."

She wrung her hands. "I'm really freaking out about the hearing, Nate. The Addisons have done an excellent job of working everyone up. Even though our expert says there's plenty of capacity left, people here are just going to believe the Addisons. On top of that, Colin's attack has all the workers edgy.

"I love this place," Maddy continued. "It has such incredible potential." She paused and let out a breath. "But, Nate, I'm almost thinking we should cut our losses and sell."

He joined her on the love seat. "Mad, you may be a first-rate hotel operator, but real estate savvy—not so much. No one in this economy is in the market for a half-restored hulking Victorian in a shabby business district for the kind of money we've already sunk into this place. We'd lose our shirts.

"Our only hope is to win that hearing. So, what do you say we buy some people off?"

She shot him a dirty look. "You're kidding, right?"

"I figure in a town like Nugget, a hundred bucks and a mule ought to do it. Come on, I'll buy you lunch."

They crossed the green to the Ponderosa and Maddy noticed that a few of the banners had been knocked askew from the storm. The one on Portia's kiosk had been shredded. Just the "Flush" part remained. A few members of the Nugget Mafia lounged in the barber shop, leading Maddy to wonder if they ever worked.

"Hey," Nate said. "Don't let me forget, I have an afghan in the car for you from Mom. She couldn't finish it in time for Christmas so she sent it home with me. Thing weighs a freaking ton."

"Okay. I'll get it out of your car after lunch. Dave called to tell me that he got the earrings back. I overnighted them."

"What'd he say?"

"He was surprised," she said. "But mostly sad. I think it's sinking in for him that I'm not taking him back."

"He's going to do everything in his power to talk you out of it, you know?"

"Even with a prenup, a divorce could wind up costing him mega bucks. Wellmonts like holding on to what they have."

Maddy could feel her face heat like a radiator. Was that why Dave had begged her to take him back—to save his damn money?

Nate reached for her. "Uh . . . that came out harsh. Hell, Maddy, I'm probably wrong. I just don't want him taking advantage of you."

"Give me a little credit, Nate." Credit for being the most gullible female on the face of the earth. Credit for having loved someone who hadn't loved her back.

"In other news," she said, wanting to change the subject from Dave. "The documentary guy from Stanford is coming to check out Nugget—wants to get the lay of the land. He has about fifteen history students working with him. Virgil and I are going to take them to Donner Lake to see where it all went down. Cool, huh?"

"Thrilling," Nate said.

They grabbed a booth in the Ponderosa. Sophie and Mariah bustled over, wanting to hear the results of the report. Maddy and Nate gave them the *Reader's Digest* version.

Mariah poured them each a cup of coffee and slid a copy of the *Nugget Tribune* under Maddy's nose.

"What's this?" she asked, quickly perusing the page where Sandy had written a long op-ed piece urging the city council to reject new businesses that would tax Nugget's sewage plant and detailing how Sierra Heights had been required to build its own septic system. Sandy had ended the article by writing, "Shouldn't the Lumber Baron have to do the same?"

As if their twenty-room inn could be compared to a development with eighty homes and a golf course. Maddy wanted to skewer the woman along with the people who had written letters to the editor, advocating that the Lumber Baron's lodging permits be revoked. She passed the paper to Nate.

"My sources tell me the Addisons and their band of merry losers are planning a demonstration a day or so before the meeting," Mariah said.

Maddy leaned her head back. "For goodness sake, will these people not give me one moment's peace?"

"Well?" Mariah asked. "What now?"

"We continue to move forward," Nate said. "Let the town see that we're not backing down. And until the hearing, spread the word that Nugget's waste system is only running at seventy-five-percent capacity. I'm also thinking that we have Josh send a threatening letter."

"Uh-uh," Maddy said. "No letters. I know this town, and it's not going to respond well to a San Francisco lawyer telling it what to do. I think threats of a lawsuit should be a last resort. Don't you agree, Soph?"

Sophie nodded her head. "Maddy's right. Folks here will see it as an affront. They'll dig in their heels just to be contrary."

"That's exactly right," Maddy said. "No, for justice, we must go to Don Corleone."

Everyone looked at her like she'd sprouted a second head. Sophie reached for the coffee carafe and refilled their cups. "What did you have in mind, Mad?"

"I'm getting a haircut."

Chapter 20

Before Nate left for the city, he and Maddy treated themselves to a couple of fried egg sandwiches at the Bun Boy.

"Anything new on the Sophie and Mariah baby front?" she asked her brother. "I wanted to talk to them about it yesterday, but I figured they'd be more likely to give you the skinny."

Nate shrugged. "They've been pretty tight-lipped. All I know is they're making a trip to the city in a few days for some medical tests."

As far as Maddy knew, Sophie had already done all the preliminaries. "You think something's wrong and that's the holdup?"

"I couldn't tell you. But as soon as I know something, I'll share it with you."

After Nate took off, Maddy walked over to Owen's Barber Shop.

Earl barely looked up from his newspaper. A few of the other guys merely glanced at her.

Steve sat in Owen's chair with a hot towel wrapped around his face. In all the times she'd walked by the shop, there'd never been a woman inside—just lots of men standing around Owen's forty-two-cup coffee urn, shooting the breeze.

"What can I do for you, missy?" Owen asked as he whetted a straight-blade razor on a suspended strop.

"I need a trim."

That got Earl's attention. He put his paper down, took a sip from his foam cup and sat back, eyes wide.

"Maddy, honey, this is a barber shop, not a beauty parlor," Owen said, removing the towel from Steve's face and reapplying a fresh coat of hot lather.

"There are no beauty parlors in Nugget." Maddy hadn't heard the term beauty parlor since her mom used to get her weekly wash and blowout. "And I don't have time to go all the way to Reno or Quincy."

Owen scraped his razor blade a little close to Steve's ear for Maddy's peace of mind, but she supposed he knew what he was doing.

"Sorry, honey, I don't do women."

"I just need my lines crisped and my ends trimmed. Come on, Owen, it's not like I'm asking for highlights."

"Wait until my daughter Darla gets her cosmetology license. She'll cut your hair."

"When will that be?" Maddy didn't know Owen had a daughter.

"At least a few months." Owen chuckled. "She's living in Roseville to go to beauty school."

"That's nice. Is she moving back here?" Maddy took a seat away from the door. Even if she couldn't convince Owen to trim her hair, she'd brought the report and planned to start campaigning before the Addisons successfully spread more of their venom.

"She says she is, but with Darla you never know." Owen finished up with Steve, and Maddy searched his face for scrapes and cuts. Not one. The town barber knew his stuff.

When Steve got out of the chair, Owen cleaned it with a towel and motioned for Maddy to hop up. She didn't know whether to be surprised or scared. In San Francisco she got her hair cut at one of the city's top salons by a stylist named JauJou. If the stares from the peanut gallery were any indication, they, too, had been stunned by Owen's sudden change of heart.

Owen didn't shampoo her, just snapped a cape around her neck, grabbed a pair of shears and started snipping. Thank goodness he had her facing away from the mirror.

"This is a good cut you got here, Maddy."

Well, it ought to be. Maddy paid JauJou, before tip, a hundred and twenty dollars for a trim alone. "Thanks."

"Sophie and Mariah pick someone yet?"

Maddy snorted. "How much you have riding on this, Owen?"

"Hundred bucks says they ditch Lithuanian Man and go with a local."

"Oh, yeah. And who would that be?" They couldn't possibly know about Nate. But then again, the Nugget Mafia seemed to know everything in this town.

"I would've gone with Clay McCreedy," Owen said. "But he's got his hands full with those two boys of his. So my money's on the police chief." The others agreed.

"Is that who you're going with, Earl? Rhys Shepard?"

"I'm still leaning toward Lithuanian Man. Best to go with an anonymous donor, no strings that way."

"You fellows really need to get a life," Maddy said.

Clippings of her hair fell to the floor as Owen trimmed away. "I guess you'll be waiting for the council's decision on your inn before continuing construction," he said.

That was her cue. "No. Why would we wait? The sooner we open for business, the sooner everyone starts benefiting."

"And how's that?" Owen asked.

"You know that shave you just gave Steve? Men up from the city would kill for a service like that." She sighed. "Nowadays it's these chichi salons taking over. They don't know the first thing about a custom shave like that."

Maddy wished she could see Owen's reaction, but he was standing behind her, trimming the back of her hair. "At the inn we'll want to play up the fact that in Nugget old-fashioned luxuries like hot-towel wraps still exist. And we'll be sending them over here, Owen."

She turned her attention to her now rapt audience. "Steve, you and Portia have got to know how many new clients the inn could bring your tour business . . . Couples who want to learn how to fly-fish . . . Families interested in river rafting. We'll keep all your literature right there at the desk."

Earl harrumphed. "So, Maddy, your guests gonna want sheep wormer from my feedstore?"

"No. But I'd definitely say order more of these jeans I'm wearing." She tried to turn back and look at the label on her butt, but Owen told her to stop squirming.

"The brand's Cowgirl Up," he said, turning red as a pomegranate. "Lucinda's been ordering 'em. Seem to do well with the younger ladies."

"I can see why. I'll be back to buy a few more pairs."

Earl got a bewildered look on his face. "Ever since I let my daughter do the buying we've got more women in the store shopping than men."

"Well, people on vacation like to shop, too, Earl." She wanted the focus to be on the inn, not designer jeans. "Study after study shows that consumers are more likely to part with their hard-earned cash when they're on holiday. Here, up in cattle country, they'll likely want a little taste of the West—especially when they go on one of Steve's trail rides. That's where the Nugget Feed Store comes in. They'll want boots, cowboy hats, and some of those cute fringe jackets."

"We're clear on the other end of town, Maddy. They won't even know we're here," Earl argued.

"Of course they will, because we'll tell them. We'll even shuttle them over."

"Tell them what? Shuttle them where?" Everyone was too involved in the conversation to hear Clay come in the door.

"Maddy, here, is telling us how her inn's going to make us all rich," Owen said.

"That a fact?" Clay swung around one of the white plastic stack chairs, straddled it, and winked at Maddy. The guy was almost as good-looking as Rhys. "Don't let me interrupt."

"The inn's going to play up the storied history of this town," she said. "Virgil Ross and I are already working with a Stanford filmmaker who's making a documentary about the Donner Party. Who knows, some of you might even get interviewed for it," she continued. "Anyway, this filmmaker has agreed that the best place to debut the movie is right here in Nugget. Do you know what kind of exposure that will bring this town—us? How many people will come to see the very place where it all happened—especially if there is a nice place for them to stay?"

0

00

"Sounds smart." Everyone turned to Clay, who looked at his watch. "You almost done there, Owen? I need a trim, but have to be out of here in forty." He made it seem perfectly normal to find a woman in Owen's chair.

"Yep. You're next." Owen brushed Maddy's neck with a soft fat brush, took off her cape, and spun the chair around so she faced the mirror.

"Wow! It looks great." And it really did. "How much I owe you?"

"Fifteen."

Maddy blinked. "Seriously?"

"That's the going rate, missy," Owen said as he swept up Maddy's locks into a pile on the floor and shoveled them up with a dustpan.

She got to her feet. "Are you kidding me? I'm going to a barber from now on."

Grabbing her wallet out of her purse, Maddy paid her bill, but lingered.

"Gracie wouldn't let me sign that petition," Earl said. "But how much good will all that extra business do us when the town's pipes start backing up?"

It was the opportunity she'd been waiting for.

"I'm glad you asked that." Maddy pulled the report from her purse. "Nugget's waste system still has plenty of capacity left. When the Addisons started this whole hullabaloo, we got pretty worried—overflowing toilets are bad for the hotel business. So we called our own experts to conduct an inspection. You know what they found?" That the Addisons are big fat liars.

She spread the report out near the cash register and a few of the men started thumbing through it.

"Look at page eleven." Maddy pointed. "The system's got a quarter of its capacity left. Even twenty Marriotts couldn't fill that."

"But right here," Earl pulled out a page, "it says that the plant's equipment could crap out at any minute—excuse the pun." That earned him a few chuckles from the guys.

"The plant's been living on borrowed time for years," Maddy continued. "One flush from you, Owen, could send it into overdrive. So you're going to hold up commerce until the city gets off its ass? Lose out on a windfall? The Addisons don't have your best interests at heart."

When they all stared at her questioningly, she said, "The Lumber Baron is bound to give their little rental cabins some competition. Too bad they're only thinking about themselves, instead of how, together, both our lodges could bring a hell of a lot more business to this town."

When she walked out the door she saw Clay up in Owen's chair, smiling.

Rhys bolted into a sitting position. At first, he'd thought the incessant pounding was part of a dream. More like a noisy nightmare. But having grown used to these all-hours-of-the-morning calls, he quickly came out of a sleep-induced fog, hung over the side of the bed to collect his clothes, and hurriedly pulled them on.

"Coming," he yelled at the continued banging.

When he opened the door, Sam stood at the entry, his face paper-white. "There's been an accident. Papa isn't breathing."

Rhys didn't wait to hear more. He ran for the house and found Shep lying on the kitchen floor, his pajama pants twisted around his ankles. It looked like he'd collided with a kitchen chair. Given the mess, he'd mistakenly thought it was the toilet.

Rhys placed two fingers on the side of Shep's neck and counted for fifteen seconds.

Lina stood over them, fear in her eyes, and if Rhys had to guess, self-condemnation. "*Ay Dios mio*, please let him be okay."

Rhys nodded. "Pop, you with us?" He was rewarded with a loud groan. "What hurts?"

"My head. My arm. Where the hell is Rosa?"

"You checked out on us for a second there." Rhys examined both arms and, sure enough, the left ulna bone was poking out at a frighteningly unnatural angle and the skin was broken.

They got him cleaned up as best they could and Rhys loaded him into the Tahoe.

"Can we put the siren on?" Sam asked.

"Nah," Rhys said. "We've had enough drama for one morning. Let's not wake the neighbors, too."

By the time they got to Plumas District, sunlight was peeking through the waiting room blinds. Besides a broken arm and a slight concussion, the doctors feared pneumonia. So they decided to run tests and keep him for observation.

Sam had managed to curl up in one of the straight-back wooden chairs and fall asleep. Lina spent most of her time pacing.

"Sit." Rhys patted the chair next to him.

She wearily plopped down. "It's my fault. I should've been watching him better."

Rhys shook his head. "You can't stay up all night, escorting him to and from the bathroom, Lina."

"Why do you dislike him so much?" she asked.

"I don't dislike him." Which wasn't precisely true. "It's complicated. He didn't have the same bond with me that he has with you guys."

The truth was Rhys didn't know diddly about the dynamics of their relationship, only that Shep went back and forth to Stockton and then abruptly stopped.

"Did he come to see you a lot?" Rhys asked.

She nodded. "When he worked for the railroad, he came all the time. Sometimes he'd bring presents for me and Sam. But he only stayed a few days."

It was infinitely more than Rhys ever got, but as far as fatherhood went, it sucked. At least he'd paid for their school.

"How come you never knew about us?" Lina asked.

"Because he never told me."

"He used to talk about you. All the time."

Rhys did a double take. "He did?"

As if to prove it to him, Lina said, "You cut your hand when you were six and had to get eight stitches."

Rhys looked at the faint scar that ran from the base of his thumb to his wrist and cleared his throat. He'd gotten that cut trying to peel an apple with Shep's pocketknife. His father used to do it in one long, curly strip, and Rhys had wanted to be just like him. But the old man had never wanted anything to do with him. For a long time, he'd wondered if his father's disdain had something to do with Rhys's mother having left Shep. Then Rhys stopped caring.

"After I moved away, we didn't really keep in good touch. I'd call him occasionally—came to see him when a friend died—but we didn't share our lives with each other. It just wasn't that kind of relationship, Lina."

Lina felt sorry for him. Rhys could see it in her eyes. "I'm going to get a cup of coffee," he said brusquely. "You want something?"

"No."

When he came back, he found her staring off into the distance. She looked so small and lost. "We've got to talk about this, Lina," he told her. "It's time to make some decisions here."

"No facility!"

"We're not set up for taking care of him. He needs to be in a place where he's right next to a bathroom and doesn't have to walk through a kitchen. He needs twenty-four-hour care. Lina, I have a job that requires me to be on call day and night. And you should be going to college."

"Where I come from we don't give our family to strangers to care for," she snapped.

He was so weary of arguing with her. "I'm sorry. But as the adult here, I have to make the decision. I'll find him a good place."

"And where will we go?" she asked angrily. But there were equal parts of fear in her voice, too.

"We'll find you a school, get you settled in, and I guess Sam can come live with me in Houston."

"So now you're taking my brother from me, too?"

"Lina, don't be so dramatic. You can go to school in Houston. There are a lot of good colleges there, and, if you want, you can even live with us. We'll call Annie from Social Services—get the whole thing worked out," he said with resignation.

"And then we'll never see Papa again."

"Oh, for Christ's sake. We'll find him a care facility in Houston. You can visit him every day."

She sat there weeping and Rhys felt lower than pond scum.

It had been a week, and the most Maddy had seen of Rhys was the exhaust from his truck as it came and went up and down the driveway. That's how busy he'd been investigating Colin's attack and the robbery at the Nugget Market.

While juggling a takeout carrier from the Bun Boy, she knocked on his trailer door.

Rhys answered, sweeping his hand across the entry for her to come in. He kicked the door closed behind her with his foot. No boots, Maddy noticed, just white athletic socks.

"What do you have there?" He eyed the bag.

"Food," she said, putting the sack on the counter and grabbing two beers out of the refrigerator.

"Yeah?" Rhys tore into the package, shoving a couple of fries into his mouth. "I knew I liked you."

"Really? Because it seems like ever since we slept together, you don't want to be my friend anymore," Maddy said teasingly, but a part of her wondered whether Rhys had regrets.

He kissed the top of her head—even when she wore high heels, the man towered over her. "I'm always your friend."

"Good," she said, knowing that she was pouting. "Because I could really use one right now."

"What's wrong?"

"Uh, where should I start? The person beating up my workers and breaking into my inn has yet to surface. Our expert's report is favorable, yet most of the town still hates my guts and wants to put the kibosh on the project to which I've dedicated my entire heart and soul—not to mention both mine and Nate's life's savings. Did your friend Clay tell you about the barber shop?"

Rhys took her beer, put both bottles on the counter, and enveloped her in his arms. "No one hates your guts."

They just stood in the middle of the trailer's small kitchen while Rhys held her. Maybe two, three minutes passed; Maddy lost track of time. But she felt like she could breathe again, like the earth had suddenly found a sense of balance.

She wanted him to keep holding her, to soothe her with his words. But he seemed to have other ideas.

He walked her backward the ten or so feet to the bedroom and flopped her onto the bed. "I like you." He nuzzled her neck and she felt the pressure of his growing arousal. "Want me to show you how much?"

"I came to talk," Maddy said, turning her head to give him better access. She moaned with pleasure as he circled her ear with his tongue.

"We'll talk later."

"I suppose I can be flexible," she murmured, trying to catch her breath. The man made her hotter than the Mojave Desert.

"I know firsthand how flexible you can be. It's all that yoga." Rhys worked his way to her mouth, clamped down, and devoured her like a ravenous man. When he was finished plundering, he started undressing her with those nimble fingers of his.

Soon, their clothes fell in a heap on the floor and his hands roamed every inch of her body until she burned and her heart raced. He moved over her with an urgency. It was like their short time apart had spanned a thousand years and they were racing to make up for lost time.

Rhys pulled her panties off, and unlike the first time, when he'd slowly taken her to heaven, they moved together frantically. Somewhere in the background she heard a drawer scrape open and a wrapper crinkle. And before she knew it, Rhys slipped inside her, moving with those glorious strokes that made all the world's troubles melt away.

He rolled onto his back so that she was on top. "Sit up, so I can see you."

She braced her hands on his shoulders to push herself upright. He reached up to fondle her breasts and tongue her nipples as she arched her back.

"Mmm," she moaned as he gripped her hips so she could sheathe him deeper.

She rode him that way, controlling the pace and the movement. He lay back, watching the way she swayed, driving himself up and into her, his hands squeezing her bottom to the rhythm of their thrusts. Within minutes she felt ready to ride the crest. But he found her center with his thumb and worked it, sending her over the edge. Her climax was so intense she had to hold on to Rhys with both hands to keep from collapsing like a rag doll.

He rolled her underneath him, bent her legs, and pumped hard and fast. She felt him begin to shudder, then he threw his head back, shouted, "Oh, Jesus," and squeezed his eyes shut.

He lay on top of her for a while, trying to even out his breathing, eventually flipping onto his side. "I think that was a record for me. I didn't hurt you, did I?"

"No." She gave him her best dreamy, sated smile. "And it was definitely a record for me."

"Yeah?" He leaned over and kissed her. "Be right back."

He headed in the direction of the bathroom and Maddy took time to admire the view. The man had the most spectacular backside she'd ever seen. Buns of steel.

He returned a few minutes later, crawled under the blanket, and pulled her against his chest. "Tell me what your expert found. I'm not really sure I want to know about what you did at the barber shop. You didn't break in, did you?"

"No. I got a haircut." She sat up so she could fluff it in the closet's mirrored doors. "You like?"

He twirled a strand around his finger. "Yeah, I like. Whaddya do, Maddy?"

"Oh, don't go getting all Johnny Law on me. I just went over there to convince the Nugget Mafia that Sandy Addison sleeps with the fishes. Brought the report."

"And what's the report say?"

"That Nugget's wastewater plant is only up to seventy-five-percent capacity—that Sandy's the only one full of shit."

He pulled her back down. "Seventy-five percent! That's great."

She ran her fingers through the mat of dark hair on his chest. "Yeah, except for the report also says the system's in dire need of an upgrade. So I don't think I made too many inroads at Owen's.

"So, what've you been up to?" Maddy asked and Rhys chuckled. "What?" She swatted him.

"I've just missed you, that's all."

"See," she said. "You have been avoiding me."

"Not avoiding, just busy."

Maddy pulled away. "What's been going on?"

"Besides working on catching your tweaker and the Nugget Market's robber? Well, let's see. Shep broke his arm while taking a dump in the kitchen."

"Oh, no." Maddy sat up. "Is he okay?"

Rhys puffed out a breath. "The big concern was pneumonia, which he doesn't have."

"How did it happen?"

"He has trouble at night, particularly with the bathroom. The apartment's not laid out well, especially for someone with dementia. So he got confused in the kitchen and toppled over a chair. An hour later, Lina got up to get a glass of water and found him."

"Rhys, if the city gives the go-ahead on the inn, I'm moving in. The caretaker's quarters are about finished, and it'll be good to have someone on the premises. You can remodel the duplex, put in a suite for Shep."

"I agree that it would be good to have someone living at the Lumber Baron. Just not you."

She tried to argue with him, but he wasn't having it. "There's no room for negotiation here, Maddy. Until I get this son of a bitch, you're not moving into the Lumber Baron."

"Rhys, Lina and Sam can't continue to live in your dad's living room. Lina's almost eighteen. She needs privacy. Shep needs a full-time caretaker—that requires space."

"Don't I know it. But in April, I'm going back to Houston," he said, propping himself up on one elbow. "I want to make lieutenant, Maddy. Those positions rarely come up. If I'm not there when one does, I'll get passed over."

"But you're chief here."

"Maddy," he said, "it's a Podunk town of six thousand people."

"But it has really good crime."

He closed his eyes and let out a breath. "You've always known that I'm leaving, Maddy. That hasn't changed."

"I know. I just don't want you to leave." Because despite every instinct telling her that this was the absolute worst time for it, she was falling in love with the man. Foolish. But unfortunately emotions didn't have the good sense to follow a neat schedule. Sometimes true love happens even in the middle of a divorce.

"Honey, look at me." Rhys tilted his head so he was eye level with her. "Maybe what we're doing here isn't such a good—"

"Stop." She covered his mouth. "You've always been honest about your situation here. We're on the same page. I just want to enjoy what little time we have together. That's all." Yeah, they'd always have Nugget.

"Okay," he said. "So we're cool?"

"We're cool." But a voice in her head screamed, "Liar, liar, liar."

Chapter 21

As soon as Maddy turned off the faucet in the shower, the phone began to ring. Cursing, she quickly grabbed a towel, wrapped it around her toga-style, and waded into the kitchen barefoot. Even with the heat cranked up, her legs sprouted goose bumps.

She dove for the cordless before whoever was on the other end gave up. "Hello?"

"Mad?"

The connection crackled, sounding long-distance. "Dave, is that you?" Crap, she should've let it go to voice mail?

"Who else would it be? I've left you about a dozen messages." Dave tried, without much success, to disguise his hostility. Ever since he'd gotten the earrings back, he'd morphed into a temperamental child. Maybe he'd always been like that when he didn't get his way and Maddy hadn't noticed it until now. Or, more likely, he'd always gotten his way. "Why are you out of breath?"

"You caught me just as I was getting out of the tub." *So, gotta go.*

"I wanted to see if you could pick me up at the airport?"

The guy was seriously off his rocker. "You flying into San Francisco? 'Cause, in case you forgot, I live in Nugget, more than two hundred miles away. And then there's that little detail of us getting a divorce."

"Mad," he said, and whatever anger she'd heard before, now sounded like sorrow. "I would just like an opportunity for us to talk—for me to make my case. We could go to that Italian restaurant you like on Russian Hill . . . discuss this."

She tried for patience. "Dave, please don't make this any more difficult than it has to be."

"You're really going through with this, aren't you?" His voice sounded hoarse. And tired.

Maddy pulled the towel tighter, not saying anything, hoping that her silence spoke for itself. This going around in circles had become incredibly tedious.

"My lawyer says you want half the proceeds from the house," Dave said with a hint of *bring it on*, which put Maddy on alert. He was going to fight her for every damn cent.

"Assets we acquired together are not covered by the prenup," she asserted, just like her lawyer had told her. "It's only fair, Dave. I gave up a career for that house."

"I paid for it."

"Fine. We'll just go to court, then." The San Francisco real estate market was red-hot. The house was worth a small fortune. She needed that money, especially if they lost their lodging permit for the Lumber Baron.

"Maddy, don't be naïve. I've got enough money to bury you. Even if you eventually win, all the proceeds will wind up going toward your legal fees. But I'll tell you what, give me one dinner to try to convince you to call off this farce. If at the end of the meal you're still hell-bent on going through with it, I'll give you the whole fucking house and sign your stupid papers."

"Why are you manipulating me like this?"

"I want you back, Maddy."

"I'm not coming back. And no dinner in the world is going to convince me otherwise. But I do need the money from the house that I spent four years of my life trying to make a home. So if you'll put this ridiculous proposal of yours in writing I'll do it."

"Yep. My lawyer'll send it right over." He rattled off a date, time, and meeting place.

"Just dinner, Dave."

"Let's see what happens."

Chapter 22

When Rhys got to the Lumber Baron a group of workers sat on the porch, basking in what little sun had peeked through the clouds, eating sandwiches and Bun Boy burgers.

"Maddy inside?" he asked, climbing the steps.

"Yeah. She's on the second floor, picking colors with the painters," someone from the crew said.

The workers made room for him to get by, and once inside, he spent a few minutes in the foyer just taking in the sheer opulence of the stained glass and the woodwork. The transformation still blew him away. The staircase, he noticed, was no longer that putrid pink. The paint had been stripped to bring the finish on the banister and treads back to its original mahogany, and it looked pretty damn outstanding. The place was shaping up, Rhys thought as he ran his palm over the silky-smooth handrail. If the city kept it from opening, it would be a travesty.

He found Maddy standing in the middle of one of the guest rooms, studying four different shades of green painted in big squares on the wall.

"Hi." She smiled up at him and went back to examining the color swatches, tilting her head first to the left and then to the right.

He started to sit on the perfectly made bed heaped with tasseled pillows, but thought better of it. "You can lie here with the fire going and watch the game." Rhys pointed at the flat-screen TV that hung above a crisp white mantel.

"That's the idea," Maddy said, gracing him with yet another one of her kick-ass smiles. "Ordinarily, I wouldn't have furnished and accessorized a room this early in the construction. But if we actually open by summer, I need to start making brochures, build a website. I need pictures."

She continued to talk a mile a minute and Rhys just stood there, struck by her sheer beauty. Not just her physical appearance, which completely did it for him, but the woman had so much vigor that he felt completely dazzled by it. Moonstruck.

"Is everything okay, Rhys? You look a little funny."

"Yeah," he said, and blinked a few times to clear his head. "Can you go for a ride? I want to show you something."

He drove her to a deserted old summer camp and they sat on the deck of an imposing lodge, watching the sun hang over the Sierra until dusk, then wandered the grounds with only the crunch of dead leaves and an occasional birdcall to fill the silence. The spicy smell of pine needles and wet dirt filled the air and Rhys had never felt so peaceful. He'd happened upon the place while doing a welfare check in the backwoods. On a lark, he'd called the agent listed on the "for sale" sign. It turned out he'd gone to high school with her. She'd told him all about the camp, a white elephant that had been on the market for years.

"I thought if the inn didn't work out, maybe you could take this place over," Rhys said. "It's on its own septic system. And it's already zoned commercial."

"You saw the op-ed piece in the paper, didn't you?" Maddy asked. "Yep."

"No doubt about it, the property has potential. It's a really great place, Rhys. But after the inn, we're tapped out financially. Nate doesn't even think we'll be able to sell the Lumber Baron for enough to break even. And this place needs a lot of work."

"It was a shot in the dark," he said, feeling disappointed. "I just thought . . ."

"You're a good man." She lifted up on her toes and kissed him.

He searched her face. "I want it to work out for you, Maddy."

"I know." She gazed up as the remaining light filtered through the trees, casting shadows on the forest floor. "The Addisons are supposedly planning a demonstration against the inn. I'm going to San Francisco in a few days, but if you hear anything, a heads-up would be greatly appreciated.

"But," she quickly added, "don't do anything unethical."

The corners of Rhys's mouth lifted slightly. "I'll try not to. What're you going to San Francisco for?"

"I have to meet Dave about selling our house." When she couldn't meet his eyes, Rhys knew he wasn't getting the full story.

He leaned against a big oak, his hands fisted at his sides. "You two getting back together?"

"No. Of course not," she said. "We have stuff to discuss—about the divorce."

"Isn't that what the lawyers are for?" He pushed off the tree and walked away.

"He said if I'd give him a chance to apologize, he'd give me the house," she blurted out.

Rhys whipped around. "Let me guess. He needs to make the apology in person."

She looked down at her shoes. "Over dinner."

"I bet. You gotta do what you gotta do." He walked briskly to his truck, but what he wanted to do was hit something.

"What? You think I'm a chump for going?" she called to his back. No, he was the chump.

"Where I come from, we have another name for it." He stopped and slowly turned. She blanched and Rhys instantly wished he could take it back.

"Ah, hell, Maddy." He rubbed his eyes with the heels of his hands. "I didn't mean that. I just don't want to see you get played, is all."

"Give me a little credit, Rhys. We're ending a five-year marriage. Possessions need to be split up, real estate decisions need to be made, bank accounts need to be closed. That's what happens when people get divorced."

He knew plenty of people who'd gotten divorced. They hadn't hashed out who got what over dinner. More like over joint restraining orders. The woman was tying him up in knots. One day everything was "Don't go to Houston, Rhys," and the next was dinner with Dave.

"Maddy," he said, knowing that for his own sanity he had to end this, "maybe this would be a good time for us to cool things off. You've got your deal with Dave. Everything's up in the air with the inn. I'm on my way out. Just seems like it would make more sense for us to go back to being platonic, focus on the stuff we need to."

She jerked back, like she'd just been sucker punched. Her bottom lip started to tremble and Rhys prepared himself for the inevitable waterworks. But her face suddenly flushed red and he could tell she was angry.

"You're right," she said. "Lots going on. I'm getting out of a bad marriage, you're going to Texas. Got to keep our eyes on the ball."

He watched her turn and walk that very fine ass of hers to his truck.

Yeah, Rhys thought, it would be easier this way.

Forty-eight hours later, Rhys sat at Connie's desk, watching Jake eat fries, feeling a little sick to his stomach. Ever since he'd decided to turn down the heat with Maddy, his lungs hadn't been working too good. Not enough air coming in and out. Ultimately, though, he knew he'd done the right thing. Better now than in three months. Or worse—when Dave talked Maddy into getting back with him.

Despite her tough talk, women didn't walk away from rich guys like him. A man who could buy her the world. A man who had a hell of a lot more history with Maddy than a couple of months of making love to Rhys in a trailer.

He hadn't even had the decency to take Maddy on a real date.

"Hey, Jake," Rhys called. "When you were going through your divorces did you ever try to reconcile with any of your wives?"

"Depends what you mean by reconcile. Candy—wife number one—and I still tumble into bed every now and again. We never could keep our hands off each other. With Laurie, yeah, a few times I thought we'd wind up getting back together. Then she met Bob. Leanne—no way in hell. Why do you ask?"

"No reason."

Jake eyeballed him for a second or two, started to say something, and seemed to think better of it. Then, seemingly unable to control himself, he said, "Once, I was interested in a woman who refused to get serious with me until my divorce from Candy was a year old. Said she'd be setting herself up for heartbreak. It turned out to be a good move—for her, anyway."

The bell over the door rang and Connie came in holding a box of grocery store donuts. "Hey, Chief, you get that message from Carol Spartan I left on your desk?"

"Yeah. Thanks." He'd asked the real estate agent about Clay's Victorian just for fun when he'd contacted her about the old camp for Maddy. She'd told him some interesting historical facts about the house—things that would've made Maddy flip. But now he couldn't take her there. "Got some paperwork to do."

"Buck up, son," Jake said. "Plenty more fish in the sea."

He heard Connie ask Jake what they were talking about and Jake responded, "Fishing."

Ten minutes later, Connie stood outside his door. "Telephone for you, Chief. It's Houston."

When she continued to loiter, Rhys told her to shut his door, then answered the phone. "This is Chief Shepard."

"Chief. That sounds damn good on you, Rhys."

"Hey, Lieutenant," Rhys said, a little surprised that his old boss was calling. He hadn't heard from him since he'd taken leave from the department. "How are things at HPD?"

"Not bad, and really good for you."

Rhys took his feet off the desk and sat up straight. "How's that?"

"Little birdy says they want you to replace Jones when he retires next month." Hell yeah! He was getting promoted to lieutenant.

"Homicide's the word, kid. But keep this on the QT until personnel calls. I just wanted to give you advance notice. So act surprised."

"No problem," Rhys said. "And hey, thanks for this. You made my day." Lieutenant at one of the largest homicide departments in the country. Hot damn!

When he got off the phone, Jake popped his head inside Rhys's office. "What did Houston want?"

Rhys chuckled. "What are you, stalking my calls? Come in and shut the door." He waited for Jake to take a seat. "It's not official yet, but I'm getting promoted to lieutenant."

"Well, how 'bout that!" Jake said. "Congratulations."

"And get this. They're sending me to homicide."

"That's a big deal. Usually they send you to patrol to get your feet wet. Houston must love your ass."

Rhys shrugged. "I don't know about that." But he'd worked hard, putting in extra hours, taking lousy shifts, making plenty of collars.

"You sure you want to leave this gig?" Jake asked.

"I wanted to talk to you about that." Rhys got up, sat on the corner of his desk, and kept his voice low. "You should go for this job. I like what we've done here so far with getting the rigs, trying to keep the sheriff out of our backyard. I'd hate to see some outsider come in and screw it up, use it as a good-old-cop's club to retire. If Nugget still likes me when I leave, I could put in a good word for you. But with your experience, you won't need my endorsement." And after Sandy Addison got done with him, Jake might not want it.

"I wasn't really looking for a job that involved a lot of politics," Jake said. "That's one of the reasons I left LAPD. Too much jockeying for position. But I'll think about it. It would be better to be chief than working for an asshole."

Rhys chuckled. Guess Jake didn't think he was an asshole. Good to know.

"I'm gonna grab a bite. Hold down the fort till I get back, wouldya?" he said, and grabbed his jacket. He'd stroll over to the Ponderosa. Maybe Maddy would be there.

Owen was sitting on a stool eating a tuna melt when he walked in.

"Figured you for a Bun Boy kind of guy," Rhys said, and grabbed the seat next to him.

"Every now and then a man likes to change it up. And Tater makes a good sandwich."

"I suppose we could use a few more restaurants in town."

Owen shrugged. "Hell, with your girlfriend's inn going up, this place is turning into a regular metropolis."

Mariah came over to take Rhys's order. "Hi, Chief."

"How you doing, Mariah? I'll have what Owen's having."

"Coming right up." She moved down the bar to yell the order into the kitchen.

Rhys swiveled on the chair. "You probably know this town better than anyone, Owen. What's your take on how the vote'll go?"

"On the inn?" Owen took another bite of his sandwich and made Rhys wait while he chewed. "I'd say at this point it could go either way. Those Addisons hold some sway. But your girl ain't no lightweight. She's managed to swing some over to her side. I hear she's organizing some sort of job fair. Planning to hire folks right on the spot."

Maddy hadn't told him anything about it, but then again he hadn't seen hide nor hair of her in the last two days. "That so?"

"Yep. My guess is that it'll rile Sandy Addison up good. The woman already walks around like she's got a firecracker up her ass."

Rhys had to stifle a snicker. It wouldn't do any good having the police chief take sides. "Just as long as everyone keeps it legal."

"And what about you and Maddy?" Owen asked.

"What about us?"

Owen rolled his eyes. "Everyone in town knows you're hot for the girl and she's divorcing her skirt-chasing husband."

Ah, small-town life. Rhys had almost forgotten what it felt like. "Yeah. Well, if you know so much, how does it end?"

Owen hopped off his stool. "In the movies: The boy gets the girl and the girl gets the inn. In real life?" Owen shrugged. "Your guess is as good as mine." He shoved a couple of bills under his empty plate. "I got to get back to cutting hair."

At the eleventh hour Maddy had to bail on Dave. Today was war.

A Deep Throat source had warned Mariah that at noon, the Addisons planned to picket the inn. Supposedly there were at least eighty protesters and they'd hired the Nugget High School marching band.

Nate had been notified and was on his way. Job applications had been printed. Tables had been set up inside the inn. And signs had been posted across town, letting everyone know that the Lumber Baron was officially hiring.

Word traveled fast because applicants from as far away as Sierraville had already started lining up outside the inn's gates. Thank goodness it was a nice day for it. Most of the snow had melted from the big storm and the sun shined. Maddy walked the floor until she thought she'd wear the soles of her shoes bare, nervous that they'd mess up the timing. The plan was to start the interviews the minute the demonstrators arrived.

She looked out over the crowd of people and mumbled, "The only thing standing between you and an hourly wage is Sandy Addison and the Nugget City Council."

Occasionally, she and Sophie would pop outside to hand out application forms to newcomers and answer questions. At eleven forty-five, just as Nate arrived, Maddy stepped out onto the veranda with a bullhorn in her hand.

"Attention, everyone," she said, her voice amplified loud enough to be heard across the square. "In fifteen minutes we'll open the doors for interviews, starting with the first five applicants. I promise there will be no hiring decisions until we've talked with every last one of you. But in order to expedite the process, we ask that you have your applications filled out and your identification ready. Thanks for coming and good luck to all of you."

"Impressive," Nate said, trying to count heads.

On the other side of the square, the Addisons and their group began assembling.

Maddy had hoped that once word got out about the job fair the Addisons would have cancelled their demonstration. But it looked like they didn't plan to surrender.

Rhys came up the walkway wearing his uniform. He probably thought looking official would help keep the peace. "Hey," he said.

"Hey, yourself." This was the first time she'd seen him since their non-breakup—because, how, really, can you break up when you're not even a couple? Just a booty call. Yet, she still felt like her heart was coming out of her chest. She tried to smile and look like he wasn't affecting her. "We got a good crowd."

"Yeah, and on short notice." He seemed a little surprised—and worried.

"You gonna be okay?" He tilted his head toward the approaching protestors.

ᴖ course," she said, with as much bravado as she could muster. All day she'd had a stomachache thinking about the pending confrontation.

"They have a permit, so it's all legal."

"I figured as much."

"Try to keep the peace, okay?" She couldn't see his eyes behind the aviators, but in his tone she detected a subtle warning.

"We're just conducting a job fair. That's all."

"Yeah, right." She saw a hint of a grin before he walked away.

Nate cornered her when she got inside. "You think Dave's going to fight you for the house now?" he asked, taking away the bullhorn she'd been gripping like a lethal weapon.

"What was I supposed to do? Drop everything and drive four hours in the middle of this?" She gazed out at the cluster of demonstrators who'd claimed a strip of land across from the line of job hopefuls. The band played Pink Floyd's "Comfortably Numb."

Sophie tapped on her watch. "It's time. Let's do it."

They opened the doors of the inn and Nate waved in the first five. Maddy had organized it so that each interviewee got an audience with both her and Nate. They put the applications of the candidates they liked in a binder and the others in a box.

The Baker's Dozen came bearing sustenance, and the women all wore T-shirts with a picture of the Lumber Baron.

"Pam had them made," Amanda said. "Aren't they cute?"

Between interviews, Maddy peered outside the window to check out the scene. Rhys had evidently posted Wyatt and Jake in front of the inn to keep tempers from flaring. As she hoped, the job candidates had become immediately territorial about the inn and their future employment prospects.

Some of them, probably in an attempt to razz the demonstrators, danced on the sidewalk to the music of the marching band. According to rumor, at least two of the protestors had jumped ship to join the job-fair crowd when they heard the Lumber Baron offered full benefits and a 401k savings plan.

After two hours, the band split for another gig in Graeagle, and the demonstrators, whose chants and rallying cries were then drowned out by the heckling of the inn's prospective employees, gave up in frustration.

Maddy and Nate won this round. But in three days, the Nugget City Council would decide who gained the ultimate victory.

In the meantime, the line of still-to-be-interviewed candidates stretched farther down the block than when they had started. By the end of the day, Maddy suffered from dry mouth and her neck and shoulders killed from sitting in a straight-back chair for hours on end.

"How many left?" she asked Nate, letting out a loud yawn.

"That was our last one."

"Boy, do I want to soak in a hot bath," she said, rubbing her aching muscles. "You staying at Sophie and Mariah's?"

"Yeah. I thought we could have an early dinner together. Tomorrow I'm heading back to San Francisco first thing in the morning. In fact, I've got to get gas before the Nugget Gas and Go closes—whoever heard of a gas station shutting down at five and not opening until nine?"

"The guy who owns it is really old, Nate. He's trying to sell the station, but no one wants to buy it. I feel so bad for him that I half wish I could buy it just so he can relax."

She rotated her neck. "How 'bout I go home, take a shower, and meet you at the Ponderosa at six?"

"Sounds good. Want me to lock up?"

"I'll do it. I've got it down to a fifteen-minute routine. Go get gas before it's too late. If I'm not in the restaurant before you, order me one of those Negronis you like."

"Okay." Nate grabbed his jacket and on his way out, paused at the door. "Hey, Mad, you done good today."

She looked up from folding the last of the card tables. "We're in it to win it."

"We sure are." The door clicked behind him.

Maddy carried the box of cast-off applications to her office. On her way back she collected the water pitchers she'd stacked on the mantel and headed to the kitchen. She stood over the sink washing glasses when someone knocked on the back door. Peering out the window she suspected the man standing on the stoop was a straggler who still wanted a shot at an interview.

She opened the door. "I'm sorry, we've finished for the evening. But if you'd like to leave your—"

Before she could finish her sentence, he shoved her back inside the kitchen and flipped the dead bolt, forcing her against the wall. "We alone?"

Her eyes slid down to where he held her throat and her knees buckled.

"Don't lie to me, bitch. Don't you fucking lie to me." He pressed against her larynx and she struggled to breathe.

She pulled at his arms, gulping for air, until he loosened his grip. "What do you want?" she asked in a scratchy voice she barely recognized.

"I want my stuff." He put his face so close to hers that his putrid breath nearly made her puke. His teeth were rotten, his eyes glazed, and his face was covered in sores.

She tried to stay calm while her eyes darted around the room looking for a possible weapon. "My purse is in the other room. Just take it and go."

He yanked her hair. "Show me."

She led him into the parlor where they'd held the interviews, praying that someone would see her through the windows and send in the cavalry.

"Where's my go, bitch?"

She didn't know what he was talking about or what his "go" was. She had never seen him before in her life. He was obviously high as a kite and had mistaken her for someone else. But now didn't seem like a good time to quibble.

"You got it somewhere in the house?" He pulled so hard on her ponytail she felt her scalp ripping.

"I don't know what it is," she cried. "If it's money you want, I can get it. I just need to go to the bank. I'll come right back."

"Do you think I'm stupid?" He slammed her against the wall and that's when fear the likes of which she'd never known hit her. *He's going to really, really hurt me, maybe even murder me.*

He found her bag, emptied it on the floor, and combed through her wallet. "Twenty fucking bucks. That's all you have, bitch?" He threw the wallet against the fireplace and turned on her with feral eyes. "You wanna live, give me my shit back."

Oh, God, focus, Maddy. Think of something. "I'm new here. Just tell me what it is and I'll find it for you. I promise."

He cackled, his flying spittle landing on her skin, making her want to scrub herself raw. "The barrels that used to be in your basement . . . the equipment."

Now she knew. This was the man who'd attacked Colin, the man who'd set up the meth lab in her inn. "I don't have it, but I could write you a check for the value."

His hand snaked out so fast she didn't see it coming before it cracked her across the face. And then he reached inside his jacket and pressed a knife against her throat.

The lights at the inn were still on and Rhys decided to stroll over. All day he'd resisted the urge to visit Maddy while she conducted her interviews. He missed her, but didn't want to send mixed messages. It was better to go cold turkey. Prolonging any kind of relationship would only make it worse when it came time for him to leave.

At least the job fair had gone off without a hitch. Honestly, he'd had some concerns that team Addison might come to blows with team Breyer. But it looked as though the protestors had left with their tails between their legs. Now Rhys could take off his damn uniform.

He was halfway to the inn when his hackles went up. He could see two people through one of the windows and although he couldn't make them out, something about the way they were standing was off. Like they were locked together, performing a peculiar slow dance.

It might be nothing, but he reached for his Glock. Rhys took a detour around the back of the inn. He found the kitchen door locked. With the butt of his gun he knocked out a pane of glass and reached for the latch.

If it turned out he had an overactive imagination, he'd make the repairs himself. But something seemed wrong—a sort of heaviness in the air. A stillness. A pall. Rhys registered the empty pitchers in the sink, when a groaning noise sent him on full-blown alert.

Slipping quietly from the kitchen, he went from room to room, crouching along the walls. The sun had set, casting eerie shadows over the empty mansion while he wended his way toward the source of the sound.

When he got to the front room he saw some son of a bitch putting Maddy in a hostage hold, the edge of a knife hovering dangerously close to her carotid artery.

Rhys drew on him, staring down the sight of his 9mm, blood rushing to his ears. He couldn't look at Maddy. If he saw her fear, he'd lose it. He needed to focus. He needed to stay in control. *Bear with me, baby. Bear with me.*

If the bastard so much as hurt one hair on her head . . . "Police! Put the knife down!"

"I'll slash her throat, you come any closer." The man swayed a little off-balance and Rhys could tell he was stoned out of his mind.

Rhys clenched his teeth, never wavering, never taking his eyes off the target. "This is your last warning. Drop the knife."

"Fuck you." The man let out a high-pitched giggle, leaning a little to the right.

That's all Rhys needed for a clean shot.

He squeezed the trigger and the man staggered back, dropped the knife as he crumpled to the ground. Blood oozed from a small hole in his head. Rhys kicked the weapon away and checked his wrist for a pulse.

He couldn't find one—just a scorpion tattoo on the back of his hand.

He reached for Maddy who stood stock-still in shock. She tottered and he held her upright. "Don't faint on me, sugar."

"I'm okay," she said, her voice so hoarse Rhys could barely make out what she'd said. "Is he . . . ?"

"Yeah," Rhys said, immediately checking her from head to toe. "Did he hurt you?"

She shook her head. "I was so scared, Rhys. Those were his drugs in the basement and he wanted them back."

He brushed hair away from her eyes and felt his gorge rise when he saw the bruises on her face and throat. "He hit you?"

"If you hadn't come when you did . . ." She looked at the dead man lying on her polished wooden floor. "Oh, God, I don't think I'll ever stop feeling that knife against my throat.

"Rhys," she said in a whisper. "I want to go home."

He stiffened. Where was home? San Francisco? "Wherever you want to go, Maddy. I'll take you."

She leaned on him for stability and he felt a shiver go through her. "You'll stay with me, right? In the trailer?"

Rhys let out the breath he hadn't even realized he'd been holding. "For as long as you want." He pulled off his jacket, so he could wrap it around her shoulders, and pulled out his cell phone.

"Jake, I'm at the Lumber Baron." He paused briefly to steady himself. "Come get my weapon—and send a coroner's van."

Chapter 23

Everywhere Maddy went the next morning someone was talking about the shooting. If she didn't know better she'd think the good folks of Nugget were bloodthirsty. Especially that Portia Cane, who at the Ponderosa had taken particular pleasure in telling the story—as if she'd been there herself.

From what Maddy had heard even Stu and Ethel were holding court at the Nugget Market, telling their customers that Chief Shepard had put a bullet in their robber. And even though they'd never see a dime of their stolen money, they could at least feel safe in their store again.

Last night, before they'd gone home, someone from the Plumas County Sheriff's Department had come to take Rhys's statement and his gun for testing. "Nothing to worry about," Rhys had assured her. "It's standard procedure in any police shooting."

Maddy had also been questioned at length by a deputy. Now she and Nate stood outside the inn, leaning against his Jaguar, drinking coffee, waiting for detectives to clear the scene. They'd promised it wouldn't be too much longer. A crime-scene cleaning crew sat in a van, ready to go. Nate had hired them. Maddy didn't even know businesses like that existed.

"You okay?" In the last hour he'd been asking her that repeatedly.

"I'm fine."

"It's not going to creep you out going back inside—like having flashbacks?"

"I hope not," she said. "I don't want to let some tweaker ruin this beautiful place for me."

She'd had a pretty rough night—lots of bad dreams, fits and turns. But Rhys had held and rocked her—made her feel safe. She kept visualizing him, both hands locked on the grip of that gun, eyes narrowed over the barrel, voice controlled and commanding. He might've seemed stoic immediately after the shooting, but while they lay in bed she'd felt the rage pulsating through him.

And when they woke up, he'd made love to her slowly, watching her surge beneath him like he was trying to commit the shape of her face, the feel of her body and the taste of her mouth to memory.

"I love you, Rhys," she'd said, clinging to him.

Because in that moment she'd realized what she felt for this man was so much more powerful than anything she'd ever felt for anyone.

She'd loved Dave with all her heart. But not like this. What she felt for Rhys took her breath away, it was that indescribable, that astounding. It made her weak and invincible all at the same time. It made her tremble and burn. It made her feel infinitely secure. Because Rhys never wavered—he was like an ancient tree trunk; anchored, solid, steadfast.

But Rhys hadn't said it back. He'd just cuddled her and told her that everything would be okay.

Nate poked her in the arm. "Where'd you go?"

She tried to clear her head, purge it of the night's dreadfulness. "I'm concerned about Rhys."

"Maddy, he's a cop. He can handle it."

"It's not just the shooting," she said. "He takes care of a lot of people and doesn't have anyone to take care of him." And the truth was, he might not be capable of letting anyone. Growing up the way he did, Rhys had good reason to want to protect his heart.

Nate knitted his brows together, guilt covering his face. The whole morning he'd been blaming himself. "Christ, Maddy. I shouldn't have left you alone to lock up. If I'd stayed, none of this would've happened. The thought that he could've . . . I can't even go there."

"Don't be an idiot, Nate. The guy nearly killed Colin. If you want to blame someone, blame that maniac."

The maniac was Robbie Salter, according to his driver's license. Apparently, he'd been living on and off in the Sierra for some time and had taken up with a circle of druggies and ex-cons.

A deputy came out of the inn and called them over. "We're done here. It's all yours."

Nate signaled the cleanup crew and he and Maddy went inside. Despite the morning chill, she felt a trickle of sweat run down the valley between her breasts and had a hard time making her legs move beyond the confines of the foyer.

"Here, hold my hand," Nate said, sensing her trepidation. "We'll go in together."

Other than a dark kidney-shaped stain on the hardwood floor, the front parlor showed no signs of a shooting. It didn't even smell bad, but Maddy opened a few windows just the same.

"I'm okay," she said, her arms folded over her chest. "Everything happened so fast last night that I guess I expected to walk in this morning to find a *Texas Chain Saw Massacre*–kind of mess. But I can deal with this. I can definitely deal with this."

After a while she got up enough nerve to wander into the kitchen where the man had first attacked her. Again, she felt nothing. No fear. No post-traumatic stress. Maybe it would come later, but for now it felt over. Done.

"Hey." Colin smiled at her through the back door's broken window-pane. He held up a new panel. "I had some wavy glass left over from the cabinets. It'll work in here."

"I didn't hear you drive up."

"You were in the parlor." He broke off the remaining jagged pieces of glass from the door. "You okay?"

People would probably keep asking her that for a while. "Yep."

"Good," he said. "I finished those chairs you wanted and put them on the front porch."

She followed him around the side of the house, where four rocking chairs and a glider sat on the veranda. "Oh, Colin," she squealed in delight. "They're spectacular." She jogged up the stairs, testing and touching each one.

More feminine than his usual work, the chairs had graceful lines—slender and somewhat ornate—without being fussy. And instead of leaving them natural pine, Colin had painted the rockers glossy white.

"I think they go," he said, standing back to assess the chairs in their new setting.

"They absolutely go. They're the most beautiful pieces of furniture I've ever seen."

His face positively glowed from the praise. Maddy wrapped her arms around him and squeezed. "Thank you. This makes the place feel like a home—not like a crime scene."

It was really too cold to sit outside, but Maddy couldn't stand the thought of being closed up inside her apartment alone. So she wrapped herself in a flannel blanket and planned to spend the rest of the day cuddled up on her glider, relaxing, since she hadn't gotten much sleep the night before. Everyone was gone, and oddly the noises from the forest helped to soothe her frayed nerves.

She'd begun to nod off when the sound of an engine brought her awake. At the top of the driveway a Lincoln Town Car sputtered to a halt. She shielded her eyes with her hands and craned her neck to get a better look.

Maddy was relieved when Rhys's truck pulled in behind the Lincoln. It would be a long time before she'd feel comfortable having encounters with strangers. A man got out of the limo, but Maddy couldn't see his face as he started down the hill. Unfortunately, she'd know that stride anywhere.

Dave!

He'd left at least three messages on her machine. But she didn't have the wherewithal to call him back.

"Maddy?"

She rose, met him halfway, and he scooped her up in a passionate embrace. "Oh, baby, you all right? I've been calling and calling."

"I'm okay." It struck her how overly polished he looked—like a mannequin in a fancy men's store. Had he always dressed so formally?

"I finally got ahold of Sophie and she told me what happened." He held her away from him. "Let me have a look at you."

Rhys came up behind them and did his head-nod thing. "Hey." There was no warmth in his salutation. Maddy presumed he'd already figured out that the man with his hands all over her was Dave.

Rhys continued to stand there, his arms akimbo, and Maddy wanted to disappear. Just let the ground swallow her up whole. She wanted to tell Dave to go home, to go back to San Francisco. But she was stuck. So she made polite introductions while silently pleading with Rhys to trust her.

Dave wasn't typically rude, but he turned on Rhys. "What kind of department are you running that a madman holds a knife to my wife's throat?"

"Dave," Maddy could feel her face flush, "Chief Shepard saved my—"

"He wouldn't have had to, if he'd been doing his job properly in the first place."

Rhys slowly appraised Dave's Hermès tie, his monogrammed shirt, his Ferragamo loafers. "I'll let y'all get reacquainted." He tipped his head—"Mrs. Wellmont"—and strolled to the fifth wheel.

"Rhys," she called after him, but he kept walking.

"Let's get you packed up," Dave said, seemingly oblivious to the tension. "I want you out of this town. Which one is yours?"

She absently pointed to her side of the duplex and started to go after Rhys. But Dave had taken it upon himself to walk right into her apartment. As if he owned the place. "Dave, where are you going?" she shouted, and jogged after him.

As soon as she got rid of him, she'd go talk to Rhys. All she could think about was the look on his face when she'd called him Chief Shepard.

"So this is where you've been living for the last four months?" He looked around the small living room and walked through Maddy's bedroom into the kitchen. She could see his disapproval and it irked her.

"I'll get you home soon," he said.

"Dave—"

"You've gotta be exhausted, baby." He grabbed her around the waist and steered her to the bed. "Lie down. I'll get Renny from the car. Together we'll pack this place up while you rest."

"Dave, I need you to listen to me." Either the man was intentionally being obtuse to get his way, or he was completely crackers.

He played with the scarf around her neck. She'd worn it to cover the bruise where the psycho had choked her. "What's this?" He lifted the locket that peeked out from under the silk and opened the pendant. "The Lumber Baron?"

He took a closer look and grinned. "It needs a paint job." Then he tried to kiss her, but she moved her face so all he caught was the side of her cheek. "I've missed you, Maddy."

"Look, Dave. This thing you're doing here. Not working. I'm sorry I stood you up, but—"

"Yeah, I know, you were busy nearly getting stabbed to death." He rubbed his face and looked at his watch. "I was hoping to get out of here before it gets dark. I'm still pretty jet-lagged."

"Well, it was great of you to come." She got up, hoping he'd take the hint. Get. Out.

"Mad, enough! I get it. You want me to feel your pain over Gabby until I grovel. Okay, you've won. I can't look at a picture of Max without making myself sick. Half my friends aren't talking to me, including Soph and Mariah. Even my own mother."

When Maddy muttered, "Yeah, right," Dave said, "She thinks you'll find a loophole in the prenup and take us to the cleaners. So game over, Maddy. I pronounce you the victor. Just come home already. When you're feeling better in a week or two, we'll come back. I promise."

"Dave, there's no *we* anymore." Why had she never noticed how self-absorbed he was?

"Look, baby, I've had a lot of experience with hotels and you're sunk. No one is going to want to stay in your inn now. It's tainted. I'll buy it off you and Nate—turn it into a halfway house or something. It'll be a good tax write-off."

She laughed. Not just laughed, roared. "Dave, you don't know anything about Nugget. These people love a story of survival. This is the home of the Donner Party, for heaven's sake."

"Okay," he said, running his hands through his perfectly coiffed hair, trying to placate her. Clearly, he suspected that she'd lost her mind. "Maybe we should stay the night. With a good night's sleep, you'll see reason in the morning."

"Dave." She wanted to rip her hair out. "Sit."

When he took his place next to her on the bed, she said, "I forgive you."

Dumbfounded, he turned and looked at her like he thought it might be a trick. "Really? For Gabby, for everything?"

"For everything."

"So, you'll stop this divorce and we can go back to the way we were?" The man was so self-entitled that it actually made him dense.

"No." Back when anger and pain had consumed her, she'd fantasized about this moment. How she would make him beg for her forgiveness. Now, she just wanted him to go away. For good.

"Why?" he asked. "Why can't we go back to the way we were?"

"Because we were never that way."

He rubbed his temples, and Maddy registered that he was trying hard to understand. Not getting his way was as foreign to Dave as Tristan da Cunha, the most remote inhabited place in the world. At least according to Wikipedia.

"So you're saying our whole marriage was a sham? Which means you haven't really forgiven me at all, have you?"

"I have forgiven you," Maddy said. She took a deep breath and let it out. "I'm just not in love with you anymore."

She watched as the color drained from his aristocratic face. "Because of Gabriella?"

"Maybe in the beginning." Now, Gabby didn't even factor into the picture. This was about her, about her evolution. "But then I changed, became a different person with different needs."

"And I can no longer fulfill those needs?" he asked, and for the first time seemed to be actually listening.

She thought about Rhys, about how he was a man to always count on, and said, "I don't think you ever could."

He leaned his head back and shut his eyes. "Is there a chance, if we tried, you could love me again?"

"No," she said, and saw the exact moment when it finally sunk into his head. It was really and truly over.

"You look like something the cat dragged in, man." Clay figured his friend was in a bad way so he came to the police station to see what he could do. "Where were you last night? I called you five times."

"Stayed in Reno. Shut off my phone."

"The shooting, or that Lincoln that drove through town?"

"You heard about that, huh?"

"There's very little in this town I don't hear about. That her husband?"

"Yup."

"Figured as much. She leave him, or did they ride off into the sunset together?"

"Dunno."

"She lives next door to you. How do you not know?"

Rhys squinted his eyes like he had a headache. "He came down the driveway all duded up in designer clothes, got in my face about Rotten Robbie attacking Maddy, and then disappeared inside her place. When I got home this morning, the Lincoln was gone."

"You didn't knock on her door?"

"She'll let me know when she's ready—send an email, a text, whatever."

Clay gave Rhys a hard perusal. "You'll be okay with it if they've reconciled."

"Sure."

Yeah, right, Clay wanted to say. The boy wore his goddamn heart on his sleeve. "My escrow closed. Let's grab lunch and I'll buy you a drink."

Rhys muttered, "Had plenty of those," and grabbed his jacket.

"And the shooting?" Clay asked on the way over to the bowling alley. "You okay with that?"

"Sure. Why wouldn't I be?"

"Don't pull that on me. I've been to war. I know what killing a man feels like. And it can fuck you up."

"I'm fine," he said. "But if it makes you feel any better, there's still plenty of time for PTSD to set in."

Once in the Ponderosa, they grabbed two menus and instead of waiting for a host, seated themselves. Mariah waved from behind the bar.

"Seems like that escrow closed pretty fast," Rhys said, after a server took their orders.

Clay shrugged. "Foreclosure—cash deal."

Rhys whistled. "Must be nice to be rich."

"Not rich anymore. It wiped me out. So buy the goddamn house. Otherwise, my boys ain't going to college."

Rhys rolled his eyes and leaned forward. "Houston wants to make me a homicide lieutenant."

"No kidding!" He high-fived Rhys. "You've been wanting this for a long time."

"Yes, I have."

"Congratulations. Then I guess you're taking it."

"Yup," Rhys said, falling back against the cushioned bench. "How are the boys? You and Justin patch things up?"

"No." Clay let out a breath. "That'll take some time. Right now he blames me for Jen's death. I figure better him blame me than having the memory of his mother sullied by the truth."

"He's going to find out eventually."

"Yeah, I know. And when that day comes, it would sure help if you lived next door."

"You fight dirty, Clay."

"I fight to win." He pulled a pen from his jacket, scrawled a figure on a napkin and shoved it at Rhys. "That's what it'll take to get in the house."

Rhys shoved the napkin back. "I have it on good authority it's worth twice that."

"Hey, if you wanna pay more, that'll work, too."

"I don't want to pay anything, since I'm going back to Houston."

"You on duty?"

"Nope—paid administrative leave until the sheriff deems that the shooting was clean. It's just a formality."

There was no doubt in Clay's mind that the son of a bitch had had a bullet coming. "Hey, Mariah," he called across the dining room, "get my friend here a Jack, neat." He turned to Rhys. "When are you going to stop running? This place needs you, Rhys. Sam and Lina like it here and God knows those two kids have been through enough.

Now you're gonna drag 'em to Texas? I'm not buying this promotion shit. Chief trumps lieutenant."

"This job's not permanent."

"Bullshit!" Clay waited for Mariah to put down the drinks and go back to the bar. "It's yours if you want it."

"Not if Sandy Addison has anything to say about it."

"Screw her," Clay said. "Now hear me out. I'll carry the note on the house." Rhys tried to interrupt him, but he wouldn't let him talk. "This is a sound business proposal for both of us." He made a few calculations on the napkin and shoved it under Rhys's nose. "Over a thirty-year fixed loan this is what you'll pay the bank in interest— even if you get the lowest rate possible. That's a hell of a lot of money and I'd prefer you pay it to me."

He reached inside his pocket again and dangled a key in front of Rhys's face. "Let's make a deal."

"Clay," Rhys said. "I appreciate what you're doing, I really do. But nothing works for me here, man. I don't belong in Nugget."

Clay wanted to tell his friend that everything was working for him here—a family, friends, a great job—but Rhys was so mired in the past, he couldn't see it. Shit happens, you move on.

But Rhys's mind was already made up. Nothing would hold him in this town.

Maddy kept looking out her front window, searching for Rhys's truck. She had stayed up most of the previous night waiting for him to come home. Now it was close to sundown and he still wasn't back. When she finally heard his tires on the gravel, she grabbed her coat and dashed outside.

"Hey," he said, climbing out of his truck.

"Where've you been? I've been freaking out, trying to find you."

"Where's Dave?" He headed to the trailer, his gait deceptively easy, like he couldn't care less about her answer. It was the stiff way he held his shoulders that gave him away.

"I sent him packing less than an hour after he got here, but you were already gone. Dammit, Rhys, I went to the police station, the Ponderosa; I even drove up McCreedy Road looking for your truck. And your phone goes straight to voice mail."

"I was in Reno," he muttered, fumbling for his house key.

"Reno? Why'd you go to Reno?"

"I was feeling lucky." He opened the door of the fifth wheel, seemed to hesitate, and then asked her to come inside.

"You cold?" He turned on the space heater, looking at her for the first time since he'd pulled up. She knew her eyes were swollen, her face mottled from crying and last time she looked, her hair had a serious case of the frizzies. But he was staring at the bruise on her cheek, which had turned a deep black and blue, and she saw him wince.

He untied the scarf that covered her discolored throat and gently caressed it with his thumb. "Hurt?"

"I'm okay. But I had trouble sleeping without you," she said. "I'm sorry about what Dave said. He's an ass. I know you think he has this magical pull on me. But it's over between us. I love you, Rhys." *Tell me that you love me, too.*

Leaning against the kitchen counter, he closed his eyes for a second and took a deep breath. "We need to talk."

She knew whatever he had to say was not good. He motioned for her to take a seat, so she perched on the edge of one of the recliners, her mouth so dry she was finding it hard to swallow.

"Maddy, I made lieutenant at Houston PD. I've been meaning to tell you . . . but . . . there just hasn't been a good time. I've accepted the position."

The trailer's walls felt like they were closing in on her and she could hardly breathe, the space heater was so hot. He'd always told her he was leaving. Nothing had changed, he was following his plan. So why then was she hyperventilating?

"Congratulations, Rhys. I'm really proud of you." She got to her feet and prayed she could make it to the door without bursting into tears.

Like a fool, she'd tricked herself into believing that the shooting had changed everything. That life was too fragile to waste worrying about perfect timing, perfect jobs, and imperfect places. But it wasn't about her and Dave, or about Houston PD, or even about Nugget. Rhys didn't love her. At least not enough to stay.

"Maddy, ah, honey, I don't know what to say." He looked so uncomfortable, like email would've been a better option. Then he wouldn't have to see her dying inside.

"It's okay." She started fanning her face as if that would hold back the tears. "It's really okay. I have to go now. Nate, Sophie, and Mariah are waiting for me."

She fumbled with the doorknob and practically ran to her car. Somehow she made it to the Ponderosa without having remembered the drive there. Nate, Sophie, and Mariah lounged in one of the back booths. For an instant, Maddy considered turning around and running out.

"Hey, Mad." Nate waved to her, and the three made room so she could squish in. "You okay? You don't look so good."

Too late.

"My face just stings a little, is all." She pointed to the bruise and slid into the banquette.

"Oh, you poor thing," Sophie said, then looked at the others questioningly.

"What?" Maddy asked.

"We have news, but maybe now's not such a hot time. You're recuperating."

Maddy examined all three of them, trying to read their faces. "No. Tell me."

"We're having a baby," Mariah blurted, and the sheer radiance emanating from her nearly blinded Maddy. It was enough to light the entire room.

"Well, not quite yet," Sophie clarified, but she, too, wore an ear-to-ear smile. She explained that she and Mariah were going to use in vitro fertilization in which Mariah's eggs would be surgically removed from her ovary, mixed with Nate's sperm in a petri dish, and transferred to Sophie's uterus.

"We'll all be connected to the baby—you, too, Maddy." Then Sophie went on to praise science and medicine and a lot of things Maddy couldn't listen to right now. It all buzzed in her head like static.

"When do you start?" Maddy asked, trying to seem as over the moon as everyone else at the table. She really was happy for her friends . . . But Rhys was leaving . . . and she loved him.

"First, Mariah has to take hormones to increase her egg production," Sophie explained. "And if all goes well, we could be pregnant in a couple of months."

Nate, who'd been quietly observing her, said, "You okay, Mad? You don't look so good."

"I'm fine. Just a little shaken up still."

"Maybe you should call it an early night." Nate cocked his head with concern. "I'm counting on you to kick us some Addison ass tomorrow."

Rhys sat inside the trailer, drinking his coffee. He could hear Sam outside, dribbling on the dirt. Every time the ball bounced against the backboard, his head felt ready to explode. He'd spent another quality night with his good friend, Jack Daniels.

Out of habit, he reached for his empty holster and decided to slip it onto his belt anyway. He stuffed his arms into his jacket and went outside.

"You ready?" he called to Sam as he made his way across the makeshift basketball court. Maddy's Outback still sat on the car pad. Typically on mornings like this she was at the inn when he got to the police station after taking Sam to school. Seeing her sitting on the mansion's veranda, waving to him from across the square, had lit him up like a bottle rocket. That's what she did to him.

She loved him and he was just walking away.

"Yep." Sam tossed him the ball and Rhys did a layup.

Lina came onto the porch with a brown paper bag. "I made you breakfast," she said, begrudgingly shoving the bag at him and walking away before he could thank her.

He peeked inside the sack to find an egg-and-bacon sandwich neatly wrapped in cellophane, and a banana. Climbing the stairs two at a time, he went inside the house and found her in the kitchen. "Stop being mad at me, Lina. I'm doing the best I can."

"Nope," she said. "You can do a lot better." For a shrimp, the girl was a real ball buster.

He swung his gaze to Shep, who sat at the Formica table, sipping coffee. "Good morning, Pop?"

Shep held up his cast. "Damn thing itches." He turned to the stove where Lina was cooking oatmeal. "I want eggs, Rosa."

Rhys caught Lina's eye, shook his head in frustration and left.

"Let's get," he called to Sam and followed the boy up into his truck. "How's school?"

"Great!" Sam said. At least someone was happy.

"You and Cody getting along?"

Sam nodded. "Since I moved here he's been my best friend."

Both boys were mourning the loss of their mothers. It was good that they had each other. When Rhys was a kid, he'd had Clay. Funny how sometimes life could come full circle.

"We're joining 4-H," Sam said. "Cody's dad said I could have a steer and keep it at their ranch until we show them at the fair."

Rhys frowned. "Hey, kid, you know we're moving to Houston, right?"

"Lina doesn't want to."

"Well, you guys are certainly free to stay here; maybe you could get yourselves jobs working on the railroad."

He crossed the trestle bridge leading to Nugget Elementary, flashing on how he used to ride his bike over the short span, intentionally hitting the cattle guards for extra bump.

"Whoa, you see that?" He pulled to the shoulder of the road and pointed at the river. "Big old steelhead jumping."

He sat there, looking out over the water, remembering sitting on the shore with his pole and bucket. "I caught my first fish in the Feather—Cody's grandpa took me."

Sam bounced up in his seat and craned his neck to see. "Can we go?"

"Fishing?" Rhys asked, and Sam nodded. "Too cold. Fall is the best time for catching steelhead. You a pretty good fisherman?" Rhys couldn't help it; he ruffled the kid's hair.

"I've never been."

"You've never been fishing?" How could a boy make it to eleven and not have had that rite of passage? It tugged at his gut that he wouldn't teach Sam how to angle in the Feather River, on the banks where he'd spent many a chilly October day as a boy, casting his line.

Sam just shrugged and Rhys shook his head. Can't play basketball. Can't fish. Neither kid could drive. Man, he had his work cut out for him.

After he dropped off Sam, Rhys went to the station.

"Congrats, Chief," Connie called from her desk.

When he gave her a what-the-hell-for look, she said, "You've been cleared and reinstated. Welcome back, though you never really left." Rhys caught her doing an eye roll as she walked away.

"Connie, don't you have some vacation time you need to take?"

"Nope. You're a slave driver."

He hung his jacket on its hook and sorted through the messages on his desk. Connie came into his office and shoved a box under his face.

"What's this?" he asked.

"Your weapon, I presume."

"Put it over there." Without looking up he nudged his head at the corner of his desk and went back to his messages. There was one from Dink Caruthers.

"Someone woke up on the wrong side of the bed," she muttered as she left.

No, someone woke up in an empty bed.

Rhys opened the box, removed his Glock, loaded it with one in the chamber and holstered it to his belt. Then he dialed the mayor.

He had no idea what his honor wanted, but given that tonight was the Lumber Baron hearing, and that he'd had that run-in with Sandy Addison, it couldn't be good.

Chapter 24

The auditorium was stuffed to the gunwales and Maddy saw no sign of Rhys.

"Quit it!" Nate pulled her down in her seat. "You're making me a nervous wreck."

Maddy found it difficult to sit still while Bud Coleman gave a forty-five minute dissertation on the capacity, or lack thereof, of Nugget's Wastewater Treatment Plant. Several audience members, she'd noticed, nodded off in their chairs.

"What's the bottom line, Bud?" Mayor Caruthers impatiently interrupted. "Can the system accommodate a twenty-room hotel, or not?"

"It's not that simple."

In Maddy's mind it was, but Bud apparently wanted to cover his ass in case of an ensuing shitstorm. Literally.

"Well, sure it is." Dink started losing his patience.

"The system's old," Bud said. "Maybe it can handle it, maybe it can't. But there's no question anything new might tax it."

Way to be as namby-pamby as possible, Bud. Maddy wanted to tell him to sit down and let their expert have the floor.

Dottie Campbell, one of the council members, dittoed that emotion a few minutes later, stopping his wishy-washy sputter midstream. "Sit down, Bud."

Bud gathered up his stack of papers from the podium and slunk away from the microphone. Maddy and Nate's specialist took to the stage, opened his laptop, and directed his laser pointer at a big screen behind the council table. The council members turned their chairs around so they could view his presentation.

Maddy craned her head to look at the back of the room for Rhys, but with the lights dimmed she couldn't see anything. Their expert spent the next hour methodically highlighting how the city's wastewater system was more than adequate to take on a small hotel. Although Doug came across much more decisive than Bud, Maddy had to admit that his primer was equally boring.

She caught a council member yawning a few times during his program, Dink stealthily text messaging, and at least one other council member doodling. Not a good sign, she feared. Even she had started to drift before the lights flicked back on.

"Any questions?" their expert asked the council members.

"I have one," Dottie said. "How much did the Lumber Baron owners pay you for your expert opinion?"

Maddy felt the audience suddenly spring to life as if it had been shocked out of a coma with a cattle prod.

Doug fidgeted with the lapel on his jacket, cleared his throat, and said, "Two hundred and twenty dollars an hour."

The room let out a collective gasp. Nate muttered a simple "Uh-oh," and Mariah winced.

"How many hours you figure you have in?" Dottie asked.

Doug appeared to be tallying it up in his head. "At least forty if you don't include my travel time to and from San Francisco."

Dottie flashed a snotty little smile. "Shall we take public comments now?" She waited for the other members of the council to agree and suggested that in order to save time, speakers should line up in the center aisle behind the microphone stand.

Sandy Addison was first up. Nate clenched Maddy's knee to stop her from rattling them out of nerves.

"That man," she pointed to Nate and Maddy's expert, "is being paid thousands of dollars to tell you a whole lot of hogwash. You heard Bud, he's been running Nugget's wastewater treatment plant for more than a decade. The pipes running underneath your homes and businesses can't take any more." Sandy squinted her eyes at Maddy. "They'll have you believe that it's only twenty rooms—not enough to break the system. I'm predicting that before long they turn that dining room into a little restaurant as a side business. There's nothing in their current permits that says they can't. That'll produce even more waste. And what about all those outbuildings? How much you wanna bet they turn those into rooms? More waste.

"Despite Mrs. Breyer's nasty accusations that Cal and I are trying to sabotage her inn because we don't want competition, we've got nothing against a new hotel coming into Nugget. We've got a loyal customer base—the same families have been returning to Beary Quaint for generations. But until the city can afford to put in a new sewage system none of us can afford the risk. If we have to shut down our cabins because toilets are backing up we'll go out of business and so will the rest of you."

A number of people applauded and Maddy wanted to crawl under her chair. For the next hour it was like open-mic night at the Improv. A steady stream of residents, merchants, and business owners made their way to the podium, some choosing to address issues that had nothing to do with the inn.

One fellow, whom Maddy had never seen before, wanted to discuss passing an ordinance that would fine residents for not cleaning up after their dogs.

"You've gotta be kidding me," Nate muttered.

"Shush," she said.

Finally, one of the council members told the man that tonight's hearing was strictly about the inn. A few more people got up, including Carl Rudd from the sporting goods store.

"I don't have anything against the Lumber Baron," he told the council. "In fact, I think it'll bring money to this town. But until we get the waste plant up to speed, it would be completely irresponsible of the city to allow any new businesses to open."

Unfortunately, unlike Sandy Addison, who in Maddy's opinion came off like a harridan with hemorrhoids, Carl sounded reasonable. Even smart. She looked across the room. The Nugget Mafia sat in a cluster and she saw a few of them nodding in agreement. Oh, this was not good. Not good at all.

Someone who didn't want to wait his turn shouted, "Has anyone looked into what the cost would be?"

Dink cleared his throat. "We've never formally opened it for bidding, but unofficial estimates have ranged in the millions—more than the town can afford, I'm afraid."

"What about putting a bond measure for the money on the June ballot?" someone yelled.

Portia kept muttering to anyone who would listen that the inn was "a hotbed of crime."

"I'd like to smack her," Maddy said between clenched teeth.

When it was Clay McCreedy's turn, Maddy squirmed. He had a lot of sway in this town, including the ear of the mob. She glanced over at the Nugget Mafia again, and this time Owen winked at her. Although Clay had always been absolutely lovely to her, Maddy got the sense he disapproved of a married woman leading on his best friend. And while the rest of the town had made it known whose camp they were in, Clay had steered clear of taking sides.

He didn't use the microphone, yet his voice boomed through the auditorium. "It's been a long night, so I'll keep this brief. My family's ranched this land since the nineteenth century—been here since the gold rush. As you well know, when Tip died two years ago, I retired from the Navy and moved back from San Diego with my family to take over. Just like he passed it on to his son, I want to pass it on to my boys. But I look around this town and I say, 'What'll hold 'em here?' All around me is decay. I watched you people shun Sophie and Mariah when they first brought the Ponderosa back to life. And now the inn."

He shook his head. "When are you people going to get it through those thick skulls of yours that we need businesses like this? People here need jobs. The town needs revenue. If it's the sewage system you're worried about, get it fixed! A bond measure's a good idea. Or hold a goddamn bake sale. Just do it! If these folks," he pointed to the five council members, "can't figure out a way, elect new ones who can."

Maddy looked over at a smiling Nate. "Don't jinx it."

"If Cowboy Clay didn't clinch it for us, your boyfriend's about to."

Maddy couldn't believe it. Rhys strode up to the podium in his uniform. He hated uniforms, said they made him itch. But for some crazy reason he'd gotten it in his head that the townspeople took him more seriously in it. They'd take him seriously in a clown suit.

"Clay's a tough act to follow," Rhys told the crowd. "I want to build on something Portia said earlier about the inn being a hotbed of crime."

There was a refrain of chuckles and Rhys's face grew stern. "I might laugh with you, if I hadn't had to take a young man's life in that inn." The hall fell silent. "I feel strongly that Robbie Salter came to Nugget because he found shelter—a place to set up his methamphetamine lab—in the abandoned Lumber Baron. You all may as well have rolled out a red carpet for him, letting that place fall to pieces the way you did. Then he terrorized the place—robbed the Nugget Market, nearly killed Colin Burke and held a knife to . . . Well, you get the picture. Bottom line: You shut that place down and it'll go vacant again. And this time, it's all decked out with hundreds of thousands of dollars' worth of upgrades. That's very attractive to thieves and vandals."

Rhys took a deep breath. "I'm not going to belabor the point, since we've been over it before." He started to walk away, stopped, then grabbed the mic again. "I know most of you are aware that me and Ms. Breyer . . . Oh, hell, how did you say it, Owen?"

"That you're hot for the girl," Owen shouted, and the room broke into uproarious laughter.

Rhys smiled. "Yeah, that pretty much sums it up. So if you think I'm biased, you're damned right. But this is the thing: when I left here eighteen years ago, I never expected to come back, let alone be the town's chief of police. Never thought in a million years I'd even like you people. And here I am, genuinely liking you—wanting to keep you safe. And I think I do a damn good job of it."

He stopped looking at the council members and turned to face the audience. "Houston PD wants me back, wants to give me a promotion."

The crowd booed and Rhys held up his hand. "But today, your mayor made me a very nice offer." Rhys nodded at Dink. "He wants me to be your permanent chief. It's where my little sister and brother want to be and it's always been Shep's home. Shep . . . Well, he needs this place now more than ever. But I'll only stay if Maddy stays."

He faced her and spoke as if they were the only two people in the room. "If you'll have me and if what you said is true, I'll stay. For you."

Maddy wiped tears from her eyes. She didn't know whether to wrap her arms around Rhys or to strangle him. What was he thinking blackmailing Nugget into voting in favor of the inn? Make no mistake about it; what he'd just done was extortion. This town loved Rhys Shepard.

The clapping of the audience filled her ears as her heart pounded. Nugget would be buzzing with Rhys's grand gesture for days. Maddy had to get to him. She started to stand up, but Nate pulled her back down.

Dink cleared his throat. "If there are no more public comments, the council will get down to business." He waited for any dawdlers, but no one had the nerve.

Maddy was so busy searching the hall for a glimpse of Rhys she almost missed the vote. It was four to one in their favor, Dottie being the single holdout.

"Remind me not to send her a Christmas card," Nate said, hugging Maddy so hard she thought she might have a few busted ribs.

Maddy broke away. "I have to find Rhys," she said.

"He went to the police station right after the vote," Mariah said. "Meet us at the Ponderosa for drinks."

She ran like the wind across the square, pulled open the door, and threw herself into Rhys's arms. "I thought you weren't coming."

"I was late—got caught up in something."

She smiled up at him. "Like a job offer."

"Yeah," he said and tilted his head to the side. "How 'bout you, you okay?"

"Are you kidding?" She started dancing around. "We got the inn, Rhys. We got it, and it's all because of you. Until you said you'd stay for good they were on the fence—I could see it in their eyes."

"Nah, Clay had them at 'elect new ones.' "

"So you were just bluffing?"

"I wasn't bluffing, Maddy." He held her away from him. "Is that what you think?"

"What you said in there . . . Oh, Rhys."

"I didn't mean to come on too strong, scare you off. I know it's too soon . . . Anyway, the whole thing's moot now that the inn's been okayed, right?"

She blinked back tears. He'd been bluffing at the hearing. Knowing that accepting the permanent police chief position would help her case, he'd thrown it out to hedge Maddy's bet. "Did you mean what you said, or were you just forcing the city's hand?"

"Now, why the hell would you ask something like that?" He pulled her inside his office and shut the door. "It's just . . . awkward."

"Why?"

Rhys's shoulders sagged. "Because I told you I was leaving, then I did a complete one-eighty in front of the whole town. You ever been to a ball game where some douche bag proposes to his girlfriend on the scoreboard while the entire park waits with bated breath for her answer?" He didn't let her reply. "I hate those guys. And tonight I was one of them. I shouldn't have made a public display of my feelings for you, backed you into a corner like that, especially on the heels of you breaking up your marriage. It wasn't right."

"So, it wasn't a bluff? You really meant that if I stayed, you would stay as chief?"

"Of course I meant it. I love you, Maddy. I've loved you since that first time we kissed on the porch. I've never felt like this about anyone before. Truth: It scares the shit out of me. But today I realized that living without you scares me a hell of a lot more."

Maddy stood on the tips of her toes and kissed him, feeling happier than she'd ever felt in her whole life.

"I love you, too, Rhys Shepard," she said. "And, in case you were wondering, my answer is yes."

He frowned in confusion. "Yes to what?"

"Yes—I'll have you. Don't worry. I know you weren't proposing. And you're right, it's too soon for that. But I want to be with you, Rhys."

The next day Maddy looked at the Lumber Baron Inn in a totally new light. The sun glinted off the copper gutters as a crew of painters set up scaffolding around the exterior of the house. Soon—if the weather cooperated—the mansion would be bathed in buttery yellows, light greens, and crisp whites.

Before, it was just a dream, Maddy mused. Now, this labor of love, once the dilapidated mansion that brought her to Nugget, would open in summer. Really open. If all went well with the Stanford professor and his Donner Party documentary, Nugget would be flooded with tourists. At least that was her hope.

And she, with a lot of help from her friends, had made it happen. She snapped a few pictures with her phone for the before-and-after album, documenting the inn's transformation.

"Hey, heard the hearing last night was a humdinger." Colin came up next to her. He was a mysterious man, but Maddy had grown incredibly fond of him.

"Where were you?" she teased.

"I don't do meetings," he said. "You got a few minutes to pick out some baseboards for those attic rooms?"

"Actually, I've got an appointment. Can it wait?"

"Absolutely."

Rhys trotted up the walkway. "You ready to go?"

"Let me just go inside and get my purse." She sprinted into the front parlor where she'd left the handbag next to a pile of upholstery swatches. Sawdust made her sneeze, the pounding of nail guns filled her head, and nothing had ever sounded better.

She raced outside. "I just have a quick errand." And before Rhys could stop her, she dashed across the square and into the barber shop.

"You won the bet, Owen," she announced to the Nugget Mafia. "Sophie and Mariah went with a local. By this time next year, Nugget could have a new baby."

"Well, I'll be damned." Owen dragged his hands through his Brylcreemed hair. "Who they finally go with?"

"My brother."

"He's not a local," Earl protested.

"He is now." By the time she swaggered out, Owen was demanding that the rest of the mob pay up.

She jumped into Rhys's truck and fifteen minutes later they drove up McCreedy Road.

"Just give me a hint," Maddy pleaded.

"Nope. It's a surprise. That's Clay's house," Rhys pointed.

"Oh, it's lovely," she said. "I don't know why, but for some reason I pictured a log cabin, not a sprawling farmhouse."

"A log cabin?" Rhys laughed. "Where did you get that idea? See all that?" He waved at pastures on both sides of the road. "That's Mc-Creedy Ranch. In the summer Clay runs cattle on this land. Then he moves them south for winter."

"Wow. I had no idea it was such a large operation."

"I'll take you over there sometime," he said. "He's got a whole menagerie—horses, milk cows, chickens."

"So is Clay's house the surprise?"

"No." Rhys laughed. "The surprise is just up the road a piece."

"The land here is so different from most of Nugget," she said, staring out the passenger window. "Not so much forest as green rolling hills . . . kind of takes my breath away."

Rhys hung a left at a birdhouse mailbox and took a brick driveway up to a picture-perfect Victorian. "This is it!"

"Oh, Rhys, it's like a smaller version of the Lumber Baron." She opened the truck door before he'd even come to a full stop. "And not so small."

Maddy jumped out of the cab and ran up the porch stairs. While he fiddled with the lock, she peered inside the windows.

"Oh, it's gorgeous. Hurry up, open the door."

As soon as he unlocked it, she rushed in and started exploring. "Have you seen this kitchen?" she called out.

He came up behind her. "Yep." Before he could say more, she was off to the next room.

After she inspected every inch of the main floor, she climbed the staircase to the second, and came bounding back down twenty minutes later. "Can I see the cottage?" She'd spied it from one of the upstairs windows along with spectacular views of the Sierra.

Rhys led her outside, down the walkway, and showed her the inside of the guesthouse. The property was stunning—vintage with so much character. She could see cows grazing in the distance and the Feather River running through a corner of the property.

"What is this place?" she asked.

He beamed liked a schoolboy divulging a secret. "It was built by one of the Donner Party survivors."

She grabbed his arm. "Get out."

"According to the original deed, Virginia Reed-Murphy and her husband John Marion Murphy built it as a summer home in the late nineteenth century."

"Oh, my God!" She couldn't believe it.

"What?"

"This is the house Virgil told me about! This is it . . . Virginia Reed." She went up onto the porch, and this time scrutinized the Victorian like a historian.

"So what was Virginia's deal?" Rhys asked.

Maddy found a comfortable spot on the veranda to sit and for the next thirty minutes gave Rhys Virgil's historical account.

When she was finished, Rhys stood up and offered Maddy a hand. "That's about the vilest story I've ever heard."

She wiped the back of her skirt as she turned again to survey Virginia's house.

"I bet this was her happy place," she said to Rhys. "Walking through it, I got a really good vibe. You think she found peace here?"

"Maybe." He grabbed her around the waist. "Do you like it?"

"Are you kidding? I love it. Who owns it?"

"I do," he said. "Well, I will, as soon as I sign the papers."

That nearly knocked her over. "Seriously? You own this? It's a piece of history, Rhys."

"I don't think it's exactly museum quality," he said. "It's been remodeled and added on to a dozen times. But I think it'll make a pretty good home."

They went inside the house to have another look around. Sunlight filled the rooms and the scent of lemon polish filled the air. It truly was a beautiful place, but more important it felt good. Safe. Like an old friend waiting to embrace them.

"It's amazing, Rhys. When did you find it?" She still couldn't believe this house belonged to him.

"Clay bought it in foreclosure. It comes with a bunch of land, so he can increase his herd. He's selling me the house and a couple of acres. It'll be good for the kids. Even when Lina goes to college, she'll always have a place to come home to. Sam, too."

"Oh, Rhys." She reached up and kissed him. "What about Shep?"

Rhys took her hand and walked her out to the porch. "Actually, I was thinking of taking your advice of hiring an in-home caregiver for my dad and offering room and board. The cottage might make a good incentive for getting someone to come to Nugget."

"How's he doing, Rhys?"

"Getting worse."

"How're you doing with Shep getting worse?"

Rhys shrugged. "It is what it is." Besides resignation, sadness tinged his voice. "Maybe under different circumstances we could've gotten to know each other. Started over. I think about all the good memories Clay has of Tip and I'd liked to have had some of my dad, too."

"He did give you a wonderful family," Maddy said. "You'll always have Lina and Sam in your life. And they love you, Rhys."

"Yeah, and I love them." A smile lit his face. "And to think I almost tossed them away." Rhys took Maddy's hand. "You never know. Shep and I may still have time to make some memories."

They sat on the porch steps for a while, just staring out into the open. "It's so beautiful here," Maddy said.

He turned her so he could look into her eyes. "I know it's too soon. But when you're ready, live with me here, Maddy. Help me make this house a home."

She pulled him close, feeling shielded and safe and loved. The sun shone on the west side of the veranda, washing it in a gorgeous halo of light.

"We'll put our rockers there," she pointed.

"Yeah?" he said, thick emotion clogging his voice.

"And maybe one of those zero-infinity pools over there."

He chuckled. "Not happening, sugar." Gathering her up in his arms, he started for the house.

"Where are you taking me?"

His voice went low and husky as he carried her up the stairs. "On our official first date," he said, his eyes glinting with happiness. "We're gonna have lots of them, sugar."

Dear Reader,

Thanks for reading *Going Home*, the first in my Nugget Series. This is my debut novel and I'm absolutely thrilled to share it with you. The setting and the characters for the series came easily. I grew up in small towns. My parents, hippies from New York City, moved our family to California when I was just a little kid. For some crazy reason that my sister, brother, and I still can't figure out, they got the farming bug. Weird for two people who grew up on concrete, taking the subway. But, then again, my dad was a Boy Scout and my mom lived above a produce stand in the East Village. So maybe that explains it.

Anyway, the best part of my life was spent in the country, raising animals for 4-H, attending rodeos, and riding my horse, Sugar. Eventually, I moved to the big city for college and to be a newspaper reporter. Now every day I curse the traffic, the smog, and people who cut in line.

Luckily my aunt owns a cabin in the Sierra Nevada where my family goes to get away and inner-tube on the Feather River, ride our bikes on gorgeous mountain trails, and eat soft-serve at the neighborhood frosty. Incidentally, it's not far from where the Donner Party got stranded in 1846.

Sound a lot like Nugget?

In the next Nugget book, I'll be telling Clay McCreedy's story and I hope you continue this journey with me. In the meantime, visit my website, www.stacyfinz.com, and follow me on Twitter @sfinz or @stacyfinz. I'd love to hear from you.

Enjoy!

Stacy Finz

Please turn the page for an exciting sneak peek of
Stacy Finz's next Nugget romance
FINDING HOPE
coming in January 2015 wherever e-books are sold!

Chapter 1

Emily gingerly wended her way around the moving boxes, each one labeled with bright red marker. Clutching a fistful of silverware, she managed to make it from the kitchen to the dining room without tripping over one of the cartons.

It was amazing how much stuff people accumulated over the years. Her cookbooks and kitchen equipment alone would take up most of a large U-Haul. At least Drew, her ex-husband, was taking the furniture, and the rest could be donated to the Goodwill. Where she was going, she wouldn't need half the contents of this big house.

She did a quick appraisal of the table with its last-minute centerpiece—a bouquet of hydrangea cut from the backyard—and began setting her best Laguiole steak knives at each of the six place settings. The knives had languished in storage since the last lunch.

Emily knew that etiquette dictated that the sharp edge of the knife face the plate. To point the blade toward a guest was an ancient sign of aggression.

Not good in a room full of FBI agents and police detectives, she reflected wryly. But this would be the last time. The last lunch. Soon she'd be leaving here, the only home Hope had ever known.

Her hands shook as she tried to rearrange the glasses. The guests were due to arrive in thirty minutes and Emily needed every second of that time to pull herself together. Even though it had been four years, the anniversaries were particularly difficult. Every painful detail of that July day—the chaos, the frenzy, the terror—looped through her brain like a skipping record.

Drew and her attorney had warned her against hosting that first anniversary lunch.

"The police will use it to try to slip you up," Drew had said. "They're not coming because they're your friends, Em. I'm a lawyer, I know." She had learned in those first few days of the investigation that the parents are always the primary suspects.

But it had been a full year since Hope had been taken from them, and even if the police weren't her friends, she needed them. The lunches had been Emily's attempt at keeping Hope's memory alive and her case file active, instead of being relegated to a dusty basement somewhere.

Later, the lunches seemed to serve as a combination vigil–healing ceremony. The investigators were no closer to solving what had happened to her daughter than they had been four years ago. And that had left indelible scars—even on jaded law enforcement.

To quote the news clips, "the trail had gone cold." The reporters had pounced on the next sensational story and the police had new, more pressing crimes to solve.

Everyone except for her had moved on. Even Drew. He was getting remarried. And more than anything she owed him a fresh start, a chance at happiness. Even if it meant relocating to the ends of the earth.

She hadn't been able to bring back their daughter, but she could at least make amends for what she'd done.

Four days later, Emily climbed the steep grade into the Sierra mountains. Her old friend Joe had certainly been right about this part of the state being unbelievably beautiful. Verdant fields and miles and miles of pine trees. Snow still dusted the highest peaks of the mountains and her ears popped from the altitude. With the back of her hand she touched the driver's side window. Surprisingly, it felt warm.

She'd been driving for nearly four hours from the Bay Area and figured she had to be close to her destination. Nugget. She'd lived in California her whole life and had never heard of the little railroad town.

Not only did the town have a paltry population of six thousand people, but she would be living in a barn. If the pictures did the place justice, it was a very nice barn indeed. Joe had gone on and on about Nugget and his friend Clay McCreedy's cattle ranch—"It's exactly what you need. Fresh air and a fresh start."

What she needed was to get her business rolling again so she could afford to pay her own way. At least in this mountain hamlet the rent was a pittance compared to the mortgage on her and Drew's Palo Alto house. Even after the hefty sum they'd sold it for, there was little left. They'd racked up a pile of debt paying lawyers and private investigators.

Not only would it be far cheaper than anything she could afford in the Bay Area, but here, her neighbors weren't likely to connect her to Hope. No longer would she have to suffer pitying looks. Or worse. Faces filled with suspicion and condemnation.

She glanced down at the directions she'd printed from Google Maps as she traveled the two-lane highway. There it was, to the left, McCreedy Road. She pulled in, drove for less than a mile, and parked on the shoulder to reread Mr. McCreedy's instructions. They said to meet him at the big, white farmhouse at one o'clock to collect the key. Up ahead in the distance she saw an outcropping of trees and assumed that must be the location of the house.

According to Joe, McCreedy Ranch, one of the first cattle spreads in the area, covered thousands of acres. He said Clay's great-grandfather drove his cattle across the Nevada desert into Plumas County in the 1800s to sell beef to the gold miners.

She had no idea where on the property her new home was located, whether it was near the house, or somewhere remote. The whole rental transaction had been done via email, and Emily braced herself for the possibility that the place would turn out to be a total disaster. Although the photographs had been lovely, she knew from experience the tricks a camera and a good stylist could play. How many times had she sprayed the outside of a cocktail glass with glycerin to make it look frosty for the lens, or drenched a day-old dried-out pastry with hair spray to make it look fresh-out-of-the-oven luscious? Too many times to count.

But she'd gotten the impression that Mr. McCreedy couldn't care less about renting out the barn, that he was only doing it as a favor to Joe. So hopefully he wasn't trying to sell her a sow's ear.

Emily glanced down at her watch. It was nearly one o'clock. She'd nosed the van out onto the road again when a man on horseback caught her attention. On the other side of the split-rail fence, in a field carpeted with orange poppies, he galloped so fast it made her heart pound. With his head and shoulders pushed forward over the horse's flowing mane, they beat across the pasture fast as a freight train. For a second, she thought her imagination had conjured him, a centaur, untamed and magnificent. From this distance she couldn't make out the man's features, just a black cowboy hat that began to blur as he faded into a copse of trees up ahead.

She sat back to catch her breath; the sight and speed, so exhilarating, stirred something dormant in Emily's breast. Something she hadn't felt in four years.

Life.

When she reached the white farmhouse, she found the man dismounting from the horse. Not a centaur at all, Emily noted, but a tall, strapping cowboy. Besides the hat, he wore leather chaps that fit snugly over his jeans and a scarred pair of brown boots. In all the time she'd known Joe, she'd never seen him ride a horse. And he'd worn tennis shoes.

"Hello." He tipped his hat, tied the horse, and deftly removed the saddle. His large hands moved quickly, like he'd done this a thousand times. "You Emily Mathews?"

A squat man with a big belly and silver hair materialized out of nowhere and started brushing the sweaty steed.

The rider took the brush. "I've got it, Ramon. I'll take Big Red back to the stable when I'm done."

The squat man seemed reluctant to relinquish the chore, but eventually wandered off.

The cowboy looked at her and arched his brows with impatience. "Emily, right?"

"Oh. Yes." There was so much to take in, she'd become distracted.

The house with its long sweeping porch and the yard's expansive lawns were gorgeous. If not for the musky smell of horses and cows, it would have felt like she had wandered onto a Hollywood set.

He continued to rub the comb in circles over Big Red's coat, occasionally scratching the horse behind his ears. "Your moving truck came this morning."

Emily nodded. The man still hadn't introduced himself, but she presumed he must be Clay McCreedy. She'd expected a much older man to own such a big cattle operation. But he was about her age, thirty-seven, forty at the most.

"As soon as I'm done here we'll put Big Red up and I'll take you over to the barn," he said, bending over to lift and clean the horse's hooves with some kind of a pick. Emily tried not to notice how the chaps nicely framed his backside.

"Great," she said, having a million questions to ask him—where's the nearest grocery store and gas station? Who did she need to call for cable? Instead, she stood there like a mute, her hands stuffed inside the pockets of her khakis. There was a time when she'd been adroit at small talk and at socializing. In fact, Drew used to call her the "belle of the ball." But years of hiding in her house had made her rusty.

Even when she'd been good at it, Emily suspected Clay McCreedy would've made her stammer. The man, with his low gravelly voice and all that rough-and-tumble cowboy thing he had going on, was larger than life.

"So you did Joe's cookbook, huh?" He untied the horse's lead and grabbed the saddle with one hand, beckoning her to follow him down the driveway. Big Red's hooves made clip-clop noises on the blacktop.

"Yes, I did," she said, hugging his side. The only thing she knew about horses was not to get behind them. They kicked.

His lips quirked. "Didn't know old Joe could cook."

"He's pretty good at it, actually." In fact, he'd been one of Emily's few clients who had recipes that worked.

Officially, Emily was a freelance cookbook editor. In truth, she was a cookbook ghost writer. The dirty little secret about famous chefs and celebrity cooks is that they couldn't formulate recipes to save their lives. She never met one who measured or weighed, paid attention to cooking times, or didn't use exotic ingredients unavailable to home cooks.

So publishing houses, and sometimes the authors themselves, hired her to do everything from creating and testing recipes to styling dishes and writing the text. Essentially, she wrote the whole book and slapped someone else's name on the cover. In Joe's case, he'd needed help telling the story of how his ranch had grown from a backyard hobby to one of the most popular gourmet beef businesses in the country. He was a cattleman, not a writer.

"You'll be writing cookbooks here, then?" Clay asked.

"Editing them," she corrected. "Yes, that's the plan."

"You don't need to be near the action?"

It figured that he would be curious why she'd come to Nugget, instead of staying close to San Francisco's thriving food scene. "Nope. All I need is a computer and a kitchen." And a fresh start.

When they reached the stables, he opened a gate to a large paddock, took off Big Red's halter and gave him a slap on the rump. The horse nickered and trotted away.

"Colin's installed your electric stove," he said. "So you're set."

The kitchen already had a gas range—it had been the first question she'd asked in her emails—but she liked to test recipes on both types of stoves so she could tweak cooking times accordingly. She'd bought an electric brand popular with home cooks online at the Sears in Reno, the nearest city, and had it delivered. "I'll write you a check for your man's labor. Thanks for letting me make the modification."

He shrugged. "No big deal. Just means you'll have fewer cabinets."

She followed him inside the stable and peered into a row of horse stalls. The man, Ramon, was laying down fresh straw with a pitchfork. Clay said something to him in Spanish and the man let out a loud belly laugh. When they got to a small room filled with saddles and bridles, Clay began to unbuckle his chaps. Although he was fully dressed under the sturdy leg coverings, she could feel her face heat and turned away.

"We can walk to the barn from here," he said. "Afterward, if you want, you can drive the van over."

"Sounds good." She was getting impatient to see the place.

Two boys came rounding the driveway as they headed back up.

"Hey, Dad," the younger boy called, and gazed at her with open curiosity. The older one never looked up from his phone.

When they reached Clay, he asked, "How was camp?"

"Okay, I guess," the boy said, while Clay waited for a reply from the eldest.

When he didn't give one, Clay pulled out one of the boy's earbuds. "When I ask you a question, I expect an answer."

"Yes. Sir." The boy clicked his heels and saluted.

"How was camp?" Clay asked, annoyance at the boy's insolence edging his voice.

"It sucked."

Clay turned to Emily. "These are my sons, Justin and Cody. This is Ms. Mathews, our new neighbor."

Cody stuck his hand out for a shake. "Good to meet you, ma'am."

Justin grunted something unintelligible.

Clay gave him a quelling look and the preteen simulated the voice of a robot. "Nice. To. Meet. You. Ms. Mathews."

Even sullen and disrespectful, he was a beautiful boy. Dark hair and deep blue eyes like his father. He was still filling out, but would eventually have his dad's frame, too. Sinewy and broad-shouldered. Cody had the same blue eyes, but fairer hair and complexion. He was maybe a year or two older than ten, the age Hope would be now.

"Nice to meet the both of you," Emily said brightly, hoping to smooth the awkwardness. Clay seemed a hair away from smacking Justin.

"There are snacks in the house," he told the boys. "Then get started on your chores."

"Are they good-for-you snacks?" Cody wanted to know.

"Brownies. Mandy brought them by earlier."

Cody raced for the house, his pack bouncing up and down against his back.

"Hey, save some for me," Clay shouted after him.

Justin also turned for the house, but not before giving Clay a spiteful glare.

Clay shook his head, let out a sigh, and led her off the driveway to a flagstone trail. They climbed a slight knoll and she could hear water, maybe a creek. Before she could ask what it was, they came to the top of the hill, and the sight stopped her in her tracks.

"The Feather River," Clay said.

"It's beautiful." The wide tributary snaked through the land, wild and rugged. Her gaze followed the river upstream where a waterfall cascaded down an outcropping of boulders.

"Glad you like it," he said, "because that's your view from the barn. But it comes with a price. There's a sandy beach down there, where the boys like to put in their tubes and kayaks. It'll cut into your privacy—at least during the summer."

"I don't mind," she lied. Watching those children so alive, playing in the water, would be a constant reminder of what she'd lost. But it was almost August. The seasons had to be short around here, she thought as she looked up at the surrounding snowcapped mountains.

A short distance later, through a grove of trees, sat the barn. It was red with white trim, had a double-dutch front door, a set of barn-door sliders, dormer windows, old-timey lantern light fixtures, and a rooster weather vane.

It was so charming from the outside that Emily held her breath in anticipation while Clay unlocked the door. He flipped on the lights, then ushered her across the threshold. All she could do was goggle. With the exception of her moving boxes, which had been neatly stacked against the rear wall, the place looked like one of those show-case houses in *Country Living* magazine.

"Those pictures you sent didn't come close to doing this place justice," she said. "My God, it's spectacular."

"Yeah, well it ought to be for all the fuh—" He stopped himself, stuck his hands in his pockets, and leaned against the wall, silently inviting her to take her fill.

Sounded like the barn was a bit of a sore spot between Clay Mc-Creedy and the missus, Emily surmised as she walked the big front room. The beams had to be a hundred years old, pitted and weathered with character. The plank walls and floors reminded her of frontier houses she'd seen on a trip to Old Baylor Park in Texas, where historians had preserved some of the state's first homes.

She stared up at the massive twig chandelier hanging over the center of the room. A stone fireplace, kilim rug, two leather couches, and a cowhide chair set off the living room, while a pine farm table and eight Windsor chairs anchored the dining area.

"Your wife must be very successful as an interior decorator. Her taste is impeccable." Emily couldn't believe all the furniture came with the place. Some of the pieces looked expensive. If they weren't antiques, they were damned good replicas.

She found the bedroom, which was small, but more than adequate. The bathroom had a clawfoot tub and tiled shower. And there was a small loft that would serve as an office. But it was the kitchen that nearly made her swoon. Open shelves galore, state-of-the-art appliances—except for her new electric range—a spacious center island, and windows that faced the river. It wasn't laid out as well as her Palo Alto kitchen, which she had personally designed. Still, she felt like she had struck gold.

"So she used this as her showroom and office?" Emily asked, chagrined that she didn't even know Clay's wife's name. She'd been dealing strictly with him.

"Yeah," he said, then walked over to the fireplace, stuck his head in the box and inspected the flue. "In the winter, I'd suggest using this as much as possible. Heating bills can get steep up here. The phone, cable and Internet are still in my name. It's a local company and they give me a package deal for the entire ranch. Since it's not costing me anything extra, I'll throw those services in for free. We can settle up at the end of each month on any extras—pay-per-view movies, whatever. That work for you?"

"Absolutely."

"I left the barn's phone number over there." He nodded his head toward the center island, where she saw a sticky note stuck to the counter. "You may occasionally get a call for Jennifer. You can refer them to the main house. That number is on there, too."

"Thanks," she said, relieved to have one fewer chore to do and happy to save the money.

"I'll let you get to your unpacking, then. If you want to bring your van around, just take the driveway past the stable. It'll loop you to the barn."

"Thank you, Mr. McCreedy."

"Call me Clay."

"Okay, Clay. Thank you." He tipped his black hat and made his way to the door. Emily, unable to believe her good fortune, couldn't help being inquisitive. "Why doesn't your wife use it anymore?"

"She's dead," he said, and slipped out.

The woman seemed reliable enough, Clay mused as he walked back to the house. Her check had cleared and according to Joe, her ex-husband was a big-time Silicon Valley lawyer. Clay might not be the best judge of character, but she certainly hadn't struck him as the type to throw wild parties, or to be so irresponsible as to burn the barn down. Hell, even if she destroyed the place, insurance would cover it.

At first, he'd balked at Joe's request to rent the barn to his lady friend. Joe had said she needed a change of scenery due to some extenuating circumstances. Clay hadn't bothered to ask about those circumstances. Didn't care. He had enough responsibilities running a cattle ranch and raising two boys. Adding landlord to the list . . . Well, he didn't need the headache.

But Joe had cajoled, and the barn was just sitting there, collecting dust. Clay didn't give two shits about the stuff in it—the antiques, the rugs, the pictures that Jennifer had purchased in one fell swoop from a design center showroom in San Francisco. The McCreedys had been living in these mountains since the gold rush. He slept in the same bed where his great-grandmother gave birth, ate off the same wake table that his ancestors brought with them on a ship from Ireland. His family's history is what mattered to him, not some meaningless bric-a-brac with a hefty price tag.

So he'd finally relented to Joe. Cattlemen helped each other, and Joe would've done the same thing for him. Clay only hoped he wouldn't live to regret his decision. He had enough responsibilities without Emily turning into a high-maintenance tenant.

At least she wasn't much to look at. Plain old mousy, if you asked him.

Granted, he was close to six-three, but she barely reached his chin. He liked statuesque women, long and leggy. Charitably, he would call Emily scrawny. Maybe, just maybe, she was hiding a voluptuous figure under all those baggy clothes. But Clay sincerely doubted it. In his experience, women liked to show off their assets. God knew Jen had—like a grand champion at the county fair, strutting all those USDA prime cuts. Especially the ones he'd paid for.

He couldn't even remember the color of Emily's hair; only that it hung around her face like a dead animal. Her eyes were a nice shade of blue, though. Just devoid of any signs of life—no twinkle, no spark. Not quite cold, just detached.

"Thank you, Joe," he said aloud, and meant it from the bottom of his heart.

Because the last complication Clayton McCreedy needed in his life right now was another hot-looking woman.